Drawn through Blood

John W. Otte

Geeky Grace Books

ISBN: 979-8-9858103-2-5 (print)

ISBN: 979-8-9858103-3-2 (ebook)

Book Cover by Kirk DouPonce, www. DogEaredDesign.com

Edited by Megan Gerig (MG Literary Services)

Map designed by Luan Bittencourt

For Mark, Keri, Sam, and Alice

PEDREVOR
The Expanse
ELSCONTIN
The Stone
Kolvese Plain
The Edge
The Cold Light Forest
The Shessu
Heartland
The Bearer's
Repose
The Far
Waters
The Diradae
Mountains
Bistion
Delah
Maotoa
The Blood
Sea
The Gyrid Flats
KSANN
The Low River
Province
RIOKA
The Right Highlands
The Weyfir Coast
Sholn
Plissk Sanctuary
Oasis
The Kronin Desert
The Cradle Ridges
THE DALARK
IMPERIUM
THE XONIEL
DYNASTY
The Elder Sea
The Plotan Expanse
The Demilitarized Zone
The Dalark Channel
The Dalark
Beachhead
Nekek the Bright
(Ruins)
Outuaa
ERECONE
The Weyfir Sea
TOMMA
The Foundation

Dramatis Personae

RULERS OF THE XONIEL DYNASTY

- Everys - Queen of the Xoniel Dynasty and secretly a toratropic mage
- Narius - King of the Xoniel Dynasty
- Quartus - Narius's younger brother, now declared outlaw

PALACE STAFF

- Challix - Everys's assistant
- Trule - Everys's chief maid
- Rewether - Commander of Everys's Queen's Guard
- Kevtho - Queen's Guard and Everys's Swordbound
- Urett - Narius's assistant
- Zar - Commander of the King's Guard
- Farga - King's Guard and Narius's Swordbound
- Turron - The Dynasty's Master Archivist

NARIUS'S ADVISERS

- Paine - Narius's Vizier
- Auriel Zammit - Governor-General of Bastion
- Bokil - Minister of Internal Security
- Elamek - Minister of Agriculture
- Filamon - Minister of Resource Management
- Istragon - Supreme Prelate of the Dynasty's official religion
- Masruq - Minister of Finance
- Tormod - The Dynasty's Spymaster
- Ventios - Ministere of Labor
- Yull - Minister of Foreign Affairs

THE ETHNARCH PARLIAMENT

- The One Who Bestrides the Darkness - Ethnarch of the Diradae and leader of the Parliament
- Assumption - Ethnarch of the Kolvese
- Chilyana - one Ethnarch of the Grerid
- Musein - one Ethnarch of the Grerid
- Sollip Huntermark - Ethnarch of the Weyfir
- Numeria - Ethnarch of the Dunestriders
- Rockflow - Ethnarch of the Ixactl
- Selestine - Ethnarch of the Plissk

THE HALL OF ALL VOICES

- Zolkin - First Speaker
- Mossglade - Ixactl representative

OTHER RESIDENTS OF THE DYNASTY:

- Viara - Former Queen and Narius's ex-wife
- Duke Brencis - Former head of the Dynasty's Military, now in rebellion against Narius
- Redtale - Former head of Everys's Queen's Guard
- Favid - Everys's father
- Galan - Everys's older sister
- Legarr - Everys's younger brother, now dead
- Ulsa - Everys's mother
- "Auntie" Kyna - Siporan con artist in Fair Havens
- Oluna Hishi - Wife of Minister Masruq
- Clarinda Gaines - CEO and owner of TelleGlin

THE COLD LIGHT YOREROOT

- Stunted Root - Second of the Yoreroot
- Tall Reach - Third of the Yoreroot
- Evergreen - Knowledge Keeper
- Firestruck - Defender of the Forest
- Seed Cluster - Liaison of the Fields
- Yllana - Grafted to Tall Reach

THE DALARK IMPERIUM

- Tirigian - Emperor of the Dalark Imperium
- Innana - Princess of the Dalark Imperium and Narius's former fiancée
- Ambassador Alezzar - Represents the Imperium's interests in Bastion
- Devroshan - Former Emperor, father to Tirigian and Innana, now dead

Introduction

The ghosts didn't bother Favid anymore. Instead, the silence drove him closer to the brink every day.

He sighed heavily and looked around at the stone walls and the floor worn smooth from centuries of use. What had this room been originally? A storeroom? A workshop? A bedroom? Did the builder come to despise this room as much as Favid did?

No, he couldn't think like that. He should be grateful. Honored. How many of his people had ever seen what remained of their homeland? And here Favid, his wife, and daughter had spent the past several years in a forgotten corner of the world, tasked with a sacred duty entrusted to his family for generations. All those details were almost enough to make him overlook the squalid conditions, the crushing loneliness, and the constant fear of being caught.

Almost.

Another sigh, and he levered himself to standing. His knees groaned in protest, and he leaned heavily against the wall until the pain subsided. He ducked through the low door into the ragged stone hallway beyond. It took some shimmying, but he eventually popped into their living space. Threadbare cushions, little better than trash, were tossed into a niche carved into one wall, creating a sofa, one that was never comfortable enough to relax on. A low table was pushed into one corner, built out of rough boards that gave him more splinters than food, with four makeshift stools on two sides. And crouched over a small wood-burning stove was his wife, Ulsa, minding three different pots as she prepared breakfast.

A wistful smile tugged at Favid's lips. Ulsa always rose hours earlier than he did to start the family's day with a hearty meal, and she never complained. About anything, truth be told. When the two had married thirty years earlier, she hadn't known about his family's status. When the scriveners had sent them, she'd gone without complaint. Just the sight of his long-suffering wife was almost enough to banish the melancholy.

Almost.

Ulsa turned and offered him a smile, one that didn't distract him from the dark circles around her eyes or the way her shoulders drooped. "Have a seat. Breakfast is almost ready."

He shook his head. "Where's Galan? Has she done the morning rites yet?"

Ulsa chuckled. "Where do you think?"

Favid bit back a grumble. He should have known.

He squeezed back into the corridor, only he didn't head for his bedroom. Instead, he descended a side passage, one that dropped him into a darkened tunnel. He stretched his arms and took a deep breath, the knot in his chest unwinding just a fraction. The shaft stretched in both directions, disappearing into shadows beyond. He carefully lowered himself to the floor—a fall from the entrance might be enough to sprain an ankle, maybe even break a bone—then followed one of the rough walls toward a flickering light. Sure enough, Galan, his oldest daughter, stood before a smooth wall, her eyes roaming back and forth. He clenched his jaw, biting back the criticism that crawled up his throat. Every morning, she was here. Every morning, staring at the same patch of wall, as if she expected it to regurgitate some deep secret.

She glanced at him, and a smile split her features. For just a moment, Favid lost his frustration. Galan was the best of both he and Ulsa: a keen mind, an open heart, and a joyful countenance. If they were back in Fair Havens, Galan would probably attract attention from every young man in the neighborhood, although once they learned she was Siporan, they'd probably lose interest quickly. But still, a young woman like Galan should be breaking hearts and blazing a path for herself, not cooped up in a darkened ruin.

"Any new names show up today?" He tried to keep his tone light and joking.

She made a face at him. "Still not funny, Papa. You know that's not why I'm here."

That was the problem: he *didn't* know why she was doing this. He stepped next to her. Scratched into a smooth part of the wall were hundreds of glyphs, written in the ancient Siporan language. When Favid, Ulsa, and Galan had arrived a year earlier, he and Galan had marveled at the wall, thinking that it was some hidden record of their people's history. Or some sort of warning, carved into the rock for future generations to digest.

But then Galan had discovered an old lexicon and uncovered the truth. No messages. No prophecies. Just names. Hundreds of them, all squished into the same space. And there was no clue as to who the people were. The workers who'd constructed their hideaway? Soldiers on campaign? Explorers who'd happened across these ruins before the area was turned into a demilitarized zone? They would never know. There was no way they could. And yet Galan insisted on beginning her morning at the wall, studying each name, running her fingers along the carvings.

He took a long breath, held it, then blew it out his nose. Best not aggravate her this early in the morning. There would be plenty of time for all three of them to poke and prod at each other's weaknesses as the day wore on. For now, he had his own morning routine to follow.

He moved past Galan's quiet contemplation until he found a particular crack in the tunnel wall. It appeared to be little more than a natural fissure, the sort of damage that would occur in a carved tunnel after centuries of neglect. But Favid knew better. Steeling himself, he walked right for the wall. Even though he knew he would be fine, his mind still screamed a warning as he approached what appeared to be an all-too-solid surface...

But he slipped through the illusion into a hidden chamber beyond.

A shiver wormed across Favid's skin. He knew he couldn't actually feel anything from walking through the glamour spell, but every morning, he was sure he felt a chill. He paused by the opening to inspect the glamour rune. One of the previous guardians had carved a template into the chamber wall, meaning he didn't have to memorize the complex pattern of whorls, slashes, and curves that cast the spell. All he had to do was make sure the template had enough ink to maintain the illusion. The rune glowed faintly as the spell slowly consumed the ink. Favid frowned. He had touched up the rune two days earlier, but it looked like the ink was fading faster than usual.

He turned away from the glamour rune and braced himself. Even though he knew he shouldn't feel a physical reaction, he swore he did, the same vertigo he felt when dangling from a great height and knowing your life hung in the balance.

And why wouldn't he? Standing in a circular chamber was a ten-foot-tall stone plinth. Carved on the outside of the curve was the template for another toratropic rune. But whereas Favid had never learned the glamour rune, he'd always known this one intimately. This was his family's heritage, the secret they had carried for the past four hundred years.

Once, this plinth was one of the eight Principalities, the most sacred of objects to his people. This plinth and seven others like it stood at the heart of the Scriptotum in Nekek the Bright, where the Singularity had revealed the secrets of toratropic magic to the Siporan people. When Nekek the Bright fell at the hands of the Xoniel Dynasty and the Dalark Imperium, their enemies had destroyed five of the Principalities. Faithful Siporan families, Favid's ancestors included, had spirited the other three out of the city before their destruction, hiding them where they could. This one, with its powerful healing rune, had been hidden in this abandoned tunnel for centuries, and Favid's family had maintained their vigil the whole time.

Without taking his gaze from the Principality, Favid picked up a bowl full of ashes and dirt and smeared the rough mixture into the template.

"Our disobedience made this necessary," Favid whispered as he worked. "In Your righteous anger, You cast us down. You brought us low so we might wake from our prideful slumber. O Singularity, who cast the world into its form, do not forget us in our dust and ashes."

He continued the litany as he worked, filling in the carving so completely that it disappeared from sight. He carefully wiped away the excess, rubbing the surface of the carving smooth. He would leave the ashes there until evening, when he would wash away the grime. Even though he had performed this ritual hundreds of times, he still struggled to keep his breathing even and his hands from trembling. How could he, a mere mortal, have the right to touch something that sacred? It didn't seem right. None of this did. Not the sacrifice, not the secrecy, not one bit of it.

"Papa?"

He jumped at Galan's voice and whirled around.

"What have I told you about interrupting me?" he snapped.

To her credit, Galan didn't wince. "Mama sent me. Breakfast is ready. And we have a guest."

A guest? He frowned. "Who?"

"Treskin."

Now that was a surprise. A fellow Siporan, Treskin was part of a team who regularly snuck into the Demilitarized Zone to bring their family supplies. But they weren't expecting him for two weeks.

Favid's frown deepened. "Tell Mama and Treskin I'll be there as soon as I finish the morning rites."

Galan left without a word. Favid turned back to the Principality to continue the morning's litany. But the words jumbled and his mind raced with questions. Why would Treskin risk getting caught by the Dynasty or Dalark to come here?

His eyes widened as a thought occurred to him. Maybe Treskin had come to tell them their time was over and they could go home.

Favid quashed the stray thought and resumed his work. But although his tone was supposed to be one of sorrow and contrition, he couldn't help the little bit of hope that bled into his voice.

Ulsa was frustrated with him. She didn't look at him as he entered the common room, seemingly focused on the pots and kettle on the stove. They'd been waiting for close to a half hour. But what else could he do? He had to perform the rite.

Maybe her anger had to do with their surprise visitor. Treskin sat at their table, sipping a steaming cup of tea. He was a wiry man, dressed in an old military uniform that was designed to blend into the Demilitarized Zone's foliage. But that wasn't the only camouflage Treskin employed. Just looking at him, most people wouldn't realize that he was actually Siporan.

Treskin raised his cup in greeting. "Good day to you, Favid. I apologize for surprising your family. I trust your vigil goes well?"

"Is this why you're here? To drink our tea and ask simple questions?" Favid stomped to the table, kicking a stray pillow back toward the sofa.

Treskin rocked back on his stool and scowled at him. "Excuse me?"

Favid sighed and sat down on the stool farthest from Treskin. "I am sorry. The past few days... I haven't slept well."

Treskin pursed his lips. "Then I'm doubly sorry that I came. I'm probably going to steal even more of your sleep."

That snapped Favid's head back. "Why?"

The other man dug in his coat pocket and set something on the table. Once he withdrew his hand, Ulsa gasped, and it felt like Favid's stomach dropped into his feet.

A small black porcelain disk sat on the table. Painted in stark white lines, a stylized eye with jagged slashes across its surface stared up at Favid. Languid squiggles poured from the bottom of the eye, coming together in a rippling pool. A death's eye rune, sent by Siporan elders to a family to express condolences at a recent loss.

"Who?" Favid whispered.

Treskin cleared his throat, rubbing the back of his neck. "Your youngest."

Favid closed his eyes and swallowed a low moan.

"How?" he asked next, although he had a good idea what the answer would be. One of his son's schemes must have caught up with him. He was always trying to find ways to skirt law and morality in an attempt to get rich.

"We don't know. His wife announced his death, but she didn't really say how he died. Almost like she couldn't... or didn't want to."

A flash of irritation cut through the grief. Of course. His daughter-in-law had always been an irritation, especially since she'd stolen their son. His moral slide could probably be blamed on her.

"But when a few of the elders asked around, they couldn't learn anything. It's almost like the whole thing is being covered up." Treskin snorted. "I suppose the royals are probably trying to avoid a scandal."

Favid frowned. "Why would you say that?"

Treskin's mouth popped open in a small circle. "D-don't you... you don't know?"

Favid exchanged a confused look at Ulsa. "Don't know what?"

"Gravedigger's trowel! I thought for sure someone would have said something when they brought you supplies."

"They used the drop-site due to increased patrols," Galan said.

"Still, to not tell you..." Treskin shook his head.

"Tell. Us. *What*?" Favid's voice was little more than a growl.

"What your other daughter's been up to," Treskin said.

"Everys?" Ulsa grabbed Favid's shoulder tightly. "She's supposed to be taking care of the shop."

Treskin laughed. "Oh, she took care of it."

"She's in trouble?" Favid could scarcely conceive of that. Everys was so quiet, such a good daughter!

"You could say that."

1

Inkstains, Everys was in trouble.

Well, not physically. For once. Four guards escorted her up the steps. To her left was Kevtho, her Swordbound, the ceremonial blade he carried bouncing on his hip with every step. To her right was Rewether, the commander of her guard. She didn't know him that well; he had taken over just a few weeks earlier. But she just couldn't bring herself to get close to him. Not that Rewether was a bad person or a bad guard. She just wished Redtale was walking with her.

"Blessed?" The gentle question snapped her out of her reverie. "Are you all right?"

Everys realized she had slowed down, and the others had paused to wait for her. Challix, her personal assistant, wore a worried expression. She was at least eight inches shorter than Everys with long, dark hair that fell just past her shoulders. As usual, she wore a sharply tailored business suit on her petite frame.

"Are you all right?" Challix repeated.

Everys forced herself to smile, a hopefully reassuring forgery. "Just reviewing what we can expect inside."

Challix's gaze sharpened, and Everys fought the urge to squirm. When she first met Challix, the other woman had been thoroughly frustrated with her. Not that Everys blamed her. By any standards, Everys was a nontraditional queen. She hadn't been a member of the nobility but a common resident of Fair Havens, a run-down neighborhood of the Dynasty's capital, Bastion. And while she was human, she was Siporan, a race the Dynasty had conquered four hundred years earlier and had oppressed ever since.

And there was the fact that she practiced illegal magic, but as far as Everys was aware, Challix didn't know about that.

While they had established a working arrangement, there were still times that Everys felt like a student facing a disapproving teacher. Like now, as Challix inspected her.

"You're right to be cautious, but this is dinner, not combat," Challix said.

Everys almost laughed. While Duchess Wendly had claimed that the night's festivities were meant to be a "friendly dinner," experience had taught Everys it would be anything but. Having Everys attend would allow the Wendly star to rise in the Dynasty's constellation, at least in the eyes of the other noble families. Most of the commoners wouldn't care who the royals ate with; they had more important matters to attend to, like not starving. But as Narius, her husband, often reminded her, logic and the nobility rarely marched in unison.

"Just remember, with the Wendlys, everything comes in layers. Until we reach the heart of the night, we won't know what their agenda really is," Challix said.

Everys nodded. Layers. Right.

Her entourage paused at the top of the stairs. Two of the Wendlys' guards snapped to attention and hauled open the front doors.

A steward led them through a long hallway dotted with elaborate portraits of long-dead Wendlys, all of whom wore the same scowl, to a lavish dining room. The walls were covered with dark wood paneling lined with gold. At least twenty crystal chandeliers brightly illuminated three rows of tables with crisp white tablecloths. Gigantic bouquets of exotic flowers sprouted every ten feet. Close to a hundred people circulated between the tables, all of them dressed in stunning attire.

As soon as the steward stepped through the door, he stomped his foot on the wooden floor, producing an impressive crack that sliced through the whispered conversations. The guests, close to a hundred of them, turned toward the doorway.

"I present Queen Everys, the Embodiment of the Water Bearer, Mother of all the Dynasty..."

Everys ignored the recitation. The nobles loved their titles, and that meant that they would have to listen to all of hers. They'd be here for at least five to ten minutes. She used the time to examine the gathered nobles.

Duchess Wendly stood at the head table. In her late eighties, she wore a black wool dress embroidered with white and gray patterns. Like most residents of the Right Highlands, she wore her hair beneath a knotted kerchief, one with jewels sewn along the edges. Predictably, she spotted the Lokreks near the head table; the Wendlys and Lokreks had been allies for four generations. The same could be said for the Tritts, although there had been rumors that the Tritts and Wendlys had been feuding over some perceived insult.

Aside from the Wendlys, Lokreks, and Tritts, there were representatives from six other major houses and twice as many minor ones. Not surprisingly, all of the guests were humans. They were mostly H inaen but with a few token darker-skinned Kolvese and Grerid with their tan skin and large, olive-shaped eyes, enough for the Wendlys and the other Hinaen nobles to convince themselves they weren't bigots. No Siporans other than her, but that wasn't a surprise. The servants and staff looked more like the community she'd grown up in—Plissk and Weyfirs, plus she thought she spotted an Elbrekkian in the mix.

As soon as the steward finished announcing her, Everys smiled and stepped forward, dipping into a formal curtsy. She thought she heard Challix make an approving noise next to her. Everys fought to keep from smiling. See, she was paying attention during the etiquette lessons!

Duchess Wendly nodded. "We welcome you to our home, Blessed, and extend our protection over you. We offer safety and protection from all that threatens us."

Everys's eyebrows shot up at the wording and Challix shifted next to her. According to protocol, Everys was supposed to show deference to the host—which she did—and then the host would make a formal declaration of hospitality. Technically, the Duchess had done that, but she hadn't used the traditional wording. Was that a warning? Or did the Duchess see her as a threat?

Challix cleared her throat quietly.

"And I accept your hospitality. May we all find shelter within these walls." Everys blurted the words and winced. So much for a friendly dinner.

Dinner turned out to be a ridiculous display of excess. But then Everys hadn't expected anything less. Even as the servants cleared away the dishes from the second course, Everys could see the layers at work. The first course had been what nobles might consider an appetizer, although most people living in the Dynasty's holdings would have considered it a full meal. Next came a hearty vegetable stew. Everys was full after the first two courses, but the third and fourth courses would likely be the richest of the six, followed by a dessert and then a final glass of wine.

The evening's entertainment had been planned out in layers as well. There was a circular stage in the middle of the dining room, one that could be seen by every guest. During the first course, a single musician had taken the stage, playing a stringed instrument. During the second course, three more musicians had joined him. Now that they were transitioning to the third course, the musicians had vacated the stage and other performers were setting up. They had cleared away the instruments and replaced them with two large trunks, one blue and one red. A rack of clothing had also been set up at the foot of the stage. Looked like a theatre troupe.

But perhaps the most maddening part of the dinner was the complete lack of conversation with her hosts. Even though she was seated with a whole squad of Wendlys, none of them spoke. At first, she thought they were snubbing her, but then she realized they weren't talking to each other either. Another family quirk? Who could tell with nobles?

As the servants finished distributing the third course, the actors took to the stage. The lead actor, an older man with a rotund belly and a crescent of brown hair ringing his bald head, bowed with a flourish of his hands. "Blessed, dear hosts, guests one and all, we beseech your attention on the story requested for the night. Tonight's matter? *The Strangler Vine*."

Whispers rippled through the dining room. Everys frowned and looked at the other guests. They seemed... surprised? Concerned? She didn't know this particular story, so she couldn't decipher the guests' reaction.

"I know, I know." The lead actor clucked his tongue. "But Klamont Wendly was most insistent, and as he provides the blades, we fulfill the demand."

Everys glanced down the table at Klamont, the Duchess's oldest son. He was easily in his sixties, with a crown of thinning white hair and a prominent nose that threatened to swallow his entire face. While the Duchess was the official head of the family, everyone knew Klamont handled the Wendlys' affairs. Why would he want a story about a plant?

But as the story unfolded, Everys realized it wasn't about a plant at all. Instead, it seemed to be a children's story about a young woman who forced her way into a family of her betters. This girl, the titular vine, overpowered the others, taking control of their finances, their personal lives, everything, until she had figuratively strangled them all. Everys froze in place, trying to keep her expression neutral and her body relaxed.

Such a transparent metaphor. No wonder the guests had reacted that way! She could see what the Wendlys were trying to say. Everyone could. But unless she challenged Klamont to a duel, she couldn't think of any way to respond to such a flagrant insult.

But wait. She did have a way she could fight back. And thankfully, she had the proper tools to do so.

As soon as the actors wrapped up their performance, Everys scooted back from the table. Most of the guests looked in her direction, their expressions ranging from worried to horrified. They were probably expecting her to make a scene, to challenge the Wendlys, to do something about the insult.

Instead, she smiled demurely and signaled for one of the servers to approach. The server, a young Weyfir boy, darted forward.

"Blessed?" he whispered. "How may I serve?"

"Point me in the direction of the nearest bathroom," she whispered back.

His eyes widened, clearly horrified at the idea of the queen using such facilities. But he gestured for her to follow him. As soon as it was clear Everys wasn't doing anything scandalous, the guests returned to their muted conversation.

The boy led Everys out of the ballroom and to a nearby bathroom. As soon as the door was closed and locked, Everys set to work. She touched the bracelet halfway up her right arm. It appeared to be made of intertwined gold and silver branches, dotted with precious gems and exquisitely carved beads. She felt along the bracelet until she found one of the correct beads and, with a little yank, pulled it from its setting. Once it was free, she rolled it between her fingers, counting to twenty.

As she did, she smiled. Tormod, the Dynasty's spymaster, had supplied her with this particular item. She was one of the few to know that Tormod was really a Siporan who had hidden his heritage. Not even her husband knew the truth. She didn't know why he had a trick like this up his sleeve, but given the way he had a tendency of appearing out of nowhere, she often suspected he used toratropic magic in his spycraft.

As she worried the bead back and forth, it became more pliable. By the time she reached twenty, she could use the gelatinous ink to sketch a rune. While most ink used in the Xoniel Dynasty had a distinctly foul odor added to it to notify anyone nearby if a Siporan was using it to cast a rune, this ink was odorless. As soon as the ink was ready, she carefully drew the lines on her hand. It wasn't easy; the ink was just a shade darker than her olive skin, allowing it to be mostly unnoticeable. If someone didn't know about the ink, it would be easy to overlook. Unfortunately, the rune Everys wanted to use was complex, using flourishes and extra lines that she had rarely practiced. Not being able to clearly see what she was drawing made it extra challenging.

Once the rune was finished, she knew she'd have to work quickly. If the ink dried, the rune would be useless. Based on her experience, she had about five minutes before that happened.

The Weyfir server led her back to the dining room. Everys nodded to some of the guests she recognized and headed for the table. As she approached the dais, Klamont stepped into her path.

"Is everything all right, Blessed?" His voice dripped with false concern.

"Perfectly fine, Klamont." She mirrored his false smile. "I just find it helps to stretch my legs to avoid boredom. Although I must admit, your choice of entertainment this evening was intriguing."

His gaze sharpened, silent laughter lurking in his expression. "I know the material was unusual, but I've always had a fondness for that story. Are you familiar with the works of the story's author? Terrosin the Large?"

"I don't believe I am."

Klamont's smile broadened. "A pity. It's a shame that most schools in the Dynasty neglect such classic literature. I've always appreciated

Terrosin's take on how society ought to function. *The Strangler Vine*, I find, is a good reminder to never let my grasp exceed my reach."

She had to force herself to keep smiling when what she really wanted to do was smack his overfed face. "A worthy thing to remember, to be sure."

"I'm glad we agree. Well, if you'll excuse me, Blessed, I must prepare to give my toast. I'm sure you'll find that just as enlightening as the story."

"I have no doubt."

As Klamont turned to go, Everys tapped the rune on her palm, activating the magic. Then she snared his hand, forcing him to turn back to her.

"Lord Wendly, I thank you for your hospitality. I hope the same generosity I've seen tonight will extend to the relationship between your house and the palace. I know the king greatly appreciates the sacrifices the Wendlys have made over the years."

A look of genuine surprise flitted across Klamont's face. Apparently he believed her. But then, why wouldn't he? The Wendlys considerable holdings were mostly farmland. They produced a good portion of the Dynasty's food, although they always complained that too much was expected of them. She knew for a fact that Narius didn't put any stock in the Wendlys' complaints, but she had to keep Klamont still as the spell transferred from her palm to him.

Klamont cleared his throat, then said, "Yes, well... I hope that you will relay the words of my toast to your husband. It is my hope he will understand us better after tonight."

"I will be paying rapt attention," Everys said, every word sincere.

She released his hand and headed back to her seat. Her heart stuttered, and she tried to keep her expression neutral. She hoped she wouldn't laugh or even smirk once the spell took hold.

As soon as she was seated, Klamont stepped to the middle of the dais and stared imperiously at the other guests. Within a minute, they had all fallen silent and turned toward him, some with curiosity, others looking apprehensive or even eager.

Once the noise had died down, Klamont signaled to one of the servers. The Plissk boy darted forward from his station and pressed a full glass of red wine into his hand. Klamont scowled at the server, then offered a more pleasant smile to the guests, raising his glass.

"A toast, my friends, to all of you for joining us tonight. And to you, Queen Everys." He nodded in her direction. "While my family never dreamed we would have a Siporan grace our home, we are delighted that you are the first."

Everys fought to keep from snorting. From his tone, he probably hoped she'd also be the last.

"We Wendlys have always prided ourselves on the sacrifices we have made to make the Dynasty strong. When the Dynasty added the Right Highlands into their holdings, we were the first to acknowledge their authority. When they called for troops to fight their wars, we were the first to send conscripts. And when the Dynasty goes hungry, we are the first to send the fruit of our labor to meet that need without complaint."

Once again, Everys fought to keep her expression neutral. She wondered how many of the other guests would agree that the Wendlys didn't complain.

"We have proudly been the foundation upon which the Dynasty was built. Our family's motto says it best: 'Ours the blood, ours the fields.' And long have we appreciated the royal family's support and friendship."

Everys could feel the "but" coming as Klamont paused for what must have been dramatic effect. He should have taken lessons from the actors on how to do it properly.

"But our Dynasty faces crises unlike any we have conquered in the past centuries. Our king promises great changes that will benefit us all. And change he has made, best illustrated in the choice of his latest wife."

Her cheeks prickled with heat. That was an unfair jab. Gossips loved to titter about how Narius had been married four times, but that simply wasn't true. His first marriage had been arranged to a horrible woman who'd walked out on him. His second had been to her, a loveless alliance that had turned into more. His third wedding hadn't actually happened, thanks to a terrorist attack. And his fourth, remarrying her, well... she didn't count that as a separate marriage.

"And yes, he has achieved some measure of greatness. Forging peace with the Cold Light terrorists is certainly impressive. But while he has claimed victory, have we reaped any benefit? No. The same agricultural quotas remain in place. And rumors swirl that another round of conscriptions are imminent to counter the Dalark threat."

Everys's stomach churned. A small part of her chafed at Klamont's statement that Narius won the peace with the Cold Light, a race of sentient trees who had rebelled against the Dynasty for decades. *She* had brokered that peace, not Narius. But the dread growing in her heart overwhelmed the annoyance. Klamont wasn't doing much to hide his disdain for Narius's rule. And why hadn't the spell taken hold yet? It should have by now. Had she botched it?

"I would never suggest that any of us be as bold as those who are currently fomenting rebellion against the Dynasty's rulers." Klamont grimaced toward Everys, another poorly acted moment. "Such shameful behavior will undoubtedly come to nothing. But I would suggest that we, the families of the Right Highlands, our friends, our allies, we make our voices heard in Bastion, the Hall of All Voices, in the palace itself. We will stand with the Dynasty, as we always have, but if they demand more, we do too!"

Everys fought to keep from frowning. This was the heart of the evening? Klamont whining about his family's usual list of grievances? Based on the reaction of the other guests, they weren't taking him very seriously. They might all forget what he said by the end of dessert.

As she realized this, a cold weight settled in her stomach. She had made a terrible mistake. But there was nothing she could do about it without casting another rune on Klamont. Hopefully the spell hadn't worked...

"There is strength in numbers. The Perfected Warrior teaches us this!" Klamont thundered, raising his glass high. "Here's to—"

Then his left leg buckled.

Everys squeezed her legs to keep from reacting. Klamont wobbled. The wine in his glass sloshed, a tiny spray flying through the air. His eyes widened, and then his right leg buckled as well. He stumbled forward, his left arm pinwheeling while he tried to hang on to his cup.

But then both of his legs gave out, and he collapsed with a loud thud. His wineglass tumbled out of his hand, spraying the dais with crimson drops.

Several of the guests bolted to their feet as a chorus of gasps and cries ricocheted through the crowd. Several of Klamont's siblings and children darted to his side, but he batted away the hands of his would-be helpers and tried to push himself up again. But as soon as he got to his knees, he collapsed again.

"My legs!" Klamont shouted. "I can't feel my legs!"

More shouts and shrieks from the other guests. More of Klamont's relatives surged from their tables, trying to help. This time, he didn't fight them. Every time he tried to stand, his legs wouldn't cooperate.

Inkstains, that wasn't what she wanted at all! Yes, the rune was supposed to make his legs numb, but only for fifteen seconds, just enough to make him stumble. Had she accidentally made the spell permanent? She had meant to embarrass him, not cripple him, and—

Oh no.

The sensation started on the back of her hand. A wave of pins and needles shot up her arm and then down into her legs, growing sharper with each passing second. Pain spasmed in her thighs and rolled down into her calves before rebounding into her chest. Fire chased the pain, burning from her heart through the rest of her body.

Everys clenched her teeth to keep from crying out against the rebuke. She should have known it was coming; the Singularity didn't tolerate what He considered misuse of toratropic magic. The pain and discomfort would pass, but she didn't want to let on that she was hurting.

Her arm twitched and she dropped her glass. The crimson wine spilled, flowing across the tablecloth, looking like blood...

Like her husband's blood, pooling under his graying body as his life slipped through her fingers.

The sudden memory slammed down on her, and she bit back a cry. The rebuke intensified and her body spasmed.

"Blessed!" Challix's voice sounded like it echoed down a tunnel.

And then people surrounded her as well, guards and servers and Wendlys. And she tried to tell them that she was okay, but her jaw was clenched too tightly and another wave of pain rolled through her.

Everys realized that the trouble she feared had shown up. And she was the cause.

2

The dinner ended shortly after Klamont collapsed. Not a huge surprise. As Everys sat in the empty dining room, a great weight settled in her stomach. She had made such a mess of things.

Thankfully, the rune had ended after ten minutes, but that had been long enough to panic the other guests, especially since Everys had seemingly been struck down as well. The rebuke hadn't lasted as long as the spell, but her reaction had only made things worse. Rumors were likely swirling about poison or illness. Within the first few moments, half the guests had fled the dinner. The other half were too stunned to move. Eventually one of Klamont's nephews spoke some hasty words to dismiss the remaining guests, who filed out of the manor in deathly silence. Everys, sitting at the dais alone, watched them all go. The Wendlys had abandoned her as quickly as they could.

Challix emerged from one of the side doors and approached the dais. Everys studied her assistant's expression. No overt signs of disappointment, which was a surprise; Challix was usually the first to point out how she had messed up. But then, she didn't know what Everys had done.

"According to the Wendlys' family physician, Klamont is likely to make a full recovery," she said.

"Have they determined what caused his collapse?" Kevtho asked.

Everys's cheeks burned as she braced herself for the answer.

Challix shook her head. "I suspect they're going to do a medical examination." She turned to Everys. "They've offered to examine you as well, Blessed."

Everys blanched at the thought. They wouldn't find anything. A rebuke never left physical evidence. She shook her head. "I'm feeling much better now. Ready to head back to Bastion."

After exchanging a look with Challix, Kevtho cleared his throat. "Rewether is insisting we keep you here until the manor grounds clear out a bit more. If this was an attack, we want to keep you somewhere secure."

She swallowed a groan. She was the one who'd caused all of the drama in the first place. But she couldn't reveal that. The only people in the palace who were aware of her toratropic abilities were her husband, Vizier Paine, and Tormod.

"You poor dear!"

The guards snapped alert and whirled at the shout. A solitary woman, old enough to be Everys's mother, rushed to the dais. She was stocky, wearing a fashionable dress of long-flowing fabrics that just bordered on garish. But the moment Everys saw her, she couldn't help but smile.

"Oluna, I didn't know you'd be here," Everys said.

Oluna Hishi dodged around one of the guards and dropped onto the dais next to her. She snared Everys's hands and squeezed. "Are you feeling all right?"

"Much better now that I've seen you."

Oluna swatted her shoulder. "You're too kind, Blessed. I'm sorry that I wasn't able to talk to you sooner, but the Wendlys love their protocol. Since Masruq wasn't with me, I got stuck in the back of the room with the sycophants and hangers-on."

"I'm sorry. If I would have known, I would have insisted you join me."

"No need. I spent my time well. I seeded three different rumors that could blossom into truly juicy scandals, although I daresay that all of my hard work has probably been forgotten by now."

Everys's smile grew broader. She didn't know if Oluna had actually done that, but she wouldn't have been surprised if she had. Everys had met her several months earlier at a Queen's Court. Oluna, the wife of finance minister Masruq, was a bright spot in the minefield of the noble houses. She could at least make these events entertaining.

"Any good ones I should help spread?" Everys asked.

Oluna shrugged expansively. "Oh, just the usual. Possible affairs, a simmering feud between two lesser houses, plus an imminent bankruptcy. Nothing truly scandalous and all of them will evaporate once the truth comes out. But then again, my stories were better crafted than those actors, eh?"

Oh. Everys had almost forgotten about that. She focused on her fingers, which twisted together in her lap.

But Oluna leaned forward and patted her knee. "Don't worry about that, Blessed. Klamont thinks himself clever. An opinion no one shares, mind you. Most guests were laughing at him rather than you."

So if she hadn't done anything, Klamont's speech wouldn't have mattered? Everys swallowed a groan. Perfect! She was surprised she didn't get hit with another rebuke.

Oluna chuckled. "Don't worry, Blessed. This will all be forgotten soon enough. I know your schedule is likely packed full, but when you find a free evening, come over for dinner. I'll make Masruq cook. Truth be told, he could rival anything we had here tonight."

Everys forced herself to smile. "That sounds wonderful."

Oluna beamed, and Everys tried to match her enthusiasm. But she didn't feel it. Narius had sent her here to strengthen their relationship with the nobility. Not only had she failed to do that, but she had learned that their support was eroding faster than anyone probably realized. But if anyone would be able to figure out what to do about it, it was Narius.

She hoped.

3

Narius could feel the day dragging at him. He should have been asleep rather than working in the Amber Office, especially this deep into Third Watch. But he had two good reasons to stay up. Officially, it was to monitor the unfolding crises that threatened to swamp the Dynasty. He refused to be the king who watched all of his ancestors' hard work come unraveled.

Unofficially, it was because he knew he wouldn't be able to sleep until Everys was back from the Wendlys' dinner.

He leaned back in his chair, stretching his arms and twisting his back. As he did, he glanced around the room. The Amber Office was overwhelming by design, the official inner sanctum of the Xoniel Dynasty's king. Momentous decisions needed a dramatic backdrop. Most of the decor hadn't changed in two centuries, with intricately carved panels on the wall, along with stately paintings and exquisite sculptures. But tucked among the ostentatious decor were less formal touches: flowers from the royal gardens or a lacy ribbon woven around the leg of one statue. At the sight of each, his heart twitched, an empty ache that radiated into his arms.

He hated it when Everys wasn't home. That happened more and more frequently. If she wasn't working on her charitable foundation, she was attending parties thrown by the nobility. And when she was available, he wasn't. Ever since they'd remarried a few weeks ago, Narius felt like they saw less and less of each other than when they were first married.

But that would change in—he checked the chrono on his desk—about fifteen minutes. He had already heard the military skimmer land at the palace's private tarmac.

"Your Strength?" Paine's quiet voice jolted him out of his mental calculations. "Are you even listening to me anymore?"

Narius jumped, turning to his vizier. In spite of the late hour, Paine looked positively regal in his robes of state. The dark skin of his bald head gleamed in the low light and the disapproval in his gaze was unmistakable.

"I'm sorry, old friend." Narius winced. "Something about Duke Brencis's rebellion?"

Paine sighed heavily, but he nodded. "We haven't been able to ascertain the duke's current location, nor do we know how much of the military might be loyal to him. We could have a coup on our hands in months. Possibly even weeks."

The reprimand in Paine's words was unmistakable, but Narius wondered how accurate his prediction really was. Yes, Duke Brencis had his supporters. Narius knew full well some in the military didn't appreciate the new direction he was trying to take the Dynasty. But was it really that dire? He made a mental note to send out feelers to the senior officers in the military to gauge the discontent.

But Brencis had other supporters to draw from. The nobility could throw in with Brencis. While noble houses no longer maintained large militias, they could send what soldiers they had to Brencis. And they could cause Narius difficulties in other ways. He clenched his jaw. Hopefully Everys's time with the Wendlys would help him there, and—

The door to the Amber Office opened, and Zar, the head of the royal guard, stepped inside. He cleared his throat.

"Sorry to interrupt, Your Strength, but the Queen's skimmer just returned home, and she's being checked out by the doctors down in the infirmary."

Narius's head snapped back. She was what?

Before Zar could finish his report, Narius sprinted from the room. He hurried through the halls, past the doors to the throne room, and into the palace's private quarters. Then down a set of stairs and into the brightly lit palace infirmary.

Everys sat on the edge of a medical bed, her face pinched into a scowl. She was surrounded by doctors and nurses who were busy taking her vitals and peppering her with questions, all of which she answered. Rewether, Kevtho, and Challix stood nearby. When Paine entered the room, Challix stepped over to him and they had a brief but heated whispered conversation. Once Challix finished, Paine turned to face Everys, his face unreadable.

"Blessed, how was the dinner party?" Paine asked.

Narius shot a look at his vizier. There was something about Paine's tone that hinted something had happened, something he didn't approve of.

"Challix says you and Klamont Wendly suffered attacks of some kind." Paine's expression sharpened.

Challix looked stricken. Everys hung her head.

Narius looked to the doctors. "Is the queen all right?"

"As near as we can tell, she is," one of the doctors said. "Based on what we've heard, she likely had a panic attack after she saw what happened to Lord Wendly. We've taken some blood samples to test for poisons, but she's not showing any problematic symptoms right now."

Everys shot Narius a look, one he understood easily. They wouldn't find anything else. This had likely been a rebuke from using a rune improperly.

He cleared his throat. "All of you, please give us the room."

The doctors exchanged a look, but the lead physician motioned for everyone to leave.

Unfortunately, Paine didn't leave with them. "Practicing your illicit arts again? And in public?"

"That's unimportant right now," Everys said.

"'Unimportant?'" Paine sneered. "The Dynasty is teetering on a sword's edge and your carelessness could slice us to pieces."

"My 'carelessness' is the least of your troubles," Everys said. "Klamont Wendly was giving the most treasonous speech I've ever heard!"

Paine crossed his arms. "Let me guess. King Narius has been asking too much of us. We need to band together and assert our rights as nobles."

"Well, yes, but—"

"Are you sure that you aren't trying to just deflect our attention from your embarrassment at being compared to a strangler vine?"

Everys sat up straighter on the bed, her eyes igniting.

Narius quickly stepped between them. He shot a glare at Paine, then turned to Everys. "I'm sorry for whatever it is Klamont said about you. But he's said this sort of thing before. We don't have to worry about the Wendlys' support."

"No offense, husband, but I'm not sure that's true," Everys said. "Things are falling to pieces, and I think it's worse than you suspect. Have you found Duke Brencis yet?"

Paine's eyes flared, but he said nothing.

"Sadly, no," Narius said.

"How about a replacement as head of the Dynasty's military?" She leaned forward. "I doubt that the delay in naming Brencis's replacement is helping matters any."

"Now you're an expert in military oversight as well as international relations?" Paine asked.

Everys fixed him with a withering glare. "Only when it's blindingly obvious."

Paine flinched at the rebuke, and Narius had to stifle a laugh. Most humans within the Dynasty worshiped the Perfected Warrior, who supposedly urged his followers to be as blunt and rude to each other as possible, if only to keep their wits as sharp as their blades. Everys had taken to the tradition with gusto.

But he didn't need a verbal sparring match this late at night, especially not in the infirmary. He held up a hand. "Choosing Brencis's replacement isn't easy. There are familial standings to consider, along with how the choice might be interpreted within the Hall of All Voices or the Ethnarch Parliament. We've been able to narrow the candidates down to six or seven possible contenders, and—"

"All of them from the nobility?" Everys asked.

"Of course," Paine replied. "Who else would we consider?"

"How about Strategist Overturn of Vetranio's First Stand? I've done some research into his background." Everys counted off her reasons on her fingers as she spoke. "He rose through the ranks from vanguard to strategist in record time. He's well-respected by both his soldiers and officers and received numerous commendations. And, as near as I can tell, he can still serve for fifteen to twenty years."

Paine scoffed. "He isn't a noble. And he's an Ixactl. Those two points alone are enough to disqualify him. Are you certain this suggestion isn't motivated by something else? Overturn is the cousin of the former captain of your guard, is he not?"

Everys's cheeks flushed bright red. "That doesn't matter. Promoting a nonhuman sends the right message and you know it."

Once again, Narius could feel the discussion was on the verge of becoming an all-out verbal brawl. He held up a calming hand. "I will take it under consideration. But it's not a decision to make right now. Why don't you head up to your room when the doctors are done? I'll be there in a little while."

Everys's body seemed to deflate. "That would probably be best. I'll see you soon." She glared at Paine. "Vizier."

"Blessed."

Narius stepped closer to Everys and kissed her, briefly, enough to stir up some deeper desire in him. But he couldn't act on those thoughts. She smiled thinly at him and settled back onto the bed. Then Narius left the infirmary with Paine in tow. He nodded to the medical staff, Everys's guards, and Challix as they passed.

"I do wish you wouldn't be hostile toward her," Narius said once they were out of earshot of the others. "She means well, and her idea does have merit."

Paine sighed and nodded. "In a perfect world, yes. But that is not the world we live in. Have you heard Supreme Prelate Istragon's latest pronouncements?"

Now Narius snorted. Why would he put any stock in a reactionary religious leader when most of the Dynasty's people didn't really believe in the traditional religion?

"We can't ignore him," Paine said. "While he may be a zealot, he still commands a great deal of respect among both the nobility and the common folk. He's already convinced the queen is a Siporan witch who brainwashed you. If you defy tradition in appointing Brencis's replacement, he could become a true threat."

"Perhaps." Narius sighed. "Regardless, we won't solve this particular problem as of right now. What is the most pressing issue that must be addressed?"

Paine nodded curtly and launched into a summary of troubling resolutions making their way through the Hall of All Voices. And while Narius tried to concentrate on his friend's words as they walked back to his office, his mind was already heading up to Everys's room.

Of all the arrogant, infuriating, insufferable... The vizier had never liked her, never even given her a chance.

Angry thoughts chased Everys through the halls of the palace until she stepped through the doors to her quarters.

"Blessed! Welcome back!" Trule, her chief maid, hurried to her side. "I know it's late, but I've brewed some sandwarmer tea for you. Good to calm the nerves before bed."

Even though Third Watch was almost over, Trule still looked bright-eyed and alert. Maybe the Plissk, her people, didn't need as much sleep as humans. Everys hadn't known many of the reptilian desert dwellers before becoming queen, but now she considered Trule one of her closest... well, maybe "friend" wasn't quite the right term. There would always be a separation between them, one carved out by her position and authority. But Trule was trustworthy, competent, and caring, and Everys did what she could to make sure Trule was well cared for in return.

"Thank you, but I'll pass this time," Everys said. "Help yourself, though. You're dismissed for the evening."

Trule paused in the kitchenette, the teapot in her hand. An uncertain look flickered across her face, but then she smiled knowingly. "I'll leave the pot here for the king, then. He may wish to try it. Good night, Blessed."

And with that, Trule hustled out of the room, shooing the guards away as well.

As soon as the door clicked shut, Everys let out a sigh. Some of the stress melted away as she flopped onto one of the couches. Her gaze roamed around the room. When she'd first moved into the palace, she'd considered the extravagance of the queen's quarters an insult to the Dynasty's poorest residents. So much wasted space! But while she still recognized them as a waste of resources, she now felt a certain amount of comfort at the familiar surroundings. She had kept most of the furniture, the clusters of couches around a fireplace, another around a vidscreen, but she'd gotten rid of Viara's many mirrors. Narius's ex-wife had them everywhere. And Everys had added some touches of her own: paintings of the Cold Light forest, another depicting the shores of the Water Bearer's Repose, and even one of the tightly packed buildings of Fair Havens. They were all reminders of why she stayed in the palace, to try to help the Dynasty. Well, that and to help Narius as well.

Her gaze hitched on one dark corner of the room and she frowned. "You might as well come out. Narius will be here soon."

A low chuckle caused a shiver to dance up her spine, and she was suddenly aware of a presence behind her. She whirled around to see an ordinary-looking man standing behind her, a smile on his face. She clenched her teeth. How did he keep doing that?

"You're getting better, Blessed," he said, his voice soothing.

"Is that just spycraft or do you use runes?" she asked.

Tormod's smile didn't falter for a moment. "Now why would you ask that?"

Everys raised her arm and pointed to the bracelet. "Why else would you have something like this lying around?"

He chuckled. "A fair point. But just as your family protects their secrets, mine protects ours."

She swallowed a grumble. "It's been a long day, Tormod. Can't this wait?"

His smile grew broader. "You would prefer I arrived later? Perhaps after Narius has come up to your room?"

Everys's cheeks burned at the thought. No, of course not.

"I merely heard about what happened at the Wendlys. And I can't help but notice that one of the beads is missing from your bracelet." Tormod shrugged. "It isn't difficult to deduce what happened."

She studied his face, searching for any hint of disapproval. "Are you going to take the bracelet back?"

Tormod shook his head. "Now why would I do that?"

"Because I misused a rune." Everys looked down, her fingers twisting in her lap. "The Singularity did rebuke me."

"True, He did," Tormod said. "But I'm not here to play disapproving schoolmaster. Instead, I want you to tell me everything that Klamont Wendly said in his toast before the... unfortunate incident."

"Don't you have this information already?"

Tormod grinned lazily. "Humor me, Blessed."

Everys frowned and tried to recall everything Klamont had said. Her words were hesitant at first, but as she recited what she remembered, she became more certain, more sure. Tormod listened to everything she said, his face grim. As she wrapped it up, his left eye twitched. Subtle, but she noticed.

"What?" she asked.

He looked away, his brow pinching into a frown. Then he sighed. "From what my sources have told me, there have been echoes of Klamont's words at parties throughout the Dynasty's holdings. Almost as if they were all reading from the same script. I suspect I could finish Klamont's speech had it not been interrupted. And while Klamont Wendly is not known for being erudite, the others who have shared the same message are. From what I've heard, their attempts have been much more effective."

"Someone is trying to stir up the nobility against Narius." Everys swallowed hard. "And me."

"That is my belief, yes."

But who would do that? There were many possible culprits. Duke Brencis, the former head of the Dynasty's military, who had tried to overthrow Narius just two months earlier. Emperor Tirigian, the head of the Dalark Imperium, who was ramping up for war with the Dynasty. Or even Supreme Prelate Istragon, the head of the Dynasty's official religion, who made no secret of his hatred for Everys and her people.

She looked around her quarters again, suddenly feeling as though she were trapped in a very pretty cage. She wanted to run, leave the palace, leave the city. Maybe even the Dynasty itself. Leave all the troubles far behind and—

Tormod touched her shoulder, jolting her out of her panicked mindset. "Of course, I could be jumping at shadows. That is my job, after all. Don't worry, Blessed, we won't go down without a fight. I have many agents in the field right now, we'll be ready should whoever is responsible escalate beyond mere toasts and speeches."

Everys's face fell. That seemed cliche. But before she could press him on it, he stepped out of the room into the hall that led to her bedroom. She hustled after him, only to discover that he had vanished. She knew he wasn't in her bedroom; he was too polite to do something that crass. But how had he done that?

She supposed that mystery would have to wait. There were too many other issues pressing in on her, and she knew that she'd solve none of them that evening. For now, the best thing she could do was be with her husband and try to ignore the dread that threatened to swallow her.

4

If he had to answer one more call about vermin, Quartus would challenge someone to a duel. But while that would be satisfying, he knew he couldn't. If he did, his skills might reveal that he was really the disgraced and supposedly exiled prince and king's brother. And that would ruin everything.

Since that wasn't an option, Quartus ground his teeth and listened to yet another complaint about a basement infested with wiggats. Quartus tried to interrupt several times, but the caller was determined to explain just how upsetting this was. Quartus leaned back in his chair and snapped his fingers to get Stoophawk's attention.

The massive Ixactl had to duck to keep from getting his horns caught in the basement's ceiling. His expression was hopeful until Quartus shook his head. "More crustmongers?"

Quartus mouthed, "Wiggats."

Stoophawk snarled. "Lots of bitin' for not a lot of blades."

"You'll get paid regardless." That statement led to a squawk from the comm. "No, sir, I wasn't talking to you. I'm sending over a team of exterminators right now."

He dropped the connection, tapped the address into a digital scriber, then sent the info to Stoophawk's.

"You know, I don't mind bein' the front for something illegal or unsavory," Stoophawk said. "Gotta make the money legitimate somehow. But I'd at least like to know what it is we're a front for in case the constables ever ask. So I know what not to say."

Quartus leaned back in his chair and considered his... not friend. He had very few of those. But Stoophawk was far too intelligent to be labeled mere muscle. His crony? Second-in-command? Whatever he was, he probably wouldn't drop this until he had an answer.

"Very true. All right. We are basically running a makeshift counterintelligence unit at the behest of Tormod, King Narius's master of shadows, searching primarily for Cold Light terrorists but also for any evidence of collusion with Dalark infiltrators. Oh, and I'm also Prince Quartus, King Narius's estranged brother."

Stoophawk blinked at him. Quartus tensed, bracing himself.

After a few quiet moments, Stoophawk snorted. "Well, if you don't think I should know, you could've told me, instead of makin' up such a dumb story."

Quartus fought a smirk. Sometimes the truth was simply too unbelievable. Thankfully, this proved to be one of those times.

"Go deal with the wiggats. I'll keep answering the calls," he said.

"Don't know why you can't go," Stoophawk grumbled.

"You have thicker skin than I do. The bites won't hurt as much."

Stoophawk grunted but didn't say anything else. Instead, he squeezed up the stairs.

As soon as he was alone, Quartus sagged in his chair with a groan. This was not what he'd expected when he'd agreed to this assignment. When Tormod had suggested that he might serve the Dynasty by going undercover, it had seemed like such a great idea. A way to redeem himself.

A few months earlier, he had been framed for an attempted assassination of the king and queen. Thanks to Everys's intervention, what should have been a death sentence was commuted to declaring him outlaw. During that time, he had gathered a small gang of thugs and petty criminals, all of whom knew him as Qulinus. Completing his mission should have been simple enough. He had served in a counterintelligence unit for his military service. He considered himself charming and clever enough to find what he needed.

But, Dented Shield, he hadn't expected the actual work to be boring!

His gaze flicked to a map of Bastion, the Dynasty's capital city. His team had started in a neighborhood called Defector's Wrath, but they hadn't stayed there. They had already found one secret laboratory in that neighborhood, and Quartus thought it unlikely there would be a second in the same neighborhood. He had considered searching Fair Havens next, but ever since Queen Everys had accidentally started a riot there, it'd been under strict scrutiny by both the local constables and the military police.

So they had set themselves up in the Everhold. While the Everhold was filled with residential areas, there were just as many commercial properties scattered throughout. Old industrial buildings clustered at the north end, along with a former military base. And the Melgor River bordered the southern edge.

The comm started blinking and Quartus sighed. After setting up as exterminators three weeks ago, they'd been swamped with jobs almost immediately. But unfortunately, none of those calls had led them to what they were actually looking for.

"Greetings, friend." Quartus tried to inject a bit of friendliness into his voice. "This is Knife's Edge Exterminators. What seems to be the problem?"

"It's about time you answered!" A woman's voice and, based on her accent, probably a Weyfir. "You've got to help us. My husband and I are trying to sell our home, and there's some sort of infestation in the neighborhood."

"We'd be happy to help." Quartus hoped the lie sounded genuine. "What part of your house is infested?"

"Well, uh, it's not our house that has the problem. It's a neighboring property."

"Why aren't they calling us?" Quartus said.

The woman sighed. "Because technically the property isn't inhabited. Someone's been building a house there for the past two decades."

Quartus sighed. "Ma'am, I hate to say it, but there's nothing we can do. We can't just go onto someone else's property. I suggest you contact the local constabulary and report the issue. They'll pass it along to—"

"Do you think we're stupid? We already did that, and the constables said the issue was outside their purview!"

Quartus frowned. Given what he had seen of most constables in Bastion, they considered everything their business. Why wouldn't they here? Had someone told them to back off?

"We just need someone to help with these bugs."

"Ma'am, I'd like to, but I'm not sure what else we'll be able to do..." The woman's last complaint caught up with his thoughts. "Wait, did you say bugs?"

"Yes!"

"What kind?"

"I have no idea."

Quartus sat up in his chair, his heart hammering against his ribs. "Describe them."

"I don't know. They're small and green?"

Had they finally found them? "And they're infesting your neighbor's property?"

"Yes, a whole cloud of them."

"Do you see them mostly in the day or at night?"

"Early evening."

He bit back a triumphant shout. This had to be it. "How large is your neighbor's property? Any trees?"

"S-some, I guess. It's a pretty large property, mostly fenced off, but I think they have some wooded areas."

"Excellent!" He winced. Who would be excited for an insect infestation? "I'll be there to inspect the problem today. In a few hours. And hopefully, I'll be able to take care of the problem for you."

"Are you sure?"

"Absolutely. Now what's the address please?"

The woman gave him the information, and he tapped it into his scriber. The moment he dropped the call, he laughed in triumph. Finally! This was the first real lead they had found, and if they were lucky, this would be exactly what they were looking for.

He hurried out of the building and found Stoophawk loading the transport with the other members of the gang. Quartus waved at them.

"Hold on, boys, we've got a different job. A better one."

Stoophawk snorted. "How so?"

"No biting with this one." And hopefully it would bring him one step closer to the answers he needed.

Quartus studied the houses as they drove past. Not the hovels you might find in the poorer neighborhoods, but definitely not the mansion the nobles inhabited either. These were mostly made of brick or dark stones, with yards surrounding them. He nodded to himself. A fair amount of privacy, and a relaxed atmosphere that wouldn't invite scrutiny.

Quartus guided Stoophawk through the winding streets until they arrived. Sure enough, a Weyfir woman waited for them outside her home. Her skin was a pale blue, and her hair was a stringy black mess.

"You got here quick," she said.

"What can I say?" He offered her his most charming smile. "You sounded like you needed help, and I am more than happy to oblige."

A smile flitted across her lips, prompting one from Quartus as well. She probably found him attractive; many women did, and he was more than aware of it. Most of them were captivated by his golden blond hair and his copper eyes, a marker of his royal heritage. Thankfully, that feature wasn't exclusive to the royal family. Many of the noble houses had just enough royal blood for metallic-colored eyes to pop up in their children too. But Quartus never turned down an advantage.

"So where is the property with the infestation?" Quartus tried to hide his anticipation. He had to play the part of a hard-working exterminator, after all.

She pointed behind him and he turned. The neighboring house wasn't even visible from the road. Instead, a tall stone wall bordered the property with an iron gate hanging open. Quartus frowned. Why was the gate open? Was someone expecting them? But no, the woman said the property was under construction. Were they expecting construction vehicles?

He turned back to the woman, fixing his smile in place. "Don't worry, ma'am. We'll look into it and see what we can find, okay?"

"Just get rid of the bugs. That's all I want." Her gaze raked up and down his body, making it clear that wasn't *all* she wanted. "Maybe you can come in and have some tea while your team works?"

Stoophawk grumbled something under his breath. Quartus bit his tongue to keep from laughing.

"While I'm flattered, ma'am, I'm afraid that wouldn't be appropriate. I appreciate the offer, though. Maybe some other time?"

She giggled, but thankfully, she took the hint and went back into her house.

"We go in and kill the bugs, right?" Stoophawk asked.

Quartus shook his head. "Not just yet. Stickler? Take a peek."

Stickler, a scrawny Grerid man, darted forward, pulling a device from his belt. Stickler was one of the best thieves Quartus had ever met, especially when it came to bypassing security systems.

A few minutes later, Stickler turned around and nodded. "Property's hot, boss. We've got camera emplacements near the gate, plus intrusion sensors in the wall. If we would've stormed in, local constables or private security would have been notified immediately."

"Can you get past it?" Quartus asked.

Stickler chuckled. "Real question is, how long you want it down?"

Quartus considered. They might have to search the whole property, maybe even the house itself. They couldn't linger for too long, though. "Two hours?"

"I'll force the system into a deep diagnostic mode. Anyone monitoring it will think it's just routine maintenance. Gimme a moment."

Stickler skulked along the wall before kneeling and fiddling with something in the ground. As Stickler worked, Quartus turned to the rest of the team.

"All we're doing here is looking for bugs. Green ones, really small. You find them, you let me know. Got it?"

The other six members of the team nodded. But Stoophawk frowned. "You making us go legit as exterminators now?"

"Hey, trust Qulinus, Stoop." Varcu was a green-scaled Plissk teenager with nimble fingers and an eagerness born of youth. "There's a reason we follow him, not you."

Stoophawk grumbled, but he nodded.

Stickler hurried back to the group. "We got two hours, but I wouldn't dawdle."

"Okay. Stoophawk, you take Stickler and Varcu and scout the house. The rest of you, spread out through the grounds and look for bugs."

The team nodded, and they hustled through the open gates with Quartus taking up the rear.

While the rest of his men scattered across the property, Quartus walked the perimeter. The main gate was one way onto the property, but if this was a secret base, he suspected there would be others. It took him at least a half hour to walk the wall, which was in surprisingly poor repair. The walls were probably built at least ten years earlier, maybe more. He spotted a few breaks where a person could squeeze through. And as he walked along the back wall, he thought he heard gurgling in the distance. The Melgor River? He'd have to check a map.

Miklat, another member of the gang, quietly hurried to his side. "Qulinus! Think we found something."

Miklat led him to two others standing in a copse of trees. Green bugs swarmed among the trees, but they seemed focused on four stumps. Quartus pulled out his scriber and pulled up the briefing information Tormod had given him. He held the device next to one of the bugs as it scuttled along the trunk of a tree and compared it to an image on the scriber.

A smile tugged at his lips. They had finally found them.

"This is good news, boss?" Miklat asked.

"Very good news."

For years, the Dynasty had been under threat of terroristic attacks by the Cold Light, a race of sentient trees that had been conquered by Quartus's grandfather seventy years earlier. Their rebellion officially came to an end a few months earlier thanks to the work of Narius and Everys. As part of the peace treaty, the Cold Light had given the Dynasty bark beetles that would be attracted to the Cold Light. The bugs had been released in Bastion to sniff out the terrorists. Tormod had asked Quartus to find them, and now, he had.

"What's next?" Miklat asked.

Quartus knelt and tried to get a closer look at the stumps, but that wasn't easy thanks to the swarming bugs. He had expected to find Cold Light trees—he thought they were called "pillar trees"—when he located the bugs. Why were they chopped down? A chill swept over him, and he felt the distinct urge to run. He snarled. This wasn't the time to retreat, not yet.

"Keep looking," Quartus said.

His men did as they were told. Quartus set off, looking for more members of the team. He found Stoophawk, Stickler, and Varcu tucked behind a low hill, staring at the unfinished manor house.

Quartus dropped down and examined it for himself. What he saw made no sense. The manor looked to have been designed forty years earlier, and yet it was still half-finished. The servants' quarters didn't even have walls, just outlines of rooms in cement. Only half the windows had been installed, seemingly at random. And yet the walls appeared to be in good repair, as were the constructed sections of the roof. If anything, the manor looked more like someone's attempt at creating a half-finished house than an actual interrupted construction.

He didn't like this. Not one bit. A fake construction site, a finished security system, plus dead Cold Light? A shiver wormed down his back. It was time to get out of here, regroup, and come back some other time.

"See any bugs?" Quartus asked.

Stickler chuckled. "You could say that."

A swarm of bark beetles darted in and out several of the open windows. There had to be something inside the house that was attracting them as well. But the fact that there wasn't any visible response from anyone in the house made Quartus even more uneasy. Definitely time to go. If the woman who called them noticed their departure, he'd just tell her they needed specialized equipment and would be back later.

"Let's go, boys," Quartus whispered.

"We found what we're looking for?" Stoophawk asked.

Quartus nodded, hoping he projected more confidence than he felt. Because he had a sinking feeling that he wasn't any closer to the answers he sought.

5

Everys nibbled on fried kulith, the fruit's overly sweet flavor tempered by the char. She was grateful. The morning after the disaster at the Wendly estate, she needed the rich treat.

The news wasn't helping. The vidscreen in her quarters displayed a local crier, a pleasant-looking young woman who shared the latest stories from around the Dynasty's holdings. No mention of how both Klamont Wendly and she had collapsed at dinner. That gossip likely hadn't percolated to Bastion just yet. But there was still plenty to unsettle her.

"Minister Bokil has confirmed the rumors of recent equipment theft from Firebase Forward Seven. A dozen soldiers have reportedly deserted, stealing just as many transports and loads of weapons and ammunition. While the motive of the deserters is still unclear, their superiors suspect they have left to join Duke Brencis's forces."

Everys swallowed a groan. Granted, twelve soldiers deserting wasn't the biggest threat. But they weren't the only ones. The last she'd heard, at least four thousand troops had joined Brencis. And with the news of what these soldiers had done, it was likely more would follow.

Everys went to a computer terminal so she could pull up everything she could on Duke Brencis. True, the Dalark threat was more serious, but it felt further off. While the Dalark had some forces stationed in their Beachhead, the majority of their military was back in their homeland across the Dalark Channel. It would take weeks for them to truly matter. But Brencis was somewhere within the Dynasty's holdings at that moment, scheming and plotting.

Everys skimmed the basic biographical information first. His family, the Dwellins, were influential, one of the most powerful of the major houses. Not only that, but one of Brencis's ancestors had been queen.

That explained his coppery eyes and resemblance to the royal family. It was also why he could make a legitimate claim on the throne. His family connections were dense and complex. The Dwellins had intermarried with almost all the major houses and a surprising number of the minor ones over the generations. As Everys studied the genealogies, lines crisscrossed to create a web with Brencis at the center, and her eyes started to hurt.

Military record next. This was a bit more straightforward. Like all nobles, Brencis had his citizenship at birth, but he had enlisted in the military anyway. Much to her surprise, he hadn't gone straight into the officer corps the way most nobles did. Instead, he'd started as a lowly vanguard and worked his way up the ranks. He had seen some serious combat, having been deployed to Maotoa to put down rebels on the island province. That had earned him his own squad, which he'd used to hunt down Dunestrider separatists. Those campaigns had vaulted him up the ranks.

However, he had truly made his name when King Girai, Narius's father, loaned him to Tomma to put down a rebellion in that nation. His exploits had been shared far and wide through the Dynasty's holdings. When he'd returned home from overseas, King Girai rewarded him by making him the head of the Dynasty's military shortly before Girai died.

That was worrisome. Brencis was a genuine war hero. And in a culture that worshiped the Perfected Warrior, a man who had spilled his blood both at home and abroad would be revered. While Narius had served in the military as well, he wasn't a war hero.

She frowned. Where would Brencis be hiding? Given his familial connections with many noble houses, any one of them could be sheltering him. But then, anyone in the Dynasty who thought he was a better example of what a true citizen of the Dynasty should be like would do the same. And he had served all over the Dynasty as well... She rubbed her eyes. Too many possibilities. No wonder no one could track him down. He could be anywhere.

Her data terminal pinged, indicating a high priority news story. She closed her research and pulled up the feed. Weighted with certain keywords to cut through the clutter, an automated alerts program always let her know if anyone published a story about herself or Narius. For her terminal to ping, the story had to be pretty—

Her mouth dropped open as she read through the information. Cold sluiced through her chest and pooled in her stomach. This wasn't possible.

"Istragon challenged you to ritual combat?"

Narius winced at Everys's tone. This wasn't how he'd hoped this conversation would go. He had hoped he'd be able to share the story himself over breakfast, putting things in context so she'd understand how trivial this was. He had only found out about the challenge the previous night himself, when Istragon's acolyte brought him the official documents. Apparently someone in the Supreme Prelate's office had leaked the story to the press.

"Well?" She crossed her arms, her eyes on fire.

He signaled for his servants to leave his quarters. They quickly vacated, the last one quietly closing the doors behind him. Narius set aside his breakfast and motioned for Everys to sit down across from him. "I can have them bring in some food for you, if you wish."

She didn't respond. Didn't even move. Just glared at him hard enough he worried her gaze would impale him. Dented Shield, she was radiant!

"Very well," he said. "Yes, Istragon has challenged me to a sort of ritual combat."

Her frown deepened. "What does that mean?"

"According to ancient traditions, if the Supreme Prelate believes the king has strayed too far from the Perfect Warrior's teachings, the prelate can demand that he prove his devotion through a ritual called *harsannon*, or the 'Path to Glory.'"

"Through a fight?"

"Usually, although 'combat' can be broadly interpreted. For example, King Pellio the Learned had to engage fifteen acolytes in a scholarly debate on what the Perfected Warrior's weaponry was made of. And a few generations before that, King Grumio defeated a dozen swordsmen and twenty archers." He smiled at Everys's puzzled expression. "He was also eighty-five years old and well loved that his opponents just swung at him and let him toddle through their ranks and gently knock them over."

"Is that what's going to happen here?" Doubt bled through her voice.

He shook his head. "Most likely not. In both of those cases, there would have been negotiations between the prelate and king. There were no such talks for this. And given the vitriol in Istragon's most recent homilies, I doubt he would agree to symbolic combat."

"Oh."

"But it's not really combat either. For the past hundred and fifty years, these combats have been more like a sporting event than warfare. Practice weapons, point scoring, that sort of thing..."

Narius's voice trailed off when he realized that Everys had gone silent. An outside observer might have thought she wasn't listening, but Narius recognized that look: Everys gazing down to her right, a small crease between her eyes, her jaw clenched so hard her lips were a thin line. He had seen it often during the first weeks of their marriage. Everys might have fallen silent, but her mind hadn't. She was likely dissecting everything he'd told her, trying to find a way to circumvent this challenge or turn it to his advantage. He wouldn't have been surprised if she volunteered to take his place in combat. That would be an interesting fight.

"How do we get you out of this?" she finally asked.

"Paine should be here any minute to craft our reply."

And he recognized that expression as well. Everys always flinched when she heard that Paine was coming.

"Everys..." he said.

She shook her head. "I know what you're going to say. He needs to be here. It's his job."

It was, but he really did wish that she would make peace with Paine. He was one of his oldest friends, one of his staunchest allies in court. If Paine and Everys could set aside their differences, he suspected that the two of them would be able to reshape the Dynasty to whatever they wanted it to be.

Although, in that case, they might decide they didn't need him anymore. He shifted in his seat. Maybe it was better that they didn't see eye to eye.

Paine strode into the room. His gaze landed on Everys and his expression soured. Narius sighed and felt a twinge in his temples.

"Blessed, nice of you to join us," Paine said, his tone cool. "I took the liberty to pull up every challenge and response that we have on record, Your Strength." Paine pulled out a scriber and slid it across the table to Narius. "According to my research, your predecessors have rarely declined a prelate's challenge. Those few times they have were due to extenuating circumstances."

"Such as?" Narius prompted.

"In two cases, the king died before he could respond. In another, the Plissk went into open rebellion and the king had to put down the revolt. After proving himself in war, the prelate withdrew his challenge. And then there was the way your grandfather handled a similar challenge. He had Supreme Prelate Artamo assassinated."

"Those are my options? Dying, war, or assassination?" Narius asked.

"I'd pick assassination," Everys said.

Paine didn't even glance in her direction. "I'm afraid so, Your Strength. Istragon could withdraw the challenge—"

"—but that doesn't seem likely, does it?" Narius stroked his chin.

"Doubtful at best."

Narius sighed. "Very well. Then let's prepare the correct response. Make sure you invoke the Perfected Warrior, saying that I will live up to my role as his personification, so on and so forth, and that we will be in contact soon to schedule the fight and—"

"That's it?" Everys asked. "A few flowery words and we just accept this as inevitable?"

"'We?'" Paine asked.

Narius held up a hand before the vizier could say anything more. "What would you suggest?"

"Don't be polite, for one thing! Point out to him that this challenge doesn't exactly live up to the Warrior's mandates. Don't the Meditations say, 'Judge your allies by how well they protect your flank. Should they quaver, mark them as less than honorable.'"

Paine looked ready to correct her, but then he blinked and said, "Ah... yes, they do."

"We lead with that," Everys said. "We take a stand on the Warrior's Meditations, remind everyone about what we're dealing with. A potential war, a rogue duke plotting a coup. And in this moment, Istragon chooses to challenge the king's fitness? What does that say about Istragon?"

"That he's performing his duties?" Paine offered quietly.

If Everys heard his comment, she didn't let on. Instead, she launched herself from her chair. "He is no ally. Not to the throne, not to the Dynasty. We expose him for what he is: a small-minded idiot with no strategic vision. We ask the public whose Dynasty they'd rather belong to. Do they want to be hidebound to ancient traditions that only fracture us further? Or do they want to side with the king and march with him into a glorious future?"

Narius squirmed in his seat. She was so alive, so full of passion. He wished that the vizier would excuse himself so he and his wife could be alone. He wanted nothing more than to take her in his arms and—

No such luck. Paine crossed his arms. "And by doing that, you'll likely erode what little support Narius has with the nobility. Many of them appreciate those 'ancient traditions' and would be gravely concerned if the king openly flouted them."

"Of course they would," Everys countered. "Those traditions are what keep them entrenched in their privilege. Smudges, we can't upset them!"

"Unless your plan is to drive more of them to Brencis's cause," Paine said.

Everys looked ready to fire back, but Narius cleared his throat.

"He has a point," Narius said. "As satisfying as refusing him might be, we can't afford to antagonize him. Instead, I've decided Istragon's challenge gives us an opportunity for some much-needed changes."

"What do you have in mind?" Paine's voice was laced with apprehension.

Narius rose from the table and went over to a nearby couch, one that was half-covered in scribers. He frowned as he looked them over. Which one had the files he needed? Everys often teased him about how he kept his quarters. Maybe she did have a point.

He snagged the correct scriber and handed it to Paine. "I've been putting together new laws I want to enact as quickly as possible."

Paine frowned as he glanced over the scriber's screen. Then he stopped and read it closer. Narius braced himself, but he kept his eyes on Everys. He wanted to see how she would react.

"'The Siporan Restoration Act?'" Paine read the title.

"That's correct," Narius said.

Everys's jaw dropped open. "What?"

He knew that Paine was scrolling through the details, but they were easy enough to share. "One of the best things my father did was repeal the Drywell Laws that discriminated against the Siporans, but he didn't go far enough. I want to finish what he started."

"By doing what?" Everys asked, her voice quiet.

"I've noticed Siporans don't have any representation in either the Hall of All Voices or the Ethnarch Parliament. The former is elected by region. There's little we can do about that. But the Parliament isn't determined by an election."

"No. It's composed of the rulers of the nations the Dynasty has conquered and—" Paine's eyes widened, and he looked up. "Your Strength, you can't mean to—"

"I do," Narius said. "We will ask the Siporan community to select someone to represent their people using whatever criteria they wish."

"And where would this new Siporan ruler live?" Paine said. "Are you going to give them the Demilitarized Zone?"

Narius had considered that. The demilitarized zone between the Dynasty's holdings and the Dalark Beachhead was where the Siporan Ascendancy once stood. Giving the Demilitarized Zone back to the Siporans would provoke the Dalark Imperium into full warfare, though, so that wasn't really an option.

"I thought we would give whoever is chosen the Dwellins's estate. Given Brencis's treason, his property should be confiscated. Or they could be given a manor in Gilded Lock like the Diradae."

Everys made a small sound, a mix between a squeak and a gasp. He smiled, savoring the sheer look of surprise on her face.

"And that's not all," Narius said. "I also thought we should lift the ban on practicing toratropic magic. Siporans would once again be able to use their magical gifts as they see fit. Of course, I'm open to other suggestions, Everys. I know you'll have additions and corrections to make to my ideas."

Everys had paled considerably. She stumbled back to her chair and sat down.

"Istragon's challenge will benefit us," Narius continued. "Think about it: I propose this radical change to our society, and yes, there are those who will object. But when I beat Istragon's challenge, we can claim the Perfected Warrior's blessing on what we've done."

"That is certainly one possible outcome," Paine said carefully. "However, I feel this would be more likely: You force these changes. You then win Istragon's challenge. But instead of supporting your initiatives, the nobility unites behind Brencis. Then you will be dealing with a coup at best or a civil war at worst. Not only that, but your open acceptance of the Siporans will inflame Dalark's animosity further, meaning you will have true war."

"We need this, Paine," Everys whispered.

"I don't discount that," Paine said. "And under other circumstances, I would announce this change myself and help my king weather whatever challenges resulted. But our circumstances are tenuous and fragile. This could shatter everything. Is that truly what you want?"

Everys glowered at him, then sighed. "No."

Narius didn't either. As much as he hated to admit it, Paine had a point. When he thought up the Siporan Restoration Act, he had envisioned the thankful Siporan populace. He'd thought about how this would be a huge step toward true justice for the Dynasty. And more than anything, he'd wanted to protect Everys. If the truth of what she could do ever came out, there would be little he could do to help her. This would ease the burden she lived under that he could never truly understand. But once again, Paine had proved why he was vizier. He had seen past the positive veneer to the harsh realities lurking beneath.

"You think I shouldn't do this?" It wasn't a question, not really, but he phrased it like one anyway.

Paine grimaced. "I do, Your Strength. As noble as your intentions are, this just isn't the time. Once you've beaten Istragon's challenge. After Brencis is captured. When we have resolved our issues with Dalark."

"When the Blood Sea has drained completely of its water," Everys muttered. "When the Plissk deserts blossom like the Cold Light's forests. When—"

"Please, Blessed, I know how disappointed you must feel," Paine said. "I wish it could be different. But this is the reality we face."

Everys didn't say anything else. Instead, her expression went cold. She wouldn't meet Narius's gaze. That hurt worse than if she had said something. Maybe he could make a small gesture. "There's more. I've given this some thought. We'll promote Strategist Overturn to be head of the Dynasty's military. You had a good point about his record, Everys. He deserves this."

She didn't respond. Paine didn't speak either, but his eyes narrowed and his lips twitched into a snarl. Narius shot him a glare to keep him from objecting. Overturn would do an excellent job, and Everys had been right. This appointment would be a strong signal about the direction he wanted to take the Dynasty.

Paine rose from his seat. "With your permission, Your Strength, I will draft a response to Istragon's challenge and ask him to sit down to negotiate the details. Unless there's anything else?"

Not for him. Narius did have one more surprise for Everys, but he wanted to share it with only her, especially since it might further soften the blow of her disappointment.

Once Paine left, Narius grabbed a chair and scooted it closer to her. He sat down and wrapped his arms around her. She resisted him, acting as though she had been carved out of stone, not moving, not acknowledging his attempt.

"This isn't fair, Narius," she whispered. "We've been waiting four hundred years."

"I know."

She looked at him, and some of the anger in her eyes faded. She leaned into his hug and rested her head on his shoulder.

"I know you do," she whispered. "And I appreciate it."

"Well, there is one more thing. And given what Paine just said, I think it'd be best to keep this between the two of us. Well, for starters."

She frowned. "Oh?"

He took a deep breath and braced himself. "I want you to find me a scrivener."

Now Everys's confusion was palpable. "Why?"

Time to jump off the cliff. "Because I want to convert to your faith."

She pulled out of his embrace and stared at him, her mouth hanging open.

"I've given this a lot of thought. The Dynasty claims to worship the Perfected Warrior and the Water Bearer, but we only ever use the names of our gods for curses and oaths. No one actually believes that any of those stories are real. But I've seen what your God can do. I've seen how you use His power. He healed me when Brencis shot me. I can't ignore that."

"But to convert—"

He held up his hands. "I can't do it officially. If news of this got out to the public, what Paine described would likely happen. That's why whoever you find has to keep it quiet. That's why the fewer people who know about it the better. I'm sorry for that. I wish I could be more open, but—"

She lunged forward and kissed him, holding him tight. At first, he only felt relief that her anger had abated. But as he returned her kiss, it stirred some of the longings he'd felt a few moments earlier.

"What say we don't worry about breakfast anymore?" he whispered.

"I thought you'd never ask."

6

Quartus knew waiting the extra time to go back to the unfinished house was a gamble. Whoever owned the property might have learned of his snooping and quietly disposed of any evidence. But waiting had been the more prudent option, mostly so people might forget about his team.

They waited well into Third Watch a few days later before returning to the property. Quartus had a feeling the team would do better if they just went in as thieves.

While the property didn't sit on the Melgor River, it did sit on a smaller tributary, little more than a stream in that neighborhood. But that was perfect. They were able to leave their transports elsewhere in the neighborhood and follow the stream to the back wall.

Stoophawk insisted on taking the lead, which seemed a bit excessive. If they ran into trouble, it would likely be with the local constabulary, and that was a fight they didn't need. But rather than argue with the Ixactl, Quartus had let him do his thing. Let him have a small victory now, in case they didn't find anything substantial in the house itself.

Once they reached the wall, Quartus had Stickler clear the way. After a few minutes of work, Stickler reported that the property's exterior security had been deactivated. That done, Stoophawk helped each member of the team up a small embankment and then over the wall.

The moment his feet hit the dirt, a sense of unease settled on Quartus. On this side of the wall, he truly felt removed from civilization, like they had dropped into some hostile wilderness instead of a backyard in Bastion. Maybe it was because they didn't know what they'd find in the half-finished house. For whatever reason, though, Quartus felt a distinct urge to leave.

But then Stoophawk stepped up behind him and patted his shoulder. "Lead the way, boss."

Quartus squared his shoulders. No retreat at this point. He signaled for the team to move forward, and they hustled through the woods, passing the ring of stumps. No sign of the bark beetles now. Maybe they had joined the swarm at the main house. Only one way to know for sure.

As they crested a small hill, Quartus signaled for the team to drop to the ground. He peeked over the edge at the house. It appeared to be dark and deserted. Quartus nodded grimly. Hopefully that would be the case.

The approach to the house was silent as well, but Quartus felt his nerves jangling with each step. When would the hidden guards spot them? When would an alarm pierce the silence? When would a trap catch them? But as they reached the house's back door, there was nothing but silence. Once again, Stickler darted forward and popped the lock, motioning for the team to move inside.

"What's the play, Qulinus?" Stoophawk whispered as the team hurried inside.

"Spread out. Move quickly. If you find anything unusual, find me immediately." He hesitated. "And keep an eye out for any hidden rooms."

Stoophawk's gaze sharpened. "Like at that factory?"

Quartus nodded reluctantly. When he and Everys had discovered a hidden lab in a factory in Defector's Wrath, he had sent the team away. Stoophawk hadn't forgotten that and, Quartus suspected, thought that he had been cut out of some illegal profits.

They spread out, moving carefully. Like the house's exterior, the interior was unfinished as well, with holes in the floor and walls, wires exposed, and piles of wood and masonry stacked seemingly at random. It created a maze that would have been tricky to navigate with light. But they didn't dare use any light. Varcu hummed in the next room, a tuneless song that set Quartus's nerves on edge.

As he explored the half-finished house, Quartus's unease grew sharper. None of this felt right. If this house was just a disguise, why was he finding toolboxes in some of the rooms? The kitchen actually had cabinets installed, which made no sense. Why go to that effort?

"Qulinus!" Stoophawk hustled into the room. "Varcu may have found something."

The Ixactl led him back through two of the rooms to one along the house's side wall. Varcu stood in the middle of the room, staring at one of the walls.

"What do you have?" Quartus asked.

Varcu glanced at him, then turned back to the wall. "Room's too small."

Quartus frowned. It was? He looked over the room.

Varcu nodded, then pointed to one of the walls. "Near as I can tell, the wall between this room and that one has to be about five feet thick. There's no closet or doors."

"A secret passage?" Quartus guessed.

"Maybe. Haven't found the entrance to it yet."

Unprompted, Stoophawk started knocking on the wall, his ear pressed up against it. While Quartus couldn't hear a difference in the sounds, apparently Stoophawk could. The Ixactl moved along the wall until he stopped, rapped against the wood a few more times, then smashed his fist through it.

Quartus jumped at the splintering sound, but Stoophawk tore large chunks of the wall away, then reached in and groped around behind it. Something clicked and the rest of the wall slid aside with a hiss.

An acrid smell flooded the room and Quartus gagged. Stoophawk stumbled away from the door.

"What is—?" Varcu asked.

But then, the room filled with a harsh buzzing, and a dark cloud roiled out of the opening. Smoke? No, bugs! Thousands of bark beetles blasted past them in the dark. Stoophawk reeled away from the hole, swatting at them while Varcu curled up in a ball on the floor. Quartus covered his face with his forearm.

Just as quickly as they came, they were gone. Quartus took a few deep breaths to calm himself. That many bark beetles in one place? He had found what he was looking for. He motioned for Stoophawk and Varcu to follow him, and he shimmied through.

Stairs descended into a darkened basement. Bark beetles scuttled along the walls. Quartus frowned at them. They looked sluggish. Maybe they were sick? Or sleeping?

The basement was made out of simple bricks, with barely glowing lights strung along the ceiling. But unlike the rest of the house, it was clear that the basement was actually finished. He wanted to crow in triumph. They had found what they were looking for, he just knew it.

"Spread out," Quartus whispered. "Let me know what you find."

Stoophawk and Varcu peeled off, ducking through open doors. Quartus went through one himself, but he stopped in the doorway.

The room was filled with bark beetles. They crawled in and out through vents near the ceiling and they coated the walls, the floors, the furniture. But they seemed particularly interested in dozens of large beakers on one table. They buzzed and flitted around them. Quartus crept through the room, trying to find open spaces where he wouldn't step on the bugs. As he closed in on the table, he caught the whiff of a rancid odor, one that caused a sour taste to rise in his throat. He shooed the bugs off the beakers and ran a finger along the inside. There was some sort of residue inside, a sticky mess that, when Quartus sniffed it, he realized was the source of the smell.

He looked over the other containers. They all seemed to have the same stuff in them. The bark beetles seemed to be attracted to it. Well, since the beetles were attracted to the Cold Light, that probably meant this was Cold Light sap. Had they harvested it from the trees in the backyard before they cut those down? Maybe.

Quartus opened the table's drawers one by one, looking for some hint of what they were doing here with these sap samples. But the drawers were all empty.

"Qulinus!" Stoophawk shouted. "Get in here!"

Quartus found Stoophawk in another room standing over three dead bodies. Two men and a woman. All three were humans, Kolvese, Grerid, and Hinaen, by the looks of them.

"What did you do?" Quartus asked.

"I didn't do it! I found them like this."

Quartus knelt next to one of the bodies and realized pretty quickly that Stoophawk was telling the truth. All three of them had clearly been dead for a while, maybe even a few weeks. Part of their bodies had started to liquify. They wore simple clothing, unfashionable and rough along the edges. And it looked like they were covered in thicker ropes.

His eyes widened. "Shattered Spear, they're thralls."

Stoophawk stumbled backward, snarling. Quartus couldn't blame him. He didn't want to risk losing his free will either. While the Cold Light themselves were sentient trees, they were able to enslave people by implanting plant matter in them. Thralls were under the direct control of the Cold Light and served their every whim. There had been reports of Cold Light thralls in Bastion for years, but none had ever been caught.

Until now.

"Hey, Qulinus, I found some other stuff and—" Varcu's voice trailed off as he entered the room. "We need to dispose of these guys?"

Quartus did a quick once-over of the bodies to see if he could determine how they'd died. No flechette wounds, but the heads of all three were at odd angles, as if their necks had been snapped. He'd have to call this in to Tormod.

When he touched one of the bodies, ghostly red lines appeared on the floor underneath. They twisted together, creating a complex pattern that he didn't understand, but he definitely recognized. A toratropic rune.

And then another appeared on the floor nearby. Followed by another one. And another. Dozens, all the same pattern.

Quartus dropped the corpse. "Run!"

They sprinted out of the room and back up the stairs. Other members of the crew poked their heads out of the rooms they were searching at the racket. Quartus shouted for them to follow him. As they did, runes appeared along the floor, along the walls. Dozens of them. Maybe hundreds.

Quartus threw himself out an open window and slammed into the ground, rolling away from the house as it burst into flames.

He popped up to his feet and turned to run, but he froze. A woman stood in front of him, dressed in an all-black bodysuit with a scarf pulled across her face. Her intense amber eyes widened at the sight of him, but she turned and dashed away from the house, weaving through the surrounding trees. He chased after her. She darted in and out of the shadows cast by the fire. Quartus almost lost sight of her twice, but then she would dart through a better lit part of the property.

He closed the distance, but just as he reached out to snare her shirt, he tripped over a tree root, tumbling to the ground. He rolled, coming to rest in a puddle of mud. When he looked up, she was gone.

He rolled over to look back at the house. Bright blue flames consumed every bit of it. He frowned. This close to the fire, he should have felt an oppressive heat, enough to drive him away. But he was barely aware of it.

A shudder washed over him. Runes. Even though he knew Everys used toratropic magic, a small part of him wouldn't have minded if the Siporans had simply disappeared entirely.

Strong hands grabbed him from behind. Stoophawk lifted him to his feet. "C'mon, boss. Constables'll be here soon."

Quartus nodded grimly. The last thing they'd want to do was explain this to them.

Something sliced through the air near his cheek. Someone grunted behind him. He whirled in time to see Stickler drop to the ground, clutching at his chest. Quartus gaped as blood blossomed on Stickler's shirt. He frantically searched the woods, then spotted a dozen men hurrying through the woods, each of them holding weapons. They fired again. Hiley and Clovis cried out, both of them dropping.

"Scatter!" Quartus shouted.

The others didn't need any more prompting. The rest of his crew ran, each one in a different direction. Quartus ducked and wove around bushes and low-hanging branches, sure that he heard the thundering of footsteps behind him. Who had that been? Not local constables; they wouldn't have shown up that fast. Private security? Backup for the woman?

He clambered over the wall and sprinted down the street. After a few minutes, he ducked behind a transport and peeked around the bumper. No sign of pursuers. That was good, but he still punched the transport. He shook out his hand, wishing he could keep hitting something. The house was gone along with any evidence. And he had lost three men. In some ways, he was starting all over again.

7

Everys should have seen her coming.

The setup was obvious. When Everys had contacted the scrivener who performed her and Narius's wedding to see if he'd be available, the scrivener had insisted on bringing an assistant with him. The scrivener had sounded nervous on the comm, but he'd also been frightened during the wedding. Old fears died hard, especially when a Siporan holy man was being invited to the king's palace.

But then Scrivener Tolistan had arrived at the palace with her in tow.

"Dear child, it is good to see you again!" Auntie Kyna strode forward, not at all hindered by the blindfold she wore.

Everys grimaced as the older woman hugged her tightly. Kyna wasn't really her aunt. Instead, the old con artist considered every Siporan her family. She was a fixture in Fair Havens, the neighborhood where Everys had lived before she'd become queen. Kyna usually begged, but her hardship changed daily. Sometimes she pretended to be unable to walk. Other times, she faked deafness. And as she brushed past Everys, leaning heavily on a cane, she groped about as if blind.

"I apologize, Blessed," Scrivener Tolistan said. "She somehow knew I was coming to the palace and insisted on accompanying me."

"Of course she did."

That was perhaps Kyna's most maddening habit: she somehow always knew when and where to make a nuisance of herself. Kyna claimed the Singularity guided her words and actions. And Everys believed that. After all, the Singularity had left the Siporans to be oppressed by the Dynasty for four centuries. It figured He would torment His people with someone like Kyna.

Everys swallowed a sigh and motioned for Tolistan to follow her. "If you'd come with me, please."

They quickly caught up with Kyna, and Everys looped her arm through the older woman's. Kyna chuckled and took Everys's hand. To an outside observer, it would have appeared to be two old friends strolling down the hall. In reality, Everys wanted to make sure Kyna couldn't escape into the palace and cause more mischief.

She led her guests to the palace's residential wing, where she handed Tolistan off to Narius. He gave her a quizzical look when he saw Kyna, but Everys shook her head. She'd tell him all about this later, because she was sure she'd have some stories to share.

As much as she didn't want to, Everys took Kyna to her quarters.

As they entered, Trule bustled out of the bedroom. "We've almost finished sprucing up your wardrobe, Blessed, and..." The servant girl's voice trailed. "M-my apologies, Blessed. We didn't know you would have company. If we had known, I would have prepared refreshments and made sure that your quarters were presentable."

Everys frowned. A quick glance around the room didn't reveal anything that could remotely be called a mess.

"It's all right, child," Kyna said. "I'm an old friend of the queen's, and she didn't know I was coming. Besides, it's not as if I can see whatever is wrong with her quarters."

Kyna punctuated her statement by waving a hand in front of her eyes. Trule looked positively aghast.

Everys swallowed a groan. "Trule, go ahead and dismiss the staff. We'll be fine."

Trule seemed hesitant, but only for a second. Then she clapped her hands and called to the others. In a burst of motion, Everys's girls hustled out of the quarters.

Once they were gone, Everys turned to Kyna and motioned toward a couch. "Would you like to have a seat, Auntie? Make yourself comfortable? Maybe take off the blindfold?"

Kyna chuckled, but she unwound the fabric and tucked it in a pocket. She blinked her eyes. "So judgmental."

"Such a faker," Everys countered.

If Kyna was hurt by the verbal jab, she didn't let on. Instead, she settled onto the couch.

"Why did you really come here, Auntie? Is Fair Havens so boring you have to branch out?"

Kyna smiled and sighed. "Oh no. Fair Havens is much the way you left it. Many still speak of you warmly, though they wonder if your outreach center will ever see fruition."

Everys's cheeks burned. She had intended to convert the building housing her family's electronics shop into a charitable outreach center, but then a riot had severely damaged the building. The last time she'd seen it, it'd been reduced to nothing but a hole in the ground. She had meant to restart the project, but after remarrying Narius, she couldn't give it the attention it deserved.

"No, the reason I came here was to check on you. To see how you are holding up." Kyna took Everys's hands in hers. "Are you happy, child?"

Everys cocked her head at the question. In some ways, the answer should have been no. She barely saw her husband, she was constantly entertaining whining and petty nobles, and she lived constantly worrying someone would discover she was a toratropic mage. But in the ways that truly counted...

"Yes, I am."

Kyna squeezed her hand. "Good. Hold on to that feeling. Dark days are ahead of you."

"Did the Singularity tell you that?"

"No, dear child. Common sense. The threat of war weighs on your former neighbors. They know too well that when the rich and powerful start a war, they are not the ones who pay the cost. It will be the children of the poor who fight the battles. If there is economic fallout, it will land on the poor first."

Everys blew a breath out through her nose. "I know that already, Auntie."

"Perhaps you do, but many around you don't." She sighed heavily. "I have asked the Singularity many times to show me how this crisis ends. And He has been largely silent about the particulars. But He has made one thing clear: 'When the craftsman wants to build something new, he must first clear the land.'"

A tremor wormed down Everys's spine. That wasn't ominous at all. What did it mean? But instead of elaborating, Kyna fell silent, carefully arranging the fabric of her skirt.

"Anything else?" Everys braced herself for more disastrous portents.

Kyna looked up at her and smiled sadly. "Just this: 'When the winds batter the house and the rain threatens to shear it to its foundation, remember that all storms eventually end.'"

Cold clamped Everys's heart. Kyna had never been a fount of joy and reassurance, but she seemed particularly dour.

But then Kyna shook herself. She leaned forward, her eyes bright. "Do not lose heart, child. While you have not always walked closely with the Singularity, rest assured that He has never stopped journeying with you. There is a reason that you are here, in this place and in this time. And though you may lose the path, if you keep Him in your sight, you will never be truly lost."

Kyna's words lingered, and Everys felt like she had to say something, respond somehow. Before she could, Kyna clapped her hands.

"You know what would do me a world of good? Some tea. Is that something you can handle or should I summon your staff?"

Everys frowned. There was the Kyna she knew and was supposed to love. But even as Everys made her way over to the kitchenette and rummaged through the cupboards for her favorite tea, she couldn't shake the feeling of dread that had settled on her shoulders like a heavy blanket. She, too, wanted to see something new built on the foundation of the Dynasty, but how painful would the clearing have to be before it could begin?

8

Scrivener Tolistan paced near the door like a cornered animal. Narius felt it was best to keep his distance. He knew that he was in no danger from his guest, but it was clear that the feeling wasn't mutual.

"Are you sure you don't want something to drink?" Narius asked. "I'll admit, I'm not sure whether or not scriveners are allowed to indulge in wine, but I have a wonderful Weyfir vintage on hand that I think is spectacular."

Tolistan paused. "I'm... I'm not even sure how to respond to that, Your Strength. I don't even know why I'm here."

"What did the Queen tell you when she invited you to the palace?"

Tolistan stopped pacing. He looked down at the floor. "That she had someone here at the palace who wanted to learn more about Siporan beliefs. Someone who might possibly want to convert. I thought it was one of her servants, but instead, she leaves me here with..." He gestured toward Narius. "I mean no disrespect, Your Strength, but you can understand why I'd be suspicious."

Sadly, Narius understood all too well. The Dynasty did not have a stellar history with the Siporan people. Not only had his ancestor destroyed the Ascendancy, but the Dynasty had then enacted the infamous Drywell Laws that severely oppressed the survivors. And even when those laws were repealed, the old prejudices lingered. He hoped his marrying Everys would eventually help exterminate those attitudes.

He held up his hands, trying to reassure Tolistan. "I understand how you feel. The queen—Everys has shared similar fears with me in the past. But do you really think she'd have invited you here if you were in danger?"

"Our history is filled with Siporans who loved power more than the Singularity or our people. The queen would not be the first to have fallen away." Tolistan's eyes widened. "Not that I'm implying that such a thing has happened, you understand. I merely speak of the possibility!"

Narius sighed. Maybe this wasn't such a good idea after all. Maybe he had been fooling himself. Tolistan still hadn't stepped away from the door, as if he wanted to stay close to the exit for a quick escape.

"I'm sorry, Scrivener. I didn't think this through very well, but what Everys told you is true. I do want to convert to your faith. What can I do to convince you?"

Tolistan regarded him skeptically, then said, "You could start by telling me why. Why convert at all? You know how the Dynasty would treat you if they learned you had become one of us. Why do that at all?"

Narius nodded and thought over his answer. Tolistan, thankfully, didn't interrupt his musing.

"I could say that I want to do this to please my wife, and that would be true. I love her more than anything and want to have more in common with her. But it's not the entire reason. I could say that I've never believed in the traditional religion and I'm searching for something better. But that's not the complete answer either. In truth, I want something real. I want something that isn't based on myths and legends. I want to serve a god who is actually there."

Tolistan chuckled. "And how can you be sure that the Singularity is?"

"Because I've seen the gifts that He's given to the Siporans. I know what He enables your people to do."

Tolistan blinked, then went pale. His legs wobbled and he almost collapsed, but Narius crossed the distance and caught him.

"Scrivener, I know more than you realize. I know what Everys is capable of. I know that right now, there are schools where Siporan youth are trained to use toratropic magic. I know that not all of the Principalities were destroyed, and that even now, certain families safeguard the missing ones." He leaned forward. "And I know that's why I've never met the queen's family."

"She told you all of that?" Tolistan whispered.

"And much more." Narius made sure to emphasize those last two words. "Why wouldn't I want to learn more about the one who gives his people real power?"

Silence fell on the room. Narius could read the struggle in Tolistan's expression—trust fighting with doubt, hope battling history. Was this what it would be like for every Siporan as the Dynasty improved?

"Scrivener, I know I'm asking for much. I do. All I want is to learn more about my wife's faith. To learn the truth that she knows and holds dear. Treat me like anyone who is interested in your faith."

Tolistan looked down at his feet, a frown puckering his face. But then he nodded and looked up at Narius, his expression grim. "Very well, Your Strength. If I am to treat you like anyone else, then I must warn you of what you're asking. In the past, we have had many who wanted to come to the Singularity looking for power or prestige. But the Singularity never promises His people any such thing. Many of us go our entire lives without drawing a single rune. And those that can are taught the gift is for serving one another. If one follows the Singularity, it is a path dedicated to helping others."

"In many ways, it's like being the sovereign of a kingdom," Narius said.

"Is that truly the way it has been for the Dynasty, Your Strength?" Tolistan asked quietly.

Heat painted Narius's cheeks, and he had to swallow a flash of irritation. But as much as Tolistan's words needled him, he saw the truth of them all the same.

Tolistan studied his face carefully, then nodded. "Very well. I am not entirely convinced this is wise, but I will instruct you in our ways. We will have to study the Ascendancy's history, the teachings of our wisest and most revered scriveners from ages past, and contemporary Siporan thought."

"Will we discuss toratropic runes?" Narius asked.

"We could." Tolistan pursed his lips. "You must understand, Your Strength. I am not a mage. I only know the most basic details of how the runes work. Your wife... well, she might be able to explain it better."

She had. At least, she had gone over some of the basics. But ever since they had remarried, Everys had been hesitant to discuss anything else about toratropic runes. Come to think of it, aside from the incident at the Wendlys', he hadn't heard anything about her using runes since their second wedding. He frowned. Had something happened that he didn't know about?

He shook his head to clear it. While he would have to investigate that later, he should really focus on whatever Tolistan could teach him.

"Where do we begin?" Narius asked.

Tolistan opened his bag and pulled out... a book. A real, ink-on-paper book.

Narius's eyes widened. While no longer illegal, his stomach soured upon seeing it. Old prejudices he thought had been long buried. Old stories about how Siporans could conjure evil from any form of ink whispered in the back of his mind. Stories of how just by being in the presence of this relic could put him in mortal danger. He shoved aside his discomfort and opened his mind to whatever Tolistan would share.

"At the beginning." Tolistan opened to the front page and started reading. "'Before the world began, when all was wreathed in darkness...'"

9

Quartus risked a look out into the street. This early in Fourth Watch, just a few transports rumbled down the street, and a few drunks stumbled through the darkening night. No sign of constables or the people who had attacked his crew. He thought he might be safe. Only one way to find out for sure.

Sticking to the alley and the shadows, he made sure with each step that no one was looking at him. After nearly an hour of skirting corners and dodging between shadows, he finally made it to the Bloodied Blade. The bar wasn't much to look at, more graffiti and cracked bricks than actual building. But it was an unobtrusive establishment, the perfect place for clandestine meetings, which was why Quartus had spent so much time here. He slipped in through the back door.

Thankfully, the bar was mostly empty, with only two tables filled and four patrons at the bar itself. Merg, the Plissk bartender, glanced up as Quartus came out of the back and then frowned. Quartus raised a questioning brow. Merg sighed heavily, then jerked a head toward one of the booths in the back of the room.

That prompted the smallest of smiles from Quartus. Good old Merg. The bartender never seemed to care what Quartus was up to. He let him work from that back corner as long as he didn't attract attention from the constables.

Quartus settled into his usual seat, with his back to the corner and the rest of the bar in plain view. He surveyed the other patrons. A few had glanced up at him, but their attention hadn't lingered. They only wanted to confirm that Quartus wasn't a threat to them and, having decided that, they wouldn't be a threat to him. The rest didn't even bother, their focus only on their drinks. Good. Now all he had to do was wait for the rest of his team to arrive.

He scratched at the tabletop idly. None of this made sense. Someone had set up a lab of some sort in the basement of that house. They had clearly worked directly with the Cold Light there, only to kill the trees and the thralls, then destroy the entire house. Why would they have done that?

The most obvious answer was because of the new peace with the Cold Light. Maybe the Cold Light they found at the manor house had learned about that and were ready to stop. Whoever they were working with didn't approve and so they killed them.

Or... Quartus's frown deepened. Or that unknown party had gotten what they wanted from the Cold Light and had silenced them permanently.

The door to the bar banged open. Varcu came in, shooting a look around the room. Once he spotted Quartus, he headed over and slid into a seat. Quartus raised an eyebrow.

"What?" Varcu asked.

Quartus nodded at the bright red kerchief around the Plissk boy's neck. "Didn't you think that'd attract too much attention?"

Varcu shook his head. "Not if you're trying to hide in plain sight."

Quartus grunted. That was true, but that could've been too risky given the circumstances.

Within a few minutes, the rest of the gang joined them. Quartus examined them. None of them looked the worse for wear, although they all wore haunted expressions. Three of their friends, gone. And for what? Nothing. Such a waste.

"Now what, Qulinus?" Varcu asked.

Quartus mopped a hand over his face. He had no idea. He supposed they could go back to hunting for bark beetles, but they had been doing that for weeks and this was the first lead that had generated any information.

Before Quartus could organize his thoughts, though, Stoophawk leaned forward. "Where's our money?"

Quartus sighed. He should have known. "I promise you'll—"

Stoophawk jabbed the table with his finger. "No more talk, Qulinus. When you took over this crew from Plion, I was okay with it because you promised that we would make some serious blades. But now Clovis, Stickler, and Hiley are dead, and we have nothing to show for it!"

"Well, not nothing exactly." Varcu produced a scriber from his pocket. "I found this in one of the rooms, and—"

Quartus perked up. Whatever Varcu found could turn out to be nothing, but at least they had something. He reached out to take the scriber.

But Stoophawk snatched it from Varcu's hand.

"Are we getting paid?" Stoophawk snarled. "I can't help but wonder if you've been setting us up, Qulinus. You put us in the vanguard, let us take the brunt of the defense, and then you dance in and keep all the money. If you want whatever is on this scriber, you're going to pay me what I think it's worth."

Quartus regarded Stoophawk carefully. Most people in the Dynasty thought the hill giants were stupid. He knew better. Stoophawk had a singular focus—money—but that didn't mean he was a fool. Quartus's cover story had already started unraveling, and Stoophawk was the one pulling on the thread. As much as he hated to admit it, he couldn't afford to keep working with this team anymore, and not just because he didn't have any money on him.

He sighed and slid out of his seat, his hands up. "Look, Stoophawk, go ahead and keep the scriber if you feel you have to. But I probably don't have near enough blades to give you, not for a while."

"How much do you have?" Stoophawk's voice had taken on a distinct growl.

Quartus tensed. "None on me right now, but I could maybe scrape together a thousand if you gave me a few hours to—"

Stoophawk exploded out of his seat, murder blazing in his eyes. Good. Just what Quartus was hoping for.

Before the Ixactl could react, Quartus grabbed him by the wrist and planted his hip below Stoophawk's. With a sharp tug, he tossed the larger man onto the floor. Then he quickly lined up his elbow and dropped it into Stoophawk's eye.

His arm exploded in pain, but he knew that there weren't many ways to stun an Ixactl. Eyes were one of their only weak spots. Stoophawk didn't react. Instead, he threw Quartus off and popped off the floor, moving faster than a being his size should. Quartus drew a knife from his belt, but Stoophawk slapped the weapon out of his hand, then backhanded him across the jaw.

Pain ricocheted through Quartus's head and he staggered. Stoophawk didn't let up, punching him once, then twice, in the stomach. Quartus crumpled to the floor with a groan. The Ixactl wasn't done, kicking him in the stomach and ribs repeatedly. Quartus curled up, tucking his head beneath his arms. He tried to shake off the pain, but Stoophawk wasn't letting up.

Quartus tried to weather the abuse, but the pain was too much. He hadn't endured a beating like this since... well, ever. He was vaguely aware of Varcu saying something, his voice pleading. Stoophawk growled something in return, but then, mercifully, the beating stopped. Quartus managed to roll on his side. His stomach roiled and he bit back the vomit that clawed up his throat.

The scriber clattered to the ground in front of him. Then Stoophawk's massive boot slammed down on it and the device shattered. Stoophawk stomped again, grinding his heel on the delicate electronics. Each blow sent a ricochet of pain through Quartus's already throbbing head. Then the Ixactl snared Quartus by the hair and lifted him off the ground. Quartus's vision swam, barely registering the others standing around him.

"We're done, Qulinus. If I ever see you again, I'll kill you."

Stoophawk punctuated his threat with a punch across Quartus's cheek, sending him back to the floor. Quartus rolled onto his back and flexed his arms, twitching his legs. None of them felt broken, but pain still sliced through him. He probed his chest next, checking for cracked ribs. Each touch ignited new agony.

Someone nudged him in the side, sending a new cascade of pains through him. Merg towered over him, his features puckered into a frown.

"Hey, Qulinus, you gotta go," Merg said.

Quartus groaned and rolled to his hands and feet. A few of the other patrons shot looks at him, probably out of worry that if he died, the constables would show up. If he overstayed his welcome, he'd probably face another beating. He rolled to his knees and took several breaths, trying to ignore the pain the chased each one. But then he spotted it: the storage drive from the scriber. Stoophawk had destroyed the device's casing and many of its circuits, but the drive appeared almost intact, just scuffed up. A surge of hope washed away most of his aches. With trembling fingers, he scooped up the drive and pocketed it.

That done, Quartus clambered to his feet and staggered out of the bar.

Where to next? He had a safehouse established in Defector's Wrath that the rest of the team didn't know about. He hadn't gone there because he was worried he was being followed. But now he needed a place to recover. Pain overrode operational security.

The safehouse was actually an apartment over a clothing store. He slipped in from the back and carefully crept up the stairs to the landing. He lifted his wrist to swipe over the lock, and the movement sent a spasm through his muscles. Thankfully the door swung open with a muted click, and he nearly collapsed against the doorway.

The room itself wasn't much to look at, just a few stray pieces of furniture, a bed, a kitchenette, and a bathroom off to one side. However, he did have a dedicated data terminal with an encrypted connection to the local network along with a few tools he might be able to use. Most spies working for Tormod probably had more resources, but this was all he could muster. And it would have to be enough.

Once the door was locked, he collapsed onto the couch with a groan. He gently probed his injuries with his fingers. Nothing felt broken, thank Chaos, but he'd be feeling the aftereffects for days. With a groan, he tipped his head back, covered his eyes with his forearm, and fell into a fitful sleep.

When he awoke several hours later, the pain radiating through his body had grown sharper, but he couldn't afford to coddle himself any longer. He pulled out the storage drive. With Chance's intervention, he might be able to salvage at least some of what had been on the scriber.

He staggered over to the computer terminal and sank into the chair, pain slicing through his back. With a wince, he retrieved his tools and pried open the storage component's casing. Then he hooked the drive to the terminal. As the screen lit up, Quartus bit back a curse. The component had been damaged. Most of what it contained was gibberish, but there were a few files that he thought he could read. He set the terminal to copying the data. Then, while it worked, he went into the bathroom to retrieve some pain relievers.

When he came back, the terminal had finished salvaging what it could. The screen lit up with strange symbols. At first, he thought that he had found another collection of toratropic runes. But as he studied the notations, the symbols, the straight connecting lines, he realized these were chemical formulas, diagrams of complex molecules. Quartus frowned. Unfortunately, the notes that went with them were fragmented. This could be the recipe for a new type of explosive or the formula for a new fizzy drink.

Quartus sagged in his chair and his breath hissed through his lips. What did he know for certain? Someone had been using that half-finished manor to work with Cold Light terrorists. There had been Cold Light pillar trees on the property as well as three thralls, but the trees had been cut down and the thralls murdered. Whoever was responsible had been conducting experiments on an unknown substance, possibly with the assistance of the Cold Light. And whoever it was had burned down the secret lab using toratropic runes.

A cold shiver danced down his back, and he glanced at the terminal. He could contact Tormod with what he found, but what had he actually learned? Some Cold Light had died, but he had no way of knowing if there were more terrorists out there. He had located another lab, but it had been destroyed. And toratropic mages were involved, but Tormod had known that already thanks to Narius's almost wedding to Princess Innana of the Dalark Imperium. He hadn't discovered anything significant.

Still, he should report his findings.

He pulled out the encrypted comm device from its hiding place under the kitchen sink and composed a short text message explaining what he had found and requesting direction. He sent it off and waited.

An hour later, the device pinged with a simple message: "Continue investigating and report any findings."

He sighed. Figured. Tormod always took pride in keeping his secrets.

Quartus sat down again at the terminal. Maybe he could find something else. He might not have a lead now, but he was going to find one. It was his way out of this mess he had created. His way to true freedom.

10

Challix bustled into Everys's quarters with a cheery, "Good morning!"

That was enough to tell Everys she was in for a bad day.

Challix pulled out a data scriber and consulted the small screen. "I've coordinated a meeting of the donors for your charitable outreach center. I've heard that the Blaccal family has been jockeying for the opportunity to contribute medical supplies."

Everys perked up at that information. She had been searching for those resources for two weeks now. "What will they want in exchange?"

"Nothing significant. Lady Blaccal will likely want an invitation to the next Queen's Court with preferential seating. Easily done. They also hope that you'll speak to the king about their proposed museum."

Everys frowned. "What museum?"

Challix consulted her notes. "The Blaccals, along with several other noble families, wish to construct something they're calling 'The Cultural Heritage Museum' here in Bastion."

"And they need my support?"

"Not yours so much as Narius's," Challix said. "They want to display the artifacts in the royal archives there."

Everys's mouth popped open. "They what?"

"Since the public learned about the archive's existence, there have been calls to reveal what the royal family has been hiding. Some within the nobility believe that it should be put on display. Then everyone can enjoy it."

The idea soured Everys's mood considerably. That wasn't wise. For one thing, many of the artifacts weren't all that interesting, like ancient totems or badly shaped sculptures. Some were revolting, like the pile of skulls a Plissk chieftain had amassed.

But others would be problematic if they were to be revealed. Like the revelation that the Dynasty had preserved five of the eight Siporan Principalities, sacred objects that had once been housed in Nekek the Bright. Most in the Dynasty believed that all eight had been destroyed four hundred years earlier. If the public learned they still existed, that would lead to uncomfortable questions and result in more hostility directed at Siporans.

"I'm not entirely comfortable with that," Everys said. "I'll think about it, but..."

Challix nodded and turned back to her list. She laughed. "Finally, they're hoping that you'll introduce your future daughter to a Blaccal son as a potential match."

Everys spluttered, thankful that she wasn't drinking anything.

Challix laughed lightly. "They probably wanted to suggest your son marry one of their daughters, but that would be an overreach, and they knew it."

"Will... will I have to do that?" The thought was maddening. She and Narius hadn't even discussed when they would have children. It seemed incredibly premature to start marrying them off already.

"Not at all," Challix said. "In this case, we make promises that we will 'consider' their family for a potential marriage when the time comes to betroth Princess whatever-her-name-will-be. But the Blaccals will understand if their suit is overridden by a more advantageous proposal."

"Oh." Everys's stomach lurched. She hadn't considered that her future children might be used as pawns in political maneuvering. She had hoped that Narius's new Dynasty would spare them from that.

Challix must have noticed her unease. She smiled sympathetically. "Don't worry, Blessed. I'll handle the wording. Let's see what else we have..." She laughed. "This should cheer you up. A fitting for a new dress! That will be fun."

Everys blanched, causing Challix to laugh even harder. When they'd first met, they had clashed over clothes and decorations. Since then, though, Challix had taken it upon herself to make many of those decisions for Everys unless there was a good reason for her to be involved.

"What is this for?" Everys grumbled.

"Something you may enjoy, Blessed: your upcoming trip to the Plissk Sanctuary Oasis."

Everys smiled. That was coming up soon, wasn't it? Several weeks earlier, Trule had invited her and Narius to attend her younger sister's Naming Day. Everys had accepted and Narius had enthusiastically agreed. Until she'd become queen, Everys had never traveled outside of Bastion. Now she was seeing all corners of the Dynasty's holdings. And Narius would come along on this one! They would both enjoy that trip.

"And that appears to be it," Challix said. "Do you have anything to add?"

Everys brightened again. "Yes! Lady Oluna invited me to dinner with Minister Masruq."

"Very good. I'll reach out to their staff and see what we can arrange." Challix nodded and made a note in her scriber. "Anything else, Blessed?"

She smiled. "Do you think you can arrange for Narius and I to have lunch together? I was hoping we could spend a few hours and—"

"Lunch will take a few hours?" Challix asked, a teasing lilt in her voice.

Everys blushed furiously. "Well..."

Challix chuckled, but her face fell when she consulted the scriber. "I'm sorry, Blessed, but it looks like Narius was summoned to a last-minute meeting with the Flail."

Oh. She didn't like it, but that made sense. The Flail Coalition was a political alliance in both the Ethnarch Parliament and the Hall of All Voices. Led by the Diradae ethnarch, the Flail had forged alliances with close to forty noble houses, both major and minor. While political alliances came and went, the Flail was one of the longest lasting, a dominant force for the past three generations. If they wanted to speak to Narius, he'd have to listen to whatever they had to say.

Everys opened her mouth to question the purpose of the meeting when Kevtho hurried into the room. "Blessed, we have a situation. A gentleman arrived at the front gates of the palace and is demanding to see you immediately."

She frowned. That someone was demanding to see her wasn't new or unusual. From what she understood, dozens of people came to the palace every day requesting audiences with just about anyone associated with the government. The palace guard screened each and every one of them, pointed them toward the proper channels, and arrested those who were clearly trying to commit fraud. Why tell her about it?

"And?" she prompted.

"According to what we can tell, he's your father."

Everys flew through the palace halls ahead of her guards. It couldn't be him, could it? Papa was supposed to be guarding her family's Principality. As far as she knew, their vigil wouldn't be over for another two or three years. Why was he back in Bastion? Why was he at the palace? Had something happened to Mama? To Galan?

She rounded a corner and almost collided with Rewether. The captain of the Queen's Guard held up his hands to steady her. She tried to go around him, searching the closed doors in this corridor. Where was he?

"Hold on, Blessed. Let's talk about this," Rewether said.

"What's there to talk about? Is it my father or not?" She tried to duck around him.

Rewether stepped in her way again. "We believe so. He has all the proper identification documents. But there are still discrepancies that we haven't accounted for yet."

"What?"

The guard pulled out a scriber and consulted it. "According to our records, your parents and older sister departed Bastion without filing proper transit papers five years ago."

"Many people do that." She wasn't about to point out that the rich and connected never filed papers at all; that was an argument for someone else at a different time.

"True, but then, most people don't completely disappear from society for five years. Granted, we only did a cursory search, but we can find no record of your family's whereabouts or activity after they disappeared. And now, without warning, a man claiming to be your father shows up at the palace? I'm sorry, Blessed, but we have to be suspicious."

"No, you don't. He has the proper identification, correct?"

Rewether shifted on his feet. "Yes, but we have to consider the possibility the documents are forgeries or stolen."

"Who would steal the identity of a Siporan electronics shopkeeper?" Everys asked. "What possible motive could they have?"

"Beyond impersonating the queen's father?" Rewether's voice had an edge to it.

Everys winced, stung by his words. That made sense. Inkstains, it made sense, no matter how much she wanted to deny it. Given the increased tensions with Dalark, given the possibility of a coup or uprising within the Dynasty, they had to be cautious. She knew that. But if it really was her father...

Someone else hurried down the corridor, footsteps accompanied by the swishing of fabric. Everys turned and had to swallow a groan as Challix stepped up beside her. Challix would likely side with the guards. Worse, she'd probably insist on jailing her father, even if it was really him.

"Is it really him?" Challix asked.

"That's what the guards said he said, but they aren't letting me see him."

"Precautions, ma'am," Rewether said to Challix, almost as if Everys wasn't there. "Until we can ascertain his true identity and what his purpose for coming here is, we have to proceed with extreme caution. I'm sure you understand."

Challix nodded absently, but instead of looking at Rewether, she was studying Everys's face, her own features pinched into a slight frown.

"Of course, Rewether, that is perfectly understandable." Then she turned to actually face the guard. "Tell me, how long has it been since you last saw your father?"

Rewether blinked, confusion flitting across his face. "About three days. He and my mom live over in Terraced Plaza."

Challix raised a brow. "Very nice."

"I try to help them out as much as I can," Rewether said. "They actually have—"

Before he could finish his thought, Challix whirled on Everys. "And you, Blessed? How long has it been since you've seen your father?"

Everys stumbled back a step at the sudden motion. She tried to keep the quaver out of her voice, but her words were still barely more than a whisper. "Five years."

"Interesting." Challix turned back to Rewether. "Tell me, if you hadn't seen your parents for five years, and suddenly, one of them was waiting just behind that door, would you want to wait to see them?"

Everys swallowed the surprised gasp. Challix was actually on her side?

"Please, Rewether, it's been so long since I've seen him," Everys added.

Rewether stammered, then swallowed hard. His eyes took on a hard edge. "Ma'am, I understand what you're saying. I do. And I understand why you would want to see your father again, Blessed. But we don't even know if it's him!"

"There's an easy way to determine that, isn't there?" Challix asked. "Is there a way for the queen to see what this man looks like? She should be able to recognize her own father, yes?"

The guard stared at Challix blankly, then turned and disappeared through one of the doors.

Challix crossed her arms, and Everys could practically feel the annoyance and anger radiating off of her. Even still, she took a step closer to her.

"Thank you," she whispered. "I don't know why you did that."

Her assistant looked at her, pain flitting through her eyes for a brief moment. "Blessed, believe it or not, I am on your side. I always have been."

Those words were like a spike through Everys's heart.

"I know how much you must miss your family. If I can do something to help lessen that pain, I'm going to do it."

Everys stared at Challix, a lump forming in her throat. "I don't know what to say. I-I'm sorry."

Challix regarded her with a blank expression, but then a smirk tugged at her lips. "Well, if that's true, maybe we can discuss updating your wardrobe for the new season."

Everys laughed, and it felt good. Challix chuckled as well, but then schooled her features as Rewether stepped through the door.

"We have moved the individual in question into an observation room. Blessed, if you would follow me, please?" He motioned toward one of the doors.

She followed him into a drab and featureless hallway to a door. He slipped it open and gestured for her to go inside.

Two guards sat at a table, staring at a large window. The moment Everys stepped inside, they popped out of their chairs and stood at stiff attention. Rewether waved them off.

"Go ahead, Blessed." He gestured toward the window.

Everys took a shaky breath and stepped up to the glass. A lone man sat in the room on the opposite side, sullenly staring at the floor. He was dressed in rough spun clothing, the sort of thing someone in a rural community might wear, and a hood was drawn up over his head, covering most of his features.

But then he sat back in his chair, and the hood fell away to reveal an all-too-familiar face.

His face was covered in new lines and wrinkles. His hair, once a jet black, had turned snowy at the temples. She gasped. When had Papa grown so old? She knew their family's vigil would be difficult, going off into the forbidden wilderness far from civilization. But seeing the toll painted across Papa's features was too much for her.

"Is it him?" Challix asked.

Everys couldn't speak. She choked back a sob and nodded.

"You're sure?" Challix prompted.

"Without any doubt," Everys whispered.

Challix turned to Rewether. "Let him go." Before he could protest, she held up a hand. "If there are any repercussions, I will deal with them. You will not be held responsible."

Everys turned to Rewether and forced a word through her tightening throat: "Please."

Rewether looked between the two of them, then sighed. He tapped the two guards on the shoulder and jerked his head toward the door. As they left the room, he said, "Go back up to your quarters, Blessed. I'll bring him there straight away."

Why couldn't she see him immediately? Everys started to protest, but Challix touched her arm, then steered her out of the room and down the hall.

As they walked back up to her quarters, Challix said, "I'll see that a guest room is prepared immediately, Blessed. I'll try to keep the guards' presence to a minimum, but until Rewether is completely satisfied that your father isn't a threat, I'm certain he'll want to post a few near him at all times. Even though he didn't mention your mother or sister, I'll make sure that we have rooms set aside for them as well should they join your father. Pardon me for saying it, but it looks like he could use a good meal and a night's rest, so I'll ask the kitchen to prepare something for him. Palane stew is a good choice, yes? I know that you've shared that meal with—"

Everys cut off Challix's words by putting a hand on her shoulder. Her assistant frowned at her, then flinched as Everys hugged her tightly.

"Thank you," Everys whispered.

Challix hugged her back. "This is what I'm here for, Blessed. Let's get you ready."

She was ready. Now. But they hurried back to her quarters. Once there, Challix barked some orders at the girls to tidy up the place as quickly as they could. At first, Trule looked puzzled as to what had happened, but once she looked at Everys's expression, Trule urged the other girls to hurry up. Everys stood in the midst of the frenzied activity, twisting her hands together and thinking about what she could say to Papa, what he might want to know. The destruction of the shop for sure. And the fact that she was now queen. But how much of that story could she share before she started crying too hard to speak?

Within a few moments, the room looked better than it had, with most everything squared away. Challix quickly dismissed the girls, then took up a position by the door rather than follow the girls through it.

"Do you have to stay?" Everys asked.

Challix grimaced. "I'm afraid I must insist, Blessed. We've already pushed the guards enough today as it is. I suspect that they'll insist on having one of them monitor the situation as well."

Everys frowned. How could they make this work? She wouldn't be able to ask Papa about anything with outsiders present.

Before she could object, there was a knock at the door. Challix glanced at Everys and, at her nod, opened the door.

Rewether strode through, then took a step to the side, revealing her father. Papa walked into the room, a wary expression on his face. But that melted into one of astonishment... then disappointment.

"So it's true. You really have betrayed us."

11

Papa's words stabbed into her heart. How could he think that she had betrayed anyone?

"When I heard that you had married—*who* you had married—I couldn't believe it. I thought that there must have been a mistake." He gestured at her. "But here you are. The Dynasty's queen. How could you?"

Tears stung Everys's eyes. What could she say? How could she answer the hurt and pain in his voice?

"Papa, I—"

Challix cleared her throat and took a step forward. "kiv Bol Tusant Favid, yes? My name is Challix. I am your daughter's personal assistant. I'm sure you're tired from your travels. Perhaps we can bring you to a guest room where you can rest and continue this conversation later?"

Papa's gaze sharpened, but he didn't look away from Everys. "What I need right now is answers. How my daughter could ever think it was appropriate to marry the direct descendant of the monster who destroyed Nekek the Bright. How she could ever justify living in this palace built on the ashes of our people. Why she didn't feel it necessary to tell us that our family's shop has been utterly destroyed, and worse, Legarr is dead!"

He spat those last words with such force that Everys's knees buckled and she almost collapsed. Her own grief over her brother's death opened again. Legarr had been a constant pain for her since the rest of their family had left, leeching off of her. But then he'd gotten caught up in the conspiracy against Narius and her, used as an experiment with toratropic runes. And yes, she should have gotten word to her family about Legarr's death, but how could she? When Siporans were performing their vigils, they were deliberately difficult to contact. And how could she, as the queen, get a message to her family without drawing too much attention?

"Papa, I..." A sob strangled her words. What could she say? What would he even accept as an explanation?

"Well?" He crossed his arms. "Explain it to me, Everys. What possessed you to side with our enemy?"

"Sir, I'm going to have to ask you to moderate your tone," Rewether said, a warning growl in his voice.

"I will not be lectured by Dynasty butchers about how to speak to my daughter!" Papa shot back.

Rewether straightened and his eyes blazed. His hand twitched toward his weapon, a flechette thrower he had strapped to his right calf. While Everys didn't think he would fire on her father in her quarters, she had to stop this from escalating.

Stepping forward, she held up her hands, and all eyes snapped to her.

"Papa, I know you're upset. I can't imagine what it must have been like to learn about Legarr's death like that." She had to choose her words carefully here. "The shop too. And I can understand why you would be concerned about my new position. But I can assure you, this is a good thing."

Papa arched a brow at her, his lips pressed into a thin line.

"It is!" Everys insisted. "But I also know that you won't just believe me at my word, and I can't blame you. What did you used to say at the Broken Sword? 'Listen to what the customer says is wrong, trust their version of events, but then verify it for yourself.'"

Papa looked even more upset, and Everys couldn't blame him. She knew how much he loved the family's second hand electronics shop. His father had been the one to open it, and Papa had built up the business from there. But his face gradually softened, as if her words were sinking in.

"That's all I'm asking you to do," she continued. "Show me a little trust, but then see for yourself what the truth is. Can you do that? For me?"

Papa shifted his weight, his uncertainty painted across his face. Everys could practically hear his thoughts warring against each other. His hatred for the Dynasty, his love for her, the divide that had grown between them thanks to their time apart.

"Very well." Papa's shoulders slumped. "Perhaps I have been too harsh without getting a clear picture of the current situation. Everys—daughter—I would very much like to see this new life you've found for yourself."

Everys smiled, and she fought back some more tears. "I would like that, Papa. Should we start with a tour?"

Papa glanced toward Rewether. "Will that be allowed?"

Rewether's jaw clenched, but Everys held up a hand to calm him. He took a step back, but she could tell that he was struggling with his own thoughts.

"Challix?" she prompted.

Challix smiled brightly, but Everys recognized the expression. She was acting as the diplomat. "I think a tour through the private residence would be most appropriate while we see to guest accommodations. Perhaps a walk through the royal gardens as well?"

Everys nodded. "That would be lovely. Papa?"

He nodded curtly. Everys let out a shaky breath and headed for the door. Her father fell into step with her, but she noticed he kept his distance, as if she was carrying a contagious disease. She tried to keep her disappointment from her face. She wanted nothing more than to hug her father, to feel his warm embrace for the first time in years. But that would have to wait.

Rewether and Kevtho trailed behind them as they left her quarters. Papa glanced at them over his shoulder and snorted.

"They don't trust their own queen within her palace?" he asked.

"It isn't that, Papa," Everys said. "A few months ago, assassins attacked the palace and tried to kill Narius and me. We were able to fight them off, but given the current tensions with Dalark and... well, everything else, the guards are being extra cautious."

"You were able to 'fight them off?'" Papa repeated, arching a brow. "How did you manage that?"

She could hear the question lurking underneath his words. Had she used her toratropic magic? What did her husband know about her? About them? Was their family secret still safe? She knew that he wouldn't like her answer to any of those questions, so she smiled.

"My husband is an excellent shot, Papa." She forced her smile wider. "I really think you'll like him. He's a wonderful man."

Once again, Papa snorted. "Oh, yes. We all know how wonderful Xoniel royalty is, building a kingdom through conquest. Why, this palace alone must have cost the lives of millions of victims."

Rewether grumbled something under his breath. Papa spared him a glance, but then he focused on Kevtho.

"You there, guard with the sword. You're a Dunestrider, correct?" Papa said.

Kevtho nodded curtly. "I am, sir."

"If I remember correctly, your people became part of the Dynasty two hundred and fifty years ago, yes?"

"That's one way of phrasing it, sir."

"The polite way. The Dynasty way!" Papa chuckled mirthlessly. "I mean, who would ever want to admit to the real history: How the Dynasty inserted themselves into your people's conflict with the Plissk, pretending to ally with both sides. Making promises to both sides so that you'd keep killing one another. And then, when you'd worn yourselves out, they swooped in and claimed your sacred deserts for themselves."

Rewether cleared his throat, a guttural sound that he probably hoped would be intimidating.

Papa regarded him coolly. "Oh, please. Even you must know that the Dynasty has always been selective in the truths it shares. How often have they conveniently left out information from news stories? How often have they glossed over atrocities that their troops committed while 'bringing peace' to our continent?"

Rewether's face turned bright red, and his jaw worked.

"Papa..." Everys said, trying to inject some warning in her voice. While she could shield him from some consequences, if he kept speaking so freely, he could wind up offending Rewether. Or worse, committing treason within the palace itself.

Papa looked at her, anger simmering in his eyes. But then his features softened, and he chuckled ruefully. "I am sorry, guard—"

"Rewether is the captain of my guard, Papa. And Kevtho is my Swordbound."

His brow twitched into a frown, but then he corrected himself. "Rewether. I'm afraid that my journey here has tired me out more than I anticipated. I seem to be out of sorts. I apologize if I offended you."

"No offense taken, sir." Rewether's voice still carried a growl to it.

For the next hour, Everys showed Papa through the private residence: the kitchens, the dining rooms, the guest wing, the private libraries, and the art galleries. He seemed suitably impressed by everything, although she could still read an undercurrent of disappointment in his attitude and posture.

As they left the palace itself and entered the royal gardens, he did seem to relax. Everys couldn't blame him. The gardens were one of her favorite parts of the palace grounds. An army of caretakers meticulously nurtured plants from all over the Dynasty's holdings in individual sections. A stroll through the gardens was like touring the Dynasty's territories, with fragrant flowers, impressive trees, and tranquil pools. They passed by pale green cacti and prickly brown bushes from the Kronin Desert, beautiful purple and white flowers from Maotoa, and cascading fruit vines from the Low River Province, plus every kind of tree imaginable.

And then they came to her favorite part of the gardens, the newest planting. In the center of a bare patch of dirt was a sapling, slender enough she could have wrapped her hands around it. She was actually surprised one of the gardeners wasn't fussing over it. Ever since the pillar tree had been planted in the gardens, it seemed to be the focus of everyone's attention.

"What's this?" Papa asked.

"A Cold Light tree."

Papa gaped at her, then at the sapling. "Why would anyone plant something from that cursed forest here?"

"Because the hostilities between the Dynasty and Cold Light are over, Papa," Everys said. "There's actual peace."

Kevtho cleared his throat. "Your daughter is being too modest, sir. While I was not present at the negotiations, I have heard from those who were that she was instrumental in achieving that peace. It's not a story the Dynasty tells openly, but it is a truth a father should hear."

Everys's cheeks burned as Papa looked at her again, this time with a mixture of skepticism and... was that respect?

"Perhaps I judged things too harshly," he whispered. "That is truly an amazing thing."

"Thank you, Papa."

They stood next to the pillar tree in silence for a few more moments before Papa grunted. "Unfortunately, it is true that I am quite tired. Your assistant mentioned something about a guest room?"

Everys led them back to the palace, where the serving staff whisked Papa off to his room. But not before she gave him a hug that felt a lot more awkward than she liked. As he walked away, she realized she still felt too much apprehension. There was no telling what would happen when he met Narius.

For the first time she could remember, she was thankful that her husband had been called away on some official business. Hopefully whatever it was wouldn't cause him too many problems. She suspected that they now had a new one visiting the palace.

12

The transition into the Ethnarch's Enclave was always jarring. The ancient walls that once surrounded this neighborhood had been torn down long ago, although there were still some vestiges protruding from the ground. The surrounding neighborhoods were common and ordinary, only to suddenly give way to sprawling manors and gilded palaces. But that only made sense. Over the centuries, it had become fashionable for the major houses to maintain a presence in this neighborhood, mixing with the rulers of the people the Dynasty had conquered. And given how limited the actual real estate was in Ethnarch's Enclave, there was a subtle but constant war going on for who could own the most land and hold on to it. It was all juvenile, ridiculous, and predictable.

It was almost enough to help Narius forget what the neighborhood's unofficial nickname was: the Gilded Lock. And Narius really couldn't forget that, especially because of where he was going.

His transport pulled to a quiet stop at the oldest manor in Ethnarch's Enclave, positioned in the direct center. Unlike its neighbors, this house wasn't impressive, little more than a squat building made of rough-hewn stones. And unlike its neighbors, this manor house would never trade hands, no matter how often the others might.

Because this was where The One Who Bestrides the Darkness, the ethnarch of the reclusive Diradae, lived. This was the first manor built here centuries earlier, when instead of ethnarchs, the inhabitants of this neighborhood were called hostages.

Much to Narius's surprise, Paine waited for him by the road. Once his guards had done a cursory sweep of the area, Narius hurried to the vizier's side.

"They summoned you as well?" Narius asked.

Paine nodded grimly. "And not just me, but most of your advisers too. I've seen Elamek already. And I believe Masruq was here before I was."

Narius frowned. The ministers of agriculture and finance. His mind started untangling the webs of house alliances and regional politics. Just having those two involved could create significant pressure for whatever the Flail wanted, and Narius strongly suspected that they weren't the only members of his council who had been contacted. The Flail was, if nothing else, thorough.

Paine and he walked to the front door of the Diradae manor, trying not to stare at the exterior's appearance. Unlike the surrounding houses, there were no decorative flairs, no signs of outward wealth. The walls were made of rough, dark stone with narrow windows blocked by metallic bars. The building was squat, as if it had sunk up to its neck into the ground. The Diradae ethnarchs had decided long ago to leave their residence in Bastion unaltered so everyone could remember what it had been from the start: a prison. That, plus the fact that the Diradae ethnarch didn't maintain homes anywhere else within the Dynasty's holdings, was a not-so-subtle rebuke to the Dynasty's history.

Two of the ethnarch's human guards snapped to attention as they approached the front doors. Zar, the captain of the King's Guard, eyed them as they descended the stairs into the manor, then muttered an insult under his breath. Narius hid a smile. Zar judged everyone else by a harsh standard, one that he thankfully strove to meet himself.

"Did you receive any hints as to what the Flail wants?" Narius whispered to Paine once they were inside.

"Unfortunately, no," Paine replied. "The impending war, Brencis's attempted coup, possibly even the price of imports. The Flail has eclectic concerns."

Narius snorted. That was one way to put it.

Stepping into the palace itself was like traveling forward through time. While the exterior appeared to be centuries old, the interior had been updated with modern amenities and comforts. The most noticeable change came as they moved through the hallway. Some of the outside humidity seeped into the halls, but the deeper they went into the palace, the cooler and drier the air became. More than that, the lights dimmed as well. Given that the Diradae lived in caves and tunnels that wound through the Diradae Mountains, they preferred cold, dark places.

They eventually entered a large, domed audience chamber. Narius glanced around the room. He knew from his history lessons that this had once been the prison cell for the Diradae ethnarch. The thick door they stepped past was reminder enough, but the bare stone walls, the large iron rings embedded in the wall, every bit of the room's decor proclaimed its former use. Narius smiled grimly. The Diradae had long memories and wanted other people to remember with them. Not that long ago, he wouldn't have approved of the Diradae displaying their long-held grief. Now, though, he understood and he hoped he could do something to lessen it.

He glanced around the room, taking stock of who else was in attendance. He counted three other ethnarchs, representing the Ixactl, the Dunestriders, and, much to his surprise, the Weyfir. Plus half a dozen representatives from the Hall of All Voices and three members of major noble houses. Mingling with them were half a dozen members of his inner council. He gritted his teeth and forced himself to smile. They were outnumbered.

Masruq, the minister of finance, waddled over to him. Masruq was an older Hinaen man, but while his outer appearance suggested he was soft and overly pampered, Narius knew better. Masruq had married into the nobility and then clawed his way up through the finance ministry's ranks by sheer determination and sly skill, and he had guided the Dynasty's economy skillfully, making them a powerhouse that few could rival.

"Your Strength, good to see you," Masruq said. "Might I suggest a taste of the Elbrekkian red tonight? An exquisite vintage, a rare treat not to be missed."

"Indeed?" Narius said.

Masruq nodded sagely. "From what I understand, Ethnarch Estrid rarely dives this deep into his wine stock. We should feel honored."

Narius's gaze narrowed as he parsed Masruq's words. The finance minister had used the ethnarch's familiar name. Most Diradae insisted on strangers using their full names, but if they knew someone well or trusted them, they allowed them to use a shortened version. That hinted that Masruq knew the ethnarch well. But more importantly, he had obviously been scouting the members of the Flail to see why they had all been summoned here. There were certain matters that people would share with Masruq rather than Narius. Was he giving a warning? An encouragement?

"I think I will indulge." He turned to Paine. "Paine?"

Paine shook his head. "No, thank you."

Masruq chuckled. "Your loss."

Narius made his way over to a side table, where he found several open wine bottles. A servant poured him a glass of the red and offered it to him with a curt bow. Narius made his way back to Paine, sipping his glass carefully. The wine was indeed exquisite, a fruity delight with a subtle foundation of earth and spice and just a hint of smoke. It was some of the best he had ever tasted. A bribe before the discussion started? An attempt to dull his wits? Or was the ethnarch merely being a good host?

He made the rounds, making sure to greet each person by name. They were polite enough, although he could sense an undercurrent of tension from the Flail's members. That suggested they were going to ask him for something big, something they worried he may not agree to.

Quiet conversations continued as he made his way back to Paine, who had made a similar circuit through the room.

"Any thoughts?" he asked.

Paine shook his head subtly. "Nothing beyond the obvious."

Narius was about to comment when he heard the rumbling of stone against stone. He recognized the sound immediately. The gong announced that The One Who Bestrides the Darkness was about to join the discussion.

The far doors ground open, sounding like the beginning of a rockslide, and the ethnarch entered the room, followed by members of his court. The Diradae looked like giant spiders, taller than Narius. They scuttled forward on four thick legs that sprouted from their thoraxes and abdomens. They also had two pairs of arms, two thicker upper arms and scrawnier lower arms, all of which ended in hands with three sharp claws. What appeared to be an even smaller pair of arms protruded from their backs above their rear legs. The ethnarch's body was a mottled black and gray color, and from the way the light undulated across his body, Narius suspected he was covered in fine hairs.

But in spite of their monstrous appearance, the most noticeable thing about the Diradae were their masks. Each Diradae wore an oval-shaped mask that completely covered their face. Each mask had the same features: a blocky human face with a rectangular nose, sharp lips, and teardrop shaped eyes. The only difference was the ethnarch's, which had a gold line painted across the mask's forehead.

As the Diradae moved through the room, the assembled guests parted and bowed to the ethnarch. He ignored them, crossing the room to a dais. He clambered up to the top and knelt with all four legs.

Once he had settled in, Narius bowed to him. Whispers rippled through the room. Technically, Narius wasn't supposed to bow to anyone. He was king, after all. But this was Ethnarch Estrid's home and his meeting. Until Narius knew what the Flail wanted, he wasn't going to antagonize them.

"Your Strength, you honor us with your presence," Estrid said. "We are pleased you were able to come and see us on such short notice."

Narius made a sweeping gesture at the other guests. "When so many prominent individuals ask for my attention, how could any king refuse?"

Estrid motioned with his lower right hand, as if shooing an insect. "But many have in the past. It heartens me to hear you say that, but we shall see how truthful your words are."

"Then shall we begin?"

"We shall." Estrid opened his upper arms and beckoned with his hands.

Rockflow, the Ixactl ethnarch, stepped forward and cleared his throat. "Your Strength, Vizier Paine, members of the king's high council. We thank you for joining us today and—"

"We've heard the pleasantries already, Rockflow," Ventios, the minister of labor, called. "Unless Ethnarch Estrid wants us to drink more of his fancy wine, get to the point."

Several of the attendees laughed, but Narius noticed that Estrid did not. Nor did most of the members of the Flail. By Dynasty standards, Ventios's sarcasm was acceptable. But clearly this wasn't the time. Narius made a subtle waving motion with his hand to his advisers, hoping they would take the hint.

"Very well." Rockflow's voice was a rumble. "We have watched these past several weeks as the tensions between the Dynasty and the Dalark Imperium have escalated. We fear that war will soon be inevitable."

"Let them come," Elamek said. "We will show them why they shouldn't challenge the Xoniel Dynasty! After all, King Narius has just appointed Strategist Overturn to head the military. With him leading our troops, we'll make short work of the Dalark!"

Once again, his advisers nodded and made agreeing noises. But the members of the Flail did not. Narius shot a look at Paine. The vizier's gaze had sharpened as he studied the room.

"That may well be, but at what cost to the Dynasty?" Numeria, the Dunestrider ethnarch, asked. "And who will pay it?"

Masruq cleared his throat. "The Dynasty's treasury can handle the expense of any hostilities. We are already increasing our spending to make sure the military is well equipped for—"

"And where does that money come from?" Numeria asked. "Doesn't it come from the pockets of our people? And it's not just a matter of blades, is it? How many of the Desert's sons and daughters will bleed and die on that battlefield? How many Ixactl soldiers will be in any battle?"

"That is the Dynasty's way," Masruq said with a dismissive flip of his hand.

Narius ground his teeth. But it didn't have to be. If he had had more time for Falling Sword. If he and Everys could have built more on the newly won peace with the Cold Light. If Duke Brencis hadn't betrayed them. So many ifs and lost opportunities. But as the Perfected Warrior once wrote, "You only fight on the battlefield in front of you, not the one you wish you had." This was the Dynasty's way. For now.

"Very true, Minister Masruq," Estrid said, his voice a soft rumble. "That is something that the Diradae understand all too well. For five hundred years, we have sacrificed ourselves for the sake of our Dynasty. For five hundred years—"

Ethnarch Estrid continued an all-too-familiar litany of his people's history. Narius had heard it before from different perspectives: Five hundred years earlier, the Dynasty had conquered the Diradae and forcibly integrated them into the Dynasty by taking their ruling family as hostages, ensconcing them in this very prison. And why? Because of visium, a rare metal found only in the Diradae Mountains. Stronger than iron, sharper than steel, visium had made the Dynasty's military all but unstoppable. Most historians credited the use of visium weapons and armor with the overthrow of Nekek the Bright and the Siporan Ascendancy.

Paine cleared his throat, interrupting Estrid. The ethnarch paused, his back appendages twitching.

"I mean no disrespect," Paine said. "We are all aware of what the Dynasty has done to your people. What is it that you want? You clearly have a suggestion or else you would not have demanded us be here."

"Very well," Estrid said. "We want peace."

Narius quirked a brow and looked at the other members of the Flail. They nodded, some of them agreeing verbally.

"That is what we would have had if the Emperor hadn't died at your wedding," Spanica Trentwether, a member of a major noble house, said.

Heat painted Narius's cheeks. Spanica was conveniently ignoring that he and Princess Innana of the Dalark Imperium had almost been assassinated as well, that that had been the intention of the attack that had killed Devroshan, the Emperor and Innana's father. But he realized that the Flail would not care about that. He kept silent.

"Perhaps." Paine's tone made it sound as though he had made a great concession. "But that is a road we will never travel down again. And I suspect that most within the Dynasty would desire peace as well. What you have shared is not new information. What is it, specifically, that you want the king to do?"

The members of the Flail exchanged wary glances. Narius braced himself. If it had been a small ask, there would have been no hesitation.

"In a week's time, we will host a dinner here at our manor," Estrid said. "We would appreciate it if you could attend."

Narius didn't relax. A social engagement didn't deserve this much buildup.

"And we intend to invite Ambassador Alezzar to this dinner as well in the hopes that you might speak with him about how to avert the impending conflict," Estrid continued.

There it was. Ambassador Alezzar represented the Dalark to the Dynasty. He had been the one who'd proposed his near marriage to Innana. He had been the one who could speak for the Emperor, whether it had been Devroshan or, now, Tirigian. He was the only path to peace that didn't involve Narius traveling to Dalark or Tirigian traveling to the Dynasty.

"Please allow me to consult with my advisers," Narius said.

Estrid nodded, and the other members of the Flail gathered around him to hold their own conference. As his councilors stepped to his side, Zar motioned for Paine to step away and talk to him. Paine looked irritated, but he went over to the guard.

"Well, gentlemen?" Narius asked. "What do you think?"

"Preposterous," Elamek said. "How dare the Flail try to make policy like this? Whether or not the Dynasty goes to war should ultimately rest with you, Your Strength."

"If King Narius were the only one fighting the war, then that would make sense," Masruq said. "But the Flail has a point. It is their sons and daughters who would fight and die, not ours. And I've made my position clear. Peace would benefit trade and our economy. If we have a chance to achieve that, how can I oppose it?"

Narius listened as the other advisers weighed in. While this wasn't his complete council, he was able to guess how the missing advisers would vote. Within a few minutes of passionate discussion, they had come to a consensus.

He stepped away from the knot of councilors and toward the Flail. Their conversation stilled and Estrid turned his masked face to Narius.

"I accept your gracious invitation," Narius said. "I would be pleased to dine with Ambassador Alezzar and try to avert the war. By the Reforged Sword, I will do all in my power to accomplish this."

That seemed to mollify their hosts.

"We thank you, Your Strength," Estrid said. "We will send details to the palace within the day."

Paine stepped away from Zar and cleared his throat. "Our apologies, Ethnarch, but I'm afraid the king must return to the palace."

"Oh? I hope all is well?"

Narius frowned at the vizier, whose face didn't betray any emotions. But he could still read the tension in Paine's posture. Something had happened. A new disaster. A wave of numbness crashed over his body, which he ignored. No need to panic until he knew exactly what it was. He bowed to Estrid one last time then followed Zar and Paine out of the manor.

"What happened?" Narius whispered.

"According to Zar, we have company waiting for us."

"Who?"

"Your father-in-law."

Narius frowned, Paine's words not really registering. Then the full importance of what he said came crashing down on him. If Everys's father was indeed waiting for him back at the palace, he probably should have stayed in the Gilded Lock, where he would find a friendlier reception.

13

The door to Everys's quarters squeaked open, and she glanced up to see Narius peering in. He hesitated in the doorway, his lips pursed, like a little child about to get scolded for sneaking sweets before a meal.

"Is he here?" Narius whispered.

Her heart sank. How had he found out about Papa? She had hoped to talk to him about it first. "He's in a room in the guest wing. He'll join us for breakfast tomorrow morning."

"Oh." Narius stepped fully into the room, but he didn't come any closer. "I've only heard a little bit about what happened from Zar. Is it true that your father almost attacked Kevtho?"

Everys winced. Was that the rumor spreading through the palace? That would make Papa's visit all the more awkward.

Narius chuckled. "From your expression, I'm guessing not. But how did it go?"

"He's..." How could she phrase this? "He's not happy."

"With you?"

"With a lot of things," she said. "I think he went to Fair Havens to look for me first."

Narius blew out a long breath, and his shoulders slumped. "Meaning he saw what's left of the shop."

Everys looked down at her lap. "I can only imagine what the neighbors must have told him."

"What else?" Narius sat down on the couch next to her and caught her hands.

How could she phrase this without absolutely destroying him? "He's not happy that I'm married."

"If we could have brought him here—"

"No, not that. Well, not entirely." She looked up. "He's not happy that I married... you."

Narius's face fell, and Everys rushed on. "It's not fair. He doesn't even know you. If he did—"

"I'd still be the direct descendant of the man who destroyed Nekek the Bright," Narius murmured. "I'd still represent the nation who oppressed your people."

The pain laced in his voice stabbed her heart. She reached out and cupped his cheek in one hand. Tears welled in her eyes, and for a brief moment, she felt a flash of irritation at Papa. If he could only see how hurt Narius was upon hearing this, maybe his attitude would change.

"You're a good man. Don't ever forget that. It's not your fault."

"But it is," Narius said. "If I hadn't forced you to marry me, you'd still be living in Fair Havens. You'd still be working in the Broken Sword, and..."

"And I would have never met the love of my life. I wouldn't trade that for anything?"

"Really?" He looked up at her, and hope glinted in his eyes. "Getting attacked by assassins is worth it?"

"Bring on a thousand assassins." Everys sat up straighter. "I've got enough runes for all of them."

"And going into the heart of the Cold Light forests?" His smile grew just a bit broader.

"Why would I ever complain about that?" She thrust her fists on her hips, tipping her head back like a triumphant warrior. "If we hadn't done that, I wouldn't have seen the real you."

"Facing the disapproval of the nobility?" He scooted a bit closer to her.

"They are, as my husband likes to point out, 'addle-brained, short-sighted wiggats.' Why would they bother me?"

"How about drinking glasses of karabek sauce?"

She laughed. "That's where I draw the line, sorry."

He started to say something else, but Everys leaned in and pressed her lips against his. She put her hand on the back of his neck to hold him there as she deepened the kiss. His fingers snaked into her hair and she clung to him. She could almost feel his sadness trying to filter through her, but she wouldn't let it take root. They had been through so much together already. She wouldn't allow anything else to hurt him. Not that night. Not ever.

She pulled back and pressed her forehead against his. "You are my husband. And I love you more than I could ever say. If Papa doesn't understand that, then that's his problem, not yours. Now, c'mon." She rose from the couch and snared his hands, pulling him toward the bedroom. "Let me remind you of how good a husband you are."

Narius rolled onto his side and studied his sleeping wife. She curled against him, a faint grin on her lips. He loved waking up next to her, loved seeing her contented and at peace. He wished this moment could last forever.

With a sigh, he carefully slipped out of the bed. As much as he might have wanted to stay with Everys, there were expectations to remember and protocols to follow. Besides, he doubted he would have slept much anyway, and he wouldn't want to rob her of her own sleep. He gathered up his clothing and quietly dressed before tiptoeing out of the bedroom.

One of Everys's serving girls jumped as he entered the living room. Not Trule, but... Shara! That was her name. She sat on one of the couches by the fireplace, reading something on the scriber. She smiled shyly at him, and he nodded to her. This wasn't the first time one of the girls had seen him leaving Everys's bedroom.

He crept over to an empty section of the wall near the vidscreen and located the appropriate knot in the wainscoting. He pressed his hand to it, and once the biometric scanner recognized him, part of the wall swung back. With one last smile at Shara, he entered the secret passageway and pulled the door shut behind him.

Echoes of what Everys had told him chased him up the stairs. She had appeared every inch the confident warrior earlier, the picture of bravado and assuredness. But he knew her too well. Her eyes always gave her away. He'd seen the way sadness lurked in their beautiful depths. And he understood how heavy a burden a father's disapproval was.

Once inside his bedroom, he sat down on the edge of the bed and let his gaze roam over the room. This had been his father's room, back when King Girai and Queen Felisa had ruled. Before he had moved in after his coronation, the room had appeared like a rustic hunting lodge, with dark wood paneling and dozens of mounted animal heads dotting the walls. He had had the rooms completely gutted and renovated, replacing the wood with lighter plaster and disposing of all the trophies. He didn't like the animals' glassy eyes staring at him all night. Now, though, he regretted removing them. It would have been nice to have reminders of his father, as grotesque as they may have been. As it was, he had trouble remembering what their voices sounded like.

He chuckled. Sure, he could have pulled up footage of his father giving a speech or his mother conducting a Queen's Court, but they'd been experts at putting on a facade for the cameras and courtiers. They only let their guard down when they were in private with each other or their sons. He didn't miss their public personas. He missed them.

Narius's gaze hitched on the frame sitting next to his bed. He picked it up and ran a hand along its length. At one time, he had used this to store pictures of Princess Innana from the Dalark Imperium. He switched it on, calling up the new pictures he had stored: Everys at the state dinner he had thrown in her honor, the first time they had danced together. Everys at their official second wedding, radiant in her dress, a flowing gown made of red Grerid silk, sparkling with hundreds of gemstones, her hair swept up in an elaborate crown of braids. Everys during their honeymoon in Bluerest, lounging on the shore of the Water Bearer's Repose, her head tipped back and her eyes closed with the faintest smile on her lips. He looked forward to filling the frame's memory with more pictures like these.

He flipped past them to pictures from his childhood. A picture of him with his infantry unit, back when he served on the edge of the Kronin Desert. There was one of Paine and him, back when they attended school together at Pellio's Legacy. His heart lurched at the next one: a picture of Quartus, an impish smile on his face as he chased a furry plainhopper through the royal gardens. He missed the days when he and his brother had actually been friends.

And then he came to the picture he wanted to see: Father and Mother, not in their royal garments, but seated on a couch in Mother's quarters, studying a scriber together. Father appeared larger than life, with thick arms, wavy red hair, and piercing silver eyes. Mother looked small next to him, what with her dusty blond hair and hazel eyes. He remembered them as stiff and formal to each other—theirs had been a marriage of political convenience, not of love. But in this picture, he could almost imagine them happy together.

Maybe that was why they were both demanding of him. Mother used to drill him relentlessly about proper etiquette and protocol. Father had insisted on him reciting details about historical military campaigns and would lecture him for hours if he left out the least significant facts. He supposed they had been trying to prepare him to be king, but then Father had died after a prolonged illness—at least, that was the official story and Narius had promised he wouldn't dwell on the truth—and Mother had followed shortly thereafter in a freak skimmer crash.

And he'd been left to rule on his own, knowing all too well that they didn't approve of him.

Just as Everys's father didn't approve of him either.

Everys insisted that he was a good man. And he wanted to be. He would be. Maybe Everys's father didn't approve of him now, but he would. One way or another, Narius would make sure that by the time Everys's father left the palace, he would be happy to have him as his son-in-law.

14

Everys couldn't remember the last time she had felt this nervous.

Inkstains, my husband is finally going to meet my father.

Her stomach lurched and grumbled, and she pressed a hand against it as the girls fussed around her. Even though she knew the palace staff would whip up an amazing meal, she doubted she'd be able to eat much of anything. For a moment, she wished Narius had spent the full night in her room. Maybe this would have been easier if they had been getting ready together. But then she realized that they might not have made it to breakfast at all, especially after what had happened the night before.

"Blessed?" Trule prompted.

She snapped out of her reverie, blushing furiously, and turned to the servant girl. Trule held up a simple dress, offering it to her for inspection. Although it looked homespun and humble, Everys knew that Challix had likely spent far too much on it. If Papa behaved the way he had the night before, he'd likely criticize anything she wore. She nodded.

As soon as the girls had her dressed and ready, Everys set out for the private dining room. Halfway there, she could smell the food and her stomach rumbled. She rounded the corner and found Narius standing near the head of the table, a concerned look on his face. She stumbled to a stop. Why was he so—

"—glory once again rise in the west, so that all may see Your light." Papa's voice was clear and strong, sounding almost like he was singing.

Her blood froze. The Evening Verses? He was reciting the traditional Evening Verses now? Nobody did that anymore! The scriveners had decided years ago that sharing those funerary words were no longer necessary, especially given how long it had been since Nekek the Bright had been destroyed. Her family had never done this in the past. Why would Papa start now?

"May Your justice roll through the ashes of our shame. May Your peace surround us in our loss. May we see Your people restored once more according to Your will. Shatter the crowns of the defilers, and may they feel your wrath across their backs!"

That explained it all. The Evening Verses included optional imprecations against the Siporans' ancient enemies, calling for their death and destruction. Papa was trying to make a point, if inelegantly.

She came around the table and found her father kneeling on the floor, almost prostrate. He looked like he was about to start writhing in pain. All part of the Verses, unfortunately. Narius stood nearby, watching with a neutral expression, although she could read the concern in his posture, the tightness around his eyes. His gaze flicked in her direction, an unspoken question passing between them. She shrugged. She had no idea how long this was going to last.

Thankfully, after a few more mumbled words, Papa rose to his feet but kept his head bowed for a few silent moments. Then he turned to Narius.

"Well, that was certainly interesting," Narius said, offering what looked like a genuine smile.

Everys wanted to kiss him right then and there. Narius could have said something snide or rolled his eyes, but she knew him well enough to know he was being fully honest.

"I apologize for the delay..." Papa frowned. "I'm not sure how to address you. Am I to call you 'Your Strength,' as your subjects are required to?"

"That is not necessary..." Narius chuckled. "I must admit, I don't know what to call you either."

They stared at each other, neither answering the other's question. Everys stepped up to Narius and threaded her fingers through his, squeezing his hand.

"Narius, this is my father, Favid. Papa, this is Narius, my husband."

That simple introduction at least helped Narius. "With your permission, I would like to call you 'father.' Mine has been dead for several years now. I would be honored if you would permit me."

Papa's expression was stony. But then he sighed and nodded. "If you wish, that would be fine."

"And please, call me Narius. I want us to be family, not adversaries."

Papa looked ready to say something. *Neither my daughter nor I will ever be part of that family*. But Everys shot him a warning glare.

He must have received the message. Sighing again, he turned toward the table. "This all smells wonderful."

Narius relaxed as well. "It does indeed. Shall we eat?"

They took their places at the table, and the servants began dishing up the food. Everys smiled at the kitchen staff as they worked, greeting them by name. Narius did the same. Papa watched them work in silence. Once they had withdrawn, Papa started eating, focused solely on his meal.

"So, Father..." Narius seemed to trip over the name, but he recovered quickly enough. "I know that Everys took over your shop when you... left Bastion. How long did you work there?"

Papa grunted. "Most of my life. The schools in Fair Havens were notoriously underfunded. To make up for the shortfall, they unofficially expelled the Siporan students."

Narius frowned. "They what?"

"You heard me. They refused to let us into the building, but they claimed they were still teaching us to receive government funding."

Everys studied her plate. She knew this story. Papa used to tell it at the end of every school term, especially whenever Legarr complained about needing to go to school.

"Who did this?" Narius's voice had taken on an angry edge.

"Does it matter? Those responsible have long since retired, as are those who enabled and rewarded them." Papa picked at his food. "Even if you were to confront them, they would lie, and the records they kept will match their stories. There's nothing you can do."

"But it's not right. This sort of thing should be exposed!" Narius said.

Her heart swelling, Everys shot Narius an encouraging smile. There was her husband. If he learned who it was, not even the Perfected Warrior would be able to stop him.

"Exposed?" Papa laughed. "Everyone knew it was happening. The parents. The neighbors. The constables. Local officials. The prelates even praised the school administrators for their ability to do so much with so little. As a result, I received a different education. From my father in the shop. From the scriveners. And I did all right for myself, in spite of what happened."

Narius looked ready to argue, but then he closed his mouth and scowled at his plate, as if the food was somehow responsible.

Everys cleared her throat. "Thankfully, that wasn't the way things were when I went to school. Although I did enjoy the lessons Papa gave me at the shop."

Papa actually smiled, the first genuine smile she had seen from him in years. "You were always eager to learn."

"And Narius is eager to learn as well." She leaned forward. "He wants to understand what we've experienced and make things better. Change is possible, Papa."

"That's why I want to know who is responsible," Narius said. "Yes, they may not be able to answer for what they did to you, but that is a story that needs to be heard, if for no other reason than to make people aware that it happened."

Papa chuckled mirthlessly. "Why bother? Yes, some people will feel pity for those poor Siporans who were denied an education, but then they'll salve their conscience by reminding themselves that this happened long ago. Or they'll point to whatever progress they can and absolve themselves of the guilt that way. And those in power? Those who could affect real change? They're too wrapped up in their own petty squabbles and maneuvers to actually see the world as it is. Unless you can break them out of that self-interested haze, they will never try to change anything."

Narius took a breath, as if ready to argue, but then the doors to the dining room burst open and Paine rushed in. Much to Everys's surprise, the vizier looked flustered. She stared at him, surprised. Paine was always cool and collected, poised and polished. But now, even she could tell that something had happened. Something bad.

Narius must have noticed as well. He rose from his chair. "Paine? What is it?"

"The criers have picked up a new story, and they're sharing it throughout Bastion. The rest of the Dynasty's holdings as well," Paine said.

"What is it?" Everys asked.

Paine didn't even flinch at her question. He didn't even seem to mind her presence. That made her more concerned.

"This." He produced a scriber and turned on the screen.

A handsome Grerid man with bright eyes and a toothy grin appeared on the screen. "In other news, Viara, King Narius's former wife, recently made a shocking allegation."

The crier disappeared, replaced with an image of Viara.

Everys's heart froze in her chest. Viara was a stunning woman, a Hinaen beauty that few could rival. She had cut her black hair short, falling to her shoulders, but her crystal green eyes were the same as the last time Everys had seen her. Even though she was no longer queen, she had an unmistakable magnetism to her, even through the screen.

"I have remained silent too long," she said. "At first, I did so out of loyalty to the Dynasty, placing our collective needs above my own. That is what we are all taught to do, yes? But as I thought about it, I realized that I couldn't keep my silence any longer. I must share this very personal news with you, my fellow citizens, for the good of the Dynasty."

Everys stifled a groan. From what she had learned about Viara, this was her way. All theatrics, all flash, very little substance. While her words were flowery and proper, she had caught the way Viara used the word "citizen." Viara may have started speaking as though she was doing this for everyone, but that little slip revealed who she thought of as her equals: those who had earned their citizenship. Those who had inherited it due to their nobility. Not the regular people. But why would Paine consider this such a crisis? Viara was merely playing her usual games for attention.

On the recording, Viara took a deep breath and gripped the sides of the podium she stood at. "My friends... I have recently learned that I am with child. And the father is King Narius."

Everys's stomach fell into her feet, and it felt as though her head was filling with cold air. She was what? And Narius was... The color had drained from her husband's face, and he looked like he was facing one of the ancient mage-kings in battle.

Viara straightened and stared into the camera, making it look like she was looking Everys right in the eye. "I hereby call on the royal family to do what is right for my child. Not for my sake. Not even for yours. For the sake of the Dynasty. Live up to the justice you claim to pursue."

The recording switched back to the crier, who summed up what Viara had just said. Paine reached down and shut off the recording.

"Paine..." Narius's voice sounded like he was being strangled.

"The council is already on their way to discuss this new development," Paine said, his tone flat and lifeless.

Silence fell on the dining room. Everys tried to take a deep breath to calm her stuttering heart, but she couldn't breathe. What would this mean for their marriage? For them? For her?

Papa cleared his throat. "Yes, I can see how well you're changing things."

15

Quartus shifted his weight back and forth, his hands shoved deep into his pockets. He surveyed the crowd gathered outside the hostel. A dozen Plissk, two Ixactl, a handful of Weyfir, even what looked like an Elbrekkian, although what he thought were neck spines might have been a trick of the light. Not too many humans, meaning he'd stand out. But all of them were dressed similar to him: shabby clothes and desperate expressions.

He had worked hard to make sure his clothes were sufficiently worn. The desperation, though, was completely genuine.

Just finding this place had been a gift from the Trickster. While he recovered from the beating, Quartus had called every exterminator he could find to report a bark beetle infestation. Without his crew to help, it took days, but he was able to cajole information about similar infestations from the people he talked to until he realized that there was a large swarm in this part of Bastion, a run-down industrial park known as Downturn. Once he'd arrived, it was simply a matter of looking for the distinctive green bugs and following them to their source, a battered hostel that looked on the verge of collapse. According to rumors, two Cold Light thralls were using the hostel as a base of operations, trying to recruit disgruntled and disaffected people.

Armed with that information, Quartus had decided the best thing he could do was confront the thralls and see what they'd be willing to share.

He adjusted his coat and started across the street. As he approached the building, two older men on the front porch noticed him and let out a low whistle. A second later, one of the Ixactl stepped into his path.

"You best turn around and find somewhere else to go," she growled.

Quartus flashed what he hoped was a charming smile. "See, that's the thing. I don't have anywhere else to go. But rumor has it that there are folks here who might be able to give my life some direction. Like they could be a light in a cold place."

He waited to see how she would react. Her gaze flicked toward the hostel and her weight shifted. Quartus fought back a smile. She might as well have confessed to everything.

"Stay here."

He almost laughed at her. By heading into the hostel to check with whoever was in there, she was basically announcing that someone important really was hiding in the hostel.

A few minutes later, the Ixactl returned and motioned for him to follow. He forced himself to be as nonchalant as possible, but once they entered the building, three other people stepped forward and roughly searched him for weapons. He held his hands out, keeping his face impassive. He had expected this as well.

Once they were satisfied, the Ixactl beckoned him forward. They wound their way through crumbling hallways into a back bedroom, one occupied by two people, a male Grerid and a female Kolvese. Both of them wore simple, homespun clothing. But what was most noticeable were the vines wrapped around their arms and chests, stretching up through their unkempt hair. In several places, it looked like the branches actually pierced their skin, diving into their bodies before emerging elsewhere. Cold Light thralls.

Quartus wanted to crow in triumph. Hopefully he'd be able to get some answers, provided the thralls didn't kill him first.

The two thralls froze, their gazes flicking up and down his body. While they scrutinized him, he took a moment to catalog the room. Bark beetles swarmed along the walls in undulating patterns, with individual bugs flying from swarm to the thralls and then back again. Two simple cots were pressed into one corner plus a small table at which the thralls sat.

"Who are you?" the male thrall asked.

"You can call me Qulinus," Quartus said. "I'm hoping you can answer some questions for me."

The woman scoffed. "And why would we do that?"

"Did you hear about the big fire a few days back in the Everhold?"

"Yes," the man said warily.

"I was there when it started. I found three Cold Light thralls in the basement of the house, along with four stumps in the backyard. And I figured you might want to know about that."

The two thralls exchanged a look, but Quartus could read the surprise and, yes, even a little fear in their expression.

"Now I have no issues with the Cold Light. I know all about how the royal family stole your Hearth and wouldn't return it until just recently. If you're here to sow some chaos and death on the Dynasty, Warrior grant you his full arsenal. I'm just here to find out what this is." He produced the scriber and tossed it to the woman.

She caught it out of the air and frowned at him. Quartus shot her what he hoped was a winning smile. Technically nothing he said was a lie. Not really. He was outlaw, after all, meaning he didn't have much of a stake in what Cold Light terrorists did to the Dynasty.

The thrall opened the file and looked it over. She showed it to her partner.

"Looks like your dead friends were working on some sort of chemical. Any idea what it was? Toxic gas? Biological agent?"

The male snorted. "It's not a weapon. It's tree sap."

Quartus frowned. "What?"

"It's a synthetic version of sap from a pillar tree," he said.

Quartus's frown deepened. "Why would anyone want to manufacture that?"

The woman started to answer, but then her body stiffened. Her head tipped back, and her eyes rolled up in her skull. A second later, the same thing happened to the man.

Quartus took a step back, dropping into a defensive posture. It looked like they were dying or hurt or something bad, and he didn't want the Ixactl to attack him in retaliation. But she didn't move from her perch at the door.

Then the woman relaxed, and her eyes cleared, but there was a definite change in her expression. She looked older.

"Enough with the questions, Quartus Prince." Her voice had taken on a more resonant tone, as if another person spoke underneath her.

"We know who you are," the man added.

"Tell us what you truly want and then leave us that we may prepare to leave this cursed city," the woman said.

Quartus took a stuttering breath. Based on what he had heard about Narius and Everys's discussions with the Cold Light, apparently the trees had assumed direct control of these thralls.

"Okay, fine. Let's drop the subterfuge, shall we?" Quartus relaxed. "For starters, I want you to leave Bastion alone. Narius gave you your Hearth back. You've got no reason to be here anymore."

The woman made a scoffing sound. "As if that were the only concern we had. The Yoreroot is willing to be grafted into the Dynasty, but not all of us agree. We wish to be free of you animals entirely."

"You've obviously found some willing partners here in Bastion." Quartus jerked a thumb toward the Ixactl. "But I'm not all that surprised. The Dynasty has made a lot of enemies over the past few centuries. I'm more interested in who's making that synthetic sap."

The thralls' eyes narrowed at the same time, making Quartus wonder if the same Cold Light was controlling both of them.

"We do not know who their partner is," the male said.

"Why would someone want that much synthetic tree sap?" Quartus asked.

The thralls hesitated, then the woman said, "We do not know that either."

"But you must have a theory."

More hesitation.

"Suspicions only," the woman allowed.

"What are they?"

She laughed. "Why would we share those with you? Matters of the Below, not the air. And if our suspicions are correct, it will mean that the Dynasty will finally pay in blood for what they have done to us and many others."

Quartus swallowed a growl. That was less than helpful. Then his mind hitched on a detail.

"You're okay with the fact that whoever these people are murdered some of your thralls and chopped down pillar trees?" he asked. "It doesn't sound like these partners are all that interested in your liberation at all. It sounds like they just wanted to figure out how to synthesize this sap and then disposed of your friends when they got what they wanted."

The woman chuckled. "Except no one inhabited the trees when they were cut down. And our thralls are easily replaced. You will not succeed in dividing us, Quartus Prince. My suggestion? Abandon this mission and flee before our vengeance strikes you down as well."

Before Quartus could respond, a change passed over the two thralls and they sagged in their chairs. They blinked several times, then the woman fixed Quartus with a scowl.

"You heard Autumn Shade," she said. "Leave."

"Fine." He held out his hand. "But I would like the scriber back. This 'Autumn Shade' may want me to give this up, but I'm stubborn."

The thralls exchanged a look, then the man stepped closer and pressed the scriber in his hand. But before he withdrew, he whispered: "Deepflow Shipping."

Quartus had to steel his features to keep from reacting. As the man stepped back, his eyes were wide, as if asking silently if he had been heard and understood. Quartus nodded subtly.

"Thank you for your help." He injected his words with sarcasm. "I'm glad our people are finally getting along."

With that, he turned and stormed past the Ixactl and out of the hostel. He didn't slow or even look back. Hopefully no one was following him. He'd do his best to lose any tails before he returned to the safehouse.

As he walked, he considered what he had learned. Someone was making synthetic Cold Light tree sap. And he had the name of a company. He doubted that Deepflow Shipping was creating the sap, but it was a connection. A lead! And that meant—

"Hey! You! Stop right there!"

Quartus turned at the shout. Four men in black uniforms stormed in his direction. He looked around, spotting several other passersby who seemed just as nervous at their shout. Who were they after?

He turned back to the men dressed in black and realized that all four were focused on him.

Whirling around, Quartus headed down the street briskly, hoping it would look like he hadn't heard them. Maybe he had been wrong. Maybe they weren't really after him.

"I said stop! You are wanted for questioning, Qulinus!"

Definitely after him. Quartus took off at a run and the four men shouted again. Who were they? Not local constables. They weren't wearing the right uniforms. But they weren't common thugs either.

Most crime lords didn't require matching outfits. That meant they had to be government agents.

He careened around a corner and tore down the new street. But after he passed the first building, someone reached out of a side alleyway and pulled him into the shadows. He stumbled around as his rescuer brought him behind a dumpster. He could hear his pursuers thunder past the alley.

A thank you formed on his lips as he turned to the one who helped him. Only his rescuer lashed out and knocked his legs out from under him.

Quartus slammed into the cement hard, the wind knocked out of his lungs. Then his would-be savior jumped onto his chest. Quartus thrashed against his attacker, who wore an all-black outfit complete with a full mask covering his face. But the attacker wasn't put off by his resistance. He knocked aside Quartus's hands and reached into his pockets.

The scriber! Quartus bucked, knocking his assailant off of him. As he did, he snared the mask and yanked, hoping to twist it around and temporarily blind his attacker.

Instead, the mask pulled free to reveal a woman's face. A beautiful woman. A woman who looked at him with wide amber eyes.

Quartus sucked in a breath. The same eyes he had seen outside the burning house. The same woman. What was she—?

She yanked the scriber free, then kicked him across the face. Pain exploded in his jaw and nose, and he rolled on the ground, biting back a scream. He was vaguely aware of footfalls as the woman ran away. By the time he got to his feet again, she had vanished.

He groaned, exploring his nose. Not broken, but he had just recovered from the beating Stoophawk had given him. Thankfully, he didn't really need the scriber anymore. He had learned what he had to. It just galled him to lose it, especially since it meant someone else had taken notice of his investigation. And that meant that he was running out of time.

16

Narius stumbled down the hall to the Amber Office, Paine at his side and his guards surrounding them, but he was only vaguely aware of his surroundings. He felt like he was asleep, drifting through a dream, one in which the whole world had flipped upside down. Viara was pregnant, said the child was his? Blunted Sword, what was this madness?

"Your Strength?" Paine's voice barely sounded like a whisper.

He couldn't answer. He shook his head and kept walking. Not until he had the rest of his advisers present. He only wanted to talk about this once. No, twice. Once with the people who could help him untangle this mess. Once with the only person in the palace whose opinion truly mattered to him.

They turned into the Amber Office, and Narius headed straight for his place. As he walked, he took note of who had already arrived. Masruq chatted quietly with Elamek. That was fine with him; Viara's news probably wouldn't impact them directly. But then there was Auriel Zammit, the Governor-General of Bastion. Zolkin, Speaker for the Hall of All Voices. Strategist Overturn stood by himself in one corner, looking at the others awkwardly. And Minister Bokil stood in an opposite corner, studying the others beneath hooded eyes. No sign of Supreme Prelate Istragon. That was both a positive and a negative. Istragon was supposed to be here to offer his counsel and aid, but Narius suspected that would only be another screed against Everys and their marriage. That would be less than helpful.

He collapsed in his chair. A few of the advisers paused in their conversations to glance in his direction.

"Your Strength?"

Narius ground his teeth together. Leave it to Tormod to sneak up on him like this.

"Are you all right?" the spymaster whispered.

"Not particularly."

Tormod smiled, kindness shining in his eyes. "And the queen?"

"We haven't talked about it yet."

"You chose to speak to us first?"

Narius's mouth popped open and he started to say something, but Tormod held up his hands to stop him.

"Forgive my impertinence, Your Strength. This is a crisis, without a doubt. But you have us to manage the situation. Who does Everys have?" Tormod patted Narius on the shoulder. "Something to think about."

Narius's stomach sank. Tormod was right. He had left Everys alone with her father in the dining room and headed right here. It had been instinct, drilled into him by his own father. Dynasty first, personal matters second. But that wasn't how he wanted to live anymore. He looked at the door, wondering if he could go talk to Everys and fix this. But just as he started to rise, his advisers turned their attention on him.

He winced, trying to push away the guilt. He'd have to make it up to her.

"First of all, I want to welcome Strategist Overturn to these proceedings," he said, nodding to the Ixactl. "I'm sorry that your first meeting won't be about military matters."

Overturn's face was grim. "Those will come. I am willing to offer what advice I can."

Narius nodded, then looked over his advisers. "I'm assuming we've all heard Viara's," he wasn't sure what to call it, "news?"

Nods all around the room.

"Initial thoughts?" he asked.

Filamon, the minister of resource management, raised a hand. "How certain are we that this is true? We're all well aware of how Viara had numerous dalliances before she left the palace."

Narius fought the urge to grimace. Technically, as far as he knew, Viara had been faithful to him during their marriage. Tormod had started rumors to the contrary when she'd left him. He shifted in his chair as he did the math. Even though it had been clear that their marriage was disintegrating in its final days, there had been attempts made by both of them to salvage what they could. They hadn't shared a bed often in those final weeks, but he could remember a few times when they had. He winced as he thought of how he and Everys had spent the previous night, his guilt churning in his stomach.

"It's within the realm of possibility," he said.

"Is there any way we can confirm paternity now?" Filamon pressed on. "Tormod?"

Bokil grunted from his perch in the corner. "No offense, Tormod, but this is more of an internal security matter, isn't it?"

Filamon rolled his eyes. "Oh, please. I doubt the thugs who work for you would know what to look for. And besides, sending them in a raid would cause more scandal, not less. This calls for a stiletto, not a maul."

Bokil grumbled again, but he fell silent.

"If such a test has been done, I suppose my agents could secure the results," Tormod said. "But then, I suspect Viara would not have made her announcement if she didn't have proof at the ready."

"Those results could be faked," Zammit said.

"Indeed they could." Tormod pressed his hands together. "By the time we untangle and verify Viara's claims, the child will likely be born."

"Why not make sure this isn't an issue?" Bokil asked quietly.

Narius sat up straighter. The others shifted, clearly uncomfortable. Was Bokil really suggesting what he thought he was?

"You cannot be serious," Masruq said with a snort.

"I am entirely serious," Bokil countered. "If Viara were to meet with an unfortunate accident before she is able to give birth, the situation resolves itself."

"As if anyone would believe it was an accident!" Masruq shot back. "We'd best all exhort Chance and Chaos nothing happens to Viara, because we will bear the blame should anything happen to her."

Narius breathed a small sigh of relief. Duke Brencis had suggested the same solution for Viara when she'd left. He was glad he wasn't the only one who rejected such a dishonorable solution.

"You seem to be taking this whole situation very lightly, Masruq," Zammit said.

"Quite the contrary," Masruq said. "This is most troubling. The Dynasty is already teetering on a blade's edge thanks to the tensions with Dalark and the threat of a coup from Brencis. Add a potential succession crisis to the mix? Dark days ahead for sure."

"What are we to do?" Bokil asked. "Just let Viara steal the throne?"

His advisers descended into arguments. Narius let them for a few minutes; he had learned that letting them debate like this not only relieved some tension but could also spark a solution. He eventually held up a hand, silencing them.

"Strategist Overturn, do you have any ideas?" he asked.

Overturn rubbed the tip of one of his horns. "Well, two, actually. When you can't face a foe on the field of battle, sometimes it's best to placate them, right? Like what King Heronus did after he and the Dalark destroyed Nekek the Bright."

Narius frowned. "I'm not sure I'm following your reasoning."

"After Nekek the Bright had been destroyed, the Dalark was ready to keep fighting. They wanted to claim the Ascendancy's territory as their own. King Heronus objected, and it looked like it would turn into an actual battle. Heronus knew he couldn't win, so he came up with a compromise. He allowed the Imperium to keep the former territory of the Elbrekkian Combine."

A murmur rippled through the room. Narius's eyebrows rose. That was an accurate description of what had happened, but—

"Let's not forget they slaughtered most of the Elbrekkians and turned that territory into their Beachhead, which is causing us problems today," Bokil said, giving voice to Narius's thought.

Overturn raised his hand. "I'm not saying it's a perfect solution, but is there a way to disarm Viara? Turn her, if not into an ally, into a non-threat?"

Narius frowned. He definitely didn't want Viara as an ally, and he was pretty sure she'd never not be a threat. "What's your other idea?"

"Well, if you can't disarm someone, you use your most potent weapon on them." His smile turned vicious. "I say you unleash the queen on her."

Narius sputtered. He should do what?

Masruq guffawed. "An entertaining proposal. I, for one, would relish the resulting clash."

"The queen would destroy Viara," Elamek added.

The others laughed and added their own commentary, but Narius caught the quiet rebuke in Tormod's eyes.

The guilt crested inside him and propelled him to his feet. What was he doing, sitting here with these men? Tormod had been right, who did his wife have in all of this? He shouldn't be here. He should be with her, trying to sort this out with her.

"Enough!" Narius snapped.

The others fell silent. Shame danced across their faces.

"I didn't mean any offense, Your Strength," Overturn said.

Narius ignored him. He turned on his heel and headed for the door. Whispers broke out behind him, and Paine called his name sharply. He didn't care. He had to find his wife.

He hurried back to the dining room, hoping that she might be there. Thankfully, she was, sitting with Favid and picking at her breakfast. She jumped at his sudden entrance, staring at him with wide eyes.

"What are you doing here?" she whispered.

Narius knelt next to her chair. "We need to talk. I shouldn't have left you alone after hearing that news. Let's go to your quarters or mine or the conservatory or *somewhere* where we can talk and figure out—"

Someone cleared his throat behind him. Narius winced. He recognized that sound.

"Your Strength, the council hasn't finished our meeting yet," Paine said quietly.

Narius glared at his friend over his shoulder. "This is more important, Paine."

"I have no doubt it is, but time is of the essence to handle this properly."

That was true. Rusted Greaves, he knew Paine was right. But still. He sighed.

"I'm sorry," he whispered to Everys.

She nodded, but then a spark flared in her eyes. "Let me come with you."

His head snapped back. "What?"

Paine cleared his throat again. "Blessed, please forgive me, but it wouldn't be appropriate for you to—"

"—to what? Participate in a discussion that would impact my marriage?" she shot back icily.

Narius grimaced. He turned to Paine. "She comes with or we delay the meeting."

Paine huffed. "Very well."

Everys tried to say something to Favid, but he glowered at Narius like he was taking his daughter away to be executed. He'd have to try to patch up that relationship another time.

Narius offered his wife his hand and she took it. Then they walked back to the Amber Office with Paine in tow. He could practically feel the frustration boiling off of his friend as they walked. Everys kept her eyes forward.

Once they arrived back at the Amber Office, his advisers were clearly startled by Everys's presence. A few rose at her entrance, mumbling greetings, although he saw a number of guilty looks. Everys found a chair. Thankfully, she sat at the edge of the room, positioning herself to observe, not participate. At least, that's what he assumed she was doing. Once she had settled, he sat down again and turned his attention back to his advisers.

"I apologize for the interruption, my friends. Before we begin again, I want to make one thing clear. I will not endorse any plan that would bring harm to Viara or... the child," Narius said. "To do so would make it look like we are panicking and we are not. Are we understood?"

The advisers nodded.

"It is my hope this will be a minor scandal when all is said and done," Narius said.

"I hope that is the case, Your Strength," Yull, the minister of foreign affairs, interjected. "And normally, I would agree. Among the noble houses, these sorts of issues do blow over quickly. But if Viara's story is true and her child was conceived while she was still queen, that would make this situation a bit more permanent. This child would be your presumed heir. I would be willing to bet the nobility is already jockeying for position for when this child comes to power. Viara may no longer be queen, but being the mother of the next king will enrich her, both financially and socially."

Narius shifted in his seat. What Yull said made sense.

"So the king disowns the child, regardless of its paternity," Elamek said. "Take him or her out of succession entirely."

"That is a tempting solution, but I fear it is impractical," Masruq said. "As of right now, this child is the king's only heir. To disown him or her would seem the height of foolishness. And consider the reaction from the nobility. Viara's family wasn't pleased with how her marriage ended. If Narius disowns the child, we could see a revolt in the nobility."

"Not to mention how the Supreme Prelate would react," Bokil added. "He already despises the queen—no offense, Blessed. Imagine how he would respond if Narius disowned his child from the non-Siporan former queen. He would rally the common folk to the revolt as well."

The discussion descended into fractured conversations, each adviser talking over the person sitting next to him. Narius couldn't keep track of what everyone was saying. A few of them still favored a quiet assassination or, at the very least, exile. Masruq and a few others apparently thought Narius and Everys should adopt the child after it was born. Elamek argued that the laws of succession should simply be rewritten to exclude Viara and her child from consideration, although Bokil rejected that idea as being too simplistic.

He glanced toward Everys. Much to his surprise, she hadn't said anything. Instead, her gaze flicked from adviser to adviser, apparently weighing what each of them said. But her cheeks were red, and he could see her restraining herself. She had an opinion, but she was keeping it to herself. He was actually disappointed.

After several minutes of fruitless arguing, he held up a hand.

"Gentlemen, I appreciate your passion and your ideas. But I don't see a path forward here. Killing Viara isn't an option, mostly because it would solve nothing. Her allegations are public. No matter how careful we are, there would always be suspicions. Exiling Viara would achieve nothing; she'd merely set up court in her new home and create problems from abroad. And I doubt she would simply allow the queen and I to adopt her child."

Masruq nodded sagely, as if conceding the point.

"What can we do?" Narius asked.

Paine cleared his throat. "Forgive me, Your Strength. I have an unconventional solution."

"Why keep it to yourself, Paine?" Bokil demanded.

"I had hoped that one of you would present a better solution." Paine turned to Narius. "And I suspect you will not like my proposal."

Narius frowned. "What is it?"

Paine took a deep breath. "We revoke Albanon's Compromise."

For the second time that day, Narius felt like his mind had become unmoored. Revoke Albanon's Compromise? Yes, that was a possibility, and he could instantly see how that would fix the situation. His gaze leaped to Everys and it felt like ice engulfed his entire body, head to toe. She stared at him blankly, her brow pinched in confusion. She had no idea what Paine's solution meant. For her. For them.

Masruq grunted and nodded thoughtfully. "An intriguing possibility."

"It would certainly clear up this situation," Bokil said.

"And it could even resolve some of the tensions with Dalark as well," Yull added.

Narius turned back to his advisers, aghast. They couldn't possibly agree with this, could they?

"What's Albanon's Compromise?" Everys asked quietly.

Paine turned to Everys. "The Compromise limits the number of king's wives to just one."

The color drained from Everys's face. "And if it were revoked?"

"It would allow Narius to have multiple wives," Paine said quietly. "It would allow him to remarry Viara."

17

He couldn't be serious.

Paine could not mean what she thought he meant.

"By revoking the Compromise, that would allow us to... massage the laws of succession," Paine went on, speaking to the group. "Right now, as they stand, the king's firstborn legitimate son is the heir. Given that this child was presumably conceived while the king was still married to Viara, that would make him the heir. But if there are multiple wives in play, then we could craft rules governing how an heir is selected, meaning—"

"—meaning the king could choose Queen Everys's future children over Viara's," Bokil said with a predatory smile.

"Precisely."

Inkstains, how could they even consider this? Bring that viper back into the palace? Make Viara what? A consort? Concubine? Half-queen?

"And Viara wouldn't be the only possibility," Yull added. "Consider: Dalark was willing to make peace if the king married Princess Innana. The attack on their wedding and the king's subsequent remarriage to Queen Everys put a stop to that. But if the Compromise were revoked, King Narius could marry the princess, allowing us to put the current unpleasantness to rest."

Wait, she would have to share her husband with two other women? Were they really suggesting that? Her stomach lurched at the very idea, and she worried she'd vomit her breakfast all over the Amber Office.

She turned to Narius, hoping he'd stop this nonsense right away. But he only sat in his chair, his brow pinched in the way that meant he was... Oh, smudges, he was thinking about it. Actually considering it! How could he?

"Narius—" she said.

His gaze flicked in her direction. "Everys... why don't you return to your quarters? I'll be up to discuss this with you soon."

What was there to discuss? How could he even consider it?

A hand touched her arm. Challix looked down at her, a concerned expression on her face. When had she arrived? Had she heard all of this? Was she going to agree with them?

"Blessed," Challix whispered. "Let's go."

Everys didn't want to move, but from the way the advisers were looking at her, it was clear that they wouldn't continue their conversation as long as she was there. Fine. She stood, took a deep breath, and then headed for the door without looking at any of them. Hopefully they could feel her anger as she passed.

Once they had left the Amber Office, though, the anger melted away to desperation. A sob rattled in her chest, and she stumbled, almost collapsing. Kevtho was right there at her side to steady her as was Challix.

"Blessed, hang on," Kevtho whispered.

They hustled her through the hallways and back up to the queen's quarters. Once they were inside, Challix set the girls to work to brew some tea and help make her comfortable. Everys appreciated their efforts, but she couldn't bring herself to say anything. Instead, her mind locked on those two words: Albanon's Compromise.

"He can't really do that, can he?" she asked Challix. "Revoke a four-hundred-year-old law?"

"He can." Challix offered her an encouraging smile. "But Blessed, I've seen the way Narius looks at you. Even if he revokes the Compromise, that won't change how he feels about you. If he were to remarry Viara or marry Princess Innana, that would just be for political convenience. Not love."

That was true, but Everys's first marriage had been one of political convenience as well, and look where that had led. She didn't doubt that Narius loved her and always would. But he had loved Innana too when he was younger. And given the chance, Viara would do anything to get her hooks into him again. Additional wives might be convenient politically, but she knew her heart wouldn't be able to handle the competition.

She took a sip of the tea Challix pressed into her hands. The warmth spread down her throat but did nothing to dislodge the ice in her chest.

18

As far as Everys was concerned, Narius's discussion with his advisers had taken far too long. He must have taken Paine's suggestion seriously. She supposed he had to. If she took her emotional reaction out of the equation, Paine's plan for the Compromise made a good deal of sense. Solving a potential succession crisis, stabilizing relations with Dalark, all worthy goals that would only build the legacy Narius wanted.

But inkstains! She couldn't share her husband with anyone else. They had come too far, endured too much, for everything unravel like this. No matter what Narius's advisers had told him, she would have to convince him not to do it.

When he finally entered her quarters shortly after the start of Third Watch, she felt like she would vomit rather than speak.

He didn't approach her. He stood near the door, his hands held tightly at his side, not even making eye contact. She waited for him to break the silence. He had made her wait, after all. It only seemed fair.

"So," he finally said.

"Shall I instruct the girls to ready more rooms for our expanding family?" she asked coolly.

"Everys..."

"You know, I've been debating about what Viara's child should call me. 'Mother' would be too confusing, of course. 'Queen' or 'Blessed' would be too formal. I was thinking maybe 'Auntie Everys.' Has a nice ring to it, doesn't it?"

"Everys!"

"What?" She launched herself from the couch and started across the room to him. His arms twitched, as if he were getting ready to defend himself. "You spent an awful long time in that meeting. Did they convince you to end the Compromise?"

He took a deep shuddering breath, and a chasm opened in Everys's chest. Was he going to say he had?

But then he shook his head. "They want me to. Some of them, anyway. A few of them even started a list of potential new wives."

Everys gaped at him. "Besides Viara and Innana?"

He winced and nodded.

"Who?" she demanded.

"Does it matter?"

"It does if you're going to do this!" she retorted. "And you haven't said if you will!"

And he hesitated. Smudges and splatters, he actually hesitated, looking down to a corner, not meeting her gaze.

"Nothing has been decided yet." His tone, so hollow, spoke louder than his words. "Every potential solution to the current crisis has to be fairly considered and evaluated."

"That sounds like you're quoting Paine!"

Narius shrugged. "He did say something similar to that just now, yes."

"Do you really think this is going to be a solution? To bring Viara back into the palace? To marry Innana? Will that really help the situation?"

"It might!" Narius said. "Paine has done some research into how the royal family could be structured if we were to rescind the Compromise. There would be a hierarchy amongst any wives, with only one holding the title of 'queen' while the rest would be considered 'consorts.'"

Everys staggered back. "Do you think any of that matters to me? You yourself have said what a horrible person Viara was! And now, you're just going to marry her again because she might be carrying your baby? Do you really think that would make her any less of a problem?"

"In the short-term, yes. It would disarm her—"

"Until she starts her schemes from within the palace itself! Even if she's only called a consort, there are plenty of people who would remember she was once the queen."

Narius nodded. "Something that Elamek pointed out almost as forcefully as you."

"And what about Innana?" Everys added. "You told me how miserable she made you while she was here. You would want that again?"

He shook his head. "But I wouldn't have to deal with either of them alone. I would have you at my side. You and I can handle Viara. You can help me tolerate Innana or anyone else."

"But why should we have to?" Everys said, then held up her hand to stop him from replying. "Look, I understand. Viara is a complication. Marrying Innana could defuse the diplomatic tension between the Dynasty and Dalark. But marrying either of them is only a temporary solution, if that. We'll just be delaying the inevitable."

"Which would give us time to plan better," Narius said. "Right now, we're scrambling. But if we can neutralize both Viara and the potential war with Dalark, even if only temporarily, that gives us time to consider better, more lasting options."

How could he say this? She could scarcely believe her ears. Not just because she didn't like his words; there was no way that she could. But before she snapped at him, she realized he didn't believe anything he was saying. He was merely repeating what he must have heard from his advisers, the ones who wanted him to go along with such an insane plan. His voice lacked conviction, any hint of passion. Narius was a shell of himself, a mere shadow. Paine's plan had gutted him.

"Why would you even consider this?" Everys whispered. "Look at how miserable just the suggestion has made you!"

"The royal family, the king especially, is expected to make sacrifices on behalf of the Dynasty. We set aside our personal wants and ambitions. We do what no one else is asked for the good of all."

Her heart tore. He looked broken and defeated already. How could Paine do this to him? Surely the vizier could see and understand how upset Narius would be with either of those women. Or both! She wanted to hug him, whisper to him that it was all going to be okay.

He made a broad gesture. "Everys, do you think I want this? Do you think I want to bring Viara back into the palace? By all the gods, no! I would rather the Gravedigger bury me in the depths of the Blood Sea than spend another moment with her! I'd rather Chance and Chaos play dice with my eyes than even look on her! Do you think I'd want any woman other than you? Everys, I love you so much! Do you really believe I'd do anything to willingly hurt you? The last thing I want to do is inflict Viara on you! If it were up to me—"

"Isn't it, though? Or did you abdicate to Paine while I wasn't looking?"

His mouth snapped shut, and fire flashed in his eyes.

She decided to press the advantage. "If you're the king, can't you just say that this isn't going to happen?"

"But what if this is the only way? We can't afford to have another crisis break in the Dynasty." He took a deep breath and made a motion with his hands like he was pushing down his anger. "Sometimes, when you're part of the royal family, you have to do things that you don't want to for the greater good. Sometimes you have to make sacrifices. I know you may not understand that. You weren't raised in a noble house. You didn't receive the same lessons that I did."

Heat flashed through her. Was he really suggesting that she didn't understand what it meant to sacrifice? Was he making a bad joke? How could he seriously suggest she didn't understand?

"Do you really think I haven't sacrificed anything?" she whispered.

To his credit, Narius seemed to understand he made a mistake. His eyes widened and he stammered an excuse, but Everys wasn't going to let him go that easily.

"I gave up everything for you! The royal guard pulled me out of the only home I knew to be your wife. My family's home and shop were destroyed not that long ago! I've become the target of Istragon's wrath, and I've been spending time with truly horrible people so I can shore up support." She hiccupped, trying to hold back her tears. "I sacrificed our marriage so you could make peace with Dalark. And when Brencis shot you, I..."

Her words caught in her throat. She couldn't say this. Not out loud. Not to him. She had kept this truth bottled up for weeks. Months, even. But even as she fought to swallow it back down, she could feel the memories clawing their way up her throat.

"What?" he prompted quietly.

She took a deep shuddering breath, looking down at his feet. Maybe if she didn't make eye contact. Maybe if she said it as quickly and as clinically as possible.

"When Brencis shot you, I used my family's healing rune," she said.

"I wondered about that," he said. "And I know you're not supposed to use it, but you had—"

She held up a hand, cutting him off. "That's not all. I didn't have any ink with me. And you were dying. And I... so I..."

She screwed her eyes shut and the memory assaulted her again. Narius on the throne room floor, his blood spreading from beneath him. His skin going pale, the life leaving his eyes. The smell of blood and death stalking him. The feel of blood on her fingertips as she...

"...I used your blood to draw the rune," she whispered, then risked a look at his face.

He frowned. "But isn't that forbidden?"

"I couldn't lose you. Not like that. Not when I had the power to do something about it."

He stepped toward her, his arms opening to embrace her. As much as she wanted to feel his strong arms around her, she didn't move. She couldn't. Not when Paine's solution stood between them.

"That's part of the reason why I don't want to do this," she said. "I've sacrificed so much to be here for you. I don't want to lose you to anyone else."

"Like you ever could!"

"Who's to say that Viara or Innana or someone else couldn't steal your heart from me?"

Narius looked positively stricken, his shoulders slumping, pain spreading across his face. And he didn't respond. That was all the answer she really needed.

Then he took a deep breath. "Look, you're right, it most likely will delay our troubles rather than solve them. And I think Paine will figure that out. Besides, we don't even know if Viara would be interested or if Dalark would agree to those terms.

"This is what I suggest: let's leave it alone. I'm not going to let it happen. How about we work together on these problems? Come with me to the talks with Alezzar at the Diradae manor. I'm sure with you at my side, we'll be able to hammer out a workable peace."

She frowned. He sounded like he was trying to soothe a petulant child, negotiating over a bedtime or an extra snack. How could they leave this alone? He could have fathered a child with another woman, who his advisers now wanted him to marry. Shouldn't they talk about this? Shouldn't they figure out what they would do about this together? But she read the determination in his expression. He thought he was doing the right thing. Even though she didn't feel right about this, she nodded.

He smiled and opened his arms again. This time, she did hug him, but not for long. She wasn't ready for that yet. He popped up on his toes to kiss her cheek, then hugged her tightly.

"It'll be all right, Everys," he whispered. "You'll see."

She hoped that was true. Because she had a sinking feeling that no matter what they did, their future held nothing but ashes and blood.

19

Everys let out a long, slow breath as the transport pulled up to the Diradae manor. Due to security concerns, she and Narius had taken separate vehicles, meaning that she had ridden in near silence while surrounded by twitchy guards. Rewether tried to plaster on a soothing smile, but it was clear he wasn't happy about this situation.

She couldn't blame him. A glance through the window revealed dozens, maybe hundreds of soldiers patrolling the manor grounds. She recognized some of the guards from her own detail, along with many from Narius's. But there were also common soldiers mixed in with members of Bastion's constabulary. From what Challix had told her, most of Narius's inner council would be here, as would prominent members of the nobility, the Ethnarch Parliament, and the Hall of All Voices. A tempting target.

As soon as the transport came to a halt, her guards burst out of the vehicle. Then Rewether motioned for her to join him. She slid out and walked at a steady but unhurried pace for the front door. Out of the corner of her eye, she spotted several press drones hovering just beyond the manor's wall. It was her job to project peace and calm, even if that wasn't how she actually felt.

Once they entered the manor itself, Everys was greeted by Narius, who was surrounded by his own flock of guards. He took her hand and tucked it in his arm, then led her deeper into the manor. Her heart fluttered as they walked past the bare stone walls, which felt like they would close in and trap her at any moment.

Then they turned into the audience chamber. She stepped a bit closer to Narius, if only to reassure herself that he was still there.

Paine appeared at Narius's side. "Your Strength, Blessed. Welcome to the party."

Was Paine actually making a joke? Because what Everys saw did not appear at all festive. She recognized most of the people in the room, although she had never met The One Who Bestrides the Darkness before. She even spotted Diplomat Alezzar standing near the buffet table, chatting with Ministers Masruq and Bokil. And while someone had decorated the audience chamber with flowers and a few festive banners, there was no cheer in the room. No warmth. No invitation at all. The gathered attendees looked like they were attending a funeral.

"Alezzar's disposition?" Narius mumbled, although he smiled and nodded at someone across the room.

"Friendly enough," Paine replied. "I haven't perceived any problematic interactions."

"I'm sure those will come soon enough." Narius turned to Everys. "Let's make the rounds, shall we?"

Before she could answer, he split off and circulated through the room with Paine in his wake. Everys looked around, not sure who she should talk to. Sollip Huntermark, the Weyfir ethnarch, stood alone, so she headed in his direction.

Halfway across the room, she spotted Masruq shake hands with Alezzar and then start toward her. As he approached, he smiled broadly.

"Blessed, glad you could join us tonight!" he said. "I'm sorry that Oluna isn't with me. She was looking forward to hosting you for dinner. She'd hoped to see you tonight, but I was told she couldn't come due to security concerns. "

Everys smiled warmly. "Well, she is a bit of a troublemaker, you know."

"Do I ever!" Masruq chuckled. "That's why I wanted her here. Tonight will become very tense, I'm sure. A well-timed social scandal like only my wife could engineer would lighten the mood."

"Or lead to war," Everys countered.

Masruq shrugged. "At least the waiting would be over."

Everys laughed, only to clamp a hand over her mouth. It felt inappropriate to laugh, especially in that space at that time. But it still felt good, a release she had needed for days.

"According to the palace gossip, I hear that you have a special guest staying with you," Masruq said.

Everys grimaced at the mention of Papa. She hadn't been able to spend much time with him since Viara had shared her news. The few times she had seen him, he hadn't said much. What little he did share dripped with disapproval. He had spent two days in Fair Havens, visiting with old friends and the scriveners. Everys felt guilty leaving him to his own devices, but she couldn't exactly clear her schedule for a surprise visitor, even if it was her father.

Masruq frowned. "I take it from your expression that this visit hasn't exactly been... enjoyable?"

"No, it's good to see him again," Everys said. "It's been years since he and the rest of my family moved away. We just don't seem to fit anymore."

"Oh?" Masruq cocked his head to one side, then smiled warmly. "You know, I'm sure this is something that, if she were here, Oluna would pounce on immediately. She'd probably drag you into an empty corner and glare at anyone who dared interrupt—including Alezzar. Unfortunately, she's not here. But I am. Shall we commandeer a corner?"

She chuckled. "I think Narius might object to that."

"I suppose he might." He gestured toward a quieter corner and fell in step with her. "How is it that you don't fit anymore?"

She gritted her teeth. She had to be very careful in how she explained this.

"When Papa left Fair Havens, I was just his daughter. I worked in the electronics shop, but he was in charge. He set the schedule, the prices, everything else. He goes away, and when he comes back, the shop isn't there anymore and his daughter is suddenly queen. And then there's the fact that he can remember when the Drywell Laws were still enforced. To him, the Dynasty is the enemy of our people. And now his daughter is married to the king. I think he's just feeling lost. Nothing is the way he expected it to be."

Masruq nodded thoughtfully. "You know, Blessed, I'm very fortunate. I do work long hours, but in the Dynasty, economics usually are a lower priority than the military. Especially these days. If you would like, I could spend some time with your father when you're unable to. Maybe introduce him to some of my friends. Would that be helpful?"

Everys hesitated. She doubted Papa would enjoy spending time with a representative of the Dynasty, even if it was Masruq. The man wasn't exactly the pinnacle of what the Dynasty wanted in men. Too round, too soft, too happy.

He must have read her hesitation. "Blessed, I know full well my presence may invite hostility. But you have so much to focus on right now, this is my small way of lightening your load. Please. It would be my greatest honor to show your father a side of the Dynasty he may have never seen before. In some ways, my family's honor depends on it. The Hishis have always prided themselves on their hospitality. This may not be exactly what they envisioned, but I am more than happy to help."

She smiled, warmth spreading through her chest. No wonder Oluna had married him. He was so genuine.

"I'll see what he thinks."

"Excellent! Perhaps he'd even like to join us when we finally have dinner together. Now, unless I'm mistaken, it would appear that tonight's festivities are about to begin."

Everys glanced over at Narius, who subtly beckoned her. She nodded to Masruq and hurried over to Narius's side.

"Everything all right with Masruq?" Narius whispered.

"Perfect," she replied. "Are you ready?"

"As much as I can be." He snared her hand and gave it a quick squeeze. "Especially since you're here."

She almost laughed at his words, but he was sincere and sweet, she smiled instead and squeezed back.

Narius squared his shoulders. "Ethnarch Estrid, shall we begin?"

The Diradae ethnarch shifted his weight and scuttled forward, his feet clacking on the stone floor. A shiver crawled up Everys's spine. She knew the Diradae was moving naturally, but a part of her mind rebelled against seeing him. She felt like his mere presence was unnatural.

"Friends, it is good for us to be here," Estrid said. "None of us are pleased by the trajectory the Dynasty or the Imperium are on. It is my fondest wish that, by hosting this discussion, we can come to an equitable peace."

Narius cleared his throat and took a step forward. "Well said, Ethnarch. That is our Dynasty's desire as well. Diplomat Alezzar, what do you say?"

Alezzar stepped into the center of the room. Everys had never formally met him; she had only seen him from a distance once before. He wore the traditional Dalark outfit: a dull gray set of robes underneath layers of twisted and intertwined ribbons, all of them a different color. The ends of the ribbons flared, some of them dragging on the floor. And while he appeared old enough to be her father or maybe even her grandfather, he carried himself like he was younger.

"Gracious hosts, Your Strength, Blessed." Alezzar bowed to the assembled guests with a flourish of his hands. "I am honored at your invitation, for the glorious Dalark Imperium wishes only peace and harmonious relations with you and yours."

Someone in the crowd made a loud scoffing sound. Nervous chuckles rippled through the room.

Alezzar quirked a brow. "Oh, I understand your doubts. While our two mighty nations were able to accomplish the impossible by overthrowing the vile Siporan Ascendancy, our relationship has been fraught, yes? Fighting over what is now the Demilitarized Zone, the war only ending due to your unfortunate Colonial Uprisings. And a two centuries-long-truce that shows no end in sight? Truly a tragedy that no one desires."

"And yet when King Narius reached out to Emperor Devroshan to bring about true peace, he was rebuffed," Paine countered. "Numerous times."

"We have spoken of this before, have we not?" Alezzar shrugged expansively. "At the time, King Narius was untested. Unproven. But his many accomplishments over the past years impressed our lamented Emperor Devroshan. You have impressed the Imperium as a whole. How can we not desire a peaceful relationship with you, yes?"

Everys frowned. Many questions warred within her, each one wanting to escape. If they wanted peace, why were they amassing troops in the Beachhead? If Devroshan had respected her husband, why had they treated him poorly when he had almost married Innana? But she didn't say anything. She knew she was here as a guest, not as a participant. But still, it would be nice if someone would ask.

"You will forgive me if I don't entirely believe you, Ambassador," Paine said coolly. "The attitude of your rulers, your military, and your people speak volumes in contradiction of your honeyed words."

Everys fought to keep from wincing. It would have been nice if someone other than Paine had said something, but she supposed she couldn't be choosy.

Alezzar chuckled. "You will forgive me, friend Paine, if I do not put much stock in your rebuke. How often has your Dynasty publicly sharpened your swords while speaking words of peace to us through more clandestine channels? Surely you understand the need for an outer posture that hides one's true feelings."

Paine's jaw clenched and he looked ready to spit fire at someone, but he fell silent.

Ethnarch Estrid rumbled, sounding like metal scraping against stone. "Perhaps we are becoming distracted by the past. What matters in the here and now is how we back away from the precipice of war."

"Well said, Ethnarch," Narius said. "Ambassador, is the Imperium willing to discuss terms with us? Can we find a path to peace?"

Alezzar's shoulders slumped. "Regrettably, Your Strength, I cannot."

Uncertain whispers rippled through the crowd. Narius tensed and he touched Everys's arm, as if he wanted to hold her away from some danger.

"Such matters are too haughty for one such as I," Alezzar said. "Instead, these are matters best discussed between you and our illustrious emperor."

More surprise whispered through the room.

"Are you proposing a summit?" Narius asked.

"Nothing so grandiose." Alezzar snapped his fingers.

Two Dalark servants hurried out of a corner, carrying a flat metal device between them. They set it in the middle of the room and one of them bent over to fiddle with unseen controls.

"My friends of the Xoniel Dynasty, may I present he who the spirits and potentates indwell, the most severe yet benevolent Emperor Tigrigian." Alezzar made a sweeping gesture toward the device.

Motes of light burst from the metal plate and then swirled into the air. A few people gasped in shock as the sparks wove together to create a towering image of a Dalark man in his early thirties. He wore even more elaborate robes than Alezzar, brilliant golden robes with multicolored gemstones woven into the fabric. His pale skin looked like porcelain drawn across his sharp cheekbones, with a prominent nose and stern emerald eyes. A twisted crown that appeared to be made of stone rested on jet black hair.

Everys fought the urge to take a step back as she gazed up at Emperor Tirigian himself.

20

The Dalark loved their drama.

Narius regarded his opposite with as much cool detachment as he could muster. Obviously Tirigian and Alezzar were hoping that this stunt would awe the attendees. And judging from the reaction he saw, it worked. Even he had to admit he was surprised.

A chill still swept through Narius, because there was a subtler message that Tirigian had already delivered. As far as he knew, no one in the Dynasty had developed holographic technology like this. Worse, the Dynasty's intelligence teams hadn't known about this new breakthrough either. Dramatic as the presentation might be, this move sent a more troubling message before Tirigian even spoke: the Empire, while smaller in terms of territory and population, was more technologically advanced than the Dynasty. What horrors could they unleash if the two militaries met in open combat?

He shot a glance at Paine, who nodded. The vizier had caught the message as well.

"Greetings, my friends across the sea," Tirigian said, his voice surprisingly loud and clear from a such a small device. "While Alezzar is most equipped to handle these talks, I felt it best if I participate. Thus we shall avoid unseemly misunderstandings, yes?"

To his credit, Ethnarch Estrid recovered from his initial shock and shuffled forward. "Great Emperor Tirigian, you honor us with your presence. You are more than welcome in my chambers, either in person or via these amazing means."

Tirigian nodded toward the ethnarch, although Narius couldn't miss the twitch of his lip into a sneer. Narius wished he could point that out. Tirigian had lived in the palace in the weeks leading up to Narius's failed wedding. During that visit, Narius had seen firsthand the Emperor's contempt for nonhuman races. But reminding Tirigian of that would be counterproductive.

Narius took a step forward and cleared his throat. "Emperor Tirigian, it is a pleasure to see you again."

"Oh, is it?" Tirigian fixed his steely gaze on Narius. "I don't quite believe you, my erstwhile brother. You made your feelings for me quite clear when last we were together."

Narius cocked his head to one side, frowning. "I'm not quite sure what you mean. We accommodated you and your party to the best of our abilities."

"Oh? Did you? Is that what you call my father dying in your palace?"

"The King was hardly responsible," Paine interjected. "It was Duke Brencis who murdered your father in an attempted coup of King Narius."

"So you say," Tirigian murmured. "And tell me, has this traitorous duke been brought to justice?"

Narius ground his teeth, resisting the urge to look at Bokil, who hovered nearby. They had been hunting for Brencis ever since he escaped the palace with little luck.

"A convenient story." Tirigian sneered. "Blame the man who is not here to defend himself."

"Oh, but I am, Tirigian."

Narius sucked in a sharp breath. He knew that voice.

"Brencis?" he whispered.

His guards exploded into action, drawing their weapons and fanning out. Several of the other guests shouted in surprise and dove for safety. Paine stepped closer to Narius and he, in turn, shielded Everys. The last time he and Everys had seen Brencis, the traitor had shot him and tried to kill her. He wouldn't allow that to happen again.

"Calm down, Narius. You're not in danger from me. Not directly, anyway."

Narius looked around the room, frowning. The voice was definitely Brencis's, but there was something off about the tone. Tinny. Scratchy. Like...

A Dunestrider servant emerged from the crowd, holding a digital scriber above his head. The man looked pale, his body shaking, as the guards converged on him.

"When I heard about this assembly, I knew I had to listen in." Brencis's voice came from the scriber.

Narius snapped his fingers to get Bokil's attention, then jerked his head toward the scriber. Bokil nodded and hurried out of the room. If his team could trace the signal to the scriber, then they could maybe—

"I'll be brief. Narius blames me for what happened to Emperor Devroshan. And well he should. My men did kill the Emperor. And they would have killed Tirigian and his sister as well."

Narius's jaw dropped. He wouldn't have expected Brencis to be open about it.

Tirigian stood up straighter, his eyes blazing, and he jabbed a finger at the servant holding the scriber. "Narius! If you wish for there to be peace between us, there is the path forward. Give me this man that I may mete out justice upon him."

Before Narius could answer, Brencis laughed.

"If he could do that, he would have captured me already. The fact that I am still free shows why our two nations have come to this point, Tirigian. In days of old, our armies would have shown who was the stronger, your 'spirits and potentates' or our Perfected Warrior." From Brencis's tone, it was clear he thought the latter was superior. "But instead, we talk at each other. Past each other. And Narius encourages this. If I could have, I would have killed him along with your father."

Much to Narius's surprise, Tirigian actually smiled. It lasted only a second, but then it was gone, chased away by a new burst of fury. "I could forgive the attempt on me. We are men, yes? But you wanted her dead as well!"

Tirigian stepped aside and someone else stepped into the image. Narius's heart seized.

Innana stared down at him. And she had changed. He had fallen in love with her when they were children. He had been drawn to her stunning beauty, her playful spirit, her genuine heart. But now she wasn't the intriguing girl he'd met. She wasn't the embodiment of the Water Bearer he'd constructed in his imagination. She wasn't even the foolish disappointment he'd almost married. She looked like a reanimated corpse, as if she hadn't slept since their wedding day. Her eyes widened when she saw him, and she started to say something, but then Tirigian stepped into the image again.

"You see? Do you see what you Xoniel savages have done to her? Ever since she saw our father die, ever since you rejected her in favor of a Siporan witch, she has not slept. She barely eats. I fear for her health and sanity if this continues."

Innana glanced at her brother and an inscrutable expression flickered over her features, but then she ducked her head and seemed to draw into herself, becoming smaller. Narius frowned. She almost looked angry. But why?

"You have much to answer for, Narius." Tirigian's voice was a growl.

"On that, we agree," Brencis responded.

"Why are you permitting this, Your Strength?" Paine whispered.

Narius shook his head, snapping him out of his mental paralysis. He signaled to Zar and the other guards to apprehend the servant with the scriber. The guards moved in, but the servant saw them coming and dodged out of the way.

"Ah, he finally decides to act, does he?" Brencis asked. "This is the problem, Narius, and always has been: You are weak. You are driving the Dynasty into ruin. But I will not permit that to happen. Send your armies, Tirigian. Do your worst! Because I will not allow the Dynasty to—"

The guards tackled the servant, and Zar shut off the scriber, cutting off Brencis's voice. But it didn't matter. The assembled guests were already buzzing so loud, they probably could have drowned out the duke's voice had he been able to keep speaking.

"Friends!" Estrid bellowed, his voice cutting through the chaos. "I apologize for this disruption, but let us not allow one man to derail the progress we have—"

"Progress?" Tirigian snorted. "There has been none, Ethnarch. All you have accomplished is revealing the chaos that lives within the Dynasty. Perhaps if you had a more decisive leader, this would be worth considering, but as it is, this has been a waste of my time and yours."

Paine nudged Narius. He glanced at his friend, and Paine gave him a significant look. The vizier nodded toward the hologram and Narius suddenly understood. Tirigian wanted decisiveness? A bold move? There was something he could do.

But then he turned to Everys. He couldn't do this to her, could he? Not after what she had said in her quarters. Not after the pain he had seen in her face.

Paine cleared his throat and nudged him again. Narius shot him a look, but then Paine nodded toward the room. Narius took a quick look around. The other attendees were arguing with each other, but a few of them were heading for the door! And Tirigian glowered at him through the hologram, a triumphant smirk on his face. Narius was losing control of the situation rapidly. The night would be a disaster. His heart sank. What choice did he have? He had to salvage this somehow. Tirigian was here—well, in a way—and so was Innana. He didn't like this possibility. But he had been prepared to make this sacrifice in the past.

He took a step forward. "Emperor Tirigian, if I may."

Thankfully, the room around him went still. Tirigian regarded him with a quirked brow.

"Clearly this evening has not gone as anyone expected. But I can assure you, regardless of the unexpected events, my dearest desire is for peace. That was why I was willing to marry your sister, that true peace could be forged between your Empire and our Dynasty."

"And yet, the first chance you got, you fled to the arms of your pet Siporan," Tirigian spat.

Narius could practically feel the rage burning in Everys. He flinched, because he knew that anger would likely erupt into a full conflagration.

"Because I believed that possibility to be dead," Narius said. "But I still desire peace. I still desire our peoples to finally set aside our hostilities. And I am willing to do whatever it takes to achieve that. The question is, are you?"

Tirigian's gaze sharpened. "What do you have in mind?"

"If Innana will still have me, I would be willing to marry her."

Gasps rippled through the room, but he could hear Everys's strangled cry over them all. Narius closed his eyes and forced himself not to look at her. He knew that if he did, he would take everything back. And he couldn't. Not anymore.

"You would divorce Queen Everys again?" Tirigian asked. "So fickle is your heart."

"No, I would not."

The Emperor frowned. "But are you not prohibited by Dynasty law from having more than one wife?"

"At present, yes. But as king, I can amend the law. And I would be willing to do so to avert the bloodshed that is coming."

Tirigian tipped his head back and stared at Narius down his nose, as if he wasn't quite sure what he was looking at. Narius met his gaze, but he spotted Innana peek out from behind her brother. She had paled even further, and her mouth was open in a small circle.

He took a deep breath to steady himself. He couldn't step back from this now. He had proposed this course of action in front of the Flail and his advisers. It was a matter of Dynasty policy now.

"Your idea is... intriguing," Tirigian finally said. "And unexpected. You truly do not wish for conflict? Does this not contradict the way of your Perfected Warrior?"

"Perhaps," Narius said cautiously. "But even the Warrior said that his followers must choose their battles and battlefields wisely. 'Not every chance to shed your blood will lead to victory.'"

Thankfully, some of the assembled guests nodded thoughtfully. Narius had been holding on to that quote for a while. He was glad he could finally use it.

"I will have to consult with my sister, of course," Tirigian said. "But this is a path I did not expect you to—"

Alezzar suddenly cried out. Narius jumped back a step, surprised by the outburst. He had almost forgotten that the ambassador was there at all. But he was impossible to ignore now. Alezzar stumbled forward, clutching at his neck. His face had turned a horrifying shade of purple and he rasped unintelligible words. He fell to his knees and clawed at his neck and face.

Without thinking, Narius hurried forward to help, but Alezzar was already surrounded by guards and servants. They helped him lie down, and Zar was shouting, calling for a medic and ordering people to stay back. But then the guards backed away from Alezzar as if he was a threat. Zar actually threw an arm across Narius's chest.

"Your Strength, stay back. There's... there's..." Zar stared at Alezzar's prone form.

Narius looked past his guard and ice sluiced through him. The ambassador had gone still, either unconscious or dead. His face appeared bloated, his skin a blotchy mix of purple and black. But Narius knew what had rattled the guards.

A trickle of light that twisted around on itself glowed on Alezzar's neck but was rapidly disappearing. And while he couldn't quite see the full pattern from where he was standing, he had no doubt what it was.

A toratropic rune. The kind that Everys could draw.

He turned and looked right at his wife, a question in his eyes. He knew she couldn't have done it; she hadn't come anywhere near Alezzar all evening. She looked just as shocked and confused as he felt.

"What is happening?" Estrid shouted. "Is the ambassador all right?"

"No," Zar said. "He's... he's..."

Narius grabbed Zar's arm and squeezed. If Zar said the wrong thing here, he would unknowingly expose Everys's secret. And that couldn't happen. He bared his teeth slightly and shook his head.

Zar, thankfully, seemed to catch the message. He swallowed hard, then released Narius. He turned to the assembled guests. "Ambassador Alezzar is dead."

"What?" Tirigian thundered. "How? Who did this?"

Zar shot a hooded look in Narius's direction. "I don't know, Emperor Tirigian."

Narius took a shuddering breath and faced the emperor. "I do not know what happened, but I promise you, there will be a full investigation into—"

"Investigation? There is no need for that!" Tirigian thundered. "You think I would be so foolish to send my sister to your Dynasty? To a place where you cannot find a traitor who threatens your throne? To a place where assassins strike down the faithful like that? No, King Narius. Do not bother with an investigation, for we all know who is responsible for Alezzar's death. You are. Just as you will be responsible for whatever happens between us.

"You wish for peace? As long as you are king of the Dynasty, there shall be no peace between us! None! We will see your Dynasty burned to the ground! Prepare yourself, Narius. For the wrath of the spirit and potentates will consume you!"

With that, the image of Tirigian and Innana vanished in a burst of light, leaving Narius to face the Flail, his advisers, and the one who worried him the most, his wife.

21

Everys didn't want to face the next day. The previous one had been such a disaster, she knew it would spill over into the morning. Especially if she had to face Narius.

When Trule bustled into her bedroom to rouse her, Everys had already been awake, feeling the weight of the previous day settling into her bones. She mechanically went through her morning routine, choosing to have a quiet breakfast in her quarters. If the girls noticed something was wrong, they didn't let on.

How could he do that? How could he, after protesting against Paine's idea so much, actually offer to marry Innana like that? She tried to convince herself that he had spoken impulsively, a heat-in-the-moment offer. And maybe it had been. But to say it out loud, in front of all of those people! What was the Bastion rumor mill making of this story?

About halfway through First Watch, Rewether stepped into the room. He nodded to Trule and the other girls and stepped close to Everys.

"I'm sorry to bother you, Blessed, but Madam Oluna is here and wishes to speak with you."

That actually brought a smile to Everys's lips. Only for a moment, but she nodded. Rewether went back to the door and barely got it open before Oluna bustled through. She hurried to Everys's side and plopped into the chair next to her.

"You poor thing!" Oluna said. "Masruq told me all about what happened last night. Brencis and seeing Innana again and then Alezzar dying! It's a miracle you made it out of bed at all!"

Oluna's words were borderline histrionic, but Everys caught an undercurrent of humor. Not that anything from the night before was funny, but it was clear her friend didn't actually expect her to stay in bed.

"But Narius's offer to Tirigian?" Oluna leaned in closer, her face somber. "I am truly sorry for that."

A sob bubbled up Everys's throat, but she swallowed it back down. She knew that if she started crying, the girls would flock around her, trying desperately to comfort her, and that was the last thing she needed.

"I don't understand how he could even consider that," Everys whispered.

Oluna patted her on the shoulder, then rubbed her back. "I know, dear. I know. But men don't often see these things the way we do. Especially when they think it's the only way to fix something. Paine suggested this because he thought it was a simple way to shore up Narius's support when he needs it most. Think of it from his perspective. Viara's claims wouldn't undercut Narius's authority anymore. And if he married Innana too, well, then we have peace with Dalark. And, come to think of it, with a noblewoman and a princess as his new wives, Narius could answer Istragon's complaints about you as well. Then all he'd have to deal with is Brencis's insurrection, but that's only one crisis instead of four. Much simpler math, isn't it?"

Everys scowled at Oluna. Yes, the math was simpler, and she supposed it did make sense. "But it's not fair to Narius. Or to..." She couldn't bring herself to complain.

"Fairness doesn't enter into it," Oluna said. "Not when it comes to the throne. Especially not with your husband. He is the most unusual king, your Narius. Dedicated to doing what is best for the Dynasty regardless of what it may cost him. Even if it means making himself miserable in the process. I remember how he looked when he was ready to marry Innana. No matter how much it hurt him, he'd do it to serve the people he rules over."

She hated to admit the truth to what Oluna said, but Everys knew her husband too well to disagree. Narius did care about the Dynasty's subjects. Deeply.

"I suppose. I just wish he didn't have to do this," Everys said.

"He likely does too," Oluna said. "But that's part of the problem: he doesn't see any alternatives. If he had some way to shore up support for his reign that didn't involve marrying the viper or the moron, he would take it. But right now, he doesn't believe he has alternatives. But if he did? I suspect he'd gladly forget about having multiple wives."

"Why doesn't he look for those alternatives?" Everys asked.

Oluna chuckled. "You don't think he is? Do you know why I'm here? I'm here to fetch my husband. He's been here all night in the Amber Office with your husband."

He was? Everys perked up at that information, just a little.

"The problem is that, like many in the Dynasty, they're too locked in to their way of thinking," Oluna continued. "Have a problem? Throw the army at it. If that doesn't work, rally the nobles to your cause if you can. And if that doesn't work? Dip back into the Dynasty's vaunted history and see if you can't find a solution there."

Everys considered what Oluna had said. She could see the truth of it. But how did any of that help?

Oluna leaned back and studied Everys's face. "How familiar are you with Plissk mythology, Blessed? Has your maid ever told you the story of the Rising Sands?"

What did that have to do with anything? Should she go get Trule to see if she would share?

"You know that the Plissk and Dunestriders have never gotten along. For many years, before the Dynasty conquered them both, they would fight, fang and dagger, for their sacred sands. Well, many centuries ago, a Dunestrider ruler subjugated the Plissk so thoroughly, the Dunestriders believed the sands would be theirs forever. But shortly after his conquest, the Plissk would send a representative to this ruler each day, delivering a single grain of sand and a message: 'A single grain is less than nothing, but when the sand rises together, nothing may stand in its way.'

"The ruler ignored the messages, even though they came every day for years, even as the pile of delivered sand grew larger and more noticeable. And then, one day, as the ruler prepared to celebrate his conquest, a storm blew out of the desert, the worst one the sacred sands had seen in centuries. The ruler and his entire family were swallowed up by the desert, never to be seen again."

Everys stared at her friend. What was she even talking about?

Oluna patted her knee. "The Dynasty has always believed that the royalty holds the power. If not them, then the nobility. And, naturally, the military is the sword in their hands. They forget there is other power out there, power that they can't control and that they can't stand against. Just as that Dunestrider ruler was buried in sand, so too, they can be buried with what once seemed small and insignificant. You just have to figure out how to summon it to your cause."

What did that even mean? What "sand" was she supposed to summon? She supposed she could think of the common folk of the Dynasty, the ones who lived in corners of the Dynasty's holdings like Fair Havens and other neighborhoods like that, people who would never become full citizens and would scrape by as best as they could. According to Challix, Everys usually had broad support with the "ordinary people," but how could she translate that into strength her husband could use? And how could she gain that support for him quickly? If only there was a way to influence large groups of those ordinary people at once, a gesture she could make or a gift she could—

Her eyes widened. Maybe there was a way she could do this. Maybe there was something she could do that no one else would think of, wouldn't even expect.

"Oluna, I'm going to be out of the palace for a while," she said. "Masruq offered to entertain my father. Could he still do that?"

"Absolutely!" Oluna said. "We'll have him over for dinner, and I'm sure Masruq would love to introduce him to all sorts of powerful and influential people."

Everys nodded absently, then what Oluna said caught up with her. She whirled on her friend. "Won't people try to curry favor with him to try to influence me?"

Oluna chuckled. "Of course they will."

Everys grimaced. That wouldn't end well. Given how hostile Papa was toward the Dynasty, having him interact with the rich and powerful would likely lead to social scandals of all sorts.

Oluna must have read the concern in her expression. She patted her knee. "Don't worry, Everys. We'll take good care of him. The last thing I want to do is undermine your position. We'll keep those interactions relatively scandal free."

From Oluna, that was a promise of being on her best behavior. Everys headed for the door to her quarters. Time to go take a walk in the gardens.

Everys made her way through the royal gardens, past the small islands of vegetation taken from various places within the Dynasty's holdings. On her left, desert plants from the Dunestrider and Plissk's sacred sands. On her right, scraggly trees from the Ixactl Highlands. She stepped around the lush vegetation plucked from the island colony of Maotoa. And there, the Cold Light sapling that had been gifted to them after their successful peace talks. She paused for a moment to drink in the mixed scents of so many different plants, the riot of greens and reds and blues and yellows.

In that strangely peaceful moment, she was struck by how unusual the royal gardens actually were. Most of these plants weren't meant to grow in this climate. Left to their own devices, most of the plants would die. The palace employed a small army of gardeners, botanists, and horticulturists to maintain the gardens and help them thrive in the unnatural climate. Many people invested time and energy to create a serene and calming atmosphere. How much work would it take to encourage that same serenity among the people of the Dynasty?

She squared her shoulders. Only one way to find out, and she was willing to make the investment herself.

Everys approached a small pile of rubble in the middle of the gardens. These were the remains of a former royal palace. But she wasn't interested in the broken masonry. She wanted what they hid.

She stepped up to a broken pillar and waved her hand over the top. A purple light flared across the jagged surface and a soft rumbling filled the air. Part of the rubble shifted, revealing a doorway that led underground. She carefully ducked through the opening and descended.

When she came up with this plan, she knew she would have to work swiftly. If Narius heard what she intended to do, he'd probably forbid her. And she'd already met fierce resistance. Challix had scheduled a number of important meetings that Everys wouldn't be able to attend. Rewether didn't like the idea of an impromptu trip out of Bastion. But thankfully, she had been able to order them to make the necessary arrangements.

She knew that the more difficult fight was about to happen.

At the bottom of the stairs, she stepped into the royal archives. Over the past several centuries, when the Dynasty had conquered someone, the kings would claim cultural treasures and precious relics as spoils of war and then secret them away to this hidden location. She walked past displays of weapons and armor, a pile of skulls, totems, and idols. And in the middle of the room were five stone plinths, shaped like stone talons, arranged in a haphazard circle, their points outward.

Everys felt a tug toward the display. These were the Principalities, the most sacred objects her people had ever created. They once stood in the Scriptotum in Nekek the Bright. Until just a few months earlier, Everys had believed these Principalities to have been destroyed four centuries earlier. The fact that they still existed both thrilled and horrified her. She didn't like that the Dynasty had captured them and hidden them away. But the fact that they were still intact gave her hope. If the Principalities still existed, maybe someday, the Siporans could reclaim them and maybe find a home of their own.

But that was beyond what she had come to do.

"Hello?" She had sent a message to the royal archivist, asking him to meet her here. That didn't mean he would actually do so; their relationship was strained at best.

She heard movement behind her and she turned. Archivist Turron stepped out from between two of the displays. He sniffed when he saw her.

"I have come, as ordered, Blessed." There was no mistaking the disdain in his tone. "How may I serve?"

Everys nodded toward the displays. "I haven't had the chance to learn what all of these are. I need your help finding one in particular."

"Which one?" the archivist asked.

"The Ixactl's *ma-se-kranna*," Everys said. "I'm going to bring it home."

22

With a heavy sigh, Narius stepped out of the Amber Office, exhaustion dragging at every part of him. He knew clinically that he must have slept at some point in the past day or two, but he couldn't remember when it had happened.

Unfortunately, he hadn't traded his sleep for answers or a plan. For the last three watches, he and his council had circled round and round the same issues with no resolution in sight. Paine naturally wanted Narius to keep his promise and actually marry Innana, but Yull was quick to point out that Tirigian had shut down that possibility with Alezzar's death. While that gave Narius some relief that his impulsive offer wouldn't be accepted, that led to speculation about who had murdered the ambassador, which led to arguments between Bokil and Tormod. And somehow, that had circled back around to whether or not he should remarry Viara.

Finally, as the beginning of Second Watch approached and Narius's stomach ached, he called an end to it. They were accomplishing nothing. They might as well stop for some food, rest up, and then regroup the next day to begin the fruitless arguments all over again.

He stumbled down the hall, nodding greetings to the passing servants and functionaries. He headed for the dining room. Maybe he'd be able to catch Everys, see how she was doing. She'd been pretty rattled when they'd returned from the Diradae manor. Hopefully she had gotten some sleep.

But Everys wasn't there. Instead, Favid sat at the table with a plate of what looked like green sausages arranged on a slice of bread covered in gravy. He had a bite halfway to his mouth, but catching Narius's gaze, he set down his fork with a heavy sigh.

"I suppose you'll want the room?" Favid asked.

Narius smiled and gestured toward the other nine chairs. "There's plenty of room. I'll even sit on the other side of the table if you want."

Favid's gaze flicked down the length of the table and he grunted. "Your table. Sit where you want."

Narius forced himself to continue smiling, but he could feel the tension in his cheeks and jaw. A servant stepped up to him, and he quietly shared his order, asking for whatever it was that Favid was eating. It was a small gesture, and Favid would probably see right through it, but he might as well try.

That done, Narius settled into a chair, not next to Favid, but not so far away that he would be accused as being hostile. Favid focused his attention on his food while Narius drummed his fingers on the table.

"So..." Narius finally ventured. "Have you seen Everys today?"

Another grunt. "Tried to. She had a friend in her room when I tried to stop by, and then that Plissk girl said she had stepped out to run an errand."

Oh. Narius frowned. He had hoped that they would be able to spend some more time together. He knew his offer to Tirigian had upset her. How could it not? They needed some time alone, some time to work things out. He wished he could take her back to Bluerest for just a few days, spend some time at his family's retreat, but he knew that was out of the question. Not with so many crises bearing down on them.

But maybe he could do something to patch things up with Favid. The servant brought him his meal and Narius tried a bite. It was surprisingly good.

He motioned toward his plate with his fork. "This is wonderful! What is it?"

"It's an old family recipe. We call it *trallagan*."

"And what does that mean?"

Favid smiled thinly. "'Whatever's left.'"

Narius quirked a brow at Favid.

"The markets in Fair Havens were notorious for running out of food. One time, my mother came back from market with whatever she could find." Favid waved his fork at the plate. "This was the result."

Narius looked down at his plate, his respect for Favid and his family increasing. He couldn't imagine taking whatever he could find in a market and turning it into a dish like this. Everys came from a truly remarkable family. And he knew so little about them! He wished he could go back in time, conduct a proper courtship with her so he could have introduced himself to Favid and Ulsa, conversed with Galan, and even met Legarr, even if that meant he'd likely be targeted for one of his scams.

They fell into another uncomfortable silence. Once again, Narius felt his weariness drag at him. He considered retreating from the room to go rest, at least for an hour or two. But he recognized this as an opportunity. He had his father-in-law alone. He had no way of knowing when this might happen again. Withdraw? Not likely. Not when there were gains to be made.

Narius wracked his brain, trying to think of what he could talk about. He considered asking about Favid's vigil, but he knew that would be unwise. Technically, he shouldn't know about that, and there were too many people around to reveal what he knew. He could ask about Everys's childhood or what growing up in Fair Havens was like, but given Favid's hostility at breakfast the other day, he doubted that Favid would answer with more than a single syllable.

Then a thought occurred to him. He leaned forward. "Have you ever played Entrench?"

Favid frowned at him. "No. What's that?"

"A card game. It's easy to learn. I'll show you." Before Favid could object, Narius sent a nearby servant to retrieve what they needed.

A minute later, the servant returned and gave Narius a dark wooden box. He slid open the top and pulled out the deck of cards and two miniature statues depicting an ancient city. He set them in front of Favid.

"These are our capitals. You can go ahead and pick one." As he spoke, he shuffled the cards.

Favid's gaze flitted between the statuettes, Narius, and the box. "What else is in there?"

"More cities. You can play this game with up to six people. It's a lot more fun with more people, but two is good as well."

Favid picked up the city depicting ancient Elregan. He squinted at it. "What's this dial on the base?"

"That sets the value of the city and helps you keep track of your capital's defenses. Turn it to fifty. That's a good starting value."

After shuffling the cards, Narius dealt five cards to both of them. He glanced at his initial hand. A Duke, a Diradae seven, a Plissk seven, a Weyfir three, and an Ixactl two. Not bad, but not the best starting hand.

"What now?" Favid asked.

Narius smiled and explained the rules: the cards represented armies that they could use to attack each other's capitals or defend their own. They could also use the cards to set reinforcements or entrench their own city, shoring up the defenses. The rules were relatively straightforward. Entrench was designed to teach basic strategy to children, although there were additional rules that could make it more complicated for older players, such as using the card's suits strategically. But he didn't want to overwhelm Favid during his first game.

Once he finished, he allowed Favid to go first. Technically, they should have drawn to determine the first player, but he figured it was the polite thing to do.

Favid looked over his cards, arranging them carefully, then tossed one on the table. An Ixactl nine. Narius nodded appreciatively. A decent attack. He could easily block it with his Duke, but he wanted to save that for an attack of his own. He countered Favid's attack with his Diradae seven, setting it on the table in front of him.

"Now what?" Favid asked.

"We can continue to play more cards, although there are diminishing returns. If we had reinforcements available, we could add those. Or you could retreat if you fear I'm going to win," Narius said.

Favid frowned. "Well, I'm beating you, right?"

"You are."

"Are you going to add more cards?"

Narius shook his head.

"Now what?" Favid repeated.

"My city loses two defense." He adjusted the number on his statuette. "We now discard the cards, and the turn passes to me."

Favid nodded. Narius considered dropping the Duke on him right then and there, but that seemed harsh. Instead, he placed the Duke face down as a reinforcement for a future attack. Yes, Favid was learning, but some lessons could only come from the heat of battle. On his next turn, he tried a probing attack with his Plissk seven, only to be turned away by Favid playing a Lady, forcing him to discard a newly drawn Ixactl ten. Narius's gaze flicked to the Duke on the table. He was glad he already had that in reinforcements.

He shot Favid a probing look. "Are you sure you've never played this before?"

Favid's lips twitched into a smile. "Are you calling me a liar?"

Narius chuckled and drew his hand back up to five cards.

As he considered his next play, Narius said, "I feel I owe you an apology, Father. From what I've been told, the royal guard didn't treat you properly when you arrived at the palace."

"Wasn't much of a surprise to me." Favid leaned back in his chair, rearranging his cards. "You get used to that kind of treatment."

"But you shouldn't have to get used to it," Narius said. "And not just because you're the queen's father. It's illegal to discriminate against Siporans now."

Favid grimaced. "And why would that stop anyone?"

"Because my father repealed the Drywell Laws!"

"Oh? And why did he do that? Do you even know?"

Narius started to answer, but his mouth clicked shut. He hadn't been born when Father repealed the Drywell Laws. The official reason he'd learned in school was that the Siporans had paid for their ancestors' crimes long enough. But after growing up in the palace, he knew there was the official explanation and then there was the real one. Given his experience, he suspected that repealing the Drywell Laws was done as part of some give-and-take with the nobles or an ethnarch or someone else. But had Father been the one giving or taking?

"Your silence speaks volumes about what you know, Your Strength," Favid said. "But at least tell me this: How did your father view us? Would he be pleased to have a Siporan daughter-in-law?"

No. He wouldn't have. Narius knew that all too well. Father loved celebrating the Night of Shards which commemorated the destruction of Nekek the Bright. He loved bringing Narius down to the archives to show him the Principalities and gloat over the Siporans' humiliation. No, Father would have been livid if he'd lived long enough to see Narius not only married to a Siporan, but absolutely in love with one.

"You can change the laws," Favid said. "But changing another person's heart isn't that easy. Almost impossible, based on what I've seen. Your turn, isn't it?"

Narius nodded absently and considered the battlefield before them. Favid had been cagey in his defense. His capital was nearly at full strength while Narius's had been whittled down to nearly half. He considered his cards, all of which were low value. But he still did have his Duke as a reinforcement...

He led off with a Weyfir two. Favid smirked and played a Diradae ten. But that smirk disappeared as Narius flipped the Duke over, using it to eliminate Favid's card from the game. Favid would likely have to play the rest of the cards in his hand to prevent his capital from being damaged for the full fifteen points.

Narius motioned toward the cards. "Maybe this is how we change hearts, Father. A little at a time until bigger gains can be made."

Favid scowled and dropped his cards onto the table. "Don't you have kingly stuff you need to do?"

Narius shrugged. He was supposed to meet with a few delegates from the Hall of All Voices that afternoon to listen to petitions from their constituents. And he was continuing lessons with Scrivener Tolistan before supper. He considered inviting Favid to attend with him, but he suspected that would be pushing things too far.

"I suppose I do." He rose from the table. "Thank you for playing with me."

Favid waved him off, and Narius headed off for his room. By his reckoning, he had an hour before the delegates would arrive. He could maybe curl up on his couch, take a brief nap, and hope that would carry him through the rest of the day.

Halfway there, Paine fell in step with him. "Have you seen the queen recently?"

"According to Favid, she was off running an errand."

Paine shook his head with a mirthless laugh.

That stopped Narius in his tracks. He knew that laugh. Paine wasn't happy about something that had happened. "Why?"

"She left by airskimmer for The Stone two hours ago."

That caught Narius's attention. Why would she be going there?

23

"Blessed? We're approaching The Stone."

Everys looked up from her scriber at Rewether's quiet words, and a thrill shot through her as she scooted closer to the window.

Before she became queen, Everys had heard of the other cities and territories within the Dynasty's holdings, but she had only ever seen them in images or video clips. Since she had become queen, she had been to the edge of her people's homeland and to the Cold Light's forests, along with dozens of manor houses in the far-flung corners of the Dynasty's holdings. She had seen plenty already, but in her mind, this was a momentous occasion: a city that had once been the capital of an independent nation, one conquered by the Dynasty centuries earlier. She couldn't wait to see—

Wait, was that really The Stone? As the skimmer banked to come in for a landing, Everys got a good look at the cityscape spread out beneath her. For a split second, she thought that they hadn't actually left Bastion at all. In her mind, she had pictured the Ixactl living in simple stone buildings, cobbled together from what they were able to find in their highlands. Maybe not all of them; clearly the Ixactl ethnarch would live in a palace. But in her imagination, even that would be rustic. But what she saw below her was a modern metropolis, all glass towers and modern buildings.

"Is everything all right, Blessed?" Rewether asked. "You look upset."

Inkstains! She quickly tamped down on her disappointment. When they landed, she would represent Narius and the Dynasty as a whole. She had to remain composed and diplomatic, no matter what.

A few minutes later, the skimmer bumped along the airhub tarmac. As soon as it came to a halt, her guards escorted her to a waiting transport which hustled her into the city.

Once again, Everys was surprised at how modern everything looked. Yes, there were small architectural flourishes to the buildings that made them different from what she saw in Bastion. Ixactl buildings had thicker columns of stone woven into them, unshaped as if someone had simply plucked them straight from the surrounding mountains. Plus she was surprised at how much plant life sprouted from the buildings. One appeared completely covered in a red moss, but rather than look neglected, it was an artistic flair that drew her eye. And there were more Ixactl on the streets than in Bastion. But she felt unsettled as they drove past glass towers and as passersby stopped to gawk at her transport. She felt like The Stone should feel more alien. Out-of-the-ordinary. Foreign.

The transport eventually turned off the main road into the grounds of the Ixactl ethnarch's palace. Everys perked up as they approached the building. The palace had been built out of native stone, all grays and browns, many of them taller than her. But they had been fitted together with such precision and artistry. The building looked as if it was part of the highlands, an outcropping of stone that just happened to be in the shape of a palace. Rather than trumpet its presence, the Ixactl palace seemed content to blend in with its surroundings.

She spotted Ethnarch Rockflow and Representative Mossglade waiting for her at the palace's front entrance. The transport eased to a stop, and once again, her guards took point. She swallowed a chuckle. She knew she was safe at Rockflow's palace—the ethnarch likely had his own cadre of guards to secure the palace—but she couldn't fault her guards' caution. Given all the threats she and the Dynasty faced, it was good for them to be careful.

Once Rewether signaled that it was safe, she emerged from the transport. Rewether and Kevtho fell in on either side of her while two other guards wrestled a large metal box out of the transport.

When she reached the top step, Rockflow and Mossglade stepped forward, wearing approximations of friendly smiles. Like most Ixactl, they both towered over her. If she had to guess, Rockflow was eight and a half feet tall while Mossglade was just a little shorter. While both of their skin appeared to be carved straight from stone, the ethnarch's was a solid gray color while Mossglade's was a dappled white and black, appearing like marble. But their most noticeable trait was their horns. The ethnarch's swept from his temple before curving back behind him. Mossglade's twisted down, curling around her ears. Most Ixactl took great pride in their horns, and they were no exception. The ethnarch's were painted with gold and silver streaks, while Mossglade had affixed metal trinkets at seemingly random points to hers.

Rockflow bowed deeply as she approached. "Blessed, you honor us with your presence."

"I'm just glad that I was in The Stone when you decided to visit us," Mossglade added while she bowed. "Had we known you were coming, we could have prepared a more fitting reception. But please, come and enjoy some refreshments."

Rockflow led them to a small patio on the side of the palace, ringed by three-foot tall stones. These hadn't been carved or shaped. They almost looked like they hadn't been moved since the palace had been built. In the center of the patio was a fire ring with rough wooden benches circling it. A table with food was set to one side. Everys eyed her choices. One plate was covered with a pile of what looked like rocks, dappled white, black, and gray. That couldn't be right. She picked one up and shot a look at her hosts. Mossglade's mouth twitched into a grin, so Everys nibbled the snack. Tartness burst on her tongue, so strong she winced. But the initial blast was chased by an intense mix of salty sweetness.

"An acquired taste, Blessed," Mossglade said.

Everys chuckled. She tried a glass of what looked like dingy water but turned out to be a refreshing, fruity drink.

"I do have to say, Blessed, we were a bit perplexed when we were notified to expect your arrival," Rockflow said. "I would have loved to show you the wonders of our city more thoroughly. As it is, we had to scramble to fit this meeting in."

"Not that this isn't important!" Mossglade added hastily.

She understood what they were saying. For a fleeting moment, Everys wished she had notified the press about what she was about to do. This moment felt historic. It should be documented. But she also knew that this was a test run. If something went wrong, she didn't want to broadcast her failure far and wide. She smiled instead.

"Please, don't apologize. We couldn't make arrangements ahead of time. This was an impetuous decision on my part, but one that I hope will have lasting benefits for your people."

Mossglade and Rockflow exchanged uncertain looks. But then Rockflow favored her with an approximation of a smile. He had clearly practiced it, but on an Ixactl, the expression was unsettling. But Everys mirrored it, hoping hers looked genuine and warm.

"Indeed." Rockflow looked over her shoulder at the crate. "Well, I certainly appreciate the gesture. Whatever bauble you've commissioned for The Stone is graciously received and—"

Everys held up a hand, cutting him off. "I think you may have misunderstood, Ethnarch. This is not a piece of artwork I've commissioned. Nor is it some trinket or bauble. Instead, I am trying to right a wrong that has lurked between the Dynasty and your people for centuries."

Once again, Rockflow and Mossglade exchanged a look.

"When the Dynasty first conquered your people, we took something from you." Well, she hadn't. But quibbling over minor details like that seemed unwise. "For generations, we have hidden this most sacred object from you and pretended like it had been destroyed when, in reality, it hadn't been. On behalf of the Dynasty, I return the *ma-se-kranna* to you and your people, Ethnarch Rockflow. May this help mend our relationship and make up for our mistakes."

Everys gestured toward the crate. The guards stepped forward and set it down between her and the Ixactl.

Rockflow gaped at her, his expression unreadable. Then he knelt in front of the crate and opened it with trembling fingers. He looked inside and then fell back, muttering something under his breath. Everys fought to keep from frowning. He reacted as though he had found a poisonous snake in the crate.

"Is it?" Mossglade whispered.

"I... I think so," Rockflow said.

Everys winced. Of course! Neither of them had ever seen it, so how would they know for certain what she was giving them was the genuine article?

"I can assure you, it is genuine. The Dynasty's archivists have preserved the *ma-se-kranna* all these years, and I took possession of it from the current archivist. That is the original *ma-se-kranna*, returned now to the Ixactl people." Maybe she should curtsy or bow or something to make the exchange more formal. She'd have to ask Challix her opinion when she returned to Bastion.

Rockflow got to his feet and dusted off his knees. He stepped away from the crate. "All the rock-shattered luck, this has to happen when the Untested are making such a mess of things."

"The what?" Everys asked.

Rockflow gestured angrily at her. "And she doesn't even know the avalanche she's triggered! Wonderful!"

Mossglade smiled, but it came off as anemic and insincere. "Your pardon, Blessed, but our people are facing something of a... spiritual crisis at present. There is a swiftly growing movement within the youngest Ixactl who are demanding..." Her voice trailed off.

Everys heart stuttered at the uncertainty on Mossglade's face. "Demanding what?"

Mossglade shifted her weight, and she actually looked scared.

"You might as well tell her." Rockflow's voice was a bare growl.

"...Ixactl independence. Given the Dynasty's... history and its current... difficulties, they feel it best for The Stone to secede and seek a separate peace with the Dalark."

Everys's strength drained away, and her head felt like it was spinning. The Ixactl secede? What would that do? Even if they made peace with Dalark, would they ally with Brencis? Or would this just be the start of the Dynasty's unraveling? First the Ixactl, then the Weyfir, then maybe the Plissk or the Elbrekkians. Where would it stop? Would anything be left to oppose the Dalark?

"If they find out about this..." Rockflow grumbled.

"I don't understand," Everys said. "I thought the *ma-se-kranna* was a common trust, held by all of the Ixactl tribes but claimed by none."

Once again, Rockflow and Mossglade exchanged uncertain looks.

"That is a very romantic view of our people's history," Mossglade said.

"Meaning that it isn't at all accurate." Rockflow jabbed a finger at the crate. "That, Blessed, is a king-maker. He who holds the *ma-se-kranna* has claim to the tribes' loyalty. One could even argue to my title as ethnarch. Before the Dynasty took the *ma-se-kranna*, we fought many bloody wars for it to claim dominion over the Ixactl and our highland. It wasn't until it was gone that we truly united."

The emotional pit beneath Everys grew even deeper and threatened to devour her completely. "By bringing it back..."

"You just created a situation where I might be overthrown," Rockflow spat.

"Now, we don't know that for certain," Mossglade said. "It has been centuries since anyone has fought for it. Our people may accept the more fanciful version of our history."

Rockflow snorted. "Do you really think that's how the Untested will behave? You've heard their propaganda." He turned his attention to Everys. "They've been repeating the same message for weeks, Blessed. 'The Ixactl have lost our way. We must return to the ancient practices, restore our old honor.' And they see both Mossglade and me as obstacles to their goals. And I'm sorry, but you just returned the one thing that could give them legitimacy just as their leader was supposed to visit with us. This doesn't bode well."

"Indeed it doesn't."

Everys froze. She knew that voice.

She slowly turned and saw another Ixactl woman approaching the patio. She had the same stony skin, although hers was flinty gray. But unlike Rockflow and Mossglade, this woman didn't have her horns. Instead, ragged stumps jutted from her temples. She wore a simple beige outfit of roughspun fabric, matching the clothing of the half-dozen Ixactl who accompanied her.

"Redtale," Everys whispered.

The former commander of Everys's Queen's Guard regarded her coolly, and in that instant, Everys realized that what she hoped would be a grand gesture that would strengthen the Dynasty had actually turned into what could tear it down completely.

24

Tolistan nodded. "Very good, Your Strength. You remembered!"

Narius fought to keep his expression neutral. Of course he remembered! For one thing, what Tolistan had asked him to memorize during their last lesson hadn't been that complex. And for another, Xoniel nobles were expected to memorize hundreds of the Perfected Warrior's aphorisms. How difficult did Tolistan think one phrase would be? "O Siporans, remember: the Singularity is supreme, the only, the whole. In Him and through Him and for Him, all was made. And we are His people, the servants of His will."

"Remembering words is one thing," Tolistan continued. "What of the meaning?"

"The Singularity created everything in the universe. He set everything into motion and still directs and sustains His creation. And He calls on His people to participate with Him in this creation and care," Narius recited. Again, this wasn't a challenge. When he served in the military, he used to memorize more complex ideas in a shorter amount of time.

But Tolistan regarded him coolly, his sudden displeasure so palpable that Narius squirmed in his chair.

"What?" he asked.

Tolistan sighed. "This isn't a test of your memory. I'm not interested to see if you can repeat my words back to me. When we teach this to our children, application is what truly matters. What does that mean *for you*?"

Narius blinked. Oh. He had completely misunderstood the assignment. His mind fumbled with potential answers. He had to impress the scrivener so he'd trust him with the deeper secrets he held.

Tolistan chuckled and sat down across from him. "Your Strength, relax. While this is important, there's no need for such stress and anxiety. Just share your thoughts."

The words should have been calming, but they only made Narius more frantic. He stammered, then blurted out, "It's why the Singularity gave your people the runes, right? To care for and sustain the world."

"True enough. But what about the rest of us?"

Narius blinked. "I'm not sure I understand what you mean."

"What about those of us who don't cast runes?" Tolistan asked. "I've already shared that I don't. If those words only apply to those who do, why would I have memorized them? Why did I have you memorize them?"

Once again, Narius stumbled over his own thoughts. How else would the Singularity expect people to care for the world? Why entrust only some of His people with power if that was the best way to fulfill His mandate? Tolistan waited, a small grin tugging at his lips, then he chuckled.

"It's all right, Your Strength. Many of us wrestle with that question. When most Siporans are children, we hope that we'll show an aptitude for the runes. Even if we can't use them openly, our people hold those who have that talent in high regard. When most of us learn we do not, we struggle with our purpose. But those ancient words still apply to us. The question becomes: how do we fulfill them?"

Someone cleared his throat. Narius turned and was startled to see that Favid watched him from the doorway. Everys's father glared, first at him, then at Tolistan.

"What do you think you're doing, Scrivener?" Favid growled.

Tolistan blanched. "F-Favid! I didn't know you had returned to Bastion."

"Does that really matter?" Favid asked. "What are you doing?"

"The queen requested... I mean, the king wanted to... well, to learn more about our people. I'm taking him through the opening catechet-icals—"

Favid's eyes flashed with anger. "Does the community know you're doing this? Sharing our ancient texts with the enemy? What would they think?"

Narius winced at the anger in Favid's voice. Maybe he should have invited him to the lesson after all. It might have insulated Tolistan from his anger.

"Kyna insisted!" Tolistan said, sounding like a child pleading with a parent for understanding.

"Smudges take Kyna." Favid spat the words like they were poisonous. "Are we to reveal our deepest secrets to the monsters who destroyed Nekek the Bright just because some old fool claims the Singularity speaks to her?"

Tolistan looked to Narius, then back to Favid. "But the queen has already—"

Narius's eyes widened as he realized that Tolistan was going to share too much. He cleared his throat, and when the scrivener looked to him, he subtly shook his head. Some things shouldn't be shared. Not when Favid was that angry.

"I understand your anger, Favid," Tolistan said. "But isn't this what we were called to do in the ancient texts? 'I am placing you at the crossroads of many nations, so peoples you do not yet know may come, have My light written upon them, and they may know Me better through you.'"

Favid's face turned bright red, and he spluttered. "The Ascendancy is gone. Nekek is ashes. And that is because of him. His family. We are no longer at those crossroads. You make a mockery of our people by teaching him these sacred truths!"

"That may be, Favid," Tolistan said. "But maybe now we are the crossroads. Our people are present everywhere within the Dynasty's holdings and throughout the other kingdoms of the world. What better way for people to see His presence through us?"

Zar peeked into the room at the sound of the thundering voice. Narius waved him off. The last thing they needed was a jumpy guard escalating the situation. A story about the guards fighting with the queen's father in the palace itself would leak out to the press, and they didn't need that kind of drama.

"Is there something we can help you with, Father?" Narius asked calmly.

Favid turned his attention to Narius, and absolute disgust flashed across his face. But he quickly hid it behind a less toxic sneer. "Your minister, Masruq, is apparently taking me to some fancy party at a noble's house tonight. I'm not sure how I'm supposed to dress for this, so I tried to find Everys, but she still isn't back from her errands. So I came to you, hoping you would be able to help me as any good son-in-law would." From Favid's tone, it was clear he thought of Narius as anything but good.

But Narius would hopefully change that opinion. He pulled out a scriber and sent a quick message.

"We'll make sure you're taken care of, Favid," Narius said. "My assistant, Urett, will see that you have the proper clothing. And he'll also go over any protocol you need to know."

"Oh."

Was that disappointment on Favid's face? Was he expecting Narius to do this personally? Or was he inviting Narius to come with him to the party? Had playing Entrench opened this door?

"You know, I do have a series of meetings after I'm done with the scrivener. But I can have Urett postpone them so that I can help you more directly. Perhaps I could even go with you to these functions. Would that be acceptable?" Narius said.

Favid frowned. "Why would I want that?"

And with that, he stormed out of the room.

Tolistan deflated in his chair.

"Are you all right, Scrivener?" Narius asked.

Tolistan chuckled ruefully. "Not completely, but I will be. Favid and... well, the queen are members of what we Siporans call 'elder families.' They're a little like the Dynasty's nobility to many of us."

Everys had never told him that. "Will you be in trouble?"

"I don't think so. His position is more one of respect than authority. It's just..." Tolistan studied Narius with a slight frown. "May I be honest, Your Strength?"

"Please."

"Some of what Favid said resonates with me. I have no doubt you are sincere in your desire to learn more about our beliefs, but there is a part of me that is still struggling with what we're doing here. We are all taught at an early age that the Dynasty can't be trusted. Yes, the Singularity instructed us to pray for your welfare, but very few people actually do. To share these deeper truths with you... it feels like a betrayal. And Favid wouldn't be the only one to see it that way."

Narius sat back in his chair and considered what Tolistan had to say. In some ways, he could understand how he felt. He had been taught similar things about the Siporans, how they were all witches who were plotting the Dynasty's destruction. While he hadn't consciously agreed with such inflammatory beliefs, they were such a part of his culture that he had unconsciously absorbed many of them. It had taken meeting Everys to see the truth, and even still, there were times when he had to fight against those old assumptions. If Tolistan was struggling with similar thoughts, maybe he had to do something to establish more trust between them.

Something drastic.

"Scrivener, would you please come with me on a walk in the royal gardens? I have something to show you."

Tolistan looked like he was going to faint.

Narius and the scrivener stood in the middle of the royal archives, where the Principalities were displayed. Narius kept a respectful distance between himself and Tolistan as well as the stone plinths. Best to give him space and time to process what he was seeing.

"These have been here the whole time?" Tolistan whispered, sinking to his knees.

"These and many other cultural treasures from the Dynasty's people." He knew the scrivener wouldn't be as interested in those, but he felt it worth mentioning anyway.

"The queen knows?" Tolistan asked.

"She does."

Tolistan regarded him with wide eyes. "Then you probably know quite a bit more than I suspected. What has she told you?"

Not as much as he would have liked, hence his request to study with Tolistan. "The Singularity taught the runes carved into the Principalities to the Siporans. The elder families were entrusted with a Principality that they would maintain, inking the runes each day. And while the Singularity allowed you some experimentation with the runes, there were limits."

As Narius spoke, Tolistan got to his feet and approached the Principalities. He never touched them, but he leaned in closer to examine the runes. Narius fell silent, giving him the time to soak in what he saw. He felt a pang of jealousy. When he looked at the runes, all he saw were lines and curves and squiggles. But Tolistan! He knew the Siporan language. He could actually read the runes.

"What do they say?" Narius blurted out the question.

Tolistan turned to him. "Excuse me?"

"The runes. What do they say?"

Tolistan looked between the Principality and Narius. "Your Strength, they don't say anything. The runes aren't a language. They're just... symbols."

Narius frowned. "That doesn't make sense."

"What do you mean?"

"Everys once used a rune to—" He clamped his mouth shut. He was thinking of the times that Everys had used her family's healing rune, both at a state dinner celebrating peace with the Cold Light and then to heal him. But he realized that she wasn't supposed to do that, so he probably shouldn't tell Tolistan. "She once used a rune and said she was able to modify it, adding in flourishes that dictated duration, area of effect, and modified its effects."

"Well, yes, but that doesn't mean the runes are a language. They're just—"

"—symbols, yes, but symbols that convey information." Narius gestured broadly. "Isn't that what a written language is?"

Tolistan frowned. "I suppose that's true, but—"

"I mean, look at these over here." Narius grabbed Tolistan's elbow and led him over to another display.

This one consisted of several wooden racks holding what appeared to be broken swords.

As they approached, Tolistan gasped and started to tremble. "Are those... are those..."

"Yes, *ur-keleshen*. The original and copies the mage-kings made." He gestured toward the topmost sword. "When I showed this to Everys, she told me the story of how...I forget his name. Ana-something."

"Annaeus," Tolistan whispered.

"Right. He fought and lost a duel with that sword, only to have his rival kill his children before his eyes. Then he took a shard of the broken blade and carved..." Narius wracked his memory. He had only heard the story once, but the wording was distinct. "...His wrath, his pain, his... vengeance, and his... future..."

"'He carved his wrath, his agony, his revenge, his empty future on the flat.'" Tolistan's voice was hollow as he recited the story.

Narius nodded. "Annaeus carved four things into the broken blade of *ur-keleshen*, and there are four runes scratched into the original. What if those four runes originally meant wrath, agony, revenge, and empty future?"

Tolistan frowned and took a closer look. "Maybe... but this is all hypothetical anyway. Even if the runes are a language—and I'm not saying that I think they are—we can't translate it. And even if we could, why would we want to?"

"The Singularity allows you to experiment with the runes, right? Find new combinations, new effects?"

"In a very limited way."

"Since you don't know what the runes mean, I assume that has to happen through trial and error. But what if it didn't have to? What if you could know, in advance, what the rune you were creating said? Couldn't you avoid making what might be costly mistakes?"

Tolistan grimaced. "I suppose, but all of this is... just hypothetical."

"It doesn't have to be. My spymaster, Tormod, has contacts with certain researchers and academics who do cryptographic analysis for him. Code breaking. What if we asked them to study the runes? We could start with what we know: the flourishes that dictate duration or area of effect. Add in what we suspect, like the four runes on *ur-keleshen*. And then we see what they can do. Maybe we won't be able to translate anything. But if it can and does..."

He could see the interest spark in Tolistan's eyes. And Narius knew.

"How do we begin?" Tolistan asked.

25

Everys knew she shouldn't have been surprised to see Redtale. When Redtale had resigned her commission, she had said she would return to the Highlands. And when Everys had decided to bring the *ma-se-kranna* back to the Ixactl, she had hoped that she would see Redtale. But not like this.

Not with such hatred in her eyes.

Redtale glared at her, as did the young Ixactls with her. Everys didn't care about their anger. Theirs was a pale imitation of Redtale's. And theirs didn't hurt nearly as much.

"Hello, Everys," Redtale said quietly.

Her cool demeanor made each word a blow to her heart. She could sense Rewether and Kevtho bristle. She waved them off. This didn't have to become a confrontation. Not if she could help it.

"What's the matter, Blessed?" one of the young Ixactl with Redtale asked. "Afraid that these Ixactl might be dangerous? You should be. Isn't that why the Dynasty conquered us in the first place? To be threatening? To fight your endless wars?"

The other Ixactl with Redtale nodded and muttered their agreement. Everys shot a glance at Rockflow and Mossglade. They appeared uncomfortable. Rockflow even looked angry. But they didn't seem truly worried. She decided to stand her ground.

"I can't speak to—" she started to say.

"Do you know how many Ixactl have died in the Dynasty's military, Blessed?" The Ixactl stepped forward. "I doubt it. No one has ever bothered to keep track. We have bled and died for your precious Dynasty. On Maotoa. In the Colonial Uprisings. In the Cold Light's forests. And for what?"

Now he loomed over her, his hands clenched in fists. She could feel the heat of his breath pour over her, and she fought to keep from stumbling back a step. Rewether and Kevtho advanced closer to her, and she could see Kevtho's hand drop to his sword...

Then Redtale snapped something in a language she didn't recognize. The Ixactl towering over her snorted and took a step back, sneering as he did. Everys shot a glance at Rockflow, but he didn't seem to understand what Redtale had said either.

The Ixactl youth guffawed. "You see, friends? Not even our vaunted ethnarch remembers our old tongue, let alone our old ways. This is why our people need to rise up against our oppressors!"

Who was he talking to? He clearly wasn't preaching to her since he kept talking about the Ixactl. And he wasn't addressing Rockflow or Mossglade. But the other Ixactl youth with Redtale already agreed with him. So why—

And then she spotted them. Data scribers. Each of the young Ixactl held one. They were either recording or broadcasting this confrontation to others. That was who the speaker was talking to.

Then that was who she had to appeal to.

She stepped forward. "You're right. I don't know how many Ixactl have bled and died in the Dynasty's wars. I don't know the depths of loss that the Ixactl have suffered. Just as I'm sure that you don't know how many Siporans have suffered and died at the hands of the Dynasty either."

The Ixactl looked ready to object, but Everys held up a hand to stop him.

"But I didn't come here to compare our peoples' histories. The suffering of my people does not lessen the sacrifices of yours. Instead, I have come to try to undo some of the harm by returning this."

Everys walked over to the crate and opened it. She then pulled the *ma-se-kranna* out and held it up so everyone could see it.

The gathered Ixactl gasped and cursed. The *ma-se-kranna* appeared to be a thick iron ring attached to a three-foot-long pole at a right angle. A dozen metal and stone horns, all of them different sizes and shapes, jutted from the ring. She wasn't sure if it was a scepter or if it had been a crown at some point. But from the way the Ixactl reacted, they clearly saw something she didn't.

The young Ixactl male recovered quickly. "How do we even know that's the real *ma-se-kranna*? No one has seen it for generations. For all we know, it's a forgery."

Everys bristled at the accusation, but before she could answer, Redtale stepped forward.

"It's real. I have no doubt of that," Redtale said. "At least, the queen believes it to be real. The better question you should ask, Bloodshale, is why is the queen bringing it back now? She's known of the royal archives for months. Why return it to The Stone? Why now? What does she have to gain?"

Cold poured through Everys as Redtale stalked forward. Her followers kept their scribers trained on her as Redtale walked a slow circle around Everys.

"They could have returned the *ma-se-kranna* right away. The same time they returned the Cold Light's Hearth to the forest. But did they? No. Instead, the Dynasty's nobility has spent these past few months discussing the building of a museum to display the historic artifacts that their ancestors plundered from ours. But now, suddenly, the queen is here to return the *ma-se-kranna* to us." Redtale came to a halt, looking down at Everys with a grim expression. "Why is that, I wonder?"

Cheeks burning, Everys tried to think of the right explanation. Yes, she was trying to strengthen the Dynasty's relations with the Ixactl, but returning the *ma-se-kranna* was the right thing to do. She knew that. But she couldn't deny her ulterior motives, the ones that Redtale had just pointed out for her audience.

Redtale turned back to her followers. "Don't let the royals or the noble lackeys fool you. They merely want to try our young in the fires of their battles once again. To that, I say that our tribes should remain untested."

Her followers thumped their chests and shouted something in the Ixactl language. Everys flinched and, she noticed, so did Rockflow and Mossglade.

Redtale held her pose for a second. When one of her followers nodded, she relaxed and the young Ixactl put away their scribers. And then they all turned and walked away from the palace.

"Wait!" Everys called after them. "That's all this was? A show?"

Redtale turned back to her. "And your being here isn't? I'm surprised you made this move without half a dozen media drones following you."

Everys's cheeks burned as she remembered her own disappointment at not bringing the press, but she quickly shoved the embarrassment away.

"Redtale, wait," she said. "I want to talk to you."

A few of Redtale's followers stepped between them, almost as if they were trying to protect her. Redtale gently moved them aside and drew closer. But then she quirked a brow at Rewether and Kevtho.

"Guards, a moment alone please," Everys said.

Rewether started to object, but Kevtho touched his elbow and nodded grimly. The guard commander clenched his jaw and followed the Swordbound away from Everys. Mossglade did the same with Rockflow, who seemed ready to object as well. Redtale motioned for her followers to give them space as well.

"What do you have to say?" Redtale asked, her voice calm.

"What are you doing?" Everys asked. "Starting an insurrection? Suggesting that the Ixactl should secede from the Dynasty?"

Redtale shrugged. "One could interpret it that way. Or you could say I'm giving a voice to a generation before they're needlessly thrown away. Or simply repeating much of what Mossglade has said in the Hall of All Voices."

Everys stared at her before finding her words. "Do you really hate us that much?"

"It's not hate." Redtale tipped her head. "More like disappointment. I thought I meant something to you. That you were different. But now I've seen that you're just like any other member of the Dynasty's elite."

"How can you say that?" Everys said. "You know that isn't true!"

"Isn't it?" Redtale asked. "Why did you return the Hearth to the Cold Light? To get them to stop attacking the Dynasty. Why are you giving us the *ma-se-kranna* now? To shore up your husband's support in The Stone and the Highlands. This is all transactional. And we both know it."

Everys couldn't meet her gaze. She did know it. As much as she wanted to tell herself that she was motivated by justice or doing what was right, she understood far too well that Redtale was pointing out the obvious truth.

Redtale sighed heavily and absently stroked the end of her horn stubs. "You remember what I told you about why I broke my horns?"

She did. When Redtale was younger, she had been consumed with anger at the Dynasty's treatment of the Ixactl, and in protest, she had broken off her own horns as a sign of deep mourning. Because she had shamed her family by doing that, she had enlisted in the Dynasty's military, eventually rising to the command of the Queen's Guard. She had been one of Everys's only friends when she'd first married Narius.

"I remember," Everys whispered. "And that's part of the reason why I brought this back to your people. But I could have started with any number of the Dynasty's people. The Plissk. The Dunestriders. The Weyfir or the Maotoans. But I came to The Stone first. Because I do remember."

For just a moment, Redtale's features softened. She looked ready to speak, but Everys didn't let her.

"And yes, maybe part of why I did this was to shore up support for Narius among the Ixactl. I won't lie and say it isn't," Everys said. How could she make her understand? She wanted so desperately for Redtale to be her friend again. "But Redtale, when I think back to my earliest days in the palace, one of the only things that made it bearable was you. No matter what it was I faced, I knew that you would protect me. Or at least be there to support me. Since you've left, I've felt... incomplete."

Was Redtale going to start crying? For a brief moment, Everys thought it might be possible. But then her features hardened, and she snorted.

"A pretty speech, Blessed," Redtale said. "Did you practice it all the way here?"

Everys started to object, but Redtale held up a hand.

"No, you've said enough. You've done enough. Your errand is over. You've returned the *ma-se-kranna* to its people. And in spite of what the Untested have done here, I'm sure that Rockflow and Mossglade will tell the story in a way that will benefit them. You may get what you want in the end."

And with that, Redtale turned and led her Untested from the palace grounds. Rockflow and Mossglade came back and, with the help of some aides, recorded footage for the criers. Everys did her best to look happy and official and... whatever a queen should appear to be. But Redtale's words lingered the whole time. Even as Rewether and Kevtho took her back to the airhub for the return trip to Bastion, she couldn't shake what her former guard—and friend, she had thought—had said.

No matter how the Ixactl received their sacred treasure, she wouldn't get what she really wanted.

26

Quartus forced himself to bounce his legs, look around the reception area, and put on the outward facade of nervousness. At least his act gave him a reason to scan the room, taking in the desks filled with harried employees, working at data terminals or talking quietly into comm units. Fairly typical, but then, he hadn't expected anything less.

Calling Deepflow's office a corporate headquarters was a joke at best or sharply ironic at worst. Instead of occupying a steel and glass tower in the heart of Bastion, Deepflow was housed in a dilapidated warehouse in the Defector's Wrath neighborhood, which made a certain amount of sense. Barges could be loaded at nearby docks on the Melgor River and then sail down to the Blood Sea, where their cargo could be transferred to freighters. Their operation wasn't large, but if they were engaged in anything illegal, they wouldn't want to attract any attention.

A bright-eyed young Grerid man approached him, all smiles. "Polorus? If you'd come with me."

Quartus offered him what he hoped would pass for a nervous smile and rose. The young man led him past some more desks. Quartus scanned the workers' data terminals as he passed. Lots of cargo manifests, invoices, numbers, and names that didn't make sense with such a cursory glance.

An office door opened and a large Hinaen man stepped out, his thinning hair wrangled into what might have been a fashionable style twenty years earlier. Based on his impeccably tailored suit and the straight-backed way he carried himself, Quartus guessed he was probably a distant cousin of a minor noble house.

"Polorus? I'm Blathaz Kardun." The man motioned for Quartus to step into the office. "Good to meet you."

"Likewise," Quartus said.

Kardun's office was cramped, half the size it should have been, with a dingy metal desk and a number of data monitors precariously mounted on the walls. Not too much clutter, but just enough to indicate that Kardun probably spent too much time in his office and not enough at home.

"So, you're a reporter." Kardun motioned for Quartus to sit in the only other chair while he settled in behind the desk.

Quartus smiled. "Freelance, unfortunately. Trying to catch the guilds' attention through some independent stories."

Kardun chuckled. "That can't be easy. You really think there's a story here?"

Oh, there was, but Quartus kept his expression friendly. "I've heard rumors of a crime syndicate hitting warehouses in Defector's Wrath."

Kardun's face paled. "H-hitting warehouses? As in breaking into them?"

Quartus nodded gravely. "The local constables haven't been any help in my investigation. I'm assuming they haven't told you anything about this?"

"Not at all!"

"Unsurprising." Quartus pulled out a data scriber and handed it to Kardun. "I've done my best to come up with a list of the businesses that have been robbed to see if there's a pattern, but quite frankly, I'm stumped. You know this neighborhood better than I. Do you see anything that connects them?"

Kardun took the scriber and looked it over. Then he frowned and tapped at the screen. Quartus held his breath, then smiled. He had purposefully bought a barely functional scriber for this part of his plan and had spent a few hours to make it act glitchy. From the frustration on Kardun's face, his efforts had paid off.

"Sorry. Independent reporter. I don't have the best equipment."

The other man smiled sympathetically, but that was quickly chased away by annoyance as the screen on Quartus's scriber flickered. Kardun finally sighed. "Do you mind if I download this to my own terminal?"

"Please."

Kardun produced a cord and plugged the scriber into the terminal. Quartus tensed and waited. A few seconds later, Kardun unplugged the scriber and handed it back to Quartus with a smile, then turned to his terminal and frowned as he looked over the list.

Quartus carefully pocketed the scriber and tried to relax. It didn't look like Kardun had noticed that, while he downloaded the list, the scriber had injected a computer virus into Deepflow's system, one that would grant Quartus access to all their records in short order. He doubted that Kardun was savvy enough to realize what he'd done.

"They really hit all of these places?" Kardun whispered. "Why haven't I heard about this?"

Quartus shrugged. "Like I said, the constables here seem less than concerned. And, from what I've uncovered, not all of these were reported."

"Why?"

"My understanding is that some of these companies are engaged in less than reputable activities. They didn't want any scrutiny from the authorities."

As Kardun digested that information, a bead of sweat trickled down his forehead and dropped into his eye. He blinked several times and his cheeks flushed. Quartus already suspected that Deepflow was doing something illegal. If he had to guess, probably smuggling. The real question was if Kardun knew about it and, if so, how well could he hide it?

Kardun continued to sweat and he looked on the verge of shaking in his chair. "Oh. Well. I wouldn't know anything about that."

"So you haven't had any trouble lately?" Quartus asked. "Nothing has gone missing?"

Kardun shook his head. "Not that I'm aware of."

Quartus feigned disappointment, but he actually felt relieved. The mystery woman must not have made it to Deepflow yet. Hopefully Quartus's virus would uncover what this company had to do with the conspiracy before she could sniff out the connection.

"I'm sorry, I don't think I'm being that big of a help," Kardun continued.

"Perfectly fine," Quartus said. "But can we still go over that list? I'd appreciate any insight you can give me."

Kardun considered it, then chuckled. "Why not? We Hinaen gotta stick together, right?"

Quartus's smile locked into place. "Right."

"Why don't I have my girl get us some refreshments?" Kardun said. "No reason why we can't enjoy ourselves while we work, right?"

"Absolutely."

Kardun pressed a button on his desk's comm then turned back to the data terminal. "You're right, at first glance, none of these companies have any obvious connections. But when you've been in the neighborhood as long as I have, you start hearing things, you know?"

Quartus fought to keep his surprise from showing. He had just chosen a bunch of businesses at random. Had he actually stumbled across a real criminal enterprise?

The office door behind him clicked open and Kardun looked up. "Merig! There you are. We need some refreshments. I was thinking that bottle of Ksann whiskey Norfil hides in his desk. Got get it for us, won't you?"

Well, that was rude, stealing another man's liquor. And acting so condescending? Quartus turned to smile apologetically. A young woman stood in the door, wearing a rumpled but colorful outfit that complimented her dusky complexion. Her auburn hair was swept up into a bun. But she stared at him with wide eyes.

Amber eyes.

The woman!

He froze as recognition washed over her face. Then she turned and ran. Without thinking, he bolted out of the chair after her.

By the time he reached the main office, she was running between the desks, the workers shouting in surprise as she slammed past them. There was no way he could catch up with her.

Unless...

Quartus vaulted onto the nearest desk and ran across the tops, ignoring the protests of the startled workers. She shot a look over her shoulder, determination burning in her eyes. Scooping up a data scriber off a nearby desk, she hurled it at Quartus's head.

He paused long enough to duck, but it took a moment to regain his momentum. One of the workers tried to block her path, but she somehow rolled up and over his shoulder and down his back, almost as if they were dancing. She paused in the door long enough to cast a triumphant look at him.

With a roar, Quartus launched himself off the desk, hoping to tackle her before she could escape. But she shoved the worker she had rolled over into Quartus's way.

He slammed into the poor man, and they went down in a tangle of limbs. Quartus fought to free himself and scrambled after the woman. But by the time he burst out onto the street. She had vanished. He groaned and bit off a curse.

"What in the Trickster's name are you doing?" Kardun stomped out of the warehouse. "What was that about?"

Quartus whirled on him, his mind racing. Clearly that wasn't how a reporter would act. He had just shredded his cover. For nothing. His quarry had escaped and now he had a mess to clean up.

"Who was that?" he snapped, injecting angry authority into his voice.

Kardun's anger evaporated. "My assistant, Merig."

"How long has she worked for you?" he demanded.

"Only a week... who are you?"

Great question. What could Quartus say?

His mind latched onto a new story. He snared Kardun by the arm and dragged him back to his office. As soon as they were inside, Quartus shoved him toward the desk and slammed the door behind him.

"Well done, Kardun." He leaned over the desk. "I'm with Internal Security. I've been working deep cover for the past several months, tracking that individual."

Kardun gave him a skeptical look, then reached for his comm. "I'm calling the constables."

"Fine. You do that." Quartus's jumped to an embellishment to his impromptu plan. He laughed and ran a hand through his hair, then straightened his clothing as casually as he could. "And while you do, I'm going to call Minister Bokil and tell him how you're interfering with a top priority investigation. I'm sure he'd be more than happy to send more of his agents here to listen to your explanation."

Kardun paused, his face paling. Quartus waited, but he knew he had him. No one wanted to deal with agents from Internal Security.

Hopefully Kardun's fear of actual agents outweighed his doubts about Quartus.

Apparently it did. Kardun leaned back in his chair, trying to hide his shaking hands in his lap. "Wh-what do you want to know?"

"You said that this 'Merig' hasn't worked here long, yes?"

Kardun nodded. "She started a week ago."

Quartus nodded thoughtfully. That could mean she hadn't found what she was looking for yet. Why else stick around this long? But this did present an opportunity to apply some pressure.

He jabbed a finger at the door. "Do you realize what this means, Kardun? Deepflow was a target. She was scouting you! I need to know, right now, what is she after?"

"How would I know?" Kardun asked.

Maybe a little more heat. Kardun obviously was doing something worth hiding. Quartus needed him to admit it. He slammed a fist on the desk. "Broken Sword, man! Don't you realize what this means? You're a part of this now! And there's two ways that this can go. You can either tell me what you're doing here that she'd be after, or I can send in a team of Internal Security agents who will tear apart your building, your computer systems, and maybe a few employees until they find the truth. So what's it going to be?"

Quartus held Kardun's gaze, hoping the man wouldn't see through the bluff.

Kardun stammered before offering a pathetic shrug. "I don't know!" Kardun's voice was a whine.

Fine. He couldn't go any further than that and he knew it. So he'd have to pivot. "You're holding out on me, Kardun, and I don't appreciate it. You can expect my colleagues to pay you a visit any day now.

Kardun squeaked and looked ready to faint.

"Or you give me all of 'Merig's' information: contact code, address, anything she gave you."

Kardun scrambled out of his office. When he returned, he handed over a scriber with everything they had on her. Quartus looked it all over. Undoubtedly this was a cover identity that would only lead to dead ends, but he might be able to sift some leads out of it.

"I need to speak with her coworkers as well. Anyone she spent any significant time with," Quartus said, his voice a growl.

Within a few minutes, Kardun had rounded up half a dozen workers who had worked "closely" with "Merig." Despite extensive questioning, most of what they shared was clearly part of her cover.

But one of them, an older Dunestrider woman who sat near her, shared that Merig went to the same Weyfir restaurant in the neighborhood for lunch every day. Quartus digested that information. Either she had a contact there or she liked the food. It was a clue. Maybe not a helpful one, but it was a start.

27

Narius hesitated outside of Everys's quarters. The previous night, Everys had slunk home from her trip to The Stone and went right to her quarters, not even bothering to check in with him. He had already heard from both Bokil and especially Paine how disastrous her trip had been, but the fact that she had isolated herself spoke volumes.

And he had given her space. He had been annoyed when he learned what she had been up to; she should have at least told him what she was doing. But he had learned that Everys's instincts on matters like this were usually good, even if she sometimes fumbled the execution. So he had decided to give her some space, let her simmer a little, and then check on her in the morning.

He gently knocked on the door, and Trule opened it. The Plissk maid jerked, startled, then gave him a nervous smile.

"She's getting ready, Your Strength." She motioned for him to enter.

Narius headed for Everys's bedroom.

Only to discover that she wasn't actually there. He frowned, then heard the sound of running water from the bathroom. He once again knocked gently on the door.

Before he could announce himself, Everys called, "Come in!"

He chuckled nervously and did as he was told.

Sure enough, Everys was taking a shower. He hesitated in the door. Under other circumstances, he would enjoy what he saw and maybe even join her. But given everything that had happened the past few days, he doubted she would be receptive.

She turned and jumped when she spotted him. "You're not Trule."

"No, I'm not."

Her gaze dropped, and she took a step deeper into the shower, almost like she was trying to hide from him. He coughed and turned away.

"Everys, I... I came here to apologize for what I said and... well, for not talking to you about Paine's idea and then what I... well, what I said to Tirigian." He wasn't going to bring up her trip to The Stone. Best not tackle that subject yet. "And I know I've said and done things that—"

His comm chirped. Narius froze. He knew that tone. It was Paine. And if the vizier was pinging him this early in the morning.

With a sigh, he pulled out the device and answered it. "Yes?"

"We have a developing situation that requires your attention. Your advisers are waiting in the Amber Office."

Trickster's glee, he should have expected this. He sighed heavily.

"I'm sorry." He winced at how empty those words sounded.

"I know." She hesitated, then took a step forward. "Can... can I come with you?"

He smiled. "I'd like that."

They stood, an awkward silence between them. He hated this. He shouldn't feel so awkward with her. But he did, and he knew it was his fault. It would take time to fix everything that he had broken. In that moment, he made a silent promise to her that he would. Somehow.

But for now, he jerked a thumb toward the door. "I'll just wait out there."

She nodded mutely and turned back to the water. He sat on a chair in the corner of the room and waited. A few moments later, she emerged and quickly picked out an outfit. He thought she didn't appear quite as skittish or awkward around him, but he still didn't let his gaze linger on her. Once she was dressed and ready, they headed for the Amber Office together.

Paine was waiting for him, along with Overturn, Bokil, and Zammit. Narius quickly checked the corners to make sure no one was hiding. Given how few of his advisers were actually present, that probably meant the situation wasn't as dire as an invasion by Dalark. Still, though, from their expressions, it wasn't good.

"Gentlemen, what is today's crisis?" he asked.

Paine's gaze flicked in Everys's direction, frustration flickering over his face. Everys sat down in an empty chair where she could observe. After watching her a moment, Paine nodded to Zammit.

Zammit cleared her throat. "Recently, my troops conducted routine inspections in the local garrisons. They found the usual amount of contraband, but they found a few unusual items they kept passing up the chain of command until they reached me."

"What were they?" Narius asked.

Zammit set something on the desk. It appeared to be a block of wood—or was that plastic?—in a complex geometrical shape. He started to reach for it, but then paused and shot a look to his advisers. Zammit motioned for him to go ahead. He hefted it up, surprised at the weight.

"We found six of those hidden in as many barracks," Zammit said. "No idea what they are, unfortunately. All we've determined for sure is that they're hollow... sort of."

Narius rapped a knuckle against the object. It felt pretty solid to him. "What do you mean?"

Zammit handed a scriber over to him. The device displayed what appeared to be a cross section of the strange object. Sure enough, it wasn't solid. Instead, a thin channel wove through the object, looking like a worm had eaten a winding path through it. It was an odd tangle of lines that crisscrossed and doubled back on each other.

But as he rotated the image, suddenly everything aligned, and he knew what he was looking at. Someone had carved a toratropic rune into the heart of this object. It reminded him of something Everys had told him about Siporan warriors carrying something they called "void shields" into combat. The shields had similar channels carved into their interior, allowing the warrior to pour ink into them before a battle. Once the rune was activated, it enhanced the shield, giving whoever carried the shield a strategic advantage. If that's what this was, what did the rune do?

Narius caught himself before his thoughts skittered down that direction. Was this even a rune to begin with? Keeping his features neutral, he handed the scriber to Everys. Thankfully, no one objected. She frowned and looked at it, but then her eyes widened. She shot a look in Narius's direction. She must have reached the same conclusion.

"You..." Narius cleared his throat. "You said that you found more than one of these? Any idea who had them? Or where it came from?"

Zammit shook her head. "Like I said, six total. Two in a kitchen, one in an armory, another in maintenance depot, the rest in bathrooms.

Public spaces, could have been left there by anyone. As for where they came from, that isn't as clear. There is one interesting piece of information. It's made from chorizan wood."

Narius's head snapped up, and he caught himself before he swore. That wasn't good.

"What's chorizan wood?" Everys asked quietly.

Paine picked up the object and hefted it. "I'm not surprised you haven't heard of it, Blessed. It's rare in the Dynasty's holdings. It can only be found in one place: the island of Maotoa."

Narius fought to keep from groaning. Maotoa. It had to be Maotoa. As if their lives weren't complicated enough as it was. But it did make a certain amount of sense: if the Dynasty was dealing with a crisis, Maotoa usually took the opportunity to make things worse. There was an old saying: if the Dynasty was a bomb, then Maotoa was the fuse.

"Is it possible that someone just used the wood?" Everys asked.

Bokil shook his head. "Doubtful, Blessed. The Maotoans don't sell it to anyone, and from what I understand, it's almost impossible to shape. They're the only ones who know how."

"Are there any Maotoans serving in those barracks?" Overturn asked.

Zammit shook her head. "No."

Overturn grunted. "That's even more problematic. And we have no idea what they are?"

Zammit shook her head again, and Narius stole a glance at Everys, who had been examining the scriber. She also shook her head, subtly, a frustrated look dashing across her face.

"What's the situation on the island presently?" Narius asked.

Bokil cleared his throat. "A bit uncertain, Your Strength. The Maotoans hate the Dynasty, same as always. And there's been an uptick in unrest and protests. But things have gone quiet with Uaso and Trevik."

Now that was problematic too. Ethnarch Uaso and Viceroy Trevik were usually at one another's throats, sending competing reports from Dreah to Bastion, detailing each other's treachery and unfitness for service. If they had really stopped reporting on each other, that was unusual.

"So what do we do?" Narius asked.

"We could send a few Internal Security agents to Dreah," Bokil said. "Give them a week, and they'll root out whoever made these things and what they're up to."

Narius blanched at the idea. What Bokil said was true, but Internal Security wasn't known for their subtlety. Given how precarious everything was at the moment, tipping Maotoa into open rebellion didn't feel like a wise choice.

"Could we send more troops to the island?" Zammit asked.

Overturn snorted. "Not a great idea, Governor-General. With the Dalark buildup in the Beachhead, I wouldn't want to relocate too many troops on a hypothetical."

Paine cleared his throat. "If I may? We don't know for certain what this object does, let alone if it's truly a threat. Uaso and Trevik's silence is concerning, so let's see if we can't shake some answers loose. I propose the king and I visit Maotoa, speak with the ethnarch and the viceroy, and see if we can learn anything."

"Won't that be kind of obvious?" Zammit asked.

"We can take a circuitous route to get there. I'm thinking we put together a last-minute goodwill tour. We make public appearances in Wrine, make a stop at the ruins of Elregan, then circle up to Dreah on the way back to Bastion. I can make the announcement this afternoon."

"How long do you think this would take?" Narius asked.

Paine considered it. "A day or two to make arrangements. Then I'd say we'd want a few days of traveling if we don't want to arouse any suspicions about our real intent. So a week at the least?"

The others nodded thoughtfully, but then Everys spoke up.

"What about Trule's sister? Her Naming Day is in a week," she said.

His heart sank. He had forgotten. He had promised to go to the Kronin Desert with her for this ritual. He had even been looking forward to it! He turned to her, excuses and explanations springing to his tongue, but at the disappointed look on her face, he realized that he couldn't say anything to make it better.

"I'm sorry," he said. And he meant it.

She wouldn't meet his gaze. Instead, she nodded, her mouth a thin line. "It's fine. It is. Compromise and sacrifice, right?"

His mouth went dry. "I'll apologize to Trule myself."

"She'd appreciate that." Everys finally met his gaze. Tears glistened in her eyes, but she smiled. "I hope you can find some answers. If you'll excuse me, gentlemen."

She left the room, not in a hurry so much as determined. Narius winced. He'd already broken his unspoken promise. He'd have to do better. But for now, he had to focus on untangling this new knot.

28

Everys paced her quarters as the crier yammered about how the Dynasty was falling apart around them.

"...protests broke out in Sholn, Wrine, and Irieling today as common citizens took to the streets to express their concern about the tensions between the Dynasty and the Dalark Imperium. While local magistrates say that the protests have been peaceful, there are reports from eyewitnesses that some of these protests have resulted in injury and property damage. This is in spite of King Narius's recent visit to Wrine.

"In related news, the Primarch of Ksann and the Congress of Erecone have both expressed concerns about mounting tensions between the Dynasty and the Dalark Imperium. While there has been no official response to these communiqués by either King Narius or Minister Yull, sources inside the palace say that the king seems 'unconcerned' about international opinion."

She whirled on the image. "How can he be worried about what Ksann and Erecone think when he's off to Maotoa?"

"Blessed?" Trule asked from the corner.

Everys sighed. "It's nothing. Just... frustrated."

Trule made a sympathetic sound, a strange trilling that was apparently common among the Plissk. That prompted a smile from Everys.

"I just wish I could do something to help," she said. "Everything seems to be on the verge of collapse and I'm just... here."

"But you have been helping, haven't you?" Trule asked. "I can't keep track of how many different noble houses you've visited in the past two months. Plus returning the Ixactl's *ma-se-kranna*. That has to count for something!"

All of that should have, but Everys still felt like she was just walking in place. Lots of motion, the illusion of progress, but ultimately meaningless. If the crier's report was true, the Dynasty was in a death spiral. It could fracture and fall apart at any moment. She had to do something to help.

But rather than take her to Maotoa, Narius had left her here. Rather than give her something—anything!—to do, he had left her at the palace. So what could she do here?

Her mind went back to the briefing about Maotoa. And suddenly an idea occurred to her. Narius may not have entrusted her to do anything specific while he was gone, but there was one puzzle she could unravel for him. There were risks, certainly, but what was that word Narius kept using? Sacrifice. She'd just have to make one of her own.

"Trule?" She squared her shoulders. "I need you and the girls to give me some privacy, please."

"Of course, Blessed," Trule said. "But is there anything we can help you with before we go?"

Everys shook her head. After all, she was about to do something incredibly foolish and risky. The less Trule knew, the better. She just hoped that this would help, at least a little.

She had privacy, but she knew she'd have to work quickly. It wouldn't be long before Rewether or another guard checked in on her or Challix stopped by with some decision she had to make. If she was going to do this, she had to hurry.

First, she retrieved the scriber she had taken from the briefing about Maotoa. She had been surprised no one had noticed. She called up the image of the strange object, focusing on the cross section. Looking at it again, she was even more convinced that this was a toratropic rune, one she didn't recognize. Oh, sure, she could decipher pieces of it, flourishes that defined the area of effect and the duration of the spell. Those were eye-opening. As near as she could tell, this spell would affect an area the size of her living room, maybe even a little larger than that. And the spell was designed to last for close to ten minutes. Granted, the purity and composition of the ink used in the object could cut back on or even enhance the spell's power and scope, but it was good to know the basics.

Then she carefully moved as much furniture as she could away from the center of the room, exposing the stone floor underneath. She wanted a good-sized area to work.

Next, she would need ink. For a moment, she wished she had some Cold Light tree sap. That could produce one of the most powerful inks known to Siporan mages. But using that kind of ink on an unknown rune? Not wise. So she grabbed some water from the kitchenette and mixed it with some ash she scraped from the fireplace. Crude, but she had had good success with it in the past.

Then she went around the room, painting runes on the walls and floors. Runes that would dampen sound, runes that would shore up the walls, runes that strengthened the floor. She mentally ran through the other runes she knew that might help. Her living quarters weren't ideal for testing a rune, especially since she didn't know what it did. But hopefully this would lessen any damage it caused.

Once all the extra runes were active, the ink slowly burning away as the spells did their work, Everys settled in the middle of the room. She knelt, with an image of the unknown rune on her left and the bowl of makeshift ink on her right. She took a deep breath, trying to settle her stomach. This was a dumb idea. Forbidden, foolish, and brash. The ancient texts and her instructors had all said the same thing about experimenting with new runes. What she was doing could easily earn her a rebuke. She hoped it would be a minor one, but regardless, she thought it a worthy price to pay, if for no other reason than to help her husband. If she could determine what this rune did, they might be able to figure out who had sent them and why.

After taking a deep breath, she set to work. She worked on the core rune first, the part she couldn't decipher. As she worked, she tried to find patterns she might recognize, but this didn't seem at all similar to the runes she knew. The runes she had been taught had a flow to them, an organic unfurling that soothed her mind just by her drawing them. This one, though, felt wrong, like needles dug into her fingertips as she traced its lines. Maybe it was just her nervousness getting the better of her. Or maybe part of her mind was already reacting to the wrongness of the rune.

Within five minutes, she had recreated the core as best as she could. Now to add the flourishes. For a moment, she considered copying them exactly as they were. But given the sheer size and duration of the rune, she didn't think that would be a good idea. So she modified them. Instead of filling the room, the rune would only affect an area in a three-foot diameter. Instead of lasting for ten minutes, it would only last ten seconds. That should be long enough for her to see what it did.

Another five minutes, and the rune was completed. Everys rocked back on her knees and studied it. Even after drawing it, she had no idea what it might do. A shiver wormed up her back and into her hair, and she flinched. This really wasn't a great idea, but what else could she do? They had to know what this did.

Everys grabbed the cup of ink and, after taking a deep breath, tapped the rune to activate it.

Nothing happened. Everys frowned. Maybe she had gotten part of it wrong. The rune in the object was three-dimensional. Maybe that made a difference in how the rune would work. If only she could contact one of her masters and—

She felt it before she heard it, a powerful thrum that clawed up her legs and into her chest. She tried to suck in a deep breath, but before she could, a loud crash sounded in the middle of the room, a clap of thunder that knocked Everys backward. The thrumming intensified, slamming out a rhythm that rattled her teeth and shook the room. She could feel the noise pushing at her, but it felt like the roar was trying to shake her to pieces. Why wouldn't it stop? Hadn't it been ten seconds yet?

Then, in a mere breath, the noise cut off. Everys remained curled in a ball, her ears ringing. Then she cautiously sat up and looked around the room.

Oh no.

The furniture had been knocked over, plaster dust rained down from the ceiling, and she thought she saw a large crack in the floor where she had painted the rune. A quick glance revealed that the rune had indeed burned away, as had all of the other runes she had drawn to mitigate any damage. Not that they apparently did much good. How was she going to—

The rebuke crashed down on her so suddenly she tried to cry out, but the sound died in her throat as if she were strangled. Pain burned through her, starting deep within her chest and then radiating out through the rest of her body. She spasmed, her back arching, and she fell onto the ground, writhing. The pain kept mounting, growing more and more intense.

And behind her closed eyes, all she could see was blood. Her husband's blood, pooling on the floor underneath him as his life drained away. And with each passing second, her pain grew sharper and more distinct.

In the distance, she heard someone pounding on the door, shouting her name. And she tried to cry out to them, to tell them to go away, but she couldn't speak, could barely breathe, as blackness nibbled at the edges of her vision, and she fell into darkness.

29

Everys was vaguely aware of voices surrounding her in the darkness. They sounded concerned.

"Should we summon a doctor?" That sounded like Shara, one of her girls.

"Already done." Definitely Kevtho. He was so attentive.

"What are you doing? Get out of my way." Papa.

Wait, Papa?

Everys's eyes snapped open, and she realized she was lying in the middle of her living room. Someone had put a pillow under her head and half a dozen people, a mixture of guards and her girls, knelt around her, concern painted across their faces. She turned her head toward the entrance to her quarters. Two guards wrestled Papa back.

"Papa?" she whispered.

Kevtho's head snapped toward the entrance. "Let him in! That's the queen's father!"

The guards stepped aside, and Papa hurried to her side. He shoved his way into the circle and knelt, grabbing her hand.

"Are you okay?" he whispered. "What were you doing?"

She clenched her jaw shut. There was no way she could say, not in front of so many people.

Then the medical team hurried in, a doctor followed by a pair of nurses. They quickly ordered everyone to back off, which everyone did except for Papa. He stubbornly refused to leave her side. Warmth spread through Everys's chest, and for a brief moment, she felt like she could soar.

The doctor set about doing a cursory exam, taking her vitals and peppering her with questions. No, she hadn't felt anything unusual before this happened. No, she hadn't hit her head. Yes, she felt fine now, just a little weak. No, she didn't know what caused any of this.

Challix suddenly appeared in the middle of the crowd. "Blessed! Are you all right?"

Everys nodded weakly. "I think so. Can someone help me up?"

The doctor clucked his tongue. "I don't think that's wise. I suggest we bring you down to the infirmary for a full exam."

Everys shook her head. "That won't be necessary, Doctor. I'm feeling much better now."

His frown deepened. "Be that as it may, I still want to run some tests. You've had several episodes like this in the past: during the king's abortive wedding to Princess Innana and again at the Wendlys' manor. It would be wise to determine what is causing this so we can attempt to prevent it from happening."

As the doctor spoke, Papa's gaze sharpened. A question formed on his face, but he glanced around at the others. Everys swallowed hard. She knew what he wanted to ask, but he wouldn't in front of everyone.

"I really am fine, Doctor," she repeated, more firmly this time. "I will come to the infirmary if I have any more symptoms, all right?"

The doctor looked ready to object, but then Papa cleared his throat. "I'll stay with her and make sure she's healthy. That good enough for you?"

Kevtho and another guard helped her up off the floor, and the girls fluttered around her, getting the nearest couch as comfortable as possible while the guards escorted her over. As they did, some of them discussed the strange tremor that had shaken this part of the palace. Kevtho nodded toward the crack in the floor and the damage to the room, but from what it sounded like, they thought it was an earthquake. Although nobody seemed to completely agree with that suggestion as earthquakes were rare in Bastion.

Once she was settled, Trule hurried to her side. "Is there anything I can get you, Blessed? Some tea? Another pillow?"

The poor girl would probably have swam across the Elder Sea to Tomma if Everys asked her to. "I'm fine, Trule. Really. I'll just sit with my father."

Papa sat next to her and smiled, but Everys recognized the expression from when she was younger. He knew she had done something wrong but couldn't say anything about it yet.

With more reassurances, Everys was able to dismiss everyone who had gathered. Most of them left with only a little protest. Challix and Rewether tried to stay, but Everys ordered them both out. The hardest to dismiss was Trule. She seemed determined to stick to Everys's side. But when Everys told her she wanted some privacy with her father, Trule finally, reluctantly, slipped out of the room.

They sat in silence, long enough to be sure that no one would overhear, before Papa turned to her and said, "What were you thinking?"

Everys flinched at his tone. She had heard Papa speak like that often enough when she, Galan, and Legarr were children, and they had done something he disapproved of.

"Papa—"

"You think I couldn't feel the magic building in the palace while you did... whatever it was you were doing? And for you to be rebuked so hard that you passed out?" Papa snapped. "I thought I taught you to be more cautious than that! If they found out what you are, what you are capable of..."

"But Narius already knows!"

That caught Papa completely by surprise. His jaw dropped open, and he sputtered a few words. "You told... you told the inkstained *king*?"

"Well, not told him so much as... saved him."

Favid went completely still. For a moment, Everys thought that maybe he had been rebuked into silence. But then he turned to her and leaned forward.

"Tell. Me. Everything." And his voice made it clear she really didn't have any choice.

So she did. She told him everything: how she had been chosen thanks to Auntie Kyna to become queen, how the early days of her marriage to Narius had been so difficult, how they had agreed to partner together out of necessity, how she had used magic to save his life when assassins attacked both of them, how their relationship had grown from a partnership to true love, but how she had left him so he could make peace with Dalark by marrying Innana.

Through the whole story, Favid listened, his face impassive. His eyebrow twitched once or twice, mostly when she told him about how she used runes to help Narius, but also when she admitted how she realized she loved him. But as she wrapped up her story, he frowned.

"None of that explains what the doctor said. He made it sound as if you had passed out before."

Oh, smudges and spatters, this was going to be bad. She had judiciously left out details of her story because she knew how mad he would be if he knew everything.

She took a deep breath. "I don't know if you heard about how the head of the Dynasty's military, Duke Brencis, betrayed Narius and tried to kill him when he was going to marry Princess Innana." From his blank expression, he apparently hadn't, so she kept going. "Well, Brencis shot Narius, and he was dying. And I was there and I... well, I couldn't let that happen. So I... so I used our family's rune to heal him."

He blinked, and his brows flicked into a frown for a brief moment. Then he chuckled. "Well, I suppose that isn't the worst thing ever. After all, the scriveners really don't forbid the use of the Principality runes. It's more a precaution than a—" His frown deepened. "But why would you be rebuked for doing that?"

"Because..." Oh, inkstains, what could she say? "Because he's the king of the Xoniel Dynasty? And his ancestor did destroy Nekek the Bright."

Papa shook his head. "No, that doesn't make sense. The prophet Analek said that we weren't restricted from using our gifts to help non-Siporans and—" His gaze sharpened. He knew she was hiding something serious, and he wasn't going to let up until he knew what it was. "What did you do?"

Everys sighed. "I didn't have any ink with me. I had used it all protecting the wedding guests. So I used the only thing I had."

Confusion danced across Papa's face for a split second, but that was chased by understanding. Then revulsion.

"You used his blood?"

"What else could I do? He was so injured, and he was going to die and—"

"That doesn't matter!" Papa practically exploded from the couch. "Using forbidden ink in such a powerful rune. No wonder the Singularity rebuked you! How could a daughter of mine do something like that for a Xoniel king?"

"But you just said..."

"Oh, the prophets mean well, but they didn't have to live in these times. They didn't understand what we would endure under the tyrants!"

"Papa..."

"Don't 'Papa' me! I knew I shouldn't have left you here. You and Legarr should have come with us. Then you wouldn't be married to that outsider and Legarr..." Papa gasped, biting back a sob.

Everys levered herself off the couch and thanked the Singularity quietly that her knees didn't buckle. She hurried to Papa and pulled him into a fierce hug. He clung to her, and sobs wracked his body.

"I know, Papa. I miss Legarr as well." She closed her eyes and took a deep breath. "I... I was there when he died."

Papa pulled away and stared at her, his mouth agape. "Y-you what?"

She nodded. "I was the one who found him. And I'm the one who had to tell Tilash."

Papa's gaze roamed over her face. "What happened?"

"Someone experimented on him. Using runes. By the time Quartus and I—"

"The king's brother?"

Everys winced. She was supposed to keep his involvement secret. He was outlaw, after all. "Yes. When he and I found Legarr, he was already too far gone."

"And you didn't try to heal him the way you healed your husband?" Papa spat the last word like a curse.

"Papa! Narius is a good man, one of the best I've ever met. If you would just give him a chance..."

Papa snorted. "Like I've given the Dynasty a chance since arriving here? I know you've been busy as queen, but what I've seen has shown me that your husband's people are corrupt beyond redemption."

She stared at him, aghast. "How can you say that?"

"Oh, please. You asked the Minister of Finances to babysit me—that's what it was, don't bother to deny it—and so he took me to a party being thrown by some noble. And do you know what I saw there? Debauchery that would have called down the wrath of the Singularity in the ancient times. Open sexual immorality. Drunkenness. Cruelty. Entitled attitudes that exalt themselves to an evil degree. All of Pedrevor could be burning around them, and all they would care about is where their next drink is."

Everys's eyes widened. She wasn't surprised to hear those accusations—everyone knew that those sorts of parties happened—but Masruq didn't strike her as the kind of person who would participate in such activities. So why would Masruq take Papa to a party like that? It made no sense!

"This is the Dynasty your husband wants to save, and you're helping him!" Papa shook his head angrily.

"That's not fair," Everys whispered. "That's not fair at all."

"Excuse me?"

"Does the Dynasty have problems? Yes. Are the nobles out of touch with what the common people go through? Absolutely. Is the Dynasty's history awash with the blood of subjugated people? Without a doubt. Narius knows all of that, Papa. And he wants to change it. He wants to make things better."

"Easy words to say. Harder to back up with action."

"But he is trying to act. He's doing the best that he can." Tears welled up in her eyes. "Papa, you don't understand. I love him so much. And I know he can do amazing things. He's not the monster you think he is."

"Maybe not, but he's descended from monsters."

How could she get through to him? How could she help him realize that he was so mistaken? There had to be a way to break through the calcified prejudice that Papa had clung to for so long.

Her eyes widened. Maybe there was something she could show him that would change his mind.

"Come with me. We need to take a walk in the royal gardens."

30

Everys led Papa through the gardens to the center. While she was tempted to linger near the fragrant displays and drink in the beauty, like they had the first time she took him through the gardens, she knew she couldn't. She had to do this, now, before she lost her nerve entirely.

She paused by the mound of rubble and took a steadying breath. Papa started to say something snide about the ruins, but his voice trailed off as Everys activated the secret entrance.

"I don't know if you've heard about the royal archives since returning to Bastion," she said. "But here we are."

Papa nodded absently. "Some of the nobles at that party mentioned something about building a museum to house all the artifacts the Dynasty plundered. But why bring me here?"

"Because I want to show you something important. When Narius and I were first figuring out our partnership, we both opened up about secrets that we've kept. And yes, I shared some details about how toratropic magic works. But what he showed me here made a big difference in our relationship."

Of course, she was leaving out how it actually prompted a fight that took several days to resolve. Details, details. From Papa's skeptical expression, she doubted that information would have made any difference to him.

She led him down the stairs and into the archives themselves. Papa examined some of the displays with wide eyes, but she led him past them without a word of explanation. There would be plenty of time for a tour later. Instead, she led him deep into the center of the archives. With each step, she fought to keep from giggling. She couldn't wait to see his reaction when he saw the five Principalities, so long believed to be destroyed, but here, safe and sound, tucked away and protected...

And surrounded by equipment and technicians and... Scrivener Tolistan?

Everys stopped short and gaped at the swarm of activity in the center of the archives. Half a dozen men and women stood in the midst of the Principalities, examining and taking pictures of the runes carved into them. A bank of computer terminals whirred nearby, images of the runes tumbling across the displays. Circles and lines danced over the carvings, along with symbols that flashed by at high speeds.

"Wh-what are you *doing*?" Everys asked.

"Oh, good. Just what my archives need." Archivist Turron was sitting on a chair near where the *ma-se-kranna* had once been displayed.

"What is..." Everys gestured toward the activity.

"Your husband's idea," Turron said. "He's the one who ordered me to let all these people into my archives and let them do whatever it is they're doing."

Scrivener Tolistan finally seemed to notice her.

"Blessed! Welcome to..." Tolistan almost tripped over his own feet, but quickly recovered. "And Favid. So good to see you as well."

"What are you doing?"

"Your husband had an interesting idea. He's convinced that the runes are some form of written language, so we're using artificial intelligence to analyze the patterns and see if we can decipher them."

Papa snorted. "That's ridiculous!"

"Not as ridiculous as it may seem," Tolistan said. "We've always understood that the runes are symbols, but symbols always have meaning. The runes may not have complex grammar or an extensive vocabulary, but it stands to reason that, at some point, the runes may have been used as a written language."

Papa spluttered, and Everys could tell that he was about to lose his temper. She placed what she hoped was a calming hand on his shoulder.

"Why wouldn't we know how to read the runes anymore?" she asked. "We've passed them on from generation to generation."

"Begging your pardon, Blessed, but that's not entirely true," Tolistan said. "We have taught what the runes do, not what they mean. If our people switched to such a utilitarian view of the runes, it would only take a few generations before the knowledge vanished. I mean, how many Siporans do you know can read the ancient texts in the original languages?"

Well, her sister, Galan, for one. But beyond that, Everys couldn't think of many.

"So what would this accomplish?" Papa asked quietly.

"For starters, we could decipher toratropic runes that much faster." One of the other researchers walked over, her hand extended. "I'm Professor Lundara P'layvo from the Irieling Scholastium."

Papa ignored her outstretched hand, so Everys shook it with an apologetic smile. If P'layvo was upset, she didn't let on.

"How did you get recruited into this project, Professor?" Everys asked.

"I occasionally do work for Minister Tormod," she said. "Apparently the king mentioned this project to him, and he suggested that I could be of help. Well, my team and I. We developed this AI to translate ancient languages. Most of my work focuses on Plissk bone carvings, another pictographic language, but I appreciated this challenge. And, don't worry, Tormod has fully briefed us on the need for secrecy. We've handled classified issues before."

Everys's eyebrows shot up. "Why would a spy need a linguist?"

P'layvo chuckled. "Our AI can also be used to decipher coded messages. I'd like to share how many ciphers my team has cracked, but I'm not sure I'm at liberty to do so."

Everys blinked. That made sense. And if Tormod trusted the professor, Everys could too. After all, she was one of the few people that knew Tormod was secretly a Siporan. He would understand the need for discretion when working with runes.

"But why?" Papa's voice had a hard edge. "Why do we need to decipher the runes at all?"

P'layvo motioned for them to walk over to a nearby table. "From what I understand, a few months ago, a team of operatives working for Minister Tormod raided a secret lab facility here in Bastion. They recovered a number of designs that the Minister believes are toratropic runes. Some of them were used in the attack on King Narius's wedding to Princess Innana."

Papa's head snapped around to look at her, an accusatory look in his eyes. Everys struggled to keep from reacting. He had obviously figured out that she and Quartus were the team of operatives. And those runes were the ones that had killed Legarr.

Spread over the table were stacks of paper that Everys recognized from that lab. Each paper had the design of an unknown rune on it. One almost appeared like a blossoming flower, all whorls and gentle curves. Everys was able to read the flourishes along the bottom, squiggles that limited the rune's duration to a half hour and focused the effects on the target's judgment. Another was more jagged, like broken glass scattered in a starburst pattern. She leaned in closer, trying to discern the intended effect. As near as she could tell, this seemed to target at least twenty people with no notations for duration. A combat spell?

"The team recovered dozens if not hundreds of unusual designs," P'layvo explained. "More critically, they recovered some notes that explained what some of the intended effects were supposed to be. We've fed all of that into the AI to see if it can find some similarities in patterns that could lead to the base meaning. That way, we would be able to understand what all of these runes were meant to do."

"Meant to..." Papa's eyes blazed with anger. "Don't you see how blasphemous this is? This is the sort of experimentation that led to Downcasting! This is what destroyed our people!"

Tolistan cleared his throat behind them. "With all due respect, Favid, I disagree. The ancient texts make it clear that the mage-kings' sin was using runes that went against the Singularity's commands. We're not creating these runes, we're merely trying to understand them. And if we better understand them, perhaps we can find ways to counter them so no one misuses them."

"Believe me, given what we know about what the mage-kings were capable of, none of us want to experiment with unknown runes." P'layvo chuckled. "No one on my team is that stupid."

Everys could feel Papa's gaze bore into the side of her head. Her cheeks heated and she cleared her throat. She could see the research's benefit, but conducting it in the archives by a researcher chosen by one of Narius's advisers? Papa obviously didn't like that. "It doesn't sound like they're doing anything wrong. If Scrivener Tolistan says—"

"I don't care what Tolistan says!" Papa thundered. "You think the mage-kings didn't have scriveners advising them? Yet they strayed from the Singularity's path all the same. And besides, what's to keep what you learn from being misused in the future? You say that this is just to understand these runes now. But someone could use what you learn to make new runes even faster!"

"Except the Singularity doesn't forbid us from creating new runes," Tolistan said. "As long as—"

"Enough!" Papa shouted. "Don't you see what you're doing? With every excuse, you open the door wider for another Downcasting. You intend this for good, but we know that the unscrupulous will only use it for evil."

"Papa..." Everys took a step toward him.

"And you! My own daughter, condoning this? Finding excuses for the king who makes a mockery of our heritage." Papa's gaze shot to the researchers, and his words turned to a snarl.

Everys looked to P'layvo and understood. No one had said anything about her ability to draw runes. Even in the heat of this moment, Papa was trying to protect her. Her heart ached at how angry he was, but he didn't need to be! If only she could find some way to show him that...

Papa raised his hands as if in surrender. "When I was told what you had become, I didn't want to believe it. Even when I arrived here and saw that what I heard was true, I held on to my hope that you had remained faithful to our people. But now I see... Now I see how far you have fallen."

And with that, he stormed out of the archives.

Everys took a step after him, wanting to call him back. But Mama always said that when Papa got this way, the best thing anyone could do was give him space and time to settle.

"Blessed?" Tolistan asked quietly. "Are you okay?"

No, she wasn't. And she wasn't going to be. At least, not until her husband returned from Maotoa and someone figured out how to bring peace to this insane situation.

31

The waitress circled back toward his table. Quartus sighed. She had gotten progressively more insistent that he actually order something. Not that he blamed her. He had been parked in the same seat for the past three hours, alternating between glasses of water and traditional Dunestrider sand-seeped tea. The smells from the kitchen were enticing; he had never really enjoyed Dunestrider cuisine before, and his stomach reminded him that he hadn't eaten anything substantial since dinner the night before. But as much as he wanted to eat, he also knew that food would be a distraction. And he needed to remain focused.

At the end of Second Watch, his focus was rewarded as the mysterious woman slipped into the restaurant.

Quartus was impressed. He almost missed her entrance. She slipped in behind a large group of university students, a mix of human races so loud and boisterous that they naturally captured everyone's attention. The woman, wearing a kerchief over her hair and bland clothing to blend in, scooted around the students and headed for the counter. She swiped her hand over the biometric reader then headed for the door with a bag. All told, she had only been in the restaurant thirty seconds, a minute at the most. And the majority of the restaurant's patrons wouldn't remember her if they had noticed her at all.

But Quartus had. He eased out of his chair, leaving a stack of blades on the table to pay for his tea and hopefully mollify the waitress.

On the street, he caught a glimpse of his quarry striding away from the restaurant, her gait determined and her head down. He started after her, trying to keep enough distance between them. Much to his surprise, she didn't look over her shoulder at all. He snorted. Sloppy.

Then she turned a sharp corner, ducking down an alley to her left. Quartus hustled down the street and made the turn as well, stepping into... an empty alleyway.

He paused at the entrance, frowning. Garbage cans piled up along either side, stains splattered across the pavement. His nose wrinkled at the nauseating blend of odors that flowed through the air. There were entrances into the buildings that flanked the alley, but they were far enough away that he should have caught her going through one of them.

Quartus took a cautious step, scanning his surroundings for any—

Someone snared his arm and spun him into a pile of garbage. He slipped on the trash and slammed into the pavement, his breath exploding from his lungs. And then his attacker was on him, straddling his chest, a knife pressed against his throat.

"Hello, Prince Quartus," the woman whispered.

Quartus considered fighting back, but the moment he tensed his body, she pressed the blade against his skin, nicking him. It didn't feel like a deep cut, just enough to get his attention, so he relaxed and opened his hands.

"Hello yourself. Not how I wanted to start this conversation," he said.

"Why would I talk to you?"

He offered her what he hoped was a disarming smile. "Because I believe you and I are actually on the same side."

She snorted. "What makes you think that?"

"I'd be happy to elaborate, but may I sit up, please? I'm lying in something wet and it's soaking into my shirt."

The woman's gaze sharpened, and she clambered off him, her knife still at the ready. Quartus carefully sat up, keeping his hands up and open.

"We both seem to be investigating the same conspiracy against my brother," Quartus said. "I don't know why the Imperium is interested, but we've run across each other how many times now? There's no way that's a coincidence."

"What makes you think I'm Dalark?" the woman asked.

He snorted. "Please. Just look at you. You're not what we usually find in the Dynasty."

She shifted her weight, a subtle hint that he was right. To her credit, she didn't deny it.

Quartus decided to press on. "As the Warrior's Meditations say, 'Your best ally may be your foe's other adversary.' I propose we put that into action."

The woman's lips twisted into a smirk. "You think I'd work with you?"

He shrugged. "Why not? Tensions between the Dynasty and Imperium are growing sharper every day. And yet your superior, whoever that may be, felt it more important to investigate this than gather intelligence on our military or sow discord through the holdings."

"The Imperium doesn't have to help much with that," she interjected.

Quartus fought to keep from wincing. She scored a point with that. He saw the reports on the criers, same as everyone.

"Regardless, I think it would be beneficial for us to work together. I have contacts throughout the Dynasty that would be helpful."

She still regarded him skeptically.

"Look, if you're Dalark intelligence, you likely know I have no love for my brother. And I'm not overly fond of his wife." Heat prickled his scalp as he said that, and he swallowed the truth. "But these conspirators tried to assassinate them and framed me for the attack. I just want vengeance. If that means I have to team up with a Dalark agent, so be it."

Her gaze sharpened, and he could practically hear her doing the mental math. He knew she wouldn't see him as trustworthy. All he could hope for was believable. Maybe one last enticement.

"We both know that Deepflow is connected to the conspiracy somehow. How much did you find out while posing as a secretary?"

"Enough," she said, but her tone betrayed the truth.

Quartus smiled. "I have a backdoor into their records system that is slowly gathering all the evidence I need. And I'm more than willing to share. I want to unravel this as much as you. So why not make both of our lives easier?"

She still considered his words, but he already knew he had her. He could read the uncertainty warring within her, slowly winning the battle until—

She sighed, then sheathed her knife. "I am allowed to cultivate the resources I need to complete my mission. I doubt my master had you in mind, though."

Quartus smiled again. "I'm sure he'll be thoroughly impressed with your initiative."

She laughed, a melodic chuckle, then rose and helped him to stand. "So now what?" she asked.

"Well, a name would be a good start. I can't just call you 'that Dalark woman,' now can I?"

She regarded him for a moment before saying, "Yusra."

A typical Dalark name. If it was really hers, he had no way of knowing. But he filed the information away. "I have an apartment I'm operating from. Why don't we go back there and compare notes?" he asked.

She laughed again. "I can smell that ambush already. You go back and get your data. I'll get what I have. And when you're ready, contact me via comm. We'll find a neutral place where we can meet."

He sighed. Not quite what he was hoping for, but it was a good start for now. They exchanged comm codes then went their separate ways. Quartus took a circuitous route back to his safehouse. On his way, he was sure that he spotted someone trying to tail him. It wasn't Yusra. But when he doubled back to confront them, they had vanished.

So he spent some time wandering the neighborhood to ensure that he wasn't being followed anymore. After all, he didn't want to jeopardize the small advantage he had finally won.

Quartus scanned the interior of the lounge as he stepped through the door. He already felt the eyes of everyone in the room on him, evaluating him as a threat or potential target. He glared at everyone he could see, trying to project as much menace as he could. He wasn't about to let anyone take advantage of him.

When he had contacted Yusra a few hours earlier, she had suggested the time and place for their meeting: beginning of Third Watch in a curcas den near the Dunestrider restaurant. The choice surprised him.

Granted, people dealing in narcotics would probably turn a blind eye. The only real danger was a raid by the local constables, but given how well-worn the room appeared, he doubted that would happen anytime soon.

Still, if he wanted to cultivate this partnership, he had to go along with her plan, no matter how ridiculous it might seem.

"Back here, Your Strength," a voice called.

Quartus froze, then turned. Yusra waved to him from a darkened corner. A few of the den's patrons glanced in his direction as well, but turned back to their business.

Grinding his teeth, Quartus slipped through the narrow door Yusra held open. Once he was through, she slid the door closed.

"I realize this might not be your usual establishment, but I've found that the people here don't ask many questions," Yusra said. "A few blades in the right hands—or the wrong ones, I suppose—and I have all the privacy I need. So what did you bring me?"

Normally he'd insist on her going first, but he produced a scriber and handed it over. "My data dredge has already found some promising leads. Not a big surprise, but Deepflow is involved with smuggling. By my reckoning, half of their ships are carrying cargo that will eventually wind up in the Imperium."

Yusra took the scriber and scrolled through the data.

"I've shown you what I have," Quartus prompted.

Yusra's gaze flicked up to him. She grumbled something in Dalark, then pulled out a scriber of her own, tossing it to him.

While she read his, Quartus pulled up the data on hers. Sure enough, they were definitely on the same trail. He didn't recognize a lot of the names in her notes, but apparently Yusra was investigating a number of researchers in the Dalark Imperium who were working on a project involving Cold Light tree sap that had been smuggled out of the Dynasty by Deepflow. She had found the address for the lab that had burned down. Upon arriving in the Dynasty, Yusra had gone to the lab only to see it destroyed. Then she turned her attention to Deepflow, hoping to learn who was sending out the samples.

He nodded to himself. She didn't have much more than him, but she had just handed him a crucial piece to the puzzle. They were both after the same quarry. People in both the Dynasty and the Imperium were conducting parallel research on Cold Light tree sap. But why?

"There are a lot of possibilities here," Yusra murmured. "Where would we even begin?"

"Our friends at Deepflow actually helped us in that regard." Quartus exchanged scribers with her and flipped to a new screen of data on his. "After I threatened your former boss, he immediately started deleting contracts and manifests. Probably hoping to hide evidence. But he's just handed us a whole list of possible leads."

He showed her the list, and she frowned at them.

"There are at least a dozen companies and names here," she said.

"Eleven, actually. I know for a fact that Grevous Logistics and Plaush Biochemicals are owned by the same person."

She glanced at him, a question on her face. He didn't offer his source: he once slept with the daughter of the man who owned both companies, and she thought he'd be impressed with that little tidbit.

"This could take a while to clear," Yusra said.

"Then let's focus on one name in particular: Sellafus Coran," he said. "Coran is one of the major noble houses, but about twenty years ago, Sellafus had his citizenship revoked due to his criminal enterprises. Everyone in Bastion knows that he has his hands in just about any illegal activity there is."

"So let's go ask him," Yusra said.

Quartus laughed. "I wish it were that easy. Coran has a ruthless reputation. I don't think we should antagonize him unless we absolutely have to. After all, the Warrior says, 'Don't provoke a fourth enemy when you already have three.'"

Yusra nodded thoughtfully.

"Here's what I propose," Quartus said. "We split the list. I check half the names. You check the other half. If we don't find anything promising, we regroup and go after Coran. Sound good?"

"All right. I agree to a limited partnership. Just as long as it remains beneficial."

He nodded. All told, this wasn't the worst arrangement. He had a partner now, one who knew who he was and what he was really investigating. And that might make just enough difference.

32

The comm in Everys's quarters chirped. She hurried over and answered it, hoping that it wasn't another preening noble with an invitation to a party or a reporter requesting an interview. But no, they wouldn't have access to her private line. That could only mean one thing.

She opened the channel. "Narius?"

"You were expecting the primarch of Ksann?" His voice came through so clearly she thought he was in the same room. An ache opened in her chest and radiated through her arms. She felt the distinct lack of Narius's presence and wished, for just a moment, she could hold him.

"Well, he did send me that lovely vase after we really got married," she said.

"Oh, he did? I may have to bring that up during our next diplomatic summit."

His voice was light, but even across the distance, she could hear the tension, the same that she felt in her chest. They had tried to make amends before he left for Maotoa, but thanks to briefings and meetings, they'd barely seen each other.

"So where are you now?" She wanted him to keep talking, just so she could bask in his voice for a little while longer.

"We just landed outside Elregan. It's mostly an opportunity for the reporters to take pictures of me examining ruined buildings while looking contemplative. All theater, of course, but Paine thinks it might help with the public's opinion."

Everys bit back a groan. Smudges and splatters, how could they do without pictures of her husband brooding?

"I wish you were here," she blurted.

He was quiet for a few moments. She worried that she had lost the connection or that he was upset with her.

"Well, that's funny, because I wish you were here."

"That would be problematic. Because you would be in Bastion and I would be in Elregan and I don't contemplate as well as you," she said.

Narius laughed and the genuine sound lifted her spirits just a fraction.

"Actually, I wish you were coming with me to the Kronin Desert." She winced as she said it. She felt so selfish.

"I wish that too. I was looking forward to the trip out. I spent some time on the edge of the Kronin when I was in the infantry. I have always wanted to see the Sanctuary Oasis."

"Well, we're not leaving until tomorrow. You could fly back tonight and—"

"Everys."

She closed her eyes and hung her head. Of course that wouldn't work.

"I wish things could be different. I really do."

"I know."

"And I'll make it up to you. I promise."

Everys choked back a sob. He had promised that he was going to leave Albanon's Compromise in place only to go back on his word when he proposed to Innana again. How could she believe his promise now? But pointing that out wouldn't help fix things between them.

She heard a voice speaking to Narius and, although she couldn't be sure, it sounded like Paine. Heat built along her back, and her fingers tightened into fists. Good thing Paine wasn't here.

"I have to go," Narius said. "But I had a thought: why not bring your father to the Desert?"

Her head snapped up and her mouth popped open. "What?"

"I'm serious. You need to spend some more time together. And think about how your perspective changed when you left Bastion. Maybe something similar could happen with him."

She started to object, but then what he said broke through her initial skepticism. Maybe that would work. Seeing more of the Dynasty had broadened her horizons. It had helped break her out of her own mistrust and even hatred of the Dynasty. Of course, it had helped that she had gone on those journeys with Narius. Maybe going on a similar trip with his daughter would help Papa.

"I'll ask him."

"Good. And Everys?"

"Yes?"

"I love you."

She started to respond, but then the line clicked. She sighed. So much more to say that she'd just have to keep until later. For now, she had to talk to Papa.

Everys slipped out of her quarters and headed down to the guest wing. There were dozens of empty rooms, each one more lavish than most homes in the Dynasty's holdings. From what she had learned when she first moved into the palace, the royal family had many relatives, a lot of them distant, and when they descended on the palace, they had to be housed somewhere. At the moment, though, the only person in the guest wing was a single recalcitrant Siporan.

She knocked on Papa's door and waited for him to answer. She didn't hear anything. So, gritting her teeth, she opened the door and slipped inside.

Papa knelt in the middle of the living area, his head bowed and his arms crossed over his chest. Everys hesitated in the doorway. She didn't remember Papa being so pious before he left on the vigil.

He growled, then turned toward the door. "I thought I said I wanted—" His voice died. Sadness flickered across his expression. "Oh."

"Hello, Papa."

"Come to check up on me?" He turned away from her. "Or maybe you want to join me so you can repent of what you've done."

Is this all he was ever going to say to her? Another reminder of her so-called betrayal, more snide comments about her husband? She sighed and walked the rest of the way into the room. She didn't join him on the floor, but she did sit down on one of the couches and waited. Papa shot a look at her out of the corner of his eye, but then bowed his head and mumbled under his breath. She didn't catch everything he said, but she thought she recognized snippets from the ancient texts, requests for mercy and cleansing after an individual's transgressions and those of his family too.

Finally, after ten minutes, Papa repositioned his legs, and turned toward her. "So are you here to tell me that you've joined an Elderreach cult? Or maybe you'd like my help to cast more forbidden runes inside the royal palace?"

Everys was tempted to object to his barbs, but she held her tongue. She knew Papa was angry. He had been the whole time he'd been here. Maybe, if she let him vent his considerable ire, he'd eventually be willing to listen.

"Actually, no. Tomorrow I'm leaving for the Kronin Desert. My chief maid, Trule, invited Narius and me to attend her younger sister's Naming Day ceremony. Narius won't be able to attend because of this impromptu goodwill tour." She couldn't quite keep the bitterness out of her voice. "So I thought that maybe you would want to come with me."

Papa tipped his head to the side, as if considering her from a new angle would help him make a decision. But he didn't say anything.

She let the silence linger, hoping he might say something. When that didn't happen, she cleared her throat. "Remember how you used to put up those static pictures of different parts of the Dynasty in our kitchen and you always promised that you'd take us to those places someday? This is a chance to go to one of those places. To explore together."

A frown twitched on Papa's brow. He pursed his lips, and for just a heartbeat, Everys thought he would say yes. But then he shook his head and dropped his gaze.

"I'm sorry, but no. I've no interest in seeing the desert." He rose to his feet with a groan, then headed toward the kitchenette. "Thank you for asking, though."

Once he had gotten a glass of water, he headed back toward his bedroom. Although he hadn't said the words, Everys knew that she had been dismissed. She collected the scriber and headed for the door. This attempt hadn't worked. Eventually, she hoped she and Narius would be able to slip past his hardened defenses and help him see how good things could be if he would only try.

33

Challix breezed into Everys's quarters with a sunny smile and a hearty, "Are you ready to go, Blessed?" While that was a fairly common occurrence, Everys wanted nothing more than to snap at her.

It wasn't Challix's fault. Everys had been in a foul mood all day. She shouldn't have been. She had been looking forward to traveling to the Kronin Desert for weeks now. She wasn't the only one. Trule had been practically vibrating with joy ever since First Watch.

Everys squared her shoulders and turned to Challix, putting on what she hoped would pass for an enthusiastic smile. "Let's go."

They stepped out of her quarters where Rewether and Kevtho fell into step with them. They descended several flights of stairs before exiting the palace onto the tarmac. A royal cloudskimmer waited for them. As soon as Everys stepped out of the palace, she tried to shed the sadness that pressed on her. Without looking, she knew that dozens of press drones hovered just outside the palace's no-fly zone as always.

Trule waited on board. She bounced on her heels and her mood was so infectious, a smile tugged at Everys's lips. She wished she could be as enthusiastic.

"Is it time?" Trule asked.

"Almost," Rewether said. "The pilots will need to finish some pre-flight checks, but once those are completed..."

His voice trailed off because it was clear that Trule had stopped listening. She was looking around the interior, her eyes bright and her smile huge.

"Why don't you come with me into the cabin?" Everys asked.

The question froze Trule in place.

"That's not necessary, Blessed," she stammered. "I'm fine staying out here with the others. You should have your privacy and—"

"That's ridiculous. You're not my servant on this trip, Trule. You're my guest." Everys's smile broadened. "Actually, come to think of it, I'm your guest. So if anyone's going to have the cabin to themselves..."

Trule's eyes widened. "No, Blessed, I couldn't possibly..."

Rewether cleared his throat. "The pilot has signaled that we're clear to leave. So whoever is going to be in the cabin should go there now."

Everys held out a hand to Trule and she took it. They went into the cabin, a richly decorated room with a plush couch, an expansive desk, and a number of luxuries that made traveling by skimmer a true pleasure. Trule sat on the couch, so Everys took a seat at the desk. And within a few minutes, the whole room shuddered as the skimmer launched into the sky and headed for the sands.

Trule gasped and squealed, startling Everys. She had been engrossed in reports about the growing unrest in the Right Highlands, but Trule's excitement had snapped her out of her reverie.

"We're here!" she said.

Everys stepped up next to her to look out the window. Given how Trule had reacted, she expected to see some breathtaking scenery, the sort of beauty that would cause poets to weep and compose epic masterpieces. Instead, white sand spread out in all directions, interrupted by pockets of brown rocks or swept into rolling dunes. Impressive, yes, enough to cause her to squint and take a step back, but not enough to generate that much excitement. For a moment, Everys wondered if maybe Trule was able to see the world differently than a human.

But then she realized that Trule was looking at the desert with different eyes. Where Everys saw desert, Trule saw home.

"Can we see any Plissk settlements?" Everys asked.

"Unlikely," Trule said. "We tend to build our homes in gullies and ravines, and our larger barrows are usually clustered around oases. As the mystics say, 'Where water flows, civilization flourishes.'"

Someone chuckled behind them. Everys turned and saw Kevtho standing in the doorway.

"What's so funny, Kevtho?" she asked.

He looked stricken. "I'm sorry, Blessed, Trule. I shouldn't have laughed. It's just..."

His voice trailed off, and Everys could feel the tension twist in the room. And then she understood. Plissk and Dunestriders had a long and bloody history with each other and even though the Dynasty enforced a peace, those old grudges still simmered.

"It's all right," Everys said. "What is it?"

He sighed, his shoulders deflating. "When Trule mentioned Plissk civilization, it reminded me of a joke my father used to tell and..."

The tension in the cabin increased, most of it radiating off of Trule. "What was it?" Trule asked quietly.

Kevtho stammered, not meeting either of their gazes. "I'd rather not..."

Trule crossed her arms. "Let me guess. 'What's the difference between a fireswarmer nest and a Plissk barrow?'"

Everys's stomach turned leaden and cold. She had never heard this joke before, but she had a feeling the joke's conclusion would be insulting.

"Fireswarmers know to clean the excrement out of their nests," Trule continued.

Kevtho gaped at her.

"You think I haven't heard that one before, Swordbound? That one and much worse, often murmured as I walk through the palace," Trule said.

Everys bristled and turned on Trule. "By who? I want names!"

Trule smiled sadly. "I couldn't name them all, Blessed. Other servants, guards, visiting members of the nobility. They think that somehow, their status means I can't hear what they're saying."

"And it doesn't bother you?" Everys asked.

"Of course it does," Trule said. "My people have a saying: 'Words can be sharp as any blade.' And when those words are filled with hate, they are that much sharper. But I can choose how I respond to their hatred. If I allow them to change who I am, they win. I refuse to let them. So we Plissk take pride in disarming those who hate us by stealing their sharp words." She fixed a stern gaze on Kevtho. "That doesn't mean that it's okay for you to tell those jokes."

Kevtho held up his hands. "I'm so sorry, Trule. I would never—"

She smiled. "I know you're an honorable man, Kevtho, Strider of the Ridge. I have never felt any hate from you."

Everys felt absolutely stunned. This was the most she had ever heard Trule speak. How had she never realized that her maid was so thoughtful and wise?

Then Trule spit a small ball of yellowish goop into her hands. Everys's stomach lurched at the sight of it. Maybe not as wise after all?

But Kevtho had gone still as Trule crossed the cabin to him. She delicately rubbed some of the goop onto his cheeks, then a line of it down his nose, and another streak across his forehead. The color quickly faded as it was apparently absorbed into his skin.

"I name you my friend," she whispered. "Be welcome in my barrow. Be guest of my hearth. Where my feet tread, may yours soon follow."

She then patted his cheek and, with a shy smile at Everys, slipped out of the cabin. Kevtho stared after her with wide eyes.

"What was that?" Everys asked.

He took a deep, shuddering breath. "I've just been invited to attend her sister's Naming Day."

Everys stared at him. Trule hadn't done that when she'd invited her!

He must have read the question in her expression, because he laughed. "You can enter the Oasis because you're the queen, and you're Siporan. But Dunestriders aren't allowed. We've spilled too much of their blood. But by marking me like that, Trule has declared me worthy. Her people will accept me... well, as one of their own."

Everys wanted to ask more questions. So many welled up inside her. But she had a feeling that whatever she might say would sully what had just happened. So she took her place behind the desk and waited to see what other wonders the desert might hold. If they were anything like what the trip had provided, she knew this would be memorable.

34

Narius stepped off the skimmer, and it felt as though the stress of the trip fell off him. Not that anything had gone wrong. He had delivered his speeches, appeared with the right people, and Paine seemed to think each had accomplished their limited goals. But the closer they got to arriving in Maotoa, the more stress Narius felt. But once he actually breathed in the sea air, the tension melted.

Tropical trees swayed in the wind, and he could smell the salt on the air. He hadn't been to Maotoa in years. He remembered that trip fondly for a variety of reasons, but the island's beauty was certainly one of them. A pristine beach of white sand stretched as far as the eye could see, waves crashing against distant rocks. Seabirds called to one another overhead. Narius took a deep breath. If the Dynasty wasn't in crisis, he would consider coming here with Everys someday. She'd love it.

"Your Strength?" Paine's quiet words snapped him back to attention.

He sighed. Back to reality. He turned to Paine, who still wore his thick robes in spite of the oppressive heat and humidity. And yet Paine didn't look at all uncomfortable.

"Our transportation is waiting." Paine gestured down the tarmac.

They strode toward a dock that jutted into a canal. A large boat waited for him, crewed by a half-dozen Maotoans. They were all broad-chested men wearing green shorts that complimented their coppery skin. They bowed at the waist as Narius and Paine boarded the ship, followed by Narius's personal guards. As soon as everyone had boarded, one of the men, who wore a thick necklace made of black rope, stepped forward with a flourish of his hands.

"King Narius, welcome to Maotoa!" His voice was deep and resonant. "I am High Steward Melat, he who serves Maragnat Trevik and his family. He has bid us speed you to Dreah with all haste."

Narius forced himself to smile. If they were supposed to be in Maotoa's capital quickly, why not allow them to land their skimmer in Dreah? But, as Paine had explained, this trip up the Arterial Canal was traditional. Ever since the Dynasty put down the Colonial Uprisings, the Maotoans insisted that any visiting king approach Dreah in this fashion. Given the painful losses during the Uprisings, the Dynasty had agreed.

"We thank you, High Steward Melat," Paine said. "We are looking forward to visiting with Viceroy Trevik and Ethnarch Uaso. At your leisure."

Melat bowed again, but Narius couldn't miss the slight twitch to the Maotoan man's lip when Paine mentioned the viceroy and ethnarch.

The other Maotoans hefted long poles and nudged the boat into the middle of the canal. As soon as they had drifted into the center, Melat shouted something, and a rumble wormed through the deckplates. The boat slid forward, and soon, the wind slipped through Narius's hair.

"So how long until we reach Dreah?" he shouted over the engine's hum.

"No more than an hour, Your Strength," Melat answered. "Until we arrive, enjoy the sights of our island. There is much to delight the body and mind on Maotoa, after all."

As Melat walked away, he guffawed, and his laughter was picked up by the other Maotoans. Narius shifted uncomfortably, so he stepped closer to Paine.

"Any thoughts so far?" Narius whispered.

Paine shrugged. "Aside from the fact that these sailors seem a gregarious bunch? No. But I do wonder about Melat referring to Trevik as 'Maragnat.' My understanding is that term is reserved for the Maotoan ethnarch."

"That's my understanding as well," Narius said. "A mistake?"

"From the High Steward?" Paine shook his head. "Doubtful."

That was a good point. That would be like Paine using the wrong honorific in referring to Narius or Everys. Possible, but so unlikely as to be ridiculous.

"I'll see if I can't dig up some information from our host," Paine said. "You just enjoy the view."

With that, Paine drifted away from the railing, leaving Narius to watch the countryside roll by.

Vast fields of kulith bushes stretched out, the thick roots plunging deep into the submerged fields. Narius knew the sweet fruit was one of Maotoa's primary exports.

But gradually, the fields gave way to more signs of civilization. Instead of rough stone, the canal was bordered by smooth pavement. Statues began to appear at regular intervals, all of them identical, but it took Narius a few glances to realize that they were all of the Water Bearer. Granted, she was more stylized, resembling a Maotoan woman rather than a Hinaen. Given the Maotoan's respect for the ocean, their reverence for the Water Bearer made sense. But why didn't they have depictions of any of the other gods? And why did each statue depict the Water Bearer holding a gem?

That puzzle quickly evaporated, only to be replaced by another. As the boat approach Dreah, smaller craft zipped out of the canals that branched off the Arterial. Calling them "boats" was far too generous. They instead appeared to be rafts as long as the riders were tall. Each one carried a Maotoan, who leisurely rowed every few seconds but, somehow were able to keep pace with the larger boat. They smiled and waved at Narius. He returned the gesture, but froze when three of the makeshift rafts sped up and passed the boat. How were they doing that?

Soon the towers of Dreah appeared on the horizon. Then houses and other buildings crowded the banks along the canal. More of the rafts crowded around the boat and sped past it. And all along the shore, those strange statues of the Water Bearer stared at him. By the time they approached a dock near the viceroy's palace, he wanted nothing more than to be on solid ground.

Within a few moments, Melat and his team had sidled the boat up to the dock and had it tied up. Zar and his team of guards headed out onto the dock the moment a ramp was extended, fanning out to sweep the area. Narius waited next to Paine until Zar signaled he could disembark, then he plastered on a diplomatic smile and strode up the ramp.

He recognized Viceroy Trevik immediately. He was a strapping man in his midfifties, with a rakish beard and shining green eyes. In some ways, he appeared to be an action vid star, all flash, muscle, and little in terms of intelligence. But Narius knew better. There was a reason why Trevik had retained control of Maotoa for two decades now. From what Narius knew of him, he was a canny political operator, shrewd and clever.

Standing next to him was Pillara, the wife of the Maotoan ethnarch. She was taller than Trevik and wore a dress that exposed her shoulders and only came down to her knees. Bright ribbons wove through her hair, creating an elaborate style of braids and colors that gave her an otherworldly appearance. She smiled at him thinly, but her gaze was sharp.

And behind her was... Narius's eyebrows shot up. Was that really Cosena? He had first met her when he was twelve. Back then, she had intimidated him. She was several years older, and had carried herself with such confidence and poise. But time had refined her beauty. She was taller, more voluptuous, with full lips and shimmering brown eyes and long black hair that hung to her waist. For a moment, he worried that, if he spoke to her, he would revert back to the stammering adolescent she had known. But he quickly shoved aside the thought.

Trevik stepped forward, smiling with his arms opened wide. "Your Strength, welcome to Maotoa! We are so grateful you could join us!"

Narius tried to shake his hand, but the viceroy enveloped him in a tight hug. Narius shot a look at Paine, who shrugged. Trevik eventually released him and laughed, loud and uproariously. The Maotoans on the dock joined in with him. Once again, Narius glanced at Paine. What was going on?

Trevik gestured to his right. "I believe you know Pillara and Cosena?"

Pillara's face appeared to have been chiseled from ice. "Your Strength, so glad we could host you again."

"As am I," Narius replied. "But please tell me, where is your husband? I would have expected him to be here to greet me."

Pillara actually offered a genuine smile. "Never fear, Your Strength. My husband is healthy and hale. Hard at work for the future of Maotoa and the Dynasty."

That didn't really answer his question, but he decided to let it go. Plenty of time for more pointed questions later. He turned his attention to Cosena.

"Your Strength, such a pleasure to see you again." Cosena's voice was as thick and sweet as honey. "Tell me, do you still have the gift I gave you?"

The gift she...? What was she talking about?

Cosena tipped her head to one side, her eyes bright with laughter. "Tell me you haven't forgotten."

Narius wracked his mind. The Dynasty had once hosted a trade summit in Dreah. Mother, Quartus, and he had accompanied Father to Maotoa, but the only thing he really remembered about the trip was meeting Innana for the first time. Yes, he had been aware of Cosena during the trip, but again, she had already been a young woman, so overwhelming in her beauty that he—

And then he remembered. On the first day of the summit, Cosena had gathered the children who'd attended with their parents and presented them with tribal masks. He had remembered the way her hand had brushed his, how his mind had locked up in her mere presence, and then how he had heard the melodic giggling of Innana and...

He smiled. "I do indeed. I have it displayed in a place of honor in my private study."

Cosena smiled, and her face became radiant. "I am so happy to hear it, Your Strength. While I know that your attention was captivated by a certain Dalark princess, I appreciated our time together. I look forward to becoming reacquainted with you during your visit."

"As do I," Narius said.

Trevik cleared his throat. "We have arranged quarters for you in the royal palace. Steward Melat will escort you there and see to your needs until the feast tonight."

"That all sounds wonderful."

"Until tonight, then."

With that, Melat motioned for Narius and his entourage to follow him. The gathered Maotoans cheered and applauded as he passed through the crowd. Narius plastered on a wide smile and waved as they walked. So many people, crowding around.

Wait, who was that?

A woman skulked toward the back of the crowd, barely visible as Narius passed. She wasn't Maotoan—too short and too pale to be mistaken for one. And while her outfit was bland and nondescript, there was something about her that still caught his attention. Something about the way she moved. The way she looked at him, with a decisive gaze that reminded him of how Everys sometimes looked at him when she was mentally dissecting him. And her brown hair, cut short to frame her heart-shaped face, definitely made her stand out among the Maotoan women.

Paine nudged him from behind, whispering for him to keep moving. Narius scanned the faces in the crowd, hoping to catch a glimpse of the woman again. He didn't see any sign of her. A frown twitched his brow. Was he overreacting? Maybe. He was tired. But given all the mysteries already swirling through Maotoa, he'd just have to add her to the list.

35

"There it is, Blessed!" Trule leaned forward against the barge's railing and pointed right ahead of them. "The Oasis!"

At first, Everys wasn't sure anything was out there in the shimmering sands, but then, she spotted the green smudge against the brilliant white. Within a few minutes, the smudge became trees and other greenery bordering a slice of brilliant blue. She released a pent-up sigh. Finally!

The trip to the Oasis hadn't been awful. After landing at a nearby military base, Everys and her party had boarded a Plissk sandbarge, a bulky craft that somehow managed to slice through the dunes like a ship through water. The craft was filled with dozens of Plissk families, all of them traveling to the Oasis for the same reason. At first, they had shot venomous glares at the non-Plissk riders, but when they realized who Everys was, their attitude changed.

Kevtho stepped up the railing next to her. He took a deep breath and then chuckled, a weightless sound that caused a happy pang in Everys's chest as well.

"Is your home near here, Swordbound?" she asked.

Kevtho laughed again. "No, Blessed. The Dunestriders only walk the desert. We don't live in it. My family actually lives in the western foothills of the Speartip Mountains. Most of them haven't ventured into the sands for generations."

"Why not? Isn't that your heritage?"

"Of a sort, yes." He rubbed the back of his neck and looked around the barge's deck. "I'm not sure it's wise for us to discuss this so openly, Blessed. Many would disagree with my perspective."

Trule snorted and waved away his words. "You are welcome here, Kevtho. All know who you are now."

That was true. When Kevtho had boarded the barge, he'd attracted the most hostility. But then the Plissk started sniffing at him, only to react with surprise or shock or, in a few cases, disgust. After they had done that, though, the other Plissk passengers seemed more accepting or, at the least, tolerant.

Kevtho sighed, shooting another look around the deck. Then he leaned in and lowered his voice. "My people didn't live in the sands, Blessed. We were escorts for those who wished to travel through them. The Weyfir and those who traded with them, for example. We ensured their cargo would arrive on the other side of the Kronin safely and not be... harassed."

"You mean stolen by savage Plissk," Trule said, her words laced with mockery.

"That is how we spoke of it, yes," Kevtho said with a wince. "Because the Plissk tended to object to foreigners in their desert, we often found ourselves in conflict with them."

"Only they didn't content themselves to just escort others." Trule jerked her head to one side of the barge.

Everys looked to where she had indicated. Off in the distance, a large outcropping of brown stone rose from the sand. A massive boulder? No, the more Everys studied it, the more unnatural it appeared. Not a single boulder, but many stones, piled on top of each other. A fortress, crumbling in the heat.

"There are many such fortresses within the sands. Places where the Dunestriders tried to assert their dominance over the Kronin," Trule said.

Kevtho grimaced. "Also true. But thankfully, all such fortresses are now unoccupied. Once both Plissk and Dunestrider were brought into the Dynasty, very few people needed our services anymore, especially once cloudskimmers and transports became the way to move cargo."

"So the Dunestriders don't go into the desert anymore?" Everys asked.

Once again, a pained expression flitted across Kevtho's face, one mirrored by Trule.

"Many don't," Kevtho said. "But there are also many who remember how our journeys through the sands enriched our people. They feel that we have lost something by not going into the desert, that we should be the masters of the Kronin the way they think we once were."

"Spill blood for sand," Trule murmured.

"So what do they do about it?" Everys asked

Kevtho snorted. "Truthfully? Not much. They're mostly old men who feel they could solve all the world's problems if people would just listen. But some of my parents' generation will offer tours of the desert to bored nobility, offering them a chance to go hunting the great beasts of the desert."

Trule laughed at that.

"But still others cling to what they feel is their heritage and speak of recapturing what they feel is our lost glory." Kevtho leaned heavily on the railing and took a deep breath. "And sometimes, I have to admit, I understand why. When the present isn't to your liking, the past—especially an imagined one—can be very attractive."

He fell silent and Trule didn't have anything to add, so Everys spent the rest of the journey mulling over what Kevtho shared. The attitude he described sounded so familiar. She had seen it in Papa. He clearly chafed against the way things were in the Dynasty and he kept dredging up past offenses and hostility. Hopefully she and Narius would be able to help the rest of the Dynasty overcome those troubled pasts and find some sort of peace. But what could she do to help Papa see the future they were trying to build as well?

Soon, she left those thoughts behind as the barge came to a shuddering halt just outside the Oasis. Everys gaped at what she saw. The Plissk's central Oasis was enormous, surrounded by lush trees. While she could only catch a glimpse of the waters beyond the trees, they were the purest blue she had ever seen. A warbling cry went up from the barge, every Plissk on board joining their voices together in an undulating cry that startled her until she caught the happy undertones. It was a homecoming, a celebration. She wanted to join them, but it cut off before she could summon her courage.

Metallic ramps extended from the lower levels of the barges and embedded themselves in the sand. The passengers streamed out, heading for the Oasis where they were met by other Plissk. Everys and the rest of her party held back, waiting for the rest to disembark. As soon as the barge had emptied, Everys's entourage escorted her off the vessel.

As soon as they had disembarked, Trule ran ahead of them, shouting something in a lilting language Everys recognized as the Plissk native tongue. She practically collided with a small knot of Plissk, who all embraced her.

"I suppose that's where we're going, huh?" Rewether asked with a chuckle.

Everys made her way over to Trule. As she approached, the loud celebration died out, and one by one, Trule's family knelt in front of her.

"Blessed, you honor us with your presence," one of the older Plissk men said. He bore a striking resemblance to Trule, with the same color scales. But Everys had no way of knowing if this was her father, uncle, or even grandfather.

"Please, you don't have to bow to me." She motioned for them to rise.

"But we do, Blessed," one of the women said. "You took our Trule into your home, you have entrusted her with so much already. We are grateful for the kindness you have shown to her."

Trule, who hadn't bowed, hissed something at her family. Apparently that was enough to get them to rise, and Trule spent the next several minutes introducing all of her relatives to Everys. Her mother and father, Gessl and Stru, her grandparents, uncles and aunts, cousins, close to a dozen siblings, all of the names and faces blending together until Everys felt overwhelmed by it all.

But the biggest surprise was the younger sister whose Naming Day they had come to celebrate. When Everys had imagined her, she'd assumed that she was an infant, but instead, she appeared to be ten or eleven years old. She offered Everys a shy smile but didn't say anything.

Once the introductions were complete, Stru motioned for Everys and the rest of her party to follow him deeper into the Oasis. As they walked, Everys fell into step with Trule and laid a hand on her arm.

"Is it normal for Plissk to not be given names for so long?" she whispered.

Trule nodded. "An old tradition. The sands can be harsh to the young and weak. My people felt that it was unwise to waste a name on a child that might not live long enough to use it."

Everys looked over at Trule's sister. That must have been hard, not having a name for so long. "So what did you call her?"

"*Ellissannah*," Trule said. "It's an old Plissk word for 'precious little one.' We call all of our children some variation of that until their Naming Day."

"And she didn't mind?"

Trule laughed. "Of course she did. No one likes being called *Ellissannah*. I know I didn't. Every Plissk youth longs for their Naming Day."

"So why still do it?"

"Traditions have long lives, don't they?" Trule asked. "Can you honestly say that the Siporans don't hold on to old traditions that no longer quite fit?"

They did. She knew it all too well. Siporan conclaves were filled with ancient rites and rituals that the elders understood and some of the worshipers appreciated, but felt out of place and strange in modern times. They had their value, but sometimes it was hard to decide what to hold on to and what to let go.

Stru led them to a complex of huts deep within the trees where the family would dwell for the ceremony. They'd stay there overnight until the Naming Day rite the next morning. The huts were circular structures built out of rough wooden poles lashed together with green ropes, the conical roofs made out of palm fronds. Everys was shown to the largest of the huts, but the interior was bare and plain, with a bed pulled up to a fire pit in the center. There was a vidscreen and computer terminal, but it appeared out of place in the rustic room. In many ways, it reminded her of the houses she had stayed in with Narius when they traveled through the Cold Light's forests several months earlier.

A pang rose up in her. Narius should have been here with her instead of on Maotoa. Hopefully his time there would be fruitful.

36

Narius felt like he had walked into a trap, and he had no idea if he was the bait or the target.

Oh, everyone in the viceroy's palace was cordial enough. Solicitous, even. He had been shown to a lovely room, the equal of any guest quarter in the royal palace. A fountain dominated one corner of his bedroom, a quarter circle of rippling water, fed by a statue of the Water Bearer. Like the other statues he had seen on the way to Dreah, this one held one of those odd crystals. The rest of his room was a reminder of where he was: fragrant tropical flowers, bright colors, and large windows that allowed the sweet breeze to flow through the room.

But Narius didn't have time to really enjoy his room. Instead, he dressed carefully, pulling on the outfit that he had chosen for the dinner. He had considered wearing his dress uniform, but given the Dynasty's fraught relationship with Maotoa, attending the feast wearing any reminder of the military would likely lead to more friction. So Narius had settled on a formal outfit, one of mostly darker blues but with a sash of brighter colors that evoked Maotoa's heritage. Narius grimaced when he examined himself in the mirror. This outfit was more flamboyant than he was used to, but he understood its value. When in a delicate diplomatic situation, sometimes the little touches made the biggest impacts.

As soon as he was satisfied he looked the part, Narius headed for the door. Zar and another guard led the way with two more behind. When they passed Paine's quarters, the vizier stepped out and smoothly fell into step with Narius.

"Your room have a huge fountain as well?" Narius whispered.

"It does seem a bit excessive," Paine said.

Narius smiled. That was as close as he'd get his friend to actually complain, but it still felt like a victory.

Maotoan servants paused in their work as Narius passed, each of them bowing or showing some sign of acknowledgment and respect. But while they seemed outwardly happy, he couldn't overlook the simmering tension and, in some cases, anger in their postures and expressions. Maotoa wasn't the fuse. It was the bomb itself. Hopefully tonight's festivities and the rest of his visit would be a positive step in disarming it.

Steward Melat met Narius's group and gave them a quick once-over. From the way he sniffed, Melat probably didn't approve of their dress. Narius straightened, irritation flashing through him. But the steward was wise enough not to say anything. Instead, he led Narius and the others through the palace hallways until they entered a large feasting hall.

The room was twice as large as the main ballroom back in Bastion, but tables and chairs filled the room, row after row, so tightly packed that Narius had no idea how anyone could navigate the space. And yet they obviously had, for hundreds of people were already seated, talking loudly with large gestures that somehow never resulted in anyone getting hit. The floors sloped down toward the middle, giving the impression that Narius stood on the lip of a huge bowl. The ceiling had a circular hole cut in the middle, revealing the darkening sky. All four walls had multiple channels carved into them with water flowing down each.

The conversation died as Narius entered the room, then all the attendees began to shout and whoop, some of them pounding on the tables. Soon the room was thundering with noise so loud Narius could barely hear himself think.

Melat signaled for them to follow him deeper into the room. Even though the guests were so tightly packed together, somehow they reached the center of the room. Viceroy Trevik, Pillara, and Cosena sat at this table. At Narius's approach, Trevik rose and gestured broadly.

"My friends! Come, join me!" His voice rang out surprisingly loud. The room had remarkable acoustics.

Narius found a narrow flight of stairs that took him into the basin where he was further shocked to discover that the basin was filled with ankle-deep water. He paused at the top of the stairs. He didn't mind the idea of sloshing through water; he had marched through much worse when he'd served in the Dynasty's infantry. But back then, he had been a soldier wearing a combat uniform. He hated the idea of ruining his expensive boots.

Trevik laughed at his hesitation. "I am so sorry, Your Strength. I should have warned you ahead of time. In Maotoan culture, it is a sign of great respect to share the ocean's blessing with your guests. Cosena, please help our guest."

Before Narius could object, Cosena sashayed over to him. With a grin and a hooded look, she knelt at his feet, apparently not caring that her dress was now soaking up the water. She carefully untied his boots and tugged them free. Then she gently rolled his pants halfway to his knees. Narius resisted the urge to squirm, especially as her fingers brushed his bare calves. She looked up at him as she worked, her grin spreading ever so slightly.

Narius's body tensed. He wanted nothing more than to pull his feet away from her. This wasn't right—not the way her touch lingered, not the obviously seductive looks she was shooting him. There was friendly, but this went far beyond that. But what could he do? If he pulled away, it could be perceived as an insult and he couldn't do that. Not if they wanted to find out what was happening on the island. So he ground his teeth together and hoped she'd finish soon.

Once she was done, Cosena walked back to her place at the table. Narius took a steadying breath. He'd have to parse what had just happened later. For now, he couldn't hold up the feast, so he stepped down into the water.

A cheer erupted around him, one that spread through the rest of the guests. Narius jumped at the outburst. He hadn't realized how quiet the room had become while Cosena had helped him. But soon the shout died away and the conversation picked up again. Trevik motioned for Narius to take a seat next to him, with Paine seated further down the table. Paine swept into place, seemingly unconcerned that his robes were dragging in the water. Narius had to hide a smile of his own. He suspected that Paine was quietly seething.

As soon as they were seated, servers made their way through the crowded room, carrying trays of fish, fruit, and other delicacies from Maotoa. For the next hour, they kept Narius's plate filled while they brought goblet after goblet of wines and other liquors, although Narius was careful not to drink too much. He'd need his wits about him.

During the dinner, he and Trevik discussed nothing of any real importance. The viceroy mostly seemed interested in regaling Narius with stories of his many hunting and fishing trips. He had so many of them that Narius seriously wondered when Trevik had time to do any governing. The few times he tried to speak to Pillara, mostly to ask about her husband's absence, she smiled demurely. For some reason, Cosena seemed to content herself with a whispered conversation with Paine. His friend seemed completely enraptured by what she had to say, to the point that Paine never looked in Narius's direction. But Cosena did, stealing glances in his direction with a coy smile. He fought to keep from grimacing in return.

After too many courses to count, Trevik stood and waved his hands. The rowdy conversations went quiet, and Trevik beamed at the guests.

"My friends, I am so pleased that you could all be here for this momentous occasion." Trevik's voice filled the room even though he spoke normally. "It has been many years since our island has been graced by our king, and we are so happy that King Narius is here with us tonight!"

A raucous cheer went up but died quickly. Narius sat up a little taller and smiled at the surrounding tables. But no one paid attention to him. He forced himself to keep smiling. This was Trevik's party. He could be the center of attention. But the atmosphere felt forced, almost like a theatrical presentation.

"His presence alone would make tonight truly historic. But this feast is more than just us welcoming the Dynasty's king. Many of you have likely heard whispers about a rivalry between myself and Ethnarch Uaso. Indeed, many of you may have not only noticed his absence here tonight, but that he has been unavailable for the past two weeks."

That caught Narius's attention. He sat up, his eyes narrowing. At least they'd finally have answers about Uaso's recent silence.

"Many of you have doubted the reports from the palace that he has taken sick. And well you should! For the truth is this: Ethnarch Uaso is dead."

Whispers rippled through the room. Narius frowned, trying to gauge what he heard. Not anger. Not fear either. Anticipation?

"He is dead by my hand," Trevik said.

Paine's head snapped around and he met Narius's gaze with wide eyes. Narius's heart stuttered and he fought to keep his expression neutral. He couldn't react, not even after hearing such shocking news. Trevik had murdered Uaso? And this was the first they had heard of it? The crowd, surprisingly, didn't grow any louder, even though the whispering continued.

"The ethnarch insulted my honor, and I challenged him to a duel. This ended with his death, run through by my sword." Trevik's voice was calm and even, as if he was describing the weather. "I regret that our relationship came to that end, but Uaso had dishonored me for months with vile accusations that needed a firm response. And a firm response he has received."

Narius's mind tumbled through how he should respond. Duels were legal, though rare. He himself traveled with a Swordbound should he need to duel someone. But the Dynasty's viceroy dueling an ethnarch? Had such a thing ever happened in the Dynasty's history?

The whispers of the guest crescendoed, and Trevik's gaze swept over them, his face seemingly chiseled from stone.

Once the noise died down, Trevik raised a hand. "But this is not all that has happened. Just last week, Pillara consented to be my wife."

The whispering silenced. Ice formed in the middle of Narius's chest, bleeding into his limbs. They were married? He looked over at Pillara, who beamed at Trevik.

"Which means, by ancient custom and rite, I am now not only the viceroy of Maotoa, but its ethnarch as well," Trevik said.

That made no sense! Trevik couldn't be ethnarch! He wasn't a native Maotoan and—

The room erupted in cheers. The guests pounded on the tables and roared their approval. Narius looked around, stunned. Apparently the technicality of Trevik's race didn't matter to the people in this room. How would the rest of Maotoa react?

"So tonight is not just a feast celebrating our esteemed guest." Trevik gestured toward Narius. "I am most pleased that he is here to celebrate my new marriage!"

More cheers, enough that Narius worried he'd be deafened. Narius felt like he was being dragged along by an inescapable tide, swept into events he couldn't control or understand. He desperately wished that more members of his council were here, if only to figure out what his next steps should be. Or, at the least, Everys. Maybe she would have been able to navigate everything that had happened.

"So let us celebrate our island's new future, my friends!" Trevik shouted, raising a glass. "For if water is strength, then Maotoa is unbreakable!"

The assembled guests echoed the toast in a thunderous shout. Narius raised his glass automatically but didn't say anything. Instead, he met Paine's gaze and the two exchanged an unspoken question. What new crisis had they walked into?

37

Narius turned fitfully in his bed, the strange thoughts prompted by the night's feast dogging him through the hours. Uaso murdered? Trevik the new ethnarch? What would any of that mean for the Dynasty?

He flipped onto his back and threw off the thin blanket that covered him. In many ways, his room was tranquil and ideal for sleeping. A breeze wafted in from the open window, not enough to truly cool the room, but enough to soothe him. And the gentle burble of the water spilling over in the fountain would normally have been a nice lullaby. But Narius's jangled nerves simply wouldn't settle.

Not for the first time, he wished Everys was with him. She probably wouldn't have understood all the political intricacies, but her keen mind would've dissected the situation in ways other people wouldn't have seen. Cosena might not have been so brazen if his wife was here. And just sharing the same bed with Everys would have been enough to calm him.

Halfway through Fourth Watch, the faintest hint of lavender on the wind, chased by something sweet and enticing, caught his attention. Narius took a deep breath, savoring the scent. There was something familiar about it, a memory that sent prickles dancing across his skin. A smile tickled his lips, and he rolled over, suddenly feeling more relaxed. He didn't know what that smell was, but it was just what he needed. And the way the sound of burbling water washed over him, he melted into the mattress and...

The softest hint of singing flowed over him, a sweet, feminine voice. A bare whisper, so quiet that at first, he thought he imagined it. But as the sound persisted, he thought that maybe it was the sound of someone singing outside the palace, echoes of the notes drifting in on the night breeze. But no, the voice was too distinct. Although he didn't understand what the singer was saying, her words, a phrase repeated over and over, were too clear to be coming from a distance. Whoever was singing was... was...

She had to be inside his room.

Narius sat up in bed and started at the shadowy figure perched on the edge of the fountain. She trailed a hand in the water, her voice dropping to a hum that carried the melody of her song.

"Good evening, Your Strength," she whispered, and her silky voice sent a shiver skittering down Narius's spine.

"Cosena?" he asked.

The woman rose and stepped into the meager light. She had changed from her feast attire into a series of gauzy veils that swished and swirled as she moved.

Sweat prickled Narius's brow. How had she gotten into his room without the guards noticing? He took a breath to shout for Zar or whoever was on duty, only to inhale that cloying scent. As the sweet fragrance flooded his mind, he slumped back in bed.

"I hope you don't mind me visiting you like this." She settled on the edge of his bed, her voice a melodic whisper. "We didn't have much of a chance to speak at the feast, and I felt there was much we have to discuss."

"Th-there is?" Narius asked.

She gestured back toward the fountain. "Did you know that the Water Bearer originally belonged to us?"

What? He shook his head. She was here to talk theology?

"It's true," she said. "She has been this island's patron for centuries. Our ancestors say the Bearer gave Maotoans dominion over all waters. Not just those of your Blood Sea or the Dalark Channel, but any lake or river. We carried her with us as we left our island in search of richer lands. When we met your ancestors in the old city of Elregan, they became enamored with her and adopted her into your pantheon."

Was that true? Narius had no idea. In the moment, he didn't much care.

"But we do not mind the relationship that was forged between your Perfected Warrior and the Water Bearer. Just as Maotoa shares her waters, we share our goddess."

Narius nearly snorted at that. The Maotoans' history was filled with examples of them not sharing. For many centuries, Maotoa was synonymous with piracy and coastal raiders.

Cosena cocked her head at him and smiled. "Tell me, Your Strength, do you remember the day we met?"

This again? She had already asked about that mask? He nodded. "Of course. You gave me the mask."

She chuckled, a throaty sound. "That's all you remember? You don't remember what you said to your mother?"

Narius frowned, wracking his brain. Even with the prompt of the mask and her question, so many of those memories were a pleasant, tingly haze that wrapped him in a cocoon.

"I'm not offended. I know how quickly Innana pulled you into her orbit." Cosena's voice didn't carry any bitterness. "But I remember. My father introduced me to you and your parents, and then you turned to your mother and told her that you thought I was the prettiest woman you had ever seen and that one day, you would marry me."

Had he? He recognized some truth in what she had said. When they'd met, he had barely emerged from childhood and she had seemed so exotic, so overwhelming in her sophistication and grace. Perhaps he had said that at one point, only to forget his childish plans when he met Innana.

"And when I heard that Viara had left you, that you searched for a new wife to rule at your side... Oh, Narius, how I begged my father to let me travel to Bastion and remind you of what you had said." Cosena shifted and crawled across the bed toward him. "My father wouldn't permit it. But if he had, I would have offered myself to you. I would have been your wife in ways that Viara had never been."

She was at his knees, and a wave of heat crested over him. He was all too aware of how her every movement rippled through the bed to him, how her presence loomed next to him, a consuming hunger carried on that sweet scent of lavender and now citrus as well.

"And I still can be," she whispered. "I would be your wife tonight and for the rest of your life if you would have me."

"Wh-what?" His tongue felt sluggish, and he had trouble speaking.

"We heard of the offer you made to Tirigian, to take Innana as your bride for the sake of peace. Such nobility, but I would expect nothing less of you, dear Narius." Her breath tickled his cheek. "If you were to marry me as well, you could gain so much."

"Oh?" His arms ached to do something. Embrace her. Push her from his side.

She leaned in close, the purr of her voice overwhelming him. "Don't you know how we Maotoans have governed ourselves? We call our ruler the Maragnat, only it is not a solitary role. No, it is invested in a husband and wife. That is how Trevik has become ethnarch. By marrying my mother, he has become part of the Maragnat and now rules with her."

That was one puzzle solved, but in the moment, it was the furthest thing from his mind.

"And when my mother and new father pass beyond to the depths of shadows, I and my spouse will inherit the Maragnat. By marrying me, sweet Narius, you would become the legitimate ruler of Maotoa. And the people of this island would welcome you. Think of it: generations of hostility erased in an instant."

That did sound nice. But he was finding it more and more difficult to think. Her hands roamed across his chest, trailing warring heat and chills in her touch's wake.

"But more than that. Any child you and I have would inherit the Maragnat. Think of it: your heirs, ruling from both Bastion and Dreah. The Dynasty securely in the hands of your family for who knows how many generations. This is what I offer you, Narius. That... and myself."

And she kissed him, hungrily and deeply, her arms snaking around him.

Narius could scarcely believe it. At first, he was too shocked to respond, but then his body did. Overwhelmed by the intoxicating aroma, her alluring voice, her sheer presence, he kissed her back, pulling her closer. By all the weapons in the Warrior's Arsenal, this felt good. The old memories of his childhood crush screamed back into his mind. Cosena would make a formidable consort, and he would be the envy of all the nobles. With her and...

Everys. The thought of his wife sliced through his desire. He swallowed hard and pulled back, disentangling her from his arms.

"Wh-what of..." He swallowed, trying to force his thoughts into some semblance of order. "What of Everys?"

Cosena chuckled, a throaty sound. "I don't relish the thought of sharing you, dearest. But who am I to object? I know you love your queen. That is clear to everyone. Bring as many queens and consorts into the palace as you wish. I just know that when the time comes, you will be spending most of your nights in my bed."

She punctuated that statement with another deep kiss, one that drew Narius in. Her hands roamed down his arms, across his chest, and his responded in kind, pulling her close, rolling her onto her back so he could...

A cold gust of air swept through the room. Narius gasped as it sliced down his back, and Cosena cried out as well. Narius turned toward the open window, surprised at the frigidity. He would have expected freezing wind like that in the Ixactl Highlands or maybe the Cold Light's forests. Not in Maotoa. What had caused...?

A shadowy figure peeked through his window, only to drop away.

Narius bolted out of bed and rushed to the window. He looked out, trying to catch a glimpse of whoever that had been, but there was no sign. And his room was very high up in the palace. As near as he could tell, there was no safe way for whoever that was to drop down safely. Had he imagined it? That blast of cold air had been real enough.

"Narius? Come back to bed, my love," Cosena said. "Let me show you everything I offer."

He turned back to her, but as he did, he spotted smoke rising from the fountain's edge. He frowned. What was that?

Cosena called his name, but he walked to the fountain. Half a dozen small white cups floated in the water, wisps of smoke drifting up from them. He fished one of them out and gave it a closer look. Brown ash coated the bottom of the cup. He ran a finger through it, rubbed it against his thumb, then took an experimental sniff. It smelled of lavender and citrus.

Raw desire sliced through him, so suddenly that his body shuddered. He wanted to leap onto the bed, gather Cosena into his arms, and—

Narius stumbled backward, shaking his head to dislodge the animalistic thoughts. He took several ragged breaths, hoping that his racing heart would calm. He turned back to the bed, where Cosena had sat up, clutching his sheets to her chest.

"Narius?" she asked, her tone uncertain.

He held up the cup. "What is this?"

"A blend of incense to help set the mood," she said with a coy smile. "I wanted tonight to be special."

That was certainly one word to describe it. Anger sluiced through him, the heat slicing through any lingering desire he might have felt. His thoughts cleared, and for a brief moment, he considered summoning Zar and having her arrested. But that would only cause a diplomatic incident. So he tossed the cup back into the fountain.

"I think it would be wise for you to leave, Cosena." He fought against his waning desire to say the words.

Her eyes narrowed, and her gaze sharpened. But then she smiled, a smirk that was both predatory and seductive. A shiver wormed through him, and he almost told her to stay. But then she slid out of bed and crossed over to him. He took an involuntary step back, if only to keep himself from doing something he knew he'd regret.

"As you wish, Your Strength," she said. "But my offer still stands. And I urge you to take it. With me as your consort, you could achieve so many of your dreams. Without me... I worry what will come of you."

A threat? On the surface, it seemed like an empty one, given that she wasn't a warrior on a battlefield. But he still felt a pang of unease twist in his stomach.

"And besides, I know how much you'd enjoy having me," she added in a sultry whisper.

She lunged forward, kissing him once again, so fast he couldn't react. But this one felt like she was punctuating her threat. She sauntered away from him, running a hand along his chest, before striding out the door.

Narius groaned. He didn't know who was standing watch outside his door, but his guards would talk. How could they not, with the ethnarch's daughter leaving his quarters dressed like that? But there was nothing he could do about it, so he returned to bed, hoping that he'd be able to at least get a little bit of sleep. Because he knew the morning would be painful, especially when Paine learned of what happened.

38

Everys stretched, the last vestiges of sleep refusing to completely release her. As much as she hated sleeping without Narius next to her, she had to admit that she hadn't slept so soundly in weeks. But now that the sunlight streamed across her bed, she knew she had to get up and get ready.

Once she was dressed, she emerged from her hut. Rewether and Kevtho fell into step with her, the guard commander indicating where she could find breakfast, a large pavilion with a roof made out of woven brown fibers standing on thick wooden poles. As they walked, Everys noticed the many Plissk families emerging from their own huts and heading for the same pavilion. She frowned when she heard a high-pitched whine in the distance. She glanced around until she found the source: a flock of press drones darted back and forth just outside of the Oasis.

When Rewether noticed where she was looking, he nodded grimly. "They started up just before First Watch."

"Why are they here?" Everys asked.

Kevtho laughed. "The first queen to ever attend a Naming Day at the Plissk Sanctuary Oasis? Can't think why that would be newsworthy."

A fair point, but it rankled her that the press would invade Trule's family's special moment.

If Trule was bothered, she didn't let on. When the maid saw Everys enter the pavilion, she hopped to her feet and waved her over. Everys made her way over to the tables where she was immediately swamped by more members of Trule's extended family. More introductions, more faces she would struggle to remember. But at the same time, she was filled with warmth and laughter. Trule's family was clearly excited for all of them to be there, and it was hard not to be caught up in it.

Trule led her over to a long table covered with bowls of food. Some Everys recognized: large fruits, skewers of meat, jugs of water. Others took her by surprise. There was a bowl of wriggling grubs, another that was filled with translucent wings, and still another of what appeared to be half-rotten orange berries as big as her thumb.

"It's all right, Blessed," Trule whispered. "No one will be offended if you don't try the food."

That gentle permission, though, prompted Everys to take at least a small sample of everything. She wouldn't want to offend anyone, especially not after they had shown her such hospitality and welcome.

Everys was seated next to Trule's great-grandfather, a wizened man with bleached scales and rheumy eyes, and yet somehow, Everys felt like he saw her clearer than anyone. He didn't say much throughout breakfast, but she knew that this was an honor, so she treated him with the deference she would show a king or ethnarch. Much to her surprise, she found that she liked most of the food she had taken. The wings carried a hot spice that caused her eyes to water but she thoroughly enjoyed. The rotten fruit was pungent and slimy, and she only ate one of them.

After an hour, the laughter and conversation faded. A Plissk woman, dressed in elaborate robes with alternating stripes of brown and white, clambered up on a platform in the middle of the pavilion. She carried a thick walking stick that she pounded on the stage.

"Dear families, honored guests, and of course, our most blessed Queen Everys, we welcome you to the Plissk Sanctuary Oasis. I am Keeper of this Oasis. A dozen of our young people have been chosen to submerge themselves in these sacred waters and emerge as full-fledged members of our society with names that befit their status." Her voice carried surprisingly well, a rich alto that felt like warm honey. "At this time, we will have the families come forward to receive their initial anointing."

A murmur of movement rippled through the pavilion. No one spoke, but twelve groups of three people moved and formed a ring around the stage. Everys recognized Trule's parents and sister among them.

The Keeper pulled a gourd from a fold in her robes and broke it over the end of her staff, a thick blue liquid seeping down the wooden shaft. That done, she flicked the staff over the gathered families, droplets of the liquid spattering across them. As she did this, she danced and sang in the Plissk native language. Her song and movements were languid, flowing, almost like water gently lapping against a shore. Everys wanted to ask someone to translate for her, but when she turned to Trule, her maid's expression was so rapt and joyous, she kept her question to herself. Comprehension would have to wait.

Once the ceremony was done, the Keeper swept her staff toward the waters. "Now let us begin!"

With a rustle, the gathered Plissk rose in unison and filed toward the waters. They didn't speak, but their faces lit with a joy that once again seeped deeply into Everys's heart and added a spring to her step. Kevtho chuckled beside her, and they exchanged a smile.

But once they stepped out of the pavilion, angry shouts pierced the joyful silence. Everys craned her neck to see where the noise was coming from. A long line of people stood just outside the Oasis's perimeter, pumping their fists in the air and shouting. At first, Everys thought they might be Plissk, but then she realized that all of them were wearing Dunestrider garb.

"Oh no," Kevtho whispered.

"What's going on?" she asked.

He looked stricken. "The question of who owns this Oasis is... controversial, Blessed. There have been confrontations about it in the past. They're probably here because... well..."

Everys winced. They were here because of her. Her presence had brought the press drones. That gave them a wider audience for their protest.

The Plissk procession came to a halt. A disgruntled murmur swept through the crowd, and Everys could feel the hostility boiling off them. She couldn't blame them. She knew how much Trule had been looking forward to this day. For it to be interrupted like this must have stung. But she also recognized the seed that had been planted. If someone didn't do something quickly, this could turn ugly.

She started forward, struggling to move quickly across the sand, but she soon reached the Keeper. The older woman was conferring with a number of young men, all of whom were armed with clubs and a few flechette throwers.

"Blessed?" the Keeper said as she approached. "I am sorry that we are delayed, but we are discussing how best to proceed."

Everys waved away her apology. "Would it help if I talk to them?"

The Keeper's eyes widened, and her escorts hissed. "That is unwise, Blessed. We have seen these fanatics surround our Oasis many times. They do not listen to reason and will likely only become more agitated if they are indulged."

"That may have been the case in the past, but perhaps they will respond better if they speak with the Dynasty's queen." Everys then caught the unintended condescension in her words. "No offense, Keeper."

The Plissk exchanged uncertain looks. But then Trule stepped forward, causing Everys to jump. She hadn't realized that the maid had followed her.

"Please, Keeper," Trule said. "Everys has performed wonders in her time as queen. I have no doubt we will see another today."

Everys blushed at Trule's words, but she stood straighter, trying to project a regal aura.

After thinking about it, the Keeper gestured toward the gathered protesters. Everys took a deep breath and headed for the line.

As she approached them, Everys took a moment to catalog what she was facing. There had to be at least two hundred Dunestriders spread out along a dune overlooking the Oasis. Like the Plissk she had seen in the Oasis, many of them were armed with clubs, swords, and flechette throwers. If this situation turned violent, she suspected it would be a bloody fight. But she wasn't going to allow that to happen.

Six Dunestriders left the line and met her at the bottom of the dune. She didn't like that; it left the majority of their friends on the high ground, and she knew how dangerous that could be. But she forced herself to remain calm, her face impassive, as they approached.

"See this, brethren?" one of them shouted to the others. "The Plissk are so frightened they sent the queen to speak to us!"

Laughter rippled through the Dunestrider ranks. Kevtho stiffened, his hand darting to his sword. Everys motioned for him to stand down.

"There is no need for such hostility." Thankfully, her voice didn't betray her nervousness. "I would know who I am speaking to."

The Dunestrider who had spoken pounded himself on the chest. "I am Elenc of the Deep Mesa, and we are those who remain faithful to our ways. Unlike your neutered pet there."

Once again, Kevtho started to react, but Everys pierced him with a glare. He clamped his mouth shut and took a step back.

"You would do wise to treat my Swordbound with respect, Elenc," Everys said. "I know he is an honorable man, whereas you and your friends seem to take great pride in yelling at children."

Elenc's mouth snapped shut and Everys felt a ripple of pride. If she could keep him off-balance, maybe she could manage him better.

"Say what you came to say, Blessed." Elenc spat her title like it tasted bad. "We will weigh your words against the blood in this sand and see if it is enough."

"I understand there is some dispute over who owns this Oasis—"

Elenc laughed. "There is no dispute except the one the Plissk manufactured. Everyone knows this Oasis belongs to the Dunestriders! We were the first to discover it, the first to use it. It only became sacred to the Plissk because we had it!"

Everys frowned. That didn't make sense to her. If the Dunestriders didn't live in the Kronin Desert while the Plissk did, how would the Dunestriders have discovered this Oasis first? She turned to Kevtho.

"Is that true?" she whispered.

He grimaced. "That's how we understand the history. I suspect the Plissk would see things differently."

They probably would, but Everys didn't have time for a history debate. So she turned back to Elenc.

"That is a claim that I can't evaluate because I do not know your history well enough. This is what I propose: when I return to Bastion, I will speak with the Plissk and Dunestrider ethnarchs. Perhaps there is a compromise that can be reached."

"There is no compromising with those savages!" Elenc said. "No, if you wish to find resolution to this situation, then you will do what you have done for the Cold Light and the Ixactl. You returned the Hearth. You returned the *ma-se-kranna*. You will return the Oasis to us now. We will secure it from further defilement!"

Everys stared at him, shock rippling through her. But the other Dunestriders hooted and cheered, agreeing with what Elenc had said.

"I cannot agree to do that," she said. "In the cases you mentioned, there was no dispute over who those objects belonged to. The Hearth belongs to the Cold Light, the *ma-se-kranna* to the Ixactl. But this Oasis is claimed by both you and the Plissk. Sorting through those competing claims will take time. I simply ask that we not disrupt this sacred day and find a peaceful solution."

Elenc shook his head. "We have waited for the Dynasty to do the right thing for generations! We have waited and waited for you to correct this mistake and you have not. So no, Blessed, we will not back down. We will not wait any longer. And if you are not willing to give us what is ours, we will take it. Now!"

He raised a fist, and a war cry went up from the gathered Dunestriders. They brandished their weapons, and their shouts grew louder and louder.

Kevtho and Rewether quickly stepped between Everys and Elenc, their weapons raised. But the Dunestrider leader laughed at them.

"You will not stop us. But don't worry, traitor, we will not hurt the pretty queen. No, she will be our honored 'guest' until her husband does what is right." He ripped a gun from his holster and raised it in the air, then shouted something in what Everys assumed was the Dunestrider language.

With a roar, the Dunestriders charged down the hill. Everys stumbled backward, her feet slipping in the sand. Kevtho and Rewether opened fire, as did her other guards, but it was clear that they were going to be overwhelmed at any moment.

"Please!" Everys shouted. "We don't have to do this! We can talk this through. We can—"

Engines roared in the distance. Transports painted with desert camouflage raced over some of the surrounding dunes, barreling into the line of Dunestrider protesters. Some of the transports had weapons mounted on their backs, and these opened fire, mowing down the advancing Dunestriders. The rest pulled to a halt in the sand and soldiers poured out, weapons up and firing. The Dunestrider charge broke and the protesters started to flee, but the soldiers chased them and shot them in the back as they ran.

Everys winced at the bloodshed. But when she looked back at the Oasis, more military vehicles had pulled into the surrounding tree line, disgorging soldiers there as well. That seemed like overkill, but then, she had been threatened with violence. The soldiers' commander was likely being overly cautious. Still, she'd have to speak with him before this turned even more violent.

"Blessed, we have a problem," Rewether hissed at her.

"Not anymore, thankfully," she said. "Thank the Warrior that these soldiers were nearby."

"That's just it, Blessed," Rewether said. "According to my intel, there weren't supposed to be any troops near the Oasis today at the request of the Plissk ethnarch. I don't know who these troops are."

Everys stared at him. In spite of the desert heat, ice pooled in her stomach.

But before she could say anything, another transport pulled up next to her. The front door opened and a middle-aged man in military fatigues slid out. His hair was black but salted with white, and he had a stylishly trimmed full beard. When his eyes landed on Everys, though, she recognized the copper glint in the desert sun.

"Hello, Blessed," Duke Brencis said through a snarl. "So good to see you again."

39

Narius looked out the window over the Maotoan palace grounds, trying to process everything that he had learned and experienced over the past day. Uaso's death, Trevik's new marriage, and Cosena's brazen attempt at seduction. He knew things in Maotoa would be chaotic, but this would be enough to cow the god who carried that name.

The door behind him opened, and he heard the swish of robes. He nodded and turned. Sure enough, Paine stood attentively near the door.

"Your Strength?" Paine asked, his voice quiet and respectful. "You summoned me?"

"I did."

"I assume this is about what we learned at the feast."

"More than that. Cosena was here last night. In my room. She offered herself to me, both for the night and as my wife."

Paine's brow quirked upward. "Indeed."

Paine walked a slow, tight circle in the room, his head bowed, a slight frown pinching his brow. Narius allowed him a few moments to process the information before he motioned for him to share his thoughts.

"For starters, we have the situation with Ethnarch Uaso. An unprecedented situation to be sure," Paine said. "But my initial thought is that Trevik hasn't done anything wrong."

Narius frowned. "What do you mean?"

"Let us begin with the duel that ended Uaso's life. If this was indeed a properly executed duel as Trevik suggests, there would be witnesses and proper documentation," Paine said. "We could question the legitimacy of the duel, but I suspect he has all of this at the ready should we ask."

"Convenient."

Paine shrugged. "Him having the evidence will not be proof that it is falsified."

That was unfortunately true. And the fact that Trevik spoke of it so openly indicated whatever evidence he had was genuine or could pass as such.

"So do I challenge the duel's legitimacy?" Narius asked.

"That is certainly an option." Paine's tone made it clear he didn't think it was a good one. "But given the reaction we just heard to the news of Uaso's death and the strategic necessity of Maotoa, it might not be wise."

Narius grunted. Unfortunately, that all made sense. And a true investigation would take time they might not have.

"As for Trevik's claim to the Maragnat, I believe that could be legitimate as well. I did some research last night, and—"

"Cosena explained it to me. By marrying Pillara, Trevik has a legitimate claim to the Maragnat." As would his potential children with Cosena, but he didn't share that bit of data.

"Ah." Paine's gaze sharpened. "Then I'm sure you realize that we don't have grounds to challenge that either."

Narius groaned. "There's going to be a revolt in the Ethnarch Parliament when this news reaches them."

"That may not be the case either, Your Strength. This situation is unique within the Dynasty. None of the other ethnarchs have had to deal with a viceroy for one hundred fifty years. And no other ethnarch shares power with their spouse the way the Maotoans do. While some aspects of these circumstances are suspicious, our position in Maotoa may be stronger with Trevik as ethnarch. And it could be even more so if..." Paine's voice trailed off and he scowled.

Narius sucked in a sharp breath. He suspected he knew what Paine was going to say, but he wanted him to actually say it. "Go on."

Paine's scowl deepened, but then he squared his shoulders and met Narius's gaze. "Our position could be even stronger if you would marry Cosena."

And there it was. Narius immediately shook his head. "Absolutely not. That's not an option."

"Why not? You made a similar offer to Princess Innana not long ago—"

"An offer made in the heat of the moment!"

"—and we still have the situation with Viara to contend with. While this is an unexpected turn of events, we would be fools to turn it down." Paine took a step closer to him. "Your Strength—Narius—think of what this would accomplish. Maotoa has always chafed under the Dynasty's control. But if you were to marry the Maragnat's daughter? Suddenly what once was a renegade holding would be fiercely loyal to you. You would be family with Trevik and Pillara. When they pass, you would be the Maragnat with Cosena, as would a child you have with her. And if you were to marry Viara and Innana as well? Stronger ties with the nobility, peace with Dalark. I don't understand why you won't consider any of that as a possibility."

"Because I don't want any more wives!" Narius said. "Blunted Sword and Tarnished Breastplate, why is that so hard to understand? I love Everys too much to risk my relationship by bringing any of those women into the palace."

Paine started to object, but Narius didn't let him.

"Do you really think Viara would content herself to stay in whatever role we devise for her? She'd constantly be working to undermine Everys at every turn. And Innana? You saw how miserable she made me during our brief engagement. And Cosena? Truth be told, Paine, there's something unsettling about that woman. Why would I willingly subject myself and the woman I love to any of that?"

Paine waited a few moments, his expression neutral, before he answered, "Because you're the king. And that means you have to make sacrifices and do what's best for the Dynasty."

Narius scoffed, but Paine took several more steps forward.

"That's been true for every one of the Dynasty's kings, Your Strength. I know you learned the same stories that I did. Think of King Heronus, who had to set aside his personal hatred of the Dalark Imperium so they could destroy Nekek the Bright. Think of Albanon, who had to marry into the Dwellin family to secure peace for the Dynasty. Think of how Pellio had to leave aside his studies and theories and dirty his hands during the Colonial Uprisings. Think how Vetranio had to content himself with conquering only the Cold Light instead of crossing the Spineridge into Rioka like he first planned. Think of how your own father—"

But then Paine's eyes widened, and he clamped his mouth shut. Narius frowned. What was he going to say? How had his father sacrificed? He was aware of all of the examples Paine had mentioned, but what had Father done?

"Paine?" he prompted, injecting some steel into his voice to make it clear he wasn't actually asking.

Paine sighed. "Forgive me, Your Strength. I shouldn't have—"

"Paine!"

The vizier winced, then hung his head. "I don't know this for sure, but my predecessor, Vizier Malcedon, left records suggesting that at one point, your father was considering disinheriting both you and Quartus in favor of another child he hoped to have with your mother."

He what? Narius felt like he might collapse. All of this was too much. Much too much. He could understand why Father would have wanted to disinherit Quartus. His brother had always been a vain pleasure-seeker with no sense of duty. But why him?

"Why?" The question slipped out of Narius's mouth.

"According to Malcedon's notes, King Girai felt that you weren't strong enough to be king. You were too sentimental, too emotional. Too much of a dreamer and not enough of a realist. Too soft for the crown."

Each word stung, especially as Narius saw the truth of what Paine was saying. He had always suspected that Father had disapproved of him. He was always so harsh, so exacting. But he would have hoped that, if Father saw what he had accomplished during his reign, he might have been proud.

"But thank Chance and Chaos and all the gods, he didn't act on those desires," Paine said. "His council convinced him that doing so would be unwise."

"Are you really comparing my desire to only be married to Everys to... to conquering other nations? To not disowning my own children? To behaving in such monstrous ways?"

"Not at all," Paine said. "Your desires, unlike those of your predecessors, are noble. I doubt that anyone in the Dynasty would fault you. But you are the king, Your Strength. Sometimes, regrettably, what you want is immaterial. Even inconvenient. Sometimes you have to set aside—"

"But why? Why is this the only way?" Narius said. "Why am I always the one who has to sacrifice?"

Paine gaped at him, his mouth slack.

"Is that really what you think?" Paine asked. "That you are the only one who has had to give up something for the sake of the greater good? You don't think that I've had to sacrifice? Or the others on your council? What of all who have died on the battlefield to bring us to this point?

"Or what about the sacrifices you would demand others make right now? Say you stubbornly refuse to marry Innana or Viara or even Cosena now. What happens then? We go to war with Dalark? Or face a civil war? How many lives would be thrown away just so you can be happy with your Siporan wife? Why are you so opposed to this?"

Narius stared at Paine. He had never seen the vizier so angry before. And yes, what Paine said made sense. He knew the safer course would be to do as Paine suggested. Marry Innana. Remarry Viara. Maybe even bring Cosena into the family. That would solve many of the short-term crises they were facing. But in his heart of hearts, he knew. He knew he couldn't do it. Not to himself. Not to Everys. Not to anyone.

"Because it isn't fair to any of us! Not to any of those potential wives, our families, or any of us! Think about it. All we would be doing with any of these women is using them as pawns at best or hostages at worst. We force Viara into another loveless marriage, making both of us miserable. Or Innana? Tearing her away from her family and her homeland on the possibility of peace? Or even Cosena! More political maneuvering, using people as a means to an end! How is that fair to any of us?

"And more than that! I made a promise to Everys and to myself that she would be my only wife! I promised her that. And if I break my word just for political gain, what does that make me? Does that make me worthy of being king? No! If anything, it proves what a horrible person I am. I can't do that to Everys. I simply cannot do that to the woman I love."

Not just Everys, though. What of the Singularity? Narius's mouth snapped shut at the thought. He didn't know what He might think of these sacrifices and compromises. And if Narius was intending to live by His mandates, shouldn't that matter too? But he couldn't bring himself to mention that to Paine.

Paine looked ready to object, but then he sighed heavily.

"I understand what you're saying, Your Strength. And you're right. But since when has the Dynasty concerned itself with what's fair?"

"Maybe we should start," Narius said.

Paine looked like he was going to object, but then his face turned stony. He bowed at the waist. "Then I bid you the gods' blessings on that new Dynasty," Paine whispered. "Because I fear none of us may see it come to fruition."

40

Duke Brencis sneered at Everys. "Have you missed me, Blessed?"

Everys glowered back at him, and she considered using one of the beads on her bracelet. She didn't care if there were witnesses. This man deserved to be set on fire through toratropic magic. She would gladly suffer any rebuke to see him burn. He had tried to kill both Narius and her. He was fomenting revolution. And now, he had invaded this sacred ceremony. But no, she couldn't risk it. She might kill him, but his troops would likely take revenge on the Plissk. She'd have to wait for a better opportunity.

Everyone had been herded together near the guest huts. Her guards had been searched and disarmed, forced to sit with the rest of the hostages. And now Brencis strutted back and forth, clearly enjoying the fear that flowed through the Oasis.

Thankfully, he seemed completely focused on her. His troops had seated her in front of everyone else, with her between Brencis's troops and the Plissk families. She didn't mind that at all. If she could give them even that little bit of cover, it was worth it. But she needed to keep Brencis's focus on her.

She took a moment to assess him. When she had known Brencis in the palace, he had shown his age. But his time on the run had transformed him. He was in better shape, the gut that had hung over his belt gone, and his hair had been cut short. Most citizens would see him as the perfect soldier, the epitome of what the Dynasty produced. Everys thought otherwise.

"Give me a weapon, Brencis," she said. "Let's see if I miss you then."

He paused in his pacing and then laughed. His soldiers joined in.

"Such bravado! Such confidence! And so misplaced. Remember, you are far from any help. Even if soldiers loyal to your husband are scrambling right now, they won't arrive for at least an hour. More than enough time for me to kill you." He squatted down in front of her and lowered his voice. "Or reveal what you truly are."

Cold sluiced through her. Brencis had seen her use her magic when Narius had almost married Innana. But she quickly calmed herself. His threat was hollow. Many had accused her of being a toratropic mage, but no one had any evidence. He didn't either. Besides, he had been under the influence of some powerful runes that day as well. Any accusation he made could be turned back on him.

So she sat up straighter. "I'm not afraid of you, Brencis. I know what you are. You're a throwback to a more barbaric age. You're the one who is frightened of what my husband is—"

Pain exploded across her cheek. She almost fell, shocked at the sting. She worked her jaw, checking to see if she had lost a tooth. Brencis towered over her, his hand pulled back to slap her again.

"Brencis!" Kevtho's shout cut through the cries of the Plissk. "If you touch her again—"

Brencis guffawed. "Spare me, guard. You're in no position to make threats."

"Return my sword and we'll see who the threat is," Kevtho retorted.

That stopped Brencis short. "Oh, the queen's Swordbound. Kevtho, isn't it? Rather foolish of you to take on an entire squad of my men with only a sword."

"I didn't intend to take on them. Just you," Kevtho said.

Brencis's eyes glinted. Everys shifted her weight, suddenly uncomfortable. She didn't like the way the duke's expression had sharpened.

"A duel? You would fight a duel for the queen?" Brencis's voice was dull and flat.

"Not just for her. For the king. For me. For all the soldiers you betrayed with your treason," Kevtho said.

Everys shot a quick look over her shoulder. Kevtho had risen to his knees. Two of Brencis's men trained their weapons on him. But then Brencis gestured, and they relaxed.

"Some would say I'd be a fool to fight a Swordbound. After all, dueling is all you're expected to do, and let's be honest, it's been a while since I've held a blade," Brencis said.

"A convenient excuse, but I see it for what it is: cowardice. You skulk in the shadows, you hide in darkened corners. And now, you attack a peaceful gathering. You, Brencis, are a coward, and I demand you face me to prove your honor."

Once again, the duke's expression hardened, and a pit opened in Everys's stomach. She didn't like what she saw in his eyes. Not a trace of fear. Only confidence.

"Very well. Return his sword and fetch mine. We shall see who the stronger warrior is." His gaze landed on Everys. "And bind her hands. We don't want her leaping into the fray."

The soldiers laughed as if he had made a joke, but Everys's heart stuttered and her breathing turned ragged. If she couldn't move her hands, she wouldn't be able to draw any runes.

Brencis's men sprang into action. Most of them formed a ring that encircled Everys and also shielded her from the other hostages' views. Two dragged Kevtho into the middle of the ring and shoved him into place. Another handed him his blade. Still another jogged forward and handed Brencis one of his own. And one of them wrenched her hands behind her back and locked her wrists in cold metal.

Without taking his eyes off Brencis, Kevtho tore his sword free of its scabbard and twirled it in a lazy circle. He smirked at Brencis, then offered him a mocking bow.

Brencis's face remained stoic as he drew his weapon. Everys frowned. There was something wrong with the sword. Half of it seemed to be the wrong color. The metal closest to the hilt was a dark matte black, scratched up and nicked. The rest was a metallic silver, shining and new.

Kevtho laughed. "Have you fallen on hard times, Duke, that you use such a poor blade?"

The duke didn't answer. Instead, he slashed the air once, then again, and dropped into a ready stance.

Kevtho matched it. They stared at each other, and then Kevtho stomped the ground and launched himself at Brencis.

Everys had a hard time following the flash of blades as the two men danced around each other, stabbing and cutting. Neither seemed able to land a blow. She frowned. While Kevtho was clearly aiming for killing blows, Brencis seemed content to parry and block, occasionally taking a swipe at Kevtho's arms or legs. Kevtho didn't make that easy, dancing and slipping to one side or another.

But then Brencis darted in and sliced the length of his blade along Kevtho's arm. Kevtho hissed and whirled, smacking Brencis's blade with his own. Much to Everys's surprise and delight, Brencis's sword snapped in two.

Kevtho danced out of reach and dropped into a defensive posture. But then he laughed. "Your sword is broken, Duke! I would entertain your surrender."

Brencis smiled sharply. "I will do no such thing."

Everys frowned. Why was Brencis still so confident? He had been effectively disarmed, and yet he didn't appear even a little worried. Instead, he dropped into a defensive stance of his own, holding the broken sword in front of him.

With dawning horror, Everys recognized the sword in Brencis's hand. It hadn't broken. At least, not in this fight. Instead, the shiny half had disguised what it really was.

"*Ur-keleshen*," she whispered.

Brencis glanced in her direction and smirked. That was all the confirmation she needed. Somehow, the duke was holding an *ur-keleshen*, a cursed weapon from Siporan history. The ancient mage-kings had crafted hundreds of these blades, scratching runes on their flats that made whoever held the weapon nigh unstoppable. All the sword needed was blood to activate the runes.

Kevtho's blood, which stained the broken sword's edge, came to life, flowing onto the flat of the blade. It pooled into six runes along the edge. Everys sucked in a startled breath. The original *ur-keleshen*, which was housed in the Dynasty's archives, only had four runes on its edge. So why did this blade have six?

A sickly green energy shimmered along the length of the jagged blade. Then it felt as though light and shadow and color and warmth bled out of the area around Brencis, drawn into his sword. Everys could feel her own strength drawn along, chased by a deep nausea that settled in her bones. She groaned, sure that the blade was somehow going to strangle her life.

The blade grew. Slowly at first, but bit by bit, a new blade emerged, one that seemed forged of darkness itself. It curved up from the broken metal and was soon as long as Kevtho's. A dark liquid dripped from the blade's edge, but it vanished before it could hit the ground. Once the blade was formed, the same green light ran along its edge, only to be reflected in Brencis's eyes. The duke smiled, an unhinged grimace that sent a shiver rippling through Everys.

"Wh-what is that?" Kevtho asked, staggering.

Brencis's answer was a cruel smile. Everys tried to speak, but her throat closed around the words. She wanted to scream for him to surrender, to lay down his sword, to save himself. Because no matter how skilled he was, he wouldn't be able to face *ur-keleshen*. But her voice refused to cooperate.

She had to do something! She fought against her restraints, but the cold metal only tightened around her wrists. Her fingers brushed against the bracelet, but she couldn't get a firm enough grip on the beads to pull one free. Even if she could, she wouldn't be able to draw any runes with her hands behind her back. But she had to do something!

As she agonized over what to do, Kevtho straightened, tightened his grip on his sword, and charged in. Brencis chuckled, ducking and dodging every swipe and thrust, not even bothering to parry. He simply flowed around Kevtho's offense, avoiding each attempted blow, the sick smile on his face never wavering. Everys got the feeling that somehow, Kevtho simply couldn't land a blow, like his attacks just kept missing.

And then Brencis backhanded Kevtho across the face. The guard stumbled and barely got his own blade up in time to parry Brencis's attack. Brencis slashed and stabbed at Kevtho. With each blow Kevtho parried, it seemed like more and more color leeched out of his body. By the time he fell to his knees, he was a shadow of his former self, barely able to hold up his sword.

Brencis, on the other hand, looked stronger and more vital than ever. His body seemed to swell with every clash of their blades. He towered over Kevtho, raining down blow after blow, until he finally battered Kevtho's sword from his hand. Kevtho grasped at it weakly, but Brencis caught him by his hair. Then, with one final sneer, Brencis drove his blade straight through Kevtho's chest.

"No!" Everys finally found her voice. She tried to clamber to her feet, but two of Brencis's soldiers shoved her back down.

Kevtho gasped and stammered, swatting at Brencis weakly. The duke held him there a moment before ripping the sword free. Kevtho grunted and fell forward, catching himself.

He looked toward Everys, his eyes glistening. "Blessed, I'm—"

He choked and shadows swam in his eyes. Horrible black lines crawled from his eyes across his face. Then his mouth opened in a soundless scream. He pitched forward into the sand, thrashing once and then going still.

Brencis stood over his fallen adversary, his chest heaving. He took a rag from his pocket and wiped it across the blade. As he did, the darkened blade vanished, reverting to its broken form.

Then Brencis staggered, clutching at his stomach. He groaned and collapsed to his knees. In spite of herself, Everys winced in sympathy. She recognized a rebuke. She could only imagine how intense it must have been.

But it didn't last nearly long enough. Brencis clambered to his feet. His smile was shaky at first, but as he crossed over to her, it became more and more sure and confident.

"Your people certainly created some interesting weapons." His voice was hoarse. "A pity you don't have the courage to use them."

She didn't know what she could say. Her mind fumbled with words: possible insults, pleas for the hostages, a dozen questions. But before she could settle on one thing, she caught the sound of engines in the distance.

Brencis heard them too. He looked up at the sky, annoyance painted across his face. "Your saviors are drawing near, Blessed. Their reaction time is better than I expected."

Not fast enough, as far as Everys was concerned. She looked past Brencis to Kevtho's body.

He followed her gaze, then chuckled and spun the *ur-keleshen*. "Still, I would have more than enough time to kill you with your people's greatest creation. Wouldn't that be fitting, Everys? A Siporan witch, killed with an *ur-keleshen*."

She tried to keep the shock from her face at hearing Brencis pronounce the blade's name so casually. She drew herself up, blinking back tears. This wasn't how she ever wanted to die, but if she did, she wouldn't give him the satisfaction of crying or begging. She only wished she could see Narius one last time.

"But I won't. Not today, at least. And do you know why?" he whispered.

She didn't trust herself to ask.

"Because my wife asked me to spare you."

His wife? As far as she knew, Brencis wasn't married. What was he talking about?

He nodded, then knelt in front of her. "That's right. I recently took a bride. And it's someone you know. Someone who loves and adores you and your husband as much as me."

Everys gasped. He couldn't have. He didn't mean—

Brencis's smile sharpened. "That's right. Last week, I married Viara. Oh, don't worry. I'll take good care of Narius's child. After all, I wouldn't want anything to happen to him before he can claim his father's throne."

41

Narius felt like he was sulking. As much as he hated to admit it, he was.

This trip had been a failure. Yes, he had traveled all along the Dynasty's western holdings. He had delivered carefully prepared speeches meant to rally support at this crucial juncture in the Dynasty's history. And all of it had been for nothing. This final stop in Maotoa was the perfect punctuation. Uaso dead, Trevik in his place, and Cosena's brazen proposal.

On top of it all, he and Paine had fought. Really argued. He couldn't remember a single other time when that had ever happened. Yes, Paine would push back on Narius's plans, just as a vizier should. But to argue the way they had that morning? Unthinkable. At least, he would have thought so. But here they were. Paine was off consulting with Trevik's staff while Narius ate lunch with Trevik, Pillara, and Cosena on his own.

Well, he shouldn't delay any further. He stepped out of his guest quarters where Melat waited for him. The steward regarded him with a knowing smirk, but then adopted a more respectful expression before leading him and his guards through the palace.

Rather than return to the room where they had feasted the night before, Melat led him to a more intimate dining room. Large landscape paintings of Maotoa lined the walls, highlighting the island's rich beauty. A table that could seat half a dozen people was centered under an elaborate chandelier, one that sparked with carefully shaped crystals. Trevik, Pillara, and Cosena were already seated, engaged in quiet conversation. But their voices died as Narius stepped into the room. Cosena looked down at the table like a scolded child.

Trevik rose. "Your Strength, I am so glad you are joining us today. I think there is much for us to discuss."

"Indeed?" Narius asked.

"I understand you had a visitor in the middle of the night," Trevik said.

Narius looked at Cosena as well. She still wouldn't meet his gaze. Neither would Pillara, but she was too busy glaring at her daughter.

"Please allow me to explain what happened," Trevik said. "We heard the rumors that you were considering revoking Albanon's Compromise and of your offer to Princess Innana. Pillara and I spoke freely of these matters in front of Cosena, and I fear she saw this as an opportunity to act on a childhood infatuation. Please know, we did not send her to your quarters."

Narius frowned. He was inclined to believe Trevik's words given how angry Pillara looked. But there was something off about the viceroy's tone. He sounded like an actor, repeating a line, rather than an abashed stepfather genuinely apologizing for what happened. But he had no evidence to accuse him of wrongdoing, so he had to accept the viceroy's words at face value.

"I accept your apology," Narius said. "Shall we eat?"

Cosena looked ready to say something to Trevik, but the viceroy held up his hand. Narius suspected she was going to point out that Trevik hadn't technically apologized and likely wasn't sorry in the least. But Trevik was right to stop her. It would have gone against protocol for her to correct him. Since Narius had deemed what Trevik did an apology, that meant that, for all intents and purposes, everyone understood that Cosena had erred.

Pillara finally looked in his direction. She smiled, but it was clearly forced. "Won't Vizier Paine join us?"

Narius glanced toward one of the empty chairs. "Unfortunately, he is indisposed."

Pillara and Trevik exchanged a look. They appeared to be disappointed. Had they hoped to convince Paine to intervene in the situation? Pillara then offered another smile to Narius, and this one looked almost genuine.

Trevik motioned for Narius to sit next to him. As soon as he had, servants flowed into the room carrying trays of food that they placed in front of him. In spite of his unease, Narius found the food delicious. More tropical fruits, a roasted fish he didn't recognize, a hearty multigrain bread, and a sweet wine that paired well with everything. And during the meal, his hosts chatted amiably about the island's many attractions and delights. Beautiful waterfalls, pristine beaches, gorgeous vistas, he had a list of places to visit should he ever return to Maotoa. He could almost let his guard down.

Almost.

"There is something we did want to talk to you about, Your Strength," Pillara said as the servants cleared away the dishes.

"Oh?" Narius steeled himself.

"While I regret what our daughter did last night, after discussing the matter with Trevik, we would like to formally propose that you marry Cosena," Pillara said.

Narius straightened in his chair, his stomach souring.

Trevik held up a hand. "Please, Your Strength. I know that this isn't why you came here, but hear us out."

Narius clenched his jaw but settled back in his chair. The first rule of diplomacy was to listen, no matter how outrageous the request.

Trevik took a deep breath. "I know we may have surprised you with many developments. Uaso's death, my marriage to Pillara, and my resulting new status. But I want to assure you, Your Strength, all of this was done with the Dynasty's best interests at heart."

"Indeed?" Narius said.

"Maotoa is the only region in the Dynasty's holdings to still be governed by both an ethnarch and a viceroy. None of the other subjugated races suffer that indignity, and it's caused nothing but friction here. I made it my goal, when I arrived at my post, to do my best to alleviate the tension.

"But Uaso did not see it that way. He benefited from keeping the Dynasty and the native Maotoans at each other's throats. I can't tell you how often we clashed over his policies and plans. He wasn't interested in defusing the tension. I suppose a different viceroy would have left things as they were. Except I couldn't, because the Dynasty is at a tipping point. The usual way of doing things can't last for much longer, can it? So I urged Uaso to finally act, to do something bold, to strengthen Maotoa's bond with the rest of the Dynasty."

Narius frowned. A laudable goal that every ethnarch and Dynasty official should be working toward.

"Instead, Uaso accused me of having an affair with his wife. He impugned my honor, Your Strength. I had no choice but to challenge him to a duel."

Pillara nodded emphatically.

"The duel, while regrettable, has had a desirable outcome. As part of the Maragnat, I have more influence to direct the island properly. But I fear that, even with that change, it won't be enough. Only radical action can solve the crises we face.

"I understand that Cosena's actions were unwelcome, and I'm sorry that she was so impulsive. But there is wisdom in her brash action. By accepting her proposal, you would take large strides toward true peace and stability. I ask you to please consider it. Revoke the Compromise. Marry Cosena. Please."

"Please," Pillara echoed.

Narius shifted in his seat. There was an unsettling undercurrent running through the room.

Even Cosena finally met his gaze. The hunger, the lust, the passion was gone. Replaced by... pleading? Desperation? Near panic?

And he wasn't sure how to react. Their urgency made him consider Cosena's offer in a new light. A new legacy. And Cosena was beautiful. Having her as a consort was enticing.

But no, he couldn't really consider it. He had made a promise to Everys. And he didn't feel he could trust these three. Something else was going on, and until he knew what it was, he couldn't possibly agree.

"While I appreciate this offer, I'm afraid I must decline." He winced at his phrasing. He sounded like he was turning down a piece of real estate instead of their daughter. "What I mean is, I'm not sure that we are going to revoke Albanon's Compromise. Until I make a decision about that, it would be inappropriate to make any plans about marrying Cosena or anyone else, for that matter."

Pillara's face froze in what Narius could only decipher as barely restrained anger. Cosena looked sick. Trevik blew out a long breath.

"Your Strength, I respectfully ask you to reconsider," he said.

What was there to reconsider? Everything he had said was true. He hadn't completely dismissed the idea, even though he wanted to. What more did the viceroy want?

Narius turned to Trevik. "Viceroy, I am flattered by your desire for me to marry your stepdaughter. I also appreciate your desire for

Maotoa to have a stronger relationship with the Dynasty. But this insistence makes me wonder what you are not telling me."

Pillara shifted in her seat, looking positively stricken. She shot a look at Trevik, who clenched his jaw so tight his mouth thinned to a line.

"I will not agree to marry Cosena. But if there is something else that you need help with, some situation that I may help you address..." He let his voice trail off as an invitation.

Trevik stared at him, and Narius could almost hear the mental battle. After a few minutes, Trevik laughed lightly. "Nothing at all, Your Strength. I understand your position, and I won't bring it up again. Since lunch is over, perhaps we should continue with your official visit. I believe that a tour of the island's kulith fields was next on your itinerary, yes?"

The viceroy's sudden change in demeanor was even more unsettling to Narius, but Trevik was likely trying to hide his disappointment and not doing a good job of it. "I believe so, yes."

"Then I propose you take a moment to return to your quarters. Perhaps change your clothes? My understanding is that the fields are particularly muddy. I would hate for your clothes to get ruined."

Narius looked down at his outfit. He wasn't wearing anything too ostentatious that couldn't get dirty. But given the conversation they just had, antagonizing Trevik didn't seem wise. Changing his outfit was a small concession to hopefully smooth over any hurt feelings.

"Very well. Where shall I meet you when I'm ready?" Narius asked.

"Oh, don't worry, I'll send someone to escort you. We'll see you in just a little bit."

Narius nodded first to Pillara, who still glared at him, then Cosena, who wouldn't meet his gaze again. Then he excused himself. Melat met him in the hallway and led him back to his quarters. But as they walked away from the dining room, Narius heard raised voices, an argument between Trevik and Pillara. He frowned. While he couldn't make out what they were saying, he could tell that Pillara was extremely angry. He sighed. He didn't relish the idea of more talks like that, but maybe he could find something that would placate the Maotoans. Greater autonomy? An official recognition of Trevik's new position? Maybe he could find a position for Trevik among his advisers. He'd have to find a way to smooth out that relationship in the future.

Once they were back in his quarters, Narius immediately went to his luggage and selected an outfit he hoped would satisfy Trevik—a simple khaki pants and blue shirt. As he draped his choices over his arm, he turned to Zar.

"Go find Paine and see if he's going to join us for the tour," he said.

Zar nodded sharply and signaled for two of the guards to remain in the room. Narius excused himself into the bathroom and quickly changed into his new outfit.

As he checked himself in the mirror, a rhythmic thrumming came from the other room. He frowned. The noise sounded familiar, but where had he...?

His eyes widened. The sound was similar to the strange, wordless song Cosena had been singing the night before. Had she come back? No, the sound was too low, a bass warble rather than Cosena's rich alto. So what was—

Then the strange thrumming was punctuated by a *puff-snap* sound that Narius instantly recognized. Someone was firing flechette throwers in the other room. He whirled around, ready to call out to the guards.

Someone slammed into the bathroom door. Narius jumped. But then his old instincts kicked in. He slid along the wall, making sure he wasn't standing directly in front of the door. He then snuck a hand out to open the door. His guard spilled onto the floor, blood splattered across his chest. The guard's flechette thrower clattered at Narius's feet. Narius didn't hesitate. He scooped up the weapon and checked the magazine. He had about twenty shots left before he'd have to reload. Hopefully that would be enough.

Narius sidled up to the door and risked a quick peek. Two men in military uniforms stood near the fountain, clearly holding position. Narius's other guard lay sprawled near the door. Narius almost pulled back into the bathroom, but then he saw something that caused him to hesitate.

A soldier clambered out of the fountain, hauling himself over the edge. How was that possible? For one thing, the fountain wasn't deep enough for someone to lay down in, let alone climb out like that. For another, the soldier's uniform was mostly dry except for the bottom of his pants.

Narius ducked back into the bathroom. Three-to-one odds. Not good. He'd have to do something about that.

He took stock of what he had at hand. His toiletries, towels, the fixtures themselves. Nothing he could use tactically. No, wait. There was a nook in the wall by the sink, with a large potted plant.

One of the soldiers snapped something in a language Narius didn't understand, but he recognized the intent. They were looking for him. He had to act. Now!

He jumped to his feet, scooped up the plant, and then spun into the doorway. He hurled the plant at one soldier and opened fire on another. The pot shattered across the soldier's head, spraying dirt and leaves. Blood erupted from the other soldier's chest. The third soldier paused, so Narius aimed for him and shot him between the eyes before dispatching the one he had hit with the pot.

Someone shouted from inside the fountain even as the strange droning continued. Narius hurried to the fountain and looked down, only to be overcome by a wave of vertigo.

The water in the fountain swirled in an eddy six feet across. A hole had opened in the center of the vortex, revealing... someplace outdoors. The ground in the hole was strangely perpendicular to his bedroom, as if Narius stood on a building's roof and everything clung to the wall. On the other side of the hole, a group of soldiers stood in knee-deep water, some of them dragging away the man he had shot. Another man in Maotoan robes knelt in the water, his hands submerged. The Maotoan chanted, the strange droning thrumming deep in Narius's chest.

If being married to Everys had taught him one thing, it was to never underestimate an unarmed person doing something unusual. He quickly shot the Maotoan square in the chest.

Blood spurted from the man's mouth, and his singing stopped. He slumped toward the water, but as he did, the waters in the fountain rushed together and the hole vanished. That's when he noticed that the jewel in the Water Bearer's statue had been glowing, a flicker dancing within the gem, but that light quickly faded.

Narius took a shuddering breath and surveyed the carnage. Both soldiers were down and apparently dead. As he examined the one closest to him, though, he frowned. There was something odd about his uniform. The soldier wasn't wearing one from the Dynasty's military. And the weapon was unusual as well. He hurried to the dead man's side and rolled him onto his back.

The moment he saw the soldier's face, he cursed. Pale skin, a flattened nose, and snow-white hair. This man wasn't from the Dynasty at all. He had Dalark features. And now that Narius got a better look at the man's uniform, he recognized it as Dalark as well.

The Imperium was invading Maotoa. And the Maotoans were helping.

42

Someone pounded on his door, shouting Narius's name. He stared at the fallen Dalark soldiers, his mind tumbling through the implications. Bad enough that Dalark troops were in the Dynasty's territory. But they had attacked him, an act of war. And he had no idea how they had breached the palace in the first place.

"Your Strength!" Zar's voice, punctuated by another slam against the door.

That snapped Narius back to reality. He hurried over and unlocked the door. Zar and three more guards rushed inside, their weapons drawn. Zar's gaze slid from Narius to the dead bodies and then through the room. The whole time, his face was impassive, but Narius had known the head guard long enough to recognize his barely restrained fear.

"Situation?" Narius prompted.

"Dalark troops everywhere, Your Strength," Zar said. "We counted at least three dozen on our way back here. Appears they're sweeping the palace room by room."

"Any idea how they got here?" Narius asked.

Zar shook his head, but one of the guards looked like she was about to say something. Narius nodded to her.

"Forgive me for saying it, Your Strength, but I thought I saw them crawl out of one of those decorative fountains," she said.

"Probably a secret passageway," Zar said.

No, that wasn't it. Narius wanted to quiz the guard over what she saw. Had she heard any of that strange droning? But he knew there'd be time to debrief after they escaped.

If they escaped.

"Any word on Viceroy Trevik and his family?"

"No," Zar said. "They're not our priority. Getting you to safety is."

Of course. But that still left one question. "What of Vizier Paine?"

"I've got two guards looking for him, but..." Zar's voice trailed off.

Narius's stomach twisted. But there were enemy combatants in the palace. Given that there was a Maotoan with the soldiers who attacked him, Narius couldn't count on the palace staff to help them. They could be completely surrounded by enemies, and it might be impossible to find Paine. He could easily lose one of his closest friends and the last conversation with him had been an argument.

But he couldn't dwell on that. He shoved aside the pang of regret. "So what's the plan?"

Zar motioned for the guards to gather up the fallen weaponry, then turned to Narius. "I've been in contact with the military airhub outside Dreah. They're not reporting any hostiles yet, but they are on alert and prepping a skimmer for us."

Surprising that Dalark would overlook a military base, but good news for them.

"So we'll try to get out of the palace and over to the base." Zar checked his weapon. "Simple as that."

Narius knew it would be anything but.

Zar motioned for the other guards to come closer. "We've trained for this. We move quick and quiet while we can. Someone shoots at the king, we take the flechette for him. Right?"

The other three guards nodded grimly.

"For the Warrior. For the Dynasty. For the king," Zar said.

The guards repeated the battle cry, then Zar motioned for them to move and Narius didn't hesitate. He raised his own weapon and did a quick check. He might have protectors, but he wasn't helpless.

Zar opened the doors and the five of them slipped into the eerily quiet halls. Narius thought he heard shouts in the distance, but he couldn't be sure if he heard more Dalark troops or palace staff. But Zar didn't hesitate. He hustled the group down the hall to a stairwell.

They descended two floors before they encountered anyone. Four Dalark troops herded some of the palace staff together on a landing. Before the enemy soldiers could react, Zar and the other guards opened fire, killing them. Some of the palace staff cried out, but a sharp look and a hushing motion from Zar cut them off. He whispered for them to run, which they thankfully did.

Narius ground his teeth. He knew what the guard was doing. By shooing the servants, he was creating confusion for the Dalark. Some of those servants might die. From Zar's perspective it made sense—better them than the king—but it still rankled him.

Within minutes, they made it to the ground floor. Zar checked the hall outside the stairwell, then motioned for them to hurry after him. As soon as they stepped outside, someone shouted behind them. The guards behind Narius whirled and opened fire. He glanced over his shoulder to see two Dalark troops dive for cover. Zar snared his arm and dragged him along. There was more fire, punctuated by a sharp scream. The two guards caught up with them, but he noticed that one of them was limping.

They burst through a door to the outside and Narius skidded to a halt. Dozens of Dalark troops prowled the palace grounds. Zar dragged Narius behind a topiary and pressed him back. The guard peeked over the hedge and then knelt.

"I see a row of transports over there." Zar jerked his head toward the road that bordered the palace. "We're going to have to move fast. Engage only if we have to. Stay low and fast. Go!"

And then they were on the move again, crouching and running along the palace wall. Narius risked a peek to his left. So many Dalark troops. How had they gotten here so quickly? Could those strange holes in the water account for all of them? Or had they made an airdrop?

One of the Dalark soldiers turned and his eyes widened. Narius bit back a curse as the man shouted and pointed in their direction.

Zar shoved Narius behind a stone planter box, then fell backward to a more defensible position. Flechettes sliced into the wall over Narius's head and he hunkered down, protecting his head with his hands. More soldiers shouted. Narius tightened his grip on his weapon. They were pinned down. No way they'd make it to the transport now. This would be his final stand. He took several deep breaths and readied himself for whatever might happen.

Then someone landed softly next to him. The young woman wore a servant's outfit, but she clearly wasn't Maotoan. Her olive skin was too light, her short-cropped hair too dark. In some ways, she reminded Narius of Everys. The same complexion, similar facial features. A Siporan? Wait, he recognized her. She had been the one on the docks when they first arrived in Dreah.

She smirked at Narius, then rose. He reached out to stop her, but she dodged his grasp. Her fingers danced, flexing and twisting together. Several flechettes thunked into the wall on either side of her, but she didn't even flinch. Instead, she moved her hands in a complex weave, twisting her arms as she did. Then, with a soft grunt, she thrust her hands toward the soldiers.

Almost immediately, the incoming fire ceased. Narius frowned and risked a peek over the barrier. The Dalark soldiers had frozen in place, like statues. He could see them straining against whatever held them. He turned to the strange woman, only to discover she had disappeared.

The other guards emerged from cover and approached the frozen soldiers. Zar turned to Narius, a question on his face. Narius vaguely motioned toward where the girl had stood, but from the blank looks on their faces, it was clear they had no idea what he'd seen. So he shrugged.

"Chaos is working too hard today," Zar muttered. "But I won't spite him. Let's go."

They hurried along the wall, the guards keeping their weapons trained on the frozen soldiers. They easily reached a row of military transports that lined the street. Narius spotted more Dalark troops further away, and they shouted when they saw them. But Zar ripped open a door and hustled Narius inside. While the other three guards laid down suppressing fire, Zar started the transport. Once the engine roared to life, the guards piled into the vehicle.

Before they could pull away, though, someone slammed into the side of the transport. Narius glanced out the window and saw two guards with Paine. The vizier looked haggard, his clothing twisted. Blood streaked his cheek and he looked dazed. Narius wanted to shout his name, hug him, apologize for their fight right then and there. The guards inside the transport kicked open the door and the rest of them piled inside.

Paine's gaze met Narius's, and his eyes sparked. "Your Strength, are you well?"

Narius laughed. "I am. And you?"

Paine touched his cheek, smearing some blood. "Slight injuries. They tried to kill me."

The transport lurched, and the tires squealed as Zar drove it onto the road. Flechettes pinged off the windows, cracking one of them.

A guard shoved Narius and Paine onto the floor. The transport shuddered as Zar drove over something. Whether it was soldiers or some other obstacle, Narius didn't know.

"What did you see?" Narius asked Paine.

Paine frowned. "In truth, Your Strength, I'm not sure. After our discussion, I found a garden so I could clear my mind and think. But then there was a strange droning sound and a... a door opened in the water. Dalark soldiers emerged, and they opened fire on me. I hesitate to admit this, but I fled and hid until Keller and Breit found me."

Narius smiled. "No one will think any less of you, my friend."

Paine grimaced because they both knew that was a lie. But Narius nodded his thanks to the guards who rescued the vizier.

"Did you have a similar experience?" Paine asked. "The door in the water?"

Narius nodded. "It seems that the Maotoans haven't exactly been forthcoming about what they're capable of."

Paine turned away, but Narius caught the grim look on his friend's face. He understood it all too well. The Dynasty liked to think itself all-powerful and all-knowing. But over the past several months, so many long-hidden secrets had been exposed. The Siporans, the Cold Light, and now the Maotoans. No wonder the Dynasty was struggling so badly. They had been groping through the world with both eyes willfully glued shut.

Narius and Paine remained pressed onto the floor, the transport bucking and careening. Narius tried to rise a few times, only to be shoved back down again. Eventually, though, Narius was able to gently coax the guard's hand off his shoulder and risk a peek.

Zar barreled through the streets of Dreah, blowing past citizens out for walks and careening between other transports. There was no sign of the violence or the invasion here. Everything appeared so normal, Narius almost wondered if what he'd experienced was a bad dream or a fevered fantasy.

But then they spotted the military airhub. Soldiers stood with weapons at the ready near the front gate. Several of them waved the transport forward and Narius felt a surge of relief. Within a few minutes, they'd be—

Something screamed through the air.

The transport bucked, jumping off its wheels and tumbling end over end. Narius slammed into the ceiling then the window, pain exploding in his arms, his head, his back. Bodies piled on top of him, and in spite of the ringing in his ears, he could hear them moaning and felt them squirming, trying to free themselves.

"Your Strength!" Zar's voice rang metallic. "Your Strength!"

Narius tried to answer, but as he shifted, pain seared through his right leg and his mind lurched through fog. What had happened to him?

Zar barked orders to the guards. Narius couldn't follow any of them. He tried to protest, because he suspected that they were going to sacrifice themselves for his safety. But he couldn't force the words out of his mouth. The transport door wrenched open with a brain-splitting screech and the guards poured out, their guns firing.

Then Zar appeared over him. "C'mon, Narius. Let's get you out of here."

Zar dragged him from the wreckage and sheer agony lanced through his legs, his back. He groaned and tried to break free of Zar's grasp. He could figure out how to make it on his own. But Zar only fumbled him, and Narius collapsed face down. Zar shouted, and a second later, strong hands clutched underneath his arms and dragged him toward the base.

Narius tried to get to his feet, but his body simply wouldn't cooperate. He was only aware of snippets of action. Dalark soldiers charging the base. The chatter of weapons fire. Paine staggering after him, but then blood blossomed in the middle of his chest. He tried to cry out, but his voice was stuck in his throat. Two more soldiers dragged Paine away as more formed a wall between the Dalark and them.

Then they were inside the base. At least, Narius thought they were. He was having a harder time keeping his thoughts straight. He blinked, trying to stay awake, but it was too hard. All he could think about was Everys. He had left Bastion with her hating him. He had to hold on. Hold on for her. To make things better. To keep his promise, the one he hadn't said out loud.

He thought he heard someone say something about evacuating, thought the world went darker, but then the shadows consumed him, and he was dead to the world.

43

Because of Brencis's attack on the Oasis, Rewether had ordered a complete communications blackout. There was no telling who else in the Dynasty's military might have been compromised. Better to retreat to the safety of the palace.

For the entire flight, Everys couldn't relax. She was certain that at any point, their skimmer would be intercepted or shot down or otherwise destroyed. She tried to comfort Trule, but the Plissk girl was almost catatonic. Challix had tried to engage both of them in hushed conversation, but Trule didn't respond and Everys didn't know what to say. She only relaxed when she spotted the Bastion skyline out the window.

But rather than descend right away, the skimmer circled the palace. Everys flagged down Rewether.

He grunted. "Not entirely sure, Blessed. Looks like there's another skimmer on the tarmac."

It had to be Narius's! She hurried to a window and tried to see it for herself. She only managed to catch glimpses as her skimmer banked and turned, but she was pretty sure she saw crew swarming around the craft.

One of the guards grunted next to her. She turned to him and noticed the concern spread across his face.

"What is it?" she prompted.

He exchanged an uncertain look with Rewether, then grimaced. "Not my place to say, Blessed, but it looks like that skimmer may have seen some combat."

What? She tried to take another look, but she couldn't see whatever the guard had noticed. The skimmer looked fine to her.

But then she spotted people darting out of the skimmer, two of them carrying something between them. It took a moment for her to realize they were hurrying a stretcher into the palace.

"Rewether!" she shouted, pointing out the window.

Rewether looked over her shoulder and spat a curse.

"Who was that?" she asked.

Rewether worked his jaw. Everys looked out the window and saw another stretcher carried out of the skimmer and into the palace. Her heart lurched. Who was that? Why wasn't Rewether saying anything?

And then she understood. This wasn't a publicly available tarmac. The only people who could use it were people associated with the palace. As far as she knew, there was only one person who might have arrived at the palace via skimmer.

She whirled on Rewether. "Land the skimmer. Now!"

He shook his head. "Until that skimmer clears the tarmac, we have to stay in a holding pattern. I'm sorry, Blessed. We'll land as quickly as we can."

Everys stared at him, his words not registering. But then she turned and pressed up against the window, trying to see who else would emerge from the skimmer, praying that even at this height, she'd be able to see Narius walk out on his own.

Finally, after what felt like years, their skimmer was able to land. She didn't wait for anyone to signal that they were secure. The moment she felt the skimmer come to a halt, she headed for the exit. Her guards protested, but she didn't want to wait. As soon as the hatch was wide enough, she hurried down the ramp to the tarmac.

What she found told her far too much. Zar and other members of Narius's guard waited nearby. They had all been injured. One had her arm in a sling. Zar had a bandage around his head. His expression was grim, unreadable. Was that good? Or a harbinger of bad news?

Zar stepped forward. "Rewether, what's going on? We tried to comm you, but you wouldn't—"

"Is Narius all right?" Everys demanded.

"He's fine, Blessed. Relatively speaking. He's in the infirmary and—"

That was all she needed to know. She brushed past him and hurried for the palace. Let Rewether explain what had happened at the Oasis. All she wanted was to see Narius.

Servants got out of her way as she hurried through the halls. All of them wore expressions conveying different levels of shock and disbelief. She overheard snatches of conversation. Something about an attack on Maotoa. Is that what had happened? How badly was Narius injured?

She burst through the infirmary doors. The doctors and nurses were clustered around two beds. Paine lay in one, Narius in the other. Both men were hooked up to medical monitors and intravenous lines. She hurried to Narius's side.

"Blessed, careful," one of the doctors said. "The king has multiple injuries, including a pretty bad concussion..."

As the doctor rattled off Narius's diagnosis, she gingerly took Narius's hand. At first, his fingers remained limp, but then he squeezed her hand gently. She looked to his face and saw a faint smile flicker across his lips.

A choking sob rattled up her throat. "What happened?"

He tried to say something, but his voice was weak and thready. She leaned in, her ear as close to his mouth as she could.

"Paine... help him... rune."

Her eyes widened. He couldn't be serious! There was no way she could do that, not in front of all of these doctors. Not when Paine was connected to so many medical devices. They would know something had happened to him.

"Please," Narius whispered. "Could be... dying. His injures... worse."

Everys's gaze flicked over to the vizier. Paine was unconscious with so many tubes running in and out of him. He probably could use some help. An itch grew in the back of her mind. After losing Kevtho, she didn't need any more loss.

But helping Paine? The man had never accepted her, barely tolerated her. She had no idea if he would help her if their positions were reversed. But that really wasn't an excuse, was it? She could help, so she should.

"Doctors, if you could please leave us for a few minutes?" she said.

The activity in the infirmary ceased. The doctors and nurses stared at her in shock.

"Blessed, that's just not possible. Both men are in critical condition and require constant monitoring—"

"Get out." Narius's voice, while quiet and barely more than a croak, still carried the weight of authority.

The doctors and nurses obeyed, but they muttered to each other as they did. Everys tried to ignore the questioning looks they shot at her. As soon as they had left, Everys blew out a held breath. She knew she'd have to act quickly.

She plucked a bead from her bracelet and considered her options. She could use her family's healing rune. Given the severity of Paine's injuries, that was the best choice. It would knit him together, ease his pain, provide comfort. As soon as it was cast, he'd essentially be remade and whole.

But she also knew that was too risky. The doctors would have questions that no one could answer if Paine was healthy in a matter of minutes.

She finally settled on using a heavily modified version of her family's rune. Rolling the bead between two fingers, she pulled back part of the smock covering Paine's chest with her other hand and got to work. The basic rune unfurled across his chest like a fern with long grasping branches. But at the bottom of the rune, she added a half circle to tie in the extra enhancements and instructions, each one a complex squiggle of lines and curves and angles. Instead of healing Paine all at once, the rune would now work over the next week, gradually strengthening him and healing him. She added a bit of glamour to make the rune blend in with Paine's skin. Part of her worried that the spell wouldn't take with so many modifications. But as soon as she activated the rune, Paine's body relaxed and he took a deep breath. His face smoothed.

Everys braced herself. She was going to get rebuked, she just knew it. Using the rune after combat, the same way she had to save Narius a year earlier, she was going to get hit hard. But nothing happened. No pain. No rebuke. She risked a peek out of one eye. The Singularity approved? She blew her breath out of her nose and turned to her husband. Good. Because she had one more patient to help.

Before she could start, though, the door to the infirmary banged open. She whirled around, expecting to see the doctors returning, but instead, Papa stood in the doorway, restrained by two of the guards.

"I'm sorry, sir, you can't go in there!" one of them said.

"You're going to keep me from seeing my daughter?" Papa thundered.

Everys's heart leaped in spite of Papa's anger. She hated the way they had left things before she had departed for the Oasis. That he had come down here to find her made her feel like maybe their relationship wasn't completely ruined.

"Let him in," she said. "It's okay."

The guards released him, and Papa shot both a dirty look. He stepped inside and emphatically shut the door behind him. Not a slam, but enough to let the guards know he wasn't happy.

Then he hurried to her side. "When I heard about the attack on the Oasis, I was so worried. One of your guards died?"

How had he heard about any of that? Oh, the press drones. A sick feeling twisted in her stomach. The entire Dynasty had probably seen what had happened. Maybe not with *ur-keleshen*, but that Brencis had attacked the Oasis.

She squared her shoulders. All the more reason to help Narius recover quicker.

Everys turned to Narius and moved part of his smock aside as well. Now that she knew the rune would work, she wanted to get it done quickly. She leaned over and started tracing the rune.

Papa hurried to her side. "What are you doing?"

"Narius and Paine need my help, Papa," she whispered. "So I'm helping."

He took a closer look but then reeled back. "You can't! You would sully our rune by using it this way? To heal them? Don't you remember what happened last time you used it?"

She did, all too well. Just thinking about saving Narius's life after Brencis shot him sent sympathetic pains ricocheting through her. But this time, she had used ink instead of blood. She would be fine. "Papa, it'll be okay. The Singularity didn't rebuke me when I used the rune on Paine, so—"

"You already used it on him?" Papa jabbed a finger at the vizier. "Are you mad? Everys, these men are our enemies! How can you not see that? They are the ones who have kept our people in the dirt for centuries! They don't care about us at all!"

"That's not true," Everys said. "Narius loves me."

Papa scoffed. "He may love you, but he is no friend of the Siporans. That much is clear."

Counterarguments welled up inside her: Narius's desire to learn with Tolistan. His suggestion legalize toratropic magic. But she knew that this was a distraction. The doctors wouldn't stay out of the infirmary for much longer. She had to act now.

"Papa, I'm doing this."

"No, you are not. As your father, I forbid you from using our family's rune on this man. As the patriarch of this rune, you may not use it."

Everys gaped at him. He couldn't possibly be serious. But from his expression, he clearly was. She shook her head. No, she wasn't going to listen. This was her husband, and Papa was being so paranoid, so angry, without reason. She had to help. She had to!

"Everys." Narius's quiet word jolted her like electricity. "Don't."

She whirled on him. "No, I'm going to!"

Narius shook his head weakly. "Not worth it. I'll be fine. The doctors all said so. I appreciate the idea, but it's not worth fighting with your father."

Everys gaped at him. And Papa looked stunned, although that quickly gave way to a smug smile.

"Fine." She rearranged Narius's smock. "As my king and husband commands."

A pained look flitted across Narius's face, and Everys immediately regretted her sarcasm. She started to say something, but the door opened and the doctors reentered the infirmary. Everys clamped her mouth shut. The opportunity had passed.

Papa gave her one last look then stormed out of the infirmary. She swallowed a sob. She had longed for her family to come back from the vigil for so long. Now that Papa was here, she wanted him to go back. And that wish hurt worse than any possible rebuke.

44

Maotoa had fallen. Quartus couldn't believe it. The Dynasty had held on to that island for centuries. Even when their other overseas colonies revolted and won their independence, the Dynasty kept Maotoa, claiming that to do otherwise would be to invite future wars. But it hadn't mattered. Maotoa had fallen to Dalark invasion, and it had happened in less than a day.

While Bastion murmured about the news, Quartus was able to parse out even more details that weren't being publicly shared. The day after the invasion, there had been a press conference delivered by Urett, Narius's assistant. That spoke volumes. Not the king. Not Paine. Something had happened during the invasion that made it necessary for a lower functionary to speak about the crisis.

The news that emerged over the next two days only added fuel to Quartus's anxiety. The second day after the invasion, reports reached the mainland that the native Maotoans had assisted the Dalark in their invasion. And the day after that, Viceroy Trevik officially surrendered the island to Dalark control, announcing that his stepdaughter Cosena would marry the Emperor Tirigian at his earliest convenience.

The more Quartus thought about it, the more concerned he became. This new development radically shifted the balance in any conflict. He knew what the Dynasty's military had been preparing for since the cease-fire had started centuries earlier. The anticipated war with Dalark would be fought through the Demilitarized Zone between the Dynasty and the Dalark Beachhead. Yes, the Dalark could attempt amphibious assaults along the Dynasty's western coast or even airdrops from skimmers deeper into the Dynasty's territory. But those strategies would be difficult at best, what with much of the Dynasty's navy stationed at Maotoa.

But now, with Maotoa in Dalark's hands? That opened a new potential front. Dalark troops were mere hours from Bastion instead of days. The Dynasty would have to shift troops from the Demilitarized Zone and elsewhere to counter this new threat. And with Brencis running loose in the Dynasty's holdings, that made the situation even dicier.

He wasn't surprised at how helpless most people within the Dynasty felt. What could they do? But he was in a unique position. He had a Dalark agent he could question. And he was going to get some answers.

Even though he messaged her immediately, Quartus didn't hear back from her for three days. Three days to stew and simmer. He did reach out to Tormod to see if this new development changed anything, but he didn't receive a return message. The spymaster likely was overwhelmed, but that only added to Quartus's frustration. He needed some direction, some idea of how all of this fit together.

Finally, Yusra invited him to join her at the curcas den. As he approached the building, he felt much better with the weight of a flechette thrower hidden in his pocket. A good precaution normally, given how run-down the neighborhood was. But he suspected having it would be extra wise.

The Weyfir guard at the door nodded for him to enter. Quartus studied his expression to see if there was a hint of what he might expect. The Weyfir glowered at him. That told him nothing.

Quartus hesitated in the entrance, waiting for his eyes to adjust to the darkness. The usual clientele. No outward sign of hostility from anyone else. He wanted to stay there and make sure, but he knew he had to confront Yusra sooner or later. So he steeled his spine and strode to the back room.

He opened the door with a hand on his weapon, ready to draw it in case—

A knife pressed against his throat.

"So that's how it's going to be, is it?" he asked quietly.

Yusra shut the door behind him then repositioned herself, her blade not wavering for a moment. "That entirely depends on you, Quartus."

"Oh? Quite a coup for you, I would think. The same week your Imperium captures Maotoa, you murder me? Your master would be quick to reward you."

"Don't presume to know what my master desires." Yusra's voice was a growl.

Quartus chuckled. "I can and will. We all know what you Dalark are like. You want nothing more than to see the Dynasty fall."

"Not all of us do," Yusra said.

"Then prove it. Put down the knife."

"Only if you give me your weapon."

Quartus clenched his jaw. Risky, but what choice did he have? She'd slit his throat if he refused. So he raised his hands and nodded. Yusra's hand snaked into his pocket and pulled the flechette thrower out. She eased around him, setting his weapon and hers on a nearby table.

He kept his hands up and didn't move until she sighed and motioned for him to. He kept his distance from her until he reached a chair and carefully sank into it.

"This isn't something I wanted, Quartus," Yusra said, her voice insistent.

"How can I trust anything you say?"

"The fact that your throat is uncut is evidence, isn't it? How can I trust you?"

"I could have notified Internal Security about where you'd be."

"For all I know, the building's surrounded right now and they're waiting for your signal."

"So then kill me. That would give you time to get away."

Her gaze flicked to the weapons. Then, with a sigh, she picked up his gun and handed it to him. She left her knife on the table.

"If you really think I'm a threat, go ahead and shoot."

He considered it, but for some odd reason, he trusted her. So he tucked the weapon away, then picked up her knife and handed it back to her. She hid it in a sheath on her back.

"I am sorry for what happened in Maotoa," she said. "I'm sorry for whatever happened to Narius there. And if you and I can prevent more of this from happening, I'm still willing to work with you. The real question is this: are you willing to trust me?"

His gaze sharpened. Part of him didn't. She was a Dalark agent, after all, most likely trained in deception and manipulation. There was no reason to trust her. But she was so sincere. He could practically taste the truth of what she said.

"I will, on one condition. You have to tell me who you work for," he said.

She grimaced, and he understood why. That information would be leverage that could be used against her in the future. But it was only a name, a gesture of cooperation.

"I... I can't," she said.

Quartus shook his head. "That's not how this works. I need that name."

"And I would give it to you, but I can't. Because I don't know it."

His head snapped back as if he had been slapped. Did she really expect him to believe something so stupid?

"It's true. I can't remember my master's name. Before I left the Imperium, they did something to me." Yusra took a shuddering breath, and then her voice took on a singsong quality. "As far as I may roam, the truth stays locked within. My master's name hidden must remain. Until my master's voice call me back, the name will be but fog."

Yusra shuddered, her body contorting, and she gasped. Quartus's mouth popped open. What kind of brainwashing had she been subjected to? He knew that the Imperium could be fanatical, but this crossed a line. Several, as far as he was concerned.

"Very well. If you can't share your master's name, I suppose I'll have to just trust you. I can do that, yes?"

Yusra nodded.

"Good. So any leads worth pursuing?"

She shook her head. "As near as I could tell, none of the people I investigated seemed connected to the conspiracy. Profit-mongers and smugglers, yes, but nothing more dire than that. You?"

Quartus clenched his jaw. He would have to trust her word for it, but given that he hadn't found anything significant either, that clinched it.

"So that means we go after Sellafus Coran," Yusra said.

He nodded grimly. He didn't like the idea, but they really didn't have any other choice. Thankfully, though, he had gleaned some information that could help them. He just needed one more piece of information.

"How well do you dance?"

45

Everys tried to focus on what the doctor was telling her. She caught most of it: Narius had been injured, some of those injuries had been severe, but with enough time and enough caution, he would make a full recovery. But try as she might, she couldn't focus on the individual words. Instead, she stared at her husband in his bed, relief mixing with dread. Because she knew that as important as his physical health was, they needed to work on healing their relationship as well. Maybe the timing wasn't ideal with him laid up in a medical bed, but both of their misadventures had shown her how easily their lives could be over. Best to not let it linger.

Besides, there was no way he could escape if he was confined in the medical wing.

She smiled at the doctor as he wrapped up his explanation then slipped into the room. Her gaze flicked to what had been Paine's bed, which was thankfully empty. She didn't need him to be an audience for this particular discussion. The day before, the doctors had declared him healthy enough to leave, even if they were mystified as to how he had recovered so quickly.

Narius sat up as she approached. Their gazes met and she came to a halt at the foot of the bed. He looked healthier than when he'd first returned to the palace. But she could read the hesitation in his expression, the uncertainty.

"May I sit?" she asked.

He gestured toward an empty chair.

"Have they been taking good care of you?" she asked, wincing at the small talk, but she had to work her way up to broaching the serious issue between them.

Narius nodded. "Well enough. They say I may get out of here in a few days."

"That's good." She twisted her fingers together in her lap. Inkstains, why was this so difficult? "I spoke to Urett about making sure that your quarters are ready for you when you are discharged. And I know you won't be happy about this, but I told him to clean up your mess. I don't want you tripping over anything when you—"

"Everys, what is it?"

She winced at the gentleness in his voice. Tears stung her eyes. What she was about to do, the demand she was about to make...

Fine. She could do this. She took a deep breath. "Narius, please don't revoke Albanon's Compromise. I know it's selfish and it may make things worse, but I can't stand the thought of—"

Narius placed a hand on his forehead and chuckled ruefully. "Don't worry. That's not even a remote possibility anymore. Maotoa put an end to that particular plan."

She frowned. "Why?"

His laughter cut off and he gave her a look, one she recognized. Bad news was coming. She braced herself.

"Something happened on Maotoa. To me." He grimaced. "And Cosena."

Everys frowned. The name sounded familiar, but where... Her eyes widened. The ethnarch's daughter? She had never met her, but she had heard rumors about her: a voluptuous, exotic beauty. Heat flashed through her and her voice turned into a growl. "Narius..."

He held up his hands. "It's not that! Well, it's sort of not that. Please, let me explain before you say anything else. She tried to seduce me because she heard about how we might revoke the Compromise. But nothing happened. I didn't want it to happen. And yes, I may have been attracted to her when I was a boy, but not anymore! And she used this strange incense to try to make me desire her, and there was this other girl—not like that, she saved me somehow—and... and the last thing I thought of before we left the island was you. How broken things were between us. And that thought hurt worse than my injuries."

She stared at him, and tears welled up in her eyes. He kept babbling, a stream of random thoughts and snippets of what had happened to him, all of it jumbled into a pastiche that would probably take hours to unravel and reassemble into some semblance of order. But in that moment, she saw past the jumble, the confusion, the near panic. And she saw her husband. She saw his heart.

Everys lunged forward and put a hand to his mouth, stopping the stream of words.

"I love you," she whispered, then punctuated the statement with a kiss.

"I love you too. And I am so, so sorry, Everys," he said. "I got so caught up in the crises that I lost sight of what really matters. I tried to excuse it by saying that I was making sacrifices for the good of the Dynasty. But I wasn't the only one making the sacrifice. I was expecting you to as well."

Everys smiled sadly and threaded her fingers through his. "That's what royals do though, right?"

"But I keep forgetting. You're not royal. Not really."

She started to protest, but he held up a hand.

"Let me explain," he said. "You carry yourself with such strength and fire. In many ways, you behave like royalty. And you've become such a part of me that I think of you like myself. Royalty, born and bred. But that isn't fair to you. The only person I should expect to make these sorts of sacrifices is me. And if I revoked Albanon's Compromise, I would be dragging you with me. I can't do that. I won't do that. I love you too much to take advantage of you like that."

She squeezed his hand. "Narius, you are the most giving person I've ever met. Your heart for your people is so incredible. It's part of the reason why I fell in love with you in the first place. And I know you weren't doing any of this to hurt me. You just had a possible way to fix everything and quickly. I can't blame you for wanting to find a solution like that, even if you did kind of drag me along with you."

He closed his eyes and nodded. "I promise I won't do that anymore. You are my wife. You are my partner. And I love you. I took you for granted and I shouldn't have. Please forgive me."

She smiled. "You can make it up to me one way."

"What's that?"

"I want Cosena assassinated."

He froze, his eyes wide. She let him marinate in the shock for a moment before she offered him a wan smile.

"I'm joking," she said, although she didn't completely mean it.

He chuckled, then took a deep breath. "That would likely make our situation worse, unfortunately."

She groaned. How was she going to tell him this? "There's more going on than you know."

Narius frowned. "What do you mean?"

"I'm assuming you heard about what happened at the Oasis. With Brencis and... and Kevtho."

His frown deepened. "Bits and pieces. Something about a duel? Zar couldn't get much out of Rewether."

Everys took a shuddering breath. "It was bad, Narius. Brencis killed Kevtho with an *ur-keleshen*."

His eyes widened. "How would he have gotten one of those?"

"I don't know. And there's more. Narius, he says that he married Viara."

The color drained from his face and his mouth popped open. For a moment, she thought that he had fainted with his eyes open, but then he groaned and shook his head.

"That's... problematic."

To say the least. But she nodded sympathetically. "I know."

They sat in silence for a few minutes. Everys wanted to say more, but anything she offered would be empty platitudes.

"So are we going to make it?" Narius finally whispered.

She smiled. "You and me? Yes. The Dynasty... I don't know."

He blew out a long breath, which blossomed into a yawn. She took that as her cue. She leaned forward and kissed him on the forehead.

"You rest. I'll be back again soon. And maybe we'll be able to figure this out."

"That would be nice."

With that, she slipped from the medical bay. She lingered outside of the door for just a moment, long enough to swipe away a tear. And then she set out for her quarters. Narius would need time to heal. He would need space to recover his strength. Until he did, she would have to do more to help. She would, because he needed her. And she needed him.

46

The next morning, Trule was silent as she laid out Everys's clothes and made sure her toiletries were ready. Most days, Trule kept up a running commentary about palace gossip, peppering in her own pithy observations.

But as the silence dragged past her shower, Everys stepped into Trule's path and caught her hands.

"Trule, are you all right?" She winced at the question. Of course she wasn't. How could she be?

"No, I am not." Trule forced a smile. "But I still draw breath and there is work yet to be done. So I am here."

"Have you heard anything from your parents?" Everys asked. "Did your sister get her name?"

"I heard from them this morning. The soldiers who responded to Brencis's attack remained at the Oasis to allow the Naming Day ceremony to take place." If Trule felt bitter about leaving before that happened, her voice didn't betray it. "And yes, my sister has now chosen a new name: Tellisandrika. Tellis for short."

Everys smiled. "That's a lovely name. Does it mean something?"

"It does." Trule looked down at the floor. "'Tears for a fallen hero.' If you'll excuse me, Blessed."

Trule brushed past her to head into the living quarters. The strength drained out of Everys's legs and she collapsed. She buried her face in her hands and wept for her fallen hero as well.

By the time Everys emerged from her bedroom, she had managed to compose herself, although she knew her emotions were frayed to the point of snapping. When she spotted Challix, her assistant gave her a brave smile that almost pushed her over the edge again.

"Please tell me we don't have anything pressing," Everys said.

Challix offered her a shaky smile of her own. "You did have a full schedule, but I have postponed everything for today, and I have excuses ready for tomorrow and the day after as well. Never fear, Blessed, we are going to give you the space and time you need."

Everys wanted to hug her, but she doubted Challix would stand for that breach in protocol. "Are you at least taking care of yourself as well?"

Challix laughed. "There's too much to do, Blessed, and—"

"Take some time off, Challix. That's an order."

Her assistant's mouth clicked shut. She looked ready to object, but then she nodded. "As you wish, Blessed. Before I go, though, there was one matter I felt couldn't be delayed."

Challix signaled to one of the guards, who opened the door to her quarters. Before the guard could get out of the way, Oluna hurried into the room with Masruq following close behind. Oluna gasped the moment she saw Everys and rushed forward, hugging her tightly.

"You poor dear! The criers were positively filled with the news of what happened! Are you all right? Are you whole?" Oluna asked.

"I doubt they would have let us in to see her if she wasn't, my dearest," Masruq commented with a wry smile.

She shot him a look. "And you wanted us to go on retreat to the Kronin!"

Masruq shrugged expansively, but before he could say anything, Oluna turned her attention back to Everys.

"Tell me truthfully: how are you?"

A sob bubbled up through her, but Everys fought it back. She had cried enough already. "I'm well, all things considered."

"Such a brave facade. Now I know I was right to come here," Oluna said.

"Why are you here? I know we have dinner at your manor coming up soon, but—"

"I'm moving in with you." Oluna beamed at her.

"Y-you're what?"

"It was Masruq's idea." She shot her husband another look. "One of the few good ones he's had in a while."

"What can I say? I was overdue," Masruq said with a chuckle.

"Not in your quarters, obviously. You and the king will still have your privacy. But given everything that is happening here, I thought it would be best if I'm here to help you. Support you. Do whatever you need me to do." Once again, Oluna beamed at her.

Everys jaw worked, trying to form words, but she didn't even know how to respond.

"Don't worry, Blessed, my wife is extremely discreet," Masruq said. "I can't tell you how many important discussions she's been privy to and she hasn't breathed a word of it to anyone. And she will stay out of your way if you need her to. I just thought, given how much King Narius will have to prepare for the *harsannon*, you might like the extra company."

Everys turned back to Oluna, who had an expectant look on her face. She knew it wasn't a question of space. They had plenty of empty rooms in the guest wing. What Masruq said made sense. She knew that Narius's recovery and training for the *harsannon* would have to take priority. And she always enjoyed Oluna's company. So she smiled and nodded.

Masruq clapped his hands. "Excellent! Well, I will have the servants bring over what you need later today, dear. For now, I have to head down to the office. The situation in Maotoa is likely going to wreak havoc on our shipping routes, and my staff is working on projections for what that could do to the economy. I'll see you both soon."

With that, Masruq retreated from Everys's quarters. Challix offered her a smile as well and followed him out. That left Oluna looking expectantly at Everys. Everys wracked her mind, trying to think of something they could do. She wouldn't want to send Oluna away, not so soon after coming to the palace.

Oluna must have read her uncertainty. She laughed. "You don't have to worry about me, dear. I can entertain myself easily enough."

Everys smiled. "The way that you amuse yourself at banquets and galas? How many rumors will you start while you're here?"

"Only harmless ones, I assure you," Oluna said. "And none about you. So tell me. What is happening?"

A sob from Everys's lips. She flailed her hands, as if groping for the right words to express herself. Oluna made a soft clucking noise and steered her for a sofa.

Before Everys knew what was happening, so much of the story spilled out of her: the Dunestriders' attack, Brencis's appearance, Kevtho's death, Narius's injuries. She struggled to filter out the details about Brencis's *ur-keleshen* and how she had healed Paine. She felt like she could have confided those secrets with Oluna, but she stopped herself. Too much of a risk, especially given Oluna's habit of gossiping. In spite of her promise, Everys knew better than to give her friend something that juicy.

Oluna listened to Everys's babbling story, gasping at the appropriate places, before she patted the back of her hand. "To have gone through so much. But what about your father? Hasn't he helped you at all?"

Everys shook her head. Not even a little.

Oluna bristled and popped to her feet. "Then I'm going to have a talk with that sandslinker right now! Where is he?"

"Oluna, no!" Everys snared her friend's hand. "Please don't."

At first, Oluna tried to pull herself free, but then she sat back down on the couch with a huff. "Fine. I won't. But I'm not happy with him. Not even a little."

Everys managed a weak smile. She wasn't either, but she doubted that Oluna attacking her father would make anything better.

Oluna sighed. "Cheer up, Blessed. You're all safe and back at the palace. And who knows? Maybe your father will come around and see things your way."

"You think so?" Everys asked.

"He might," Oluna said, then patted her legs and stood up. "Now if you'll excuse me, I'm going to go make a nuisance of myself to the palace steward until he finds me a room. And don't worry, I'll steer clear of your father until you say it's safe to talk to him. Agreed?"

Everys smiled and nodded. And for just a brief moment, she felt like her situation would improve. With a friend like Oluna at her side, how could it not?

47

Once again, Everys found herself wandering the halls of the palace. There was no meeting to crash, no decisions for her to make. All she could do was wait and stew in the tension.

She turned a corner into the palace library. At one time, this room had probably been filled with actual ink-on-paper books. But since the advent of digital scribers, those had been disposed of. Because of that, the library was now just a large room with rows of empty shelves, punctuated by nooks with chairs and desks. She kept thinking that maybe they should find a different use for the room, but for now, this was a good place to disappear when you didn't want to be bothered.

Soft footfalls came from around one of the shelves, then, much to her surprise, Papa rounded the corner, reading from a scriber as he walked. He almost passed by her, so absorbed by what he carried. And for a fleeting moment, he looked happy, at peace. Memories welled up inside Everys, of Papa sitting in his chair in the cramped apartment, reading something off a scriber after a long day's work, injecting his own humorous commentary into gossip stories or explaining something happening in the news.

He must have noticed her out of the corner of his eye because his gaze hardened, and he turned to her. Her heart lurched at his expression.

"I hope you don't mind," he said. "I wasn't sure if there were rules about who could use this."

"There aren't," Everys said. "Honestly, I've never heard of anyone using this room for much more than a place to hide for an hour or two."

He grunted, then looked around. His expression turned wistful. "Galan would have loved it here if these shelves were still full."

Tears stung Everys's eyes. "She definitely would."

They stared at each other. Words tumbled through her mind, and she tried to sort them into something she could say, something she could offer to fix whatever was broken between them. But nothing she stitched together seemed helpful. Just empty platitudes or half-serious promises.

Then Papa sighed. "This isn't what I wanted for us."

"What?" she asked.

"This." He gestured between them. "Whatever this is. None of this. Not for any of you."

She tipped her head to one side, confused. He had made his feelings about her marriage perfectly clear. And yes, they had both grieved over Legarr's death. But what else did he regret? "What do you mean?"

Papa stammered a bit, then brightened. "Do you have any ink?"

Everys shot a worried look around the library, but no one had entered. And really, no one would. She plucked a bead from her bracelet and passed it to Papa. His eyes widened.

"You have ink on you right now?" he whispered.

The last thing she wanted to do was fight with him. "You did ask me for some."

He looked ready to object, but his mouth clicked shut. He rolled it in his finger, then crushed it. He tested the ink between his fingers, then chuckled.

"Clever. Where'd you come up with this?"

Everys hesitated. She couldn't tell him the truth. Tormod's secret wasn't hers to share.

Thankfully, Papa didn't dwell on it. He motioned for her to follow him deeper into the stacks to two chairs in a secluded corner.

"I know a rune. It's one my father taught me, an ancient rune used by Siporan troubadors. It was used to enhance their performances, but he used it to tell me bedtime stories." He motioned for her to sit down. As she did, he daubed some ink onto his finger and traced a rune onto his opposite wrist. Then he pressed his wrist to the side of her head. A tingle wormed through her head from the point of contact, and she gasped...

She sat in the middle of a misty void, with no floor below or ceiling above. She lurched, but oddly, she didn't feel like she was in danger.

"Strange, isn't it?" Papa's voice surrounded her.

He coalesced out of the mist and smiled at her. Her heart lurched at his appearance. He no longer looked so haggard and tired. There was no trace of his anger or bitterness. This was her father as she knew him before, when she was just a child first learning how to sketch the runes.

"It's been a while since I've used this. Hold on." Papa closed his eyes and his features twitched in concentration.

When he opened them, a foggy maelstrom swirled around them, then retreated, revealing furniture, walls, and shadowy people that resolved into...

"Mama?" Everys gasped.

It was her mother, but older than she had ever seen her. Round and matronly, she bustled through a phantasmal kitchen, humming. Then another person stepped out of the mists, revealing himself as Papa. He, too, looked older, but stouter and happier, with more gray at his temples and smile lines around his eyes.

Everys looked around and realized where they were: the apartment over the Broken Sword Shop, the one she had lived in before she'd become queen. A kitchen was tucked into one corner of the main room, with a table sitting nearby, eight chairs surrounding it. She turned to see the living area, a long couch facing a vidscreen on a plain white wall. To her right were three doors, the center one leading to a bathroom, flanked by the entrances to Mama and Papa's bedroom and then Galan and hers.

Her heart leaped at the familiar sight, only this wasn't the dilapidated near wreck she had known. Yes, the apartment was nothing fancy, the furnishings simple, but the whole room exuded care and well-maintained love.

She started to ask a question, but she was cut off by the sound of someone knocking at the door. Mama hurried over to the apartment door and opened it, revealing Galan. Like their parents, Galan was older, but Everys still recognized the excitement in her expression.

"Good day at work?" Papa asked.

Galan laughed. "You could say that. I think I finally have my students interested in translating that Plissk travelogue, but then they got me distracted—"

"Imagine that!" Mama said with a chuckle.

Galan gave her an annoyed look, but it was so obviously faked. "—by asking about how what Irrke wrote lines up with the official histories of the Dynasty. So we spent some time discussing textual criticism and how to actually read ancient stories properly..."

Galan rambled on, discussing her favorite academic topics. Everys's eyes teared up. She hadn't seen her older sister in years, and while she knew she didn't look like this, it felt good to see her again.

There was another knock on the door. Before anyone could answer it, Legarr, her younger brother, bustled in. Everys's breath caught in her throat. The last time she had seen him, he was being consumed by a toratropic spell, his voice cracked and dry. But there he was, alive and overflowing with energy. Like Galan, Legarr was older, but instead of his usual sly grin, he wore an easygoing smile.

Much to her surprise, a woman wearing traditional Siporan clothing followed him into the shop. At least, Everys thought she was supposed to be a woman. The person's body had that shape, but the person's face was featureless and indistinct, a hazy, pale blank. She glanced at Papa, the real Papa, who shrugged.

Oh, of course. Papa had never met Tilash, Legarr's wife. The family hadn't approved of him marrying a non-Siporan and hadn't attended the wedding. Then they'd left for the vigil shortly thereafter. But warmth washed through Everys at the thought of her sister-in-law. Tilash had taken her in after Everys's first marriage to Narius had ended.

Something prickled in her mind and she frowned. It felt like something was rifling through her thoughts. Then a ripple of light flowed over Legarr's imaginary wife and, when it faded, Tilash stood next to her husband, holding on to his arm and laughing at something that Galan had said. Her clothing transformed as well, changing into the well-worn outfits Tilash owned. Papa startled, looking between the image and Everys.

"Is that what she looks like?" he whispered.

Everys gaped at the changed woman. "How did that happen?"

"It's a collaborative spell," Papa said. "I control the narrative, but you can help fill in the blanks as needed."

Interesting. She glanced around the room and focused on the walls around the vidscreen. The blank white space rippled, and a second later, pictures appeared on the wall, showing a view of the palace gardens, the Cold Light's forest, the skyline of Bastion. She smiled, pleased with the results.

The five figments sat down at the table, chatting and laughing and gossiping.

"This is what I wanted for us." Papa walked into the scene, circling the table. "The shop, our family. Galan working in a university somewhere. Legarr working in the shop with me. And you..."

Another knock at the door. An image of Everys bustled into the apartment, carrying a basket of what looked like groceries. Everys's eyes widened at the sight of herself. Papa's imagined Everys was pregnant, at least six months along if not more. She looked at Papa, who again shrugged.

"I always thought you would be the best mother out of our children," he said.

Everys chuckled and followed him into the images. She circled his illusion of her, examining his version. She was older, like the others. But happiness and contentedness radiated from her. She laughed at something Legarr said, and Everys could hear the simple joy in the sound. She swooped over to the Papa-illusion and kissed him on the cheek before setting the contents of her basket out on the table.

"All I ever wanted for us was to be a family," Papa whispered. "Happy. Together. Faithful. That's it."

Tears welled in Everys's eyes. She wanted that too. Watching it play out like that, she understood Papa's disappointment. None of their lives had turned out like this. And she wished they had too—maybe not the pregnant part; she wasn't ready for that yet—but she couldn't deny the longing that pulled at her, to be in this simpler version of her life.

The door to the apartment banged open and a formless man walked in. He, too, wore Siporan clothing, and like Tilash had been, his face was indistinct and vague. But the moment Everys focused on him, a ripple of light washed over him and, a second later, Narius stood in the apartment. But unlike Tilash, his clothing hadn't changed. He still wore Siporan garb as he walked up behind the Everys-illusion and hugged her from behind.

Everys's heart lurched to see him, healthy and whole. He was so strong, so sure of himself, every bit the man she had fallen in love with. She wanted nothing more than to gather him into her arms, cling to him, and never let go. It didn't matter that he wasn't real. She wanted him to be like this again.

Papa gasped and the idyllic scene vanished. Everys blinked as the library spun around her, and a wave of dizziness crashed over her. The disorientation quickly faded.

"Is that... is that how you see him?" Papa asked quietly. "As one of us?"

She considered it. She had never really thought about it, but yes, she did. Narius was so respectful of her beliefs, so curious about her culture. So she nodded.

Papa grunted. "But what he's doing in the archives..."

Everys sighed. "I know, Papa. I'm not happy about that either. But I think we need what he's doing."

"Why would we ever need that abomination?"

"Because other people are creating new runes, and we don't know what they do. The one I experimented with. And do you remember how..." She swallowed hard, then forced the words out. "...how my Swordbound, Kevtho, died?"

Papa nodded.

"The official story is that he died fighting in a duel. And that's true. But Brencis used an *ur-keleshen* in the fight. One with six runes on the blade."

Papa's eyes widened. "But the original only had four."

"Right. Papa, someone is already experimenting with toratropic magic, and we don't know what they're doing. I'm not saying that we should create our own—I know that's a path that leads back to the mage-kings—but shouldn't we be able to prepare ourselves?"

He grunted and shifted in his chair. He stared at the floor.

"Papa, please." Everys reached over and lightly rested her hand over her father's. "I'm not saying Narius is perfect, but give him another chance."

Before Papa could respond, the door to the library opened and Challix hustled in.

"Blessed!" she called. "Strategist Overturn was hoping he could speak with you about what happened at the Oasis."

Overturn had been interviewing everyone at the Naming Day, trying to glean information about what units had been with Brencis. She didn't know what she'd be able to contribute, but she had agreed to give whatever she could. She started to follow Challix, but then turned back to Papa.

"Papa, Oluna—Masruq's wife?—she just moved into one of the guest rooms. I bet she'd love to explore the royal gardens with you," she said.

Papa looked up, but shook his head. "No, thank you. I have a lot to consider."

48

"Your Strength?" Tormod prompted.

Narius stared past the spymaster, not blinking. Not caring if he didn't focus. There was just too much to process. Maotoa, conquered by the Dalark. Brencis first saving Everys from Dunestrider violence and then murdering one of her guards with an ancient Siporan weapon. And then...

"Tell me again," he whispered.

Tormod looked down. "My sources have confirmed that what Brencis told the queen is true. Two weeks ago, before a prelate in the Low River Province, Duke Brencis married Viara. There are multiple witnesses willing to attest to it."

"How did we miss this until now?" Narius asked.

Tormod grimaced. "In truth, Your Strength, I don't have a good explanation. Several of my teams have reported difficulties while working in the Dynasty's holdings. Interference. Complications. A few even suspect they're being targeted."

"By the Imperium?"

"That's one possibility," Tormod said. "I don't have enough information to speculate, I'm afraid. All I can do is apologize for our lapse and promise to do better."

Narius considered upbraiding him right there, but he held off. Yes, Tormod should have found out, but then, Bokil should have as well. Or the noble families who controlled the Low River Province. There was plenty of blame to go around.

"What do you want me to do, Your Strength?" Tormod asked.

Narius considered it, then came to a decision. "Focus on Maotoa. We need to know how Dalark invaded so swiftly and thoroughly. The Maotoans obviously helped, but—"

"But that doesn't explain the nature of their help." Tormod nodded. "Consider it done, Your Strength. Now rest. I'm sure Vizier Paine will keep things well in hand until you're fully recovered."

Narius grunted and looked at the vacant bed next to him. Thankfully, Everys's healing rune had done the trick and Paine recovered far faster than anyone had anticipated. That allowed him to leave his bed and return to limited duty, taking over from Challix and trying to steer the Dynasty during the midst of this crisis.

When he turned back, Tormod had vanished. Instead, the door to the infirmary opened and Professor P'layvo and Scrivener Tolistan bustled through. He quickly dismissed the doctors and nurses so they could talk freely. The medical personnel obeyed, although with a bit of grumbling.

"Scrivener, Professor, any news?" He levered himself up to sitting.

Tolistan shook his head. "Unfortunately not, Your Strength."

P'layvo laughed. "That's not entirely accurate. We have made some progress. It's tangential to our original goal."

"What do you mean?"

The professor settled onto Paine's former bed with a sigh. "We haven't made any progress with the runes themselves, Your Strength. The sample size we're working with is too small. While the AI has flagged numerous possible connections, we simply don't have enough data to make any conclusions."

"So what progress have you made?" Narius couldn't understand why she was so optimistic.

"Well, two weeks ago, Scrivener Tolistan made an interesting observation. He wondered if the ancient Siporan language, the one used in their holy texts, was somehow derived from the runes. Given what we know of linguistic taxonomy, that's entirely likely. And we have far more data for the AI to process with the ancient Siporan language. We've been scanning in as many texts as we can, along with recordings of Siporan elders speaking in that language."

Narius barely understood what she had just said, so he looked at Tolistan for an explanation.

The scrivener frowned. "She's being far too generous. While the AI has a lot to analyze and we may even discover some insights about my people's ancient language, we're not going to learn much at all."

"Why not?" Narius asked.

"Because we're missing a bridge." He held out his right and left hands a far distance apart. "On this side, we have the runes. On the other, we have the ancient language. The AI has indicated there might be connections, but we're missing a bridge between the two, a written vocabulary that is halfway between them. Until we find that, all of this will remain theoretical."

P'layvo chuckled. "I'm not quite so pessimistic as Tolistan, but he does have a valid point. We may be reaching an unfortunate but natural endpoint in this research project, Your Strength. Unless we find more examples of Siporan runes or Tolistan's bridge, we won't make any more progress."

Narius mulled it over. There likely were more examples of runes out there, scattered throughout the Siporan Ascendancy's former territory. Their fallen capital, Nekek the Bright, probably contained a treasure trove. But all of it was within the Demilitarized Zone, and given the current tensions with Dalark, there was no way to send anyone to look.

"Then I thank you for your assistance, Professor. I will make sure that you and your team are fairly compensated. But I have to insist you keep your findings to yourself."

"I am quite aware of how this works, Your Strength," P'layvo said. "I will submit all of our preliminary findings to you via an encrypted scriber. You will have sole access. And if you should come into possession of additional data that can continue our research, my team would be more than happy to pick up where we left off."

Narius smiled, but he definitely felt some sadness. He had thought he was on to something with this research. To have it sputter out like this was more than disappointing.

Professor P'layvo excused herself, but Tolistan lingered.

"Is there something else, Scrivener?" he asked.

Again, Tolistan hesitated. "Forgive me for bringing it up, Your Strength, but I've found that rumors travel faster in the palace than in Fair Havens. I understand that you had some sort of argument with Favid?"

Narius smiled. "Not me, but the queen. A disagreement about whether or not she could cast her family's healing rune on me."

"I see." A frown flitted across Tolistan's face. He turned to leave.

"You have something else to add?" Narius prompted.

Tolistan sighed and turned back to him. "I'm sorry, Your Strength. It's really not my place to comment on this. It's a family matter. According to ancient Siporan tradition, the patriarch of a family entrusted with a Principality rune has final say on how it's used. I'm just sorry you got caught up in that."

"It's all right," Narius said. "I'm on the mend, and I'll be out of here soon."

"Be that as it may, Favid's behavior is..." He shook his head. "I've said too much already."

"Then consider this part of my lessons," Narius said. "Why would a patriarch forbid the use of a rune? Hypothetically?"

Tolistan smiled weakly. "According to tradition, for any number of reasons. If they worried that the rune's use would result in a rebuke. If they felt that the rune's user wasn't of sound judgment. If they felt the recipient of the rune wouldn't appreciate it. And then there are the unwritten reasons, many of which stem from hatred."

His voice trailed off, but Narius could easily connect the dots. Favid hated him. That was all too clear. And that hatred was spilling over into Everys.

"So if I was Siporan, he... I mean, a patriarch might not object?" Narius said.

"One would hope, but I've often found that when we try to judge another's worthiness, we're rarely satisfied. There's always a flaw, an... impurity we find disqualifying. In your case, it's the fact that you're king of the Dynasty that tried to destroy my people. If it wasn't that, it would be that you're a non-Siporan. Even when you officially convert, people will still see you as an outsider. And even if you were a full-blooded Siporan, they would judge you by your actions and your attitudes. Purity of belief and thought is a self-consuming obsession. It's never satisfied."

Narius thought of what Tolistan had said. He certainly saw that same line of thinking within the Dynasty's politics as well. Supreme Prelate Istragon, for example, railing against Narius for not being faithful enough to the Warrior's ways. Or Brencis, saying that he wasn't strong enough to face Dalark. Was there a way out of that vicious cycle? He started to ask that question, only to have his thoughts blossom into a yawn.

Tolistan chuckled. "I had best let you rest, Your Strength. From what I understand, you'll have to start training for the *harsannon* soon."

Narius swallowed a groan. His doctors wouldn't like that, but what else could he do? He had to fight. But yes, maybe taking a nap wouldn't be the worst thing. Summon his strength. As the scrivener excused himself, Narius hunkered down in the bed and allowed sleep to overtake him.

Everys watched as Narius slept.

She had come down, hoping to spend some time with him. When she found him sleeping, she let him. It was more important for him to rest, But she still maintained a quiet vigil at his side, hoping that maybe, just her presence would be enough.

But it wasn't. Clearly. He shifted, groaning and wincing as if he was in pain. He was still so heavily bandaged, and although the doctors tried to present his condition in the most positive light, it was clear they were frustrated. He needed time to heal, to recuperate, to gather his strength. With all the crises facing the Dynasty, though, he wasn't going to be given that time.

She frowned. But maybe there was something she could do about that.

She quietly slipped out of the infirmary and strode through the palace until she came to Challix's office, a modest-sized room, so orderly that it almost made Everys's eyes hurt looking at it. Challix sat at her desk, working on a computer terminal with quiet concentration. Once Everys stepped inside, though, she looked up and offered a friendly smile. "How can I help you, Blessed?"

"I need to know who is going to be on the panel judging Narius's combat."

"That's not supposed to be public knowledge to keep them impartial, but that's easily done." Challix turned to the computer terminal and started to pull up the information, but then she hesitated. "And?"

"And then we need to invite them all over for a little chat," Everys said.

Challix smirked and nodded. "Consider it done."

Everys nodded to herself. If Istragon wanted to play his little game, let him. She liked games. And she was going to show him she could play too.

49

Everys ran a hand down the front of her dress, smoothing out the fabric. For this particular social get together, she had chosen a conservative outfit: a floor-length gown with sleeves that came down midway between her wrists and elbows, with simple green-gray fabric with minimal brocade and embroidery along the bodice. Her hair hung loose and she wore minimal jewelry. Trule and the girls had succeeded again, creating a casual look. Because that's what this should appear to be: a casual conversation between potential friends.

She glanced out of the corner of her eye at Challix. Once again, her assistant had done her job admirably. According to her research, the four judges for the *harsannon* were supposed to be kept secret, even from each other. In theory, this was to keep them free from outside influence. But Narius and Paine had worked with Istragon in selecting them: two suggested by Narius, two selected by the prelate. Getting the names had been easy enough.

Getting them to the palace without them figuring out why they had been invited was trickier. The four judges had little in common when it came to their personalities, politics, or family connections, so there really wasn't a good reason to summon the four of them together. She didn't want them to be on their guard, but she also didn't want to resort to elaborate cover stories or excuses either. In the end, she went with a simple explanation: she hadn't met any of these nobles yet, and she was correcting the problem with an informal get together.

"The last of the judges arrived just ten minutes ago," Challix whispered to her as they moved to the doors of the western conservatory.

"Who is it?" Everys asked.

Challix made a face. "Tupa Mellisan."

Everys understood immediately. Lady Tupa Mellisan was one of Istragon's choices, a member of a noble family who, until just twenty years ago, had been considered one of the major houses. But due to some bad investments and the machinations of their rivals, their standing had been severely damaged. Challix suspected that Tupa had agreed to being a judge in the hopes of currying favor on behalf of her house. Challix clearly didn't approve, but Everys saw an opening. Hopefully she'd find more with the others.

The servants at the door hauled them open, and Everys braced herself as a wave of warm, humid air rolled over her. She coughed discreetly at the sweet smells that chased the wave. The conservatory was a rarely used room in the palace, an outgrowth of the royal gardens where less hearty plants could be grown in a more controlled environment. The room was bright thanks to the thick glass panels that served as both walls and ceiling. But the clusters of thick greenery and flowers that peppered the interior made the space feel cramped. Everys wound her way past fragrant bushes and clumps of flowers before finding her guests standing in a cluster near a small stone fountain. Three servants circulated among them, carrying trays of food and drinks.

Everys paused to take stock of the judges. She singled out Tupa Mellisan right away. She was a tall woman, almost as tall as her, with broad shoulders and thick black hair. Rumor had it her grandfather had been an Ixactl servant. The story had clinched her house's downfall, but Everys understood why people believed it. She looked like she could tear a stone in half with her bare hands. Given the way she harangued one of the servants, Everys immediately understood Challix's distaste.

Spanica Trentwether stood nearby, watching Tupa's tantrum through thick glasses. He was a middle-aged Hinaen man, hunched over and small in stature, with thinning red-and-gray hair. The Trentwethers were an interesting house; rather than focus on making money, they seemed intent on generating knowledge. The Trentwethers had founded half a dozen universities throughout the Dynasty's holdings over the past three hundred years, and they supported a hundred more. How they parlayed that into a family fortune was something of a mystery. They were a minor noble house, but they seemed content with their status and could be counted on to not cause drama. That was part of the reason why Narius chose Spanica to be one of his judges.

Lady Anadda Leedeke sipped at a glass of wine while she chatted with the fourth judge, Count Elsrick Bathogin. Lady Leedeke was an older woman, maybe in her midforties, with silver-blonde hair and a sharp gaze that dissected the entire room with a glance. Her holdings were situated just outside the ruins of Elregan, the Dynasty's ancient capital. Technically, no one owned those ruins. Instead, they were held in "common trust" for the good of the Dynasty. But everyone knew the Leedekes were the ruins' wardens and caretakers, which gave them a good deal of clout within the noble families. She would have expected Lady Anadda to side with Istragon, but Narius had chosen her instead.

Count Elsrick was a younger Grerid man, dressed in a sharp business suit, with piercing blue eyes and a shock of dyed-blue hair that stood on end. Technically, the Bathogins didn't have any real estate holdings and their family was relatively new, being added to the peerage only a hundred years earlier. But what gave them their influence was their stranglehold on most media in the Dynasty. They had heavily invested in the crier guilds, they financed book publishers and entertainment companies. That had been enough to catapult them into the major houses, much to the consternation of many of the more established houses. And while she would have expected someone so unconventional to be more open to Narius, Elsrick had been chosen by Istragon.

As Everys looked over the conservatory, Oluna sidled up to her, already sipping from a glass of wine. "Are you ready, Blessed?"

Everys nodded with determination. "Any advice?"

"Oh, I've been chatting them up as best as I could. Tupa is in her usual friendly mood. Annada is hard to read. Spanica has been droning on about his latest research projects. And Elsrick is... well, let's just say I'm not planning on inviting him into my home anytime soon." Oluna shuddered.

Everys pressed her lips together into a thin line. But she had invited them all here for a specific reason. She plastered on a smile and stepped forward. "My friends, it's so good of you to join me. I know this is rather unusual—"

Tupa snorted and actually rolled her eyes.

"—but I felt it good to get to know you all better." Everys turned to Tupa. "For example, Lady Mellisan. I understand that your family recently invested in a fleet of fishing boats out of Sholn."

Tupa straightened and looked pleased with herself. She nodded. "We did indeed, Blessed. A significant investment, but we felt it was important to contribute to the Dynasty's resources given the current uncertainties."

"You mean you saw a chance to fleece the people should food prices go up due to a war," Elsrick said with a snort. "But I can't help but wonder how careful you were when you bought them. You might find it to be a more costly investment than you anticipated."

At first, Tupa spluttered at his words, but then her face paled. "What do you mean?"

"I have my sources, Lady Tupa, and they've told me some interesting things about your new boats. Let's leave it at that." Elsrick smiled and took a sip of his wine.

Everys quickly turned to Spanica. "And Lord Trentwether. I hear that your family recently opened a new series of libraries in the Low River Province. You must be very proud as well."

"Knowledge should be shared, Blessed. That's actually why I'm glad to have received your invitation. I'm hoping I might persuade the royal family to search the royal archives for a specific type of artifact." Spanica pulled out a scriber and activated it. The small screen displayed an image of a blue-green crystal embedded in a bronze crescent, held in place by large iron spikes. Spanica beckoned for Annada to look as well. "I recently came into possession of this piece and find it fascinating. I was hoping I might be able to acquire similar objects for further research. If either of you have artifacts such as this, I would be most interesting in making a trade for them."

Everys fought to keep from laughing. Perfect! This was the opening she would need and—

"Oh, why settle for that, Spanica?" Elsrick said. "I'd be willing to bet you'd be able to get a lot more from the queen if you just asked. I suspect she's in a particularly generous mood today."

Cold sluiced through Everys's body. Lady Annada quirked a brow at her but didn't say anything. She didn't have to, though, as Tupa whirled on Elsrick, her confusion splashed across her face.

"What do you mean?" Tupa asked.

Elsrick chuckled and downed the rest of his wine. "You haven't figured out why we're here yet? We don't have anything in common. The queen gave us the excuse of wanting to meet us, but why like this? Why now? And why us four specifically?"

Everys exchanged a look with Oluna. The other woman shrugged, but Everys could read the worry painted across her face.

Spanica looked at the other guests, his gaze sharpening. "A valid question, to be sure."

"So I'm going to tell you about something that happened recently. Tell me if this sounds at all familiar," Elsrick said. "A few weeks ago, I was contacted by Supreme Prelate Istragon. He informed me that the king would soon be participating in ritual combat to determine his worthiness to rule, and he asked me to help judge the competition when the time came."

Comprehension dawned on Tupa's face. Spanica nodded thoughtfully. And Lady Annada remained just as impassive as ever. Everys twisted her fingers together in hopes that it would help rein in her near panic. She turned to Challix, who regarded her with wide eyes. She made a calming motion and gestured for her to continue.

Everys nodded and turned to her guests. "All right, it's true. All four of you are judges for the upcoming combat. And I did bring you here to talk to you about what will happen."

"Is that what we're calling bribery now?" Elsrick asked.

Everys's cheeks blazed with heat, but Spanica held up a hand.

"Let's not judge her too harshly," he said. "She hasn't done anything improper. At least, not yet."

She couldn't miss the emphasis he put on those last two words.

"Oh, I'm not objecting," Elsrick said. "This is how the Dynasty has done things for generations, isn't it? I'm just curious what she's going to offer."

Everys swallowed a sigh and rose to her full height. "What is it you would want, Count Elsrick?"

He smiled lazily. "Actually, I don't want anything. Istragon has already granted me exclusive broadcast rights to the combat. The entire Dynasty will see the combat thanks to me, and I'll bring in a decent profit in doing so. I doubt there's much more that you could offer me."

From his tone, it was clear that he wouldn't mind her making suggestions. She wracked her brain, trying to come up with the right bait. What would Elsrick want?

"Well, I know what I want," Tupa said. "Everyone knows who's responsible for what happened to my family. It was the Uwendis. They manufactured the whole scandal, and they nearly destroyed us. You want my support for the king, Blessed? I want the Uwendis' blood. I want their house to be dissolved. I want them wiped off the face of the Dynasty!"

A weight settled in the depths of Everys's stomach. She could probably do that. A few well-placed calls, the right social pressures, and the Uwendis would be quickly abandoned by the other noble houses. She glanced over at Oluna. If she unleashed her friend on the Uwendis, their fall would happen that much faster. But none of that felt like a good idea. For starters, the Uwendis were responsible for producing the Dynasty's armored land vehicles. Destroying their family would likely result in weakening the Dynasty's military, and she just couldn't do that. Plus she wasn't about to destroy another family to satisfy Tupa.

"I'd like to amend my previous request," Spanica said. "In addition to donations for my new libraries, I'd also like access to any special collection of volumes that the royal family might have for my own private research."

Everys turned to him and frowned. "What do you mean?"

Spanica tapped his glasses back in place. "I've often been fascinated by the sweep of history, Blessed. I used to focus on the what of history, but now I'd like to know the why. Why were your people defeated during the Night of Shards? Why did the Cold Light need their Hearth back? Why did the Weyfir choose to peacefully integrate with the Dynasty? We all know the official stories, but I want to get to the truth of the matter. And I know I won't be able to do that with records available to the public. But I suspect there are documents and primary sources that the palace has that no one else does. I want to see them."

That seemed more doable, but from Tupa's expression, she was going to want an answer to her demand and quickly. But before Everys could say anything, Lady Annada cleared her throat.

"I've been quite interested in seeing where the king has been taking us as a Dynasty," she said. "As the keepers of Elregan, we Leedekes are all too aware of what the Dynasty has been. It's been refreshing to see someone intent on moving us toward a better future.

"But at the same time, I fear that in the rush toward progress, we are losing sight of who we are and have been. So I have a request that I believe is in everyone's best interest. Several noble families have broached the idea of creating a museum to house the objects contained within the royal archives. If you want my guaranteed support, Blessed, you will officially endorse this idea and suggest that the museum be built in my family's holdings near Elregan. We will incorporate the ruins with the museum and hold the artifacts there as a common trust for all."

Everys's stomach twisted. There was no way she could agree to that, was there? No, not really. After all, the objects in the archives should never have been taken. She was more convinced of that than ever, especially after she had returned both the Hearth and the *ma-se-kranna* to their rightful owners. And there was no way that she would allow the Principalities to be housed in a museum near Elregan. She could already hear Papa's conniption at the very idea.

But she had to say something. "I am definitely... open to possibilities. I'm sure we can find something that will be agreeable to all of you if we just—"

"I've told you what I want, Blessed," Tupa snapped. "You give me the Uwendis, and my support is yours."

"Be reasonable, Tupa," Spanica replied. "Certainly there's something else you would be interested in."

"Says the *kathartin* who is only interested in books!"

Spanica bristled at the insult, an old Dynastic word for "commoner." Elsrick guffawed.

Everys balled her hands into fists. She would find a way through this. She would. She had to.

She couldn't. And she didn't.

By the time the guests had left, Everys realized she had made a bigger mess than she'd intended. Tupa wouldn't let go of her demand that the Uwendis pay for their supposed crimes against her family. And Everys suspected that now her name had been added to Tupa's list of enemies as well. And while Lady Leedeke hadn't demanded any sort of promises, the knowing look she had given Everys as she left spoke volumes. She knew that Everys wouldn't cooperate with her request. Hopefully she would continue to support Narius in the *harsannon*.

Spanica, though, had agreed to vote for Narius. Granting him access to the records would be easy enough, although Everys suspected it wouldn't be as simple as that. It never was. As for Count Elsrick, he had promised to be fair and impartial in judging the contest. Given how disastrous this meeting had been, Everys supposed that was as good as it would get with him.

"It was a valiant try, Blessed," Oluna said. "I'm sorry it didn't work out."

Everys sighed and ran a hand through her hair. She felt like she had just wasted several hours she would never get back.

"So now what?" Challix asked as the servants cleaned up the conservatory.

Everys weighed her options. She supposed she could visit with Lady Leedeke and Lady Tupa in more private settings, but she knew that would be futile. She couldn't give them what they wanted and that would likely undercut whatever standing Narius had with them. She could leave it all alone and hope for the best, but that didn't seem wise either. Really, the more Everys thought about it, there was only one thing she could do. Something she should have done right away.

"No more games," she said, mostly to herself. "Time to take the fight directly to Istragon."

50

Quartus tugged at his collar. For a flickering moment, he remembered parties at the palace. Yes, they were often stuffy affairs, filled with self-important people congratulating each other for victories they didn't achieve. But at least at the palace, he had a staff who picked out his clothing and made sure it fit. As an outlaw, Quartus had to find an appropriate suit for the party he and Yusra were going to infiltrate. So he had scoured secondhand clothing stores until he'd found an outfit. The tan pants, dark blue shirt, and overcoat smelled vaguely of age and neglect. They'd never pass as fashionable among the nobility, but thankfully, he wouldn't be mingling with them. He had used what few skills he had to spruce it up. But he hadn't been able to get the collar to stretch any further. It pinched his neck and made him feel like he was choking.

He scanned the crowd that flowed around him. According to his intel, Sellafus Coran was going to have a get together for his sycophants and hangers-on at his compound just outside of Bastion to the east of the city. Plenty of the rich and influential maintained second residences here, and apparently, that included people who made their fortunes illegally like Coran. Getting here hadn't been easy. The city's skyrail didn't reach out this far. Why would it? Most of the residents in this neighborhood had their own transports. And he was still hampered by a lack of funds. But he had managed, arriving just a bit early. Yusra had said to meet him at this corner. So where was she?

"Quartus?" Yusra's voice easily cut through the crowd.

He turned and stopped short. Yusra wore a long dress made of a rich blue material, one that showed off her every curve. Small, pale blue flowers had been embroidered along the bodice, and she wore a number of bracelets and bangles on each arm. Her hair had been arranged to create a screen, covering part of her face. She was probably hoping to hide her Dalark features, but instead, she had made herself more mysterious, more alluring.

Suddenly Quartus found it even more difficult to breathe.

She hurried to his side and looked him over. "Missing your clothing budget, eh?"

That snapped him out of his mental fog. He laughed. "Did you smuggle that all the way from Utuaa?"

Her smile turned impish. "Do you think the spirits and potentates would approve of something so decadent?"

"More's the pity."

She smiled, which dazzled him. But then he noticed that she had a long tube slung over her shoulders.

He frowned and pointed to it. "What's that?"

She glanced over her shoulder at it. "I did some research on Coran's interests. This is insurance in case we need it."

Quartus frowned at the tube. What kind of insurance did she have? Weapons? Alcohol? Another slinky dress? Hopefully they wouldn't have to find out.

He offered her his arm. "Shall we?"

She slid her hand into the crook of his arm, and he walked her down the street toward Coran's house. Quartus studied the crowd waiting to get in and found a small knot of partygoers who had clustered together, laughing and chatting while they waited. At least a dozen of them. Perfect. He steered Yusra over to the fringe of that group, close enough to appear connected but not so close that the members of the group would object to their presence. He turned to Yusra and smiled and laughed. Confusion flitted across her face, but she quickly caught on.

"So I said something funny to you?" she asked.

"Apparently so. I had no idea you were so witty, my dear," he said.

"It that because I'm a woman, or because I'm Dalark?"

His laughter died at the pointed question.

Her eyes were hard, but then a mischievous sparkle appeared in them. She turned to one of the guests they stood near and joined in the group's laughter.

Thankfully, they didn't have to wait long. When the group they were following reached the front doors, the guests walked past the two well-dressed security guards standing watch at the door, who glowered at everyone and consulted a data scriber. Probably a guest list. But Quartus knew how to handle this. It was a simple rule that served him well over the years: pretend you belonged there, and you could go just about anywhere. He kept his head up and laughed at Yusra once again as they walked past.

Once they were inside, Quartus quickly scanned the interior. It looked like the party was limited to the house's first floor. Dozens of people, most of them human, wandered from room to room. Food and drink were set on tables in the room to the right, and music drifted out of the room to the left.

He turned to Yusra. "I'll go right, you go left. Meet back here in fifteen?"

She nodded and headed for the room with the music. Quartus went the opposite direction, sidling through the guests, scanning their faces as they passed. He didn't recognize any of them, which wasn't much of a surprise. While he had an unsavory reputation, he hadn't actually hung out with real criminals all that often. He did pass by a few members of minor noble houses, all of whom didn't notice him. And why would they? No one would expect the disgraced former prince to show up in a rumpled suit. He was impressed by what he saw of Coran's home, though. The rooms were tastefully decorated in rich dark woods and deep colors. But rather than be oppressive, Coran had added splashes of color with vibrant paintings, most of which were just splatters of paint on canvas.

Once the fifteen minutes were up, he headed back to the main entrance. Yusra already waited for him. She shook her head. No sign of Coran, but that wasn't surprising. He probably was holed up somewhere with the truly important guests. They'd have to do something drastic then. A plan quickly formed in his mind.

"The music. Live or recorded?" he asked.

Yusra frowned. "Live."

Perfect. He snared her hand and dragged her into the room.

It turned out to be a ballroom. A quintet of musicians had set up in one corner, playing mellow tunes as a dozen people milled about, chatting amiably. Quartus flagged the group's leader. He paused in playing.

"Take a request?" Quartus asked.

"Depends on what it is," he returned.

Quartus smiled. "'The Lass from the Eastern Shore.'"

The musician's eyes widened. He sputtered for a moment. "I'm not sure—"

Quartus sighed and pulled the last of his money out of his pocket, passing it to the musician. "Please. My girl really wants to hear it."

"I what?" Yusra asked.

The musician pocketed the money with a nod, then Quartus grabbed Yusra's hand and led her to the edge of the mostly vacant dance floor.

"What are you doing?" she whispered.

"Hopefully getting the attention of our host," he returned.

She gave him an uncertain look. He gently removed the case she was carrying. She started to object, but he brought it over to the stage and set it at the foot of the leader. The leader rolled his eyes but gestured for him to go ahead.

Then Quartus dragged Yusra to the middle of the dance floor. The first notes of his requested song hit, a brassy fanfare that caught the guests by surprise. Quartus relished the gasps, especially as people turned to see what was going on. He had been relegated to the shadows for too long. It would be nice to return to his usual haunt, namely the spotlight.

He pulled Yusra in close, standing behind her with her arms wrapped around herself. Once the song began playing in earnest, Quartus spun Yusra from his embrace. He worried a bit as he tried to remember the complex footwork. He hadn't danced like this in years. Thankfully, a Riokan courtship dance wasn't about precise movements. It was all about style. Attitude. Confidence. And he was brimming with all three.

And thankfully, Yusra overflowed with more. At first, her movements were clumsy, but soon, she loosened up. He took her through a complex set of twirls, which she embellished with flicks of her wrist and small kicks. Her smile was energizing, bright, and warm. Quartus found it hard to remember why he was doing this in the first place, especially as she sidled up to him, running her hands over his back and chest.

Throughout the song, more and more guests filtered into the ballroom. Quartus couldn't concentrate on them, but from what he saw, they appeared at first confused by the dancing—probably not what they were expecting at this party—but soon they were applauding and cheering them on, especially when he or Yusra added a particularly large flourish.

Within a few minutes, the song came to a dramatic conclusion, and Quartus snapped Yusra back into their original pose. Their faces were so close, he could feel her sweet breath on his cheek and the way his heart thudded against her back. A thrill shot through him.

The crowd surrounding them burst into applause. Sweeping Yusra around, he urged her to bow with him. She did. The guests waited to see what else might happen, but when it became clear that the show was over, they filtered away, back to conversations or food or whatever else they had been doing. But one man caught Quartus's attention. He stood at the edge of the crowd, flanked by two Ixactl goons. He was a short, wiry man with thinning white hair, but he projected a mixture of authority and menace that instantly identified him as Sellafus Coran.

Once enough of the crowd had dispersed, he stepped forward, a scowl on his face. "When I saw who was dancing, I thought it couldn't possibly be you, Quartus."

Quartus winced at the mention of his real name. He fought the urge to look around and see if any of the other guests had heard.

Coran sneered at him. "Why would a disgraced prince sneak into my humble gathering? And yet, who else would be so audacious as to disrupt my pleasant evening like that?"

"I was hoping I could talk to you about the attempted assassination of my brother," Quartus said.

Coran's eyes widened and he looked around, probably seeing if anyone heard what Quartus had said. Then he motioned for Quartus to follow him. Yusra quickly grabbed her case before following them.

The crime boss led Quartus and Yusra away from the party and into a private study. Quartus stopped short as they entered. The room was filled with artwork, paintings, and statues. He recognized three of them immediately. How could he not? One had been stolen from an art museum in The Stone, another from a noble family's estate, and the third had reportedly vanished from the president of Elscontin's palace. If he had to guess, probably everything in the room had been stolen.

Coran walked over to a small table and poured three drinks. He gave one to Quartus, the second to Yusra, and then downed the third in one gulp.

"So let me see if I understand this," Coran said. "You thought it was a wise idea to invade my party and what? Accuse me of assassination?"

The men flanking Coran flexed, making it clear that there would be consequences if Quartus didn't answer correctly.

"Not exactly, no," Quartus said. "I'm sure you know that someone tried to have my brother and his wife killed recently. I've been trying to track down the responsible party. My investigation has led me to you."

Coran glared at him, his eyes simmering. Quartus plastered on what he hoped was an amiable smile and kept talking.

"Now, I don't think you're behind the attempt." He held up his hands in a placating gesture. "I think you just helped the real conspirators smuggle certain items from one place to another. Something from the Dalark Imperium, perhaps, or Cold Light trees and thralls from their forest?"

Coran's eyebrow twitched. That was probably all the confirmation he'd get.

"Like I said, I'm not interested in you. I just want a name. A direction. Someone I can go talk to who is responsible. Give me that, and I walk out that door and you'll never hear from me again."

Coran guffawed. "Is that how this works?"

"It can," Quartus said.

"All right. I heard your story, now you listen to mine. You're outlaw, right? That means my men end your miserable life, and for once, the constables will have no reason to question me. As for your friend, I'm sure I can find something... appropriate for her to do."

The goons started to advance on him. Quartus took a step back, his gaze darting around the study for some sort of weapon. But all he saw was the art! Could he maybe use one of the statues as a makeshift club? Only if he found one small enough, and most of them were made out of big blocks of stone.

But then Yusra stepped in front of him, holding up her hands. "Please, let me speak for a second. I'll make it worth your while."

Much to Quartus's surprise, Coran actually hesitated. Then he chuckled and motioned for his men to back down. Once they did, Yusra stepped away from Quartus, moving toward the display of art.

"This is very impressive." She ran a hand along a statue depicting a Plissk man crouching with a knife. "You have quite the collection.

Tell me, have you ever heard of *Winter Leaves on a Stilled Stream* by Bolatar?"

Coran laughed. "Might have, yeah."

That was an understatement, and Quartus knew it. Bolatar was a Dalark artist who was rumored to have only produced twenty paintings in his tragically short life. Each one was supposed to be a priceless masterpiece. Only two Bolatars had ever made it out of the Imperium, neither of which were in the Dynasty's holdings. *Winter Leaves* was said to be Bolatar's greatest work, and very few outsiders had ever seen it. It was rumored to be kept in a special vault somewhere in Utuaa.

"How about this?" Yusra unslung the case and twisted off the end. "Just give us a name. Then this is yours."

She tapped the end of her case, and a roll of canvas fell into her hands.

Coran frowned, took the canvas, and unrolled it. His eyes widened and the color drained from his face. "Trickster's guile!"

Quartus stepped behind him and peeked over his shoulder. The painting Coran held depicted a stunning mountain vista. A distant waterfall fed a river that branched off to a stream that flowed into the painting's foreground. Brown and yellow leaves floated on the placid waters. Such a simple scene, but there was something compelling about the painting. Quartus felt drawn in, like he could have studied it for hours or even days and not seen enough of it.

Coran looked up at Yusra, his jaw slack. "This is... This can't be real!"

"It is." Yusra produced a data scriber. "Tell you what. Don't give us the information now. Have the painting examined. When you're convinced it's authentic, send me what you can."

Coran set the painting aside and mopped a trembling hand across his face. He turned back to her. "Who are you?"

She smiled. "Someone who wants to be your friend, Sellafus Coran. A better friend than the conspirators have ever been to you."

Her words were friendly, but there was a bite to her tone.

Quartus cleared his throat. "I fear we may have overstayed our welcome. Coran, it was a pleasure talking to you. I hope to hear from you soon."

He offered Yusra his arm and she took it. Thankfully, Coran's men didn't object to them leaving. They moved quickly through the party and out the front door. Quartus tried not to rush, but his heart thudded in his chest.

"I have to know, how confident are you in your forger's skills? Because I don't want Sellafus Coran as an enemy," he said as they hustled back toward the corner where they'd met.

She tipped her head to one side. "Why do you assume it's a forgery?"

He snorted. "Because there's no way that's a genuine Bolatar, and definitely not *Winter Leaves*."

She regarded him quietly. Doubt gnawed at him. It couldn't be the real thing, could it?

"Unlike you, I was sent on this mission with sufficient resources. My master sent me a number of items that could be used as gifts or trade. Rare art, exotic liqueurs, more esoteric items, all the sorts of things that people in the Dynasty might find precious."

"But a Bolatar!"

Yusra sighed. "I realize that might be too much, but I figured it was worth the investment. My master will as well." He started to protest, but she kept talking. "Now, I don't know about you, but I'm starving. Why don't we go find somewhere to eat?" She looked him up and down again and smirked. "And I'll buy."

As they walked from Coran's house, his mind raced. Who was Yusra's master? That question should have been enough to keep him from following her. But when she looked over her shoulder at him with a smirk, his doubts faded, and he followed her into the darkening evening.

51

Everys rarely visited the armory in the palace. She had peeked inside it once shortly after she had moved into the palace the first time. It was gaudy and smelled like a musty old warehouse. Even though there were supposed to be services held daily, she knew the armory stood empty most of the time. She wouldn't find her adversary there.

No, if she wanted to face Istragon, she'd have to face him in his den.

The Grand Armory of the Dynasty stood just outside the palace walls, a little ways down the hill, placing it in the shadow of the palace, the Hall of All Voices, and the other government buildings. And yet, in spite of its lowlier perch, it was in many ways more ostentatious than its neighbors.

As Rewether led Everys up the front steps toward the entrance, her gaze swept over the squat building. She recognized what inspired the architecture. The armory looked like an ancient fortress, the kind that the Dynasty had built throughout its holdings centuries earlier. In some ways, it reminded her of the Dunestrider outposts she had seen in the Kronin Desert. That comparison caused a shudder to worm through her, chased by a wave of sadness for Kevtho. But she shook her head and winced. Stay focused on what really matters. Not architecture, but helping Narius.

Five entrances, large oval doors bordered by intricately carved stone archways, opened into the Grand Armory. Flanking each of the doors were a pair of ceremonial guards. They wore thick purple robes with gold filigree woven into the edges that completely covered their bodies. Solid bronze helmets with jagged horns and edges shone in the sunlight and looked uncomfortable. Each one carried a large halberd that appeared more decorative than dangerous. The guards stood still as statues until she approached the center door. Then they came to life and quickly moved to block her way.

Every stopped short as two of them crossed their weapons in front of her. "What's the meaning of this?"

One of the guards stepped forward. His voice was gruff but apologetic. "Blessed, we have standing orders to not allow any Siporans into the Grand Armory."

Her mouth popped open. Why hadn't they heard about this? But then, she shouldn't have been surprised. Istragon had never approved of her marriage to Narius, not the first time and definitely not the second. She had heard recordings of his homilies where he railed against how Siporans were a threat to the Dynasty and always had been. But those had been mere words. Now, though, the prelate had escalated to actions. Symbolic and unimportant—she didn't care if she could enter the Grand Armory or not—but troubling nonetheless.

Fine. If Istragon wanted to butt heads, she could play along. She crossed her arms. "I have important business to discuss with the Supreme Prelate. If he is unwilling to allow me entry, he may come out here and speak on the front steps where everyone may see. And if he finds that inconvenient, I can always speak to the king about his refusal."

The guard who had spoken to her shifted uncomfortably. Then he whirled to the men blocking her path, whispered something to them, and disappeared through the main entrance. The remaining guards raised their weapons, but they didn't move out of her way.

"Laying it on a bit thick there?" Rewether murmured.

She fought to hide a smirk. Maybe so, but she thought she had Istragon weighed and measured. She had no idea if there were press drones watching her. There probably were, but even if there weren't, she knew that Istragon would not want the public to see him speaking to her. If anything, he'd want it to look like she had come to his territory as supplicant.

Sure enough, a few moments later, the guard returned and held open the door. "The Supreme Prelate will see you now."

She started moving the moment he spoke, brushing past the guards that blocked her way. Rewether grunted at them, his disdain clear.

The interior of the Armory was indeed grand. Whereas the outside looked like an ancient fortress, the interior gleamed with gold and silver implements. She stepped into a circular foyer and paused in spite of herself.

Like most armories throughout the Dynasty's holdings, the Grand Armory's foyer was filled with statues of the lesser gods, the ones defeated by the Perfected Warrior. The Gravedigger, the Trickster, Chaos and Chance, the Moons. But where most armories had smaller statues, these were larger than life. Each one was at least twenty feet tall, every one a masterpiece. Whereas the statues back in Fair Havens looked old and worn, these looked like living creatures that had somehow been transformed into marble. She could practically feel the Gravedigger's morose presence or hear the Trickster's snicker. Probably the most impressive were the statues of Chance and Chaos. Whoever had carved them imbued their expressions with such life that she couldn't tell if they were looking at each other with disdain or longing. Given what the Dynasty's mythology said about those two, that fit.

But Istragon wasn't in the foyer, so she headed for the sanctum. She found herself in a long hallway that twisted around the exterior of the building. On her right were huge stained glass windows depicting stories about the Perfected Warrior's war with the gods. She recognized most of them, although a few were completely unknown to her, like the one depicting the Water Bearer playing dice with Chance and one of the Moons. At least, that's how she interpreted it.

On her left, though, were dozens of panels, each one fifteen feet long and ten feet high. They were arranged in columns five high. Each one had a series of carvings, pictographs of battles and kings draped in glory. She quickly realized what she was seeing: a visual record of what each king had accomplished for the Dynasty. The first she walked by appeared ancient, the carved images worn nearly smooth and almost unreadable. The further she walked, the more recent the images. She easily spotted Heronus destroying Nekek the Bright and decided she didn't want to linger on that one.

About two-thirds of the way down the hall, she came to the last panel. Based on what she saw, it was clearly King Girai, Narius's father. It was second from the bottom, and the last in that column was blank. She frowned. They hadn't put anything on Narius's yet? Did they wait until his reign was over?

But she couldn't dwell. She continued as the hallway curved sharply and deposited her in the inner sanctum. Once again, she was stunned at the grandeur. There were two enormous statues, each at least a hundred feet tall, on opposite sides of the circular room. The one on the left was the Water Bearer, the Perfected Warrior on the right. They stood in the same pose, their left hands on their hip, their right stretched upward to hold up the ceiling. The statues sparkled in a strange way until Everys realized that they were covered in precious metals and jewels, the treasure used to create their clothing. She gasped. They were clothed with a fortune.

Rows of benches encircled a central dais, where a smaller statue of the Perfected Warrior stood. Every armory had a similar statue. Each day, the local prelates and his or her acolytes would dress the Warrior in armor and give him the appropriate weapon to hold in his outstretched hand. Today, the Warrior held a mace.

Istragon stood on the dais, but much to Everys's surprise, he wasn't wearing his usual flowing robes. Instead, he wore what looked like a naval uniform. At first, Everys thought it was just a costume, but as she approached, she realized it was genuine. That made sense; most high ranking government officials served in the military in their early years. While not officially required, it was an understood expectation. But Everys knew that Istragon usually wore the elaborate robes that indicated his office. So why was he wearing that uniform instead?

That question would have to wait. The Supreme Prelate glowered at her with unmasked hatred.

"You must understand that I do not approve of you invading this sacred space, Queen Everys." Istragon's voice carried easily through the room. "But I've found that you have a habit of worming your way into places where you don't belong. So I deigned to make an exception today."

Everys's back stiffened at the condescension in his voice. But she couldn't get distracted. Istragon's disrespect, while annoying, didn't ultimately matter.

"Thank you for seeing me, Supreme Prelate. I was hoping we could speak about the upcoming *harsannon*," she said.

Istragon's brows arched. "Indeed. And did your husband send you to beg for leniency? Because he shan't find any from me."

Everys almost laughed at the overly dramatic statement, but she caught herself just in time.

"Please reconsider," she said. "You know the king was recently injured on Maotoa and he's still recuperating. With everything that is happening, all of the uncertainty, the last thing we need is to sow any doubts about Narius's fitness."

Istragon laughed. "Quite the opposite. It is precisely because of the uncertainty that this has to happen. Right now, there are so many who live within the Dynasty's holdings who question the king's fitness to rule. The *harsannon* will put any such doubts to rest once and for all."

Everys's lips twitched into a snarl. "They're doubting him because of what you're saying about him."

Again, Istragon laughed. "You give me too much credit. I am merely giving voice to the thoughts of our citizens and nobles. Narius has been too timid during his reign. Seeking peace with both Dalark and the Cold Light. Defunding our military. Marrying beneath his station."

She bristled at that, because she knew how close he had come to saying something truly despicable.

"You believe I am the problem. No, Queen Everys, I am not. I merely point out the truth that everyone already knows: King Narius is unworthy to rule. Look at what has happened in just the past few days. Duke Brencis marries Viara, claiming the king's only legitimate heir. Dalark steals Maotoa from the Dynasty's holdings. What will Narius allow to happen next? No, Everys, if anyone is to blame for what has happened, it is you."

Rewether took a step forward, his hand darting for his weapon. Everys frantically signaled for him to stand down. The last thing they needed was for this conversation to turn violent.

Istragon stabbed a finger at the statue behind him. "Our Perfected Warrior is clear about the qualities of a good ruler. Decisive. Strong. And able to recognize his enemies for what they are. While Narius was showing signs of weakness before he married you, his decline accelerated once you were in his life. I and so many pious citizens rejoiced when he set you aside for Princess Innana and wept when you returned. You Siporans have been a blot on our conscience for too long. That is why you will be the last to ever set foot in an armory. From this day forward, no Siporan will ever approach our beloved Warrior again!"

Everys's first thought was that was no huge loss. Most Siporans didn't attend armory services anyway. But then she realized how problematic this was. Attendance was recorded, not just by the government, but by nosy neighbors as well. If all of the Siporans in the Dynasty suddenly stopped attending, that would raise questions about their loyalty. And Everys understood all too well how suspicious the Dynasty was toward their ancient enemies. This could easily escalate to open hatred and maybe even violence.

But she had to set aside those concerns. Troubling as they were, Narius could easily countermand Istragon's decision, especially if he won the *harsannon*. She had to focus on that.

"Please, Supreme Prelate." She struggled to keep her voice even. "Surely there has to be something we can do. A compromise we can reach. Like King Grumio. Or King Pellio."

Surprise flitted across Istragon's features. Was he impressed she knew those cases? Maybe. Best to keep pressing on.

"I understand you have concerns about the direction the Dynasty has taken under Narius's leadership. And I know that he would be willing to not only listen to you, but address whatever he can." She hoped he wouldn't hear the lie in her voice. She was making promises on Narius's behalf. "But please, he can't fight in his current state."

Much to her surprise, Istragon's features actually softened. He nodded thoughtfully, then crossed the distance between them.

"Your words are persuasive. I can't promise anything. So many plans are in motion. But I will see what I can arrange. Believe me, what I do will be what's best for Narius."

Everys wanted to laugh at his transparent attempt at a lie. He would do no such thing. But she also knew that confronting him would accomplish nothing. Fine. If he didn't want to be honest, she could match him.

She forced a friendly smile to her face. "Then I'll leave you to your preparations. Thank you, Supreme Prelate."

Everys motioned for Rewether to lead the way. And as they left, she shot one more look up at the massive statue of the Perfected Warrior that soared overhead. For just a moment, she wished that he was real, because she had a feeling that Narius would need all the help he could get.

52

Frustration from her conversation with Istragon chased Everys's transport as she left Bastion. Minister Masruq lived on the outskirts. His house, a surprisingly modest manor, was situated in the middle of a wooded lot. As Everys's transport wound through the trees, Everys could feel the tension unwinding from her head and shoulders. She should have accepted Oluna's invitation long ago.

Her hosts were waiting for her at their front door. Oluna had left the palace earlier that day to make sure everything was ready. As soon as Everys slid out of the transport, Oluna hurried over and enveloped her in a big hug.

"Welcome to our humble sanctuary, dear. I'm so glad you could come out and join us."

Everys smiled. She didn't even have to go through the door to relax. It was as if the dark clouds that hovered over her and the rest of Bastion had rolled back, allowing just a sliver of sunlight to pour down. It wasn't much, but in that moment, it was enough.

Masruq didn't hug her, but he did bow. "Blessed, you honor us with your presence. I hope my cooking will be sufficient for you."

She laughed in spite of herself. She would never have pictured the finance minister as being a cook. "I'm sure it will be fine."

Rewether cleared his throat. "Uh, pardon me for intruding, but will your staff be getting the same meal?"

Masruq regarded the guard captain with a twinkle in his eye. "I made enough for you and your men as well, Rewether."

Rewether looked ready to cheer, but he composed himself. He leaned over to Everys. "The men were fighting over who got to come with us tonight."

Oluna led Everys inside their house and gave her a quick tour. Once again, Everys was surprised at how modest the house was, but then she realized, with a start, that Masruq and Oluna's home was modest by the palace's standards. Compared to the Dynasty's average resident's standards, they lived in wealth and comfort. And yet, in spite of the opulence, the house still felt comforting and homey. Unlike the sterile museums of wealth and power she had visited in recent months, she could tell people actually lived here.

They paused by a large painting of Masruq, Oluna, and a teenage girl. The girl was clearly related to Oluna and Masruq; Everys could see their features in the girl's. She had Masruq's eyes, Oluna's smile.

"Who's this?" she asked.

Oluna went quiet next to her. "That's Zivah, our granddaughter."

Everys looked at her friend in surprise. They had known each other for months now, and she had never mentioned anything about having children.

"Excuse me. I'm going to check on dinner preparations." Oluna's voice sounded hollow as she hurried away.

Everys watched her go, then turned to Masruq. He grimaced and rubbed the back of his neck.

"I'm sorry, did I do something to offend her?" Everys asked.

Masruq sighed. "Not at all, Blessed. Zivah is a sore subject for Oluna. We have... or rather, had a daughter, Blessed. Alianna. A sweet girl but very much like her mother. Very headstrong, very opinionated."

Everys smiled at the description. That was definitely Oluna.

"As much as they clashed, it still broke Oluna's heart when Alianna left home when she turned eighteen. We didn't hear from her for ten years. No idea where she was or what she was doing."

"What did they fight about?" Everys asked, then caught herself. "If you don't mind me asking."

He smiled sadly. "No, it's all right. Oluna had some very strong opinions about what Alianna should do with her life and Alianna disagreed. I think, in her mind, her choice was to either give in or leave. So she left.

"Then about twelve years ago, there was a knock on our door. A young man stood there, holding a two-year-old girl. He introduced us to Zivah, explained that his friend, Zivah's mother, could no longer raise her, and that Zivah was our responsibility now. He shoved her into my arms and then left. And so we found ourselves raising our granddaughter."

Everys looked at the painting again. As she examined it, she realized that Masruq and Oluna were younger. Masruq had more hair and had more brown peppered into it. Oluna had fewer lines on her face.

"So where is Zivah now?" Everys asked.

Once again, Masruq fell silent and Everys winced inwardly. She had stepped into another painful topic.

"She's here," Masruq whispered. "Upstairs."

Everys blinked. Zivah lived here? Then why didn't Oluna ever talk about her?

"You have to understand, we don't know if Alianna knew how sick her daughter was when she abandoned her. But it turned out that Zivah has a rare medical condition that has worsened as she's grown older. She's been in a vegetative state for years now and she's slowly fading."

Tears welled in Masruq's eyes, and Everys hurried to his side and gave him an awkward hug. He chuckled.

"Thank you for your concern, Blessed. But this is the world I live in. My daughter, gone. My granddaughter soon to depart as well. That's why I keep hoping that, at some point, we can solve the many problems we're facing. We owe it to others to make the world better, yes?" He blinked and swiped at his eyes. "Now I need to check on dinner. Care to join me in the kitchen?"

Everys smiled and followed as he led her deeper into the house, but she cast one more look at the painting as they walked away. Zivah smiled back at her. Everys stood up a little straighter and touched her bracelet. Maybe she could do something to help Masruq and Oluna.

No wonder Rewether was so excited to eat dinner. The food was exquisite, some of the finest she had ever eaten. And the conversation had been a treat as well. While they struggled to overcome their sadness at first, Oluna and Masruq soon regaled Everys with stories of how they met and courted, how she had actually proposed to him, and how she had been the one to suggest he enter government service in the first place.

"If not for her, Blessed, I may have wound up a chef in a high-priced restaurant in Gilded Lock." Masruq patted the back of his wife's hand.

Oluna chuckled. "That may be, but I think the Dynasty is the better for it, dearest."

Everys smiled as well. "I know Narius would agree. He always speaks highly of your counsel."

"You're too kind." Masruq smiled sadly. "And how is the king doing?"

Everys sighed. "Fully recovered and getting ready for that ritual combat."

Oluna snorted. "Outrageous that Istragon is still insisting on it. If you ask me, Narius should conscript Istragon back into the military and send him to the Demilitarized Zone. If he's so concerned about Siporans, let him patrol the wasteland and find out what's there."

Everys laughed, but Masruq looked positively sick.

"Oluna..." His voice had an edge to it.

She swatted away his words. "Istragon knows what I think of him. And who here is going to tell him what I said?"

Everys raised her hands in surrender. Masruq relaxed, but she could tell that he was still disturbed. But he turned to her and fixed on a fake smile.

"And your father? How is he handling the current crises?"

A pang of regret stabbed her. "Not well, I'm afraid."

"I'm sorry for that," Masruq said. "Water Bearer knows I tried to help him acclimate, but he seemed so dour, so closed off. I'm sorry, Blessed, I really did try."

Everys frowned. "The way he made it sound, you took him to some sort of debauchery."

Oluna guffawed. "Masruq, did you take Favid to Beyond-the-Wall?"

Masruq reddened at the mention of the infamous Bastion neighborhood. "Hardly. We went to Depib's house for drinks and a few friendly games of Entrench. Very tame, all things considered."

"'Tame?'" Oluna's voice betrayed her skepticism. "And tell me, did Depib use those pornographic cards like last time?"

Masruq wouldn't meet his wife's gaze. "He may have, yes."

"And I assume that Lenz was there with his collection of exotic drinks?"

Masruq nodded sullenly. Oluna speared him with a glare.

"It really wasn't that bad, Blessed!" Masruq insisted.

Everys sighed. She shouldn't have been surprised. A group of nobles gambling and drinking probably appeared to be the height of revelry to Papa. He was so stubborn, so blind to the way things were now. So stuck in his narrow mindset. He didn't realize who his attitude hurt.

She squared her shoulders. Papa may have still been stuck like that, but she wasn't.

"I'm sorry to ask this, but where's the bathroom?" she asked.

Oluna chuckled. "No need to apologize, Blessed. We all know royalty needs that from time to time."

Masruq gave her directions which were simple enough. Everys excused herself and left the dining room.

But instead of following Masruq's directions, she hurried down the hall to the stairs. She crept up them and into a hallway bordered by thick wooden doors. A quick search revealed the master bedroom, a guest room, but then she found a darkened room dominated with pristine white medical equipment, all clustered around a bed. A young woman lay in the bed, tubes and wires snaking from her body to the humming and beeping machines. Everys recognized Zivah from the portrait in the entryway, but only barely. The girl's skin, instead of being ruddy, was pale, broken by dark lines that clawed across her skin. Instead of a luminous halo of gold, her hair was now stringy and matted to her head.

The room itself seemed like it had been decorated for a little girl. The walls were painted with bright pastel colors. Pictures from popular children's programs dotted the walls. A shelf full of toys sat in one corner, gathering a layer of dust. And was that makeup on the end table? She blinked at it. That seemed like an odd waste. It seemed cruel to purchase something Zivah would never be able to use.

But then Everys looked around the room again, and she realized that there were other hints of a future Zivah would never experience. Some of the clothes hanging on the rack were meant for a young woman entering aristocratic society. It was as if Masruq and Oluna were preparing Zivah for a future she'd never have. Maybe it was a lie they told each other. Zivah wasn't dying. She'd use these things one day.

Everys knelt next to the girl and plucked a bead from her bracelet. She checked the jewelry. Only a few left. Hopefully she'd be able to get more from Tormod soon. She cracked the bead between her fingers and started drawing the lines on Zivah's cheek.

Minutes dragged by like hours. She added more details: a delay to the spell, ensuring that it wouldn't truly activate for three more days, thus ensuring that no one would connect any healing with her presence. An anesthetic to ease her pain in the interim.

She pulled her hand away, regarding her efforts with a tipped head. She should do more. But without knowing Zivah's diagnosis, she'd only be guessing. And she had been gone long enough. This would have to do.

She activated the rune. Light rippled along the pattern. The glow then spread from the rune into Zivah's cheek, then down through her face, flowing through her body.

Everys waited a few more seconds to see if a rebuke would chase the rune, but there was nothing. She let out a shaky breath. Time to get back to dinner then. She smiled down at Zivah one more time and then slipped out of the room.

Masruq and Oluna waited for her in the dining room. And they had even brought her dessert.

"Is everything all right, my queen?" Masruq asked.

Everys struggled to hide a satisfied smile. "I'm sorry it took me so long."

"We were getting ready to send out a search party for you!" Oluna said. "But I'm glad you're back. You'll love Masruq's fire honey trifle."

"That would be wonderful," Everys said. Especially since, if all went as she hoped, next time Zivah might have experienced, if not a miraculous recovery, then a step in the right direction.

53

Sweat slicked Narius's brow. He set his feet, adjusting his stance for better balance, and hefted the weighted training sword. His lips twitched into a snarl, but he forced himself to relax his face. Don't show weakness. Don't acknowledge the pain.

"Your Strength, begin." His Swordbound, Farga, stomped his foot on the floor.

Narius lunged forward, swinging his sword through the Eighth River Form. He had learned this particular sequence of lunges, slashes, and feints when he was only seven. And yet, even though he had practiced this routine for most of his life, he felt like a beginner again. His hands trembled, and his arm felt like it could wilt at a moment's notice. As he lunged into a low stab, his left foot caught on his right, and he stumbled forward, dropping the sword.

"Gravedigger's luck!" he snarled.

Farga stepped forward, a sympathetic look on his face. "There's no shame in any of this, Your Strength. Your mind remembers. Your body just needs to catch up."

Easy for him to say. Farga had been mirroring his motions all night and had barely broken a sweat. Clinically, Narius understood. Farga had made it off Maotoa uninjured. Narius was still technically recovering from his injuries. But he couldn't coddle himself. The *harsannon* was coming up in a few short days. If he couldn't do better, and quickly, he was guaranteed to lose.

"Perhaps we should call it a night, Your Strength." Farga held out a towel.

Narius snatched it out of his hand and swiped it across his forehead. "We could always spar."

Farga looked ready to object, but then grimaced and sighed. "If you wish, Your Strength."

Narius tossed the towel to one side, then swung his arm around, hoping that maybe loosening up his joint would make the difference. Then he fell into a ready stance that Farga mirrored.

But before Narius could make a move, someone cleared his throat from the door. Narius peeked to one side and saw Scrivener Tolistan lurking in the doorway.

"Or we could take a break," Narius said.

The relief on Farga's face was palpable. "An excellent suggestion."

Annoyance flickered through Narius. He was almost tempted to duel Farga anyway. But finally, with a sigh, he tossed the practice sword aside and turned to Tolistan. "What brings you here, Scrivener?"

Tolistan shot a look at Farga, then stepped forward and held out a data scriber. "The professor asked me to bring you this. It's everything we compiled."

Narius reached for the scriber, but then hesitated. He didn't intend to go back to his quarters or the Amber Office any time soon. And it didn't feel right to just have that scriber sitting out while he exercised. So he pulled his hand back.

"Why don't you hold on to it for me?" he suggested. "And if you have any more thoughts, maybe record them on the scriber as well."

Tolistan looked at the scriber, then up at him again. "B-but, Your Strength... this is your project. Your idea."

"Yes, but it's your people's heritage," Narius replied. "The last thing I'd want to do is steal something more from the Siporans. Please. Keep it. If I ever need it, I'll know who to ask."

The scrivener's mouth popped open, then he tucked the scriber away in his robes. His gaze flicked toward Farga, and a question formed in his expression.

"Farga? Can you give us the room?" Narius asked.

The Swordbound nodded and ambled out of the room.

As soon as they were alone, Tolistan took a tentative step forward. "I feel I owe you an apology, Your Strength. When Kyna first asked me to come to the palace, I feared that you were wasting both of our times. And while our lessons have veered into the unorthodox at times, you have been nothing but respectful."

Narius smiled. He refrained from saying, "I told you so." Instead, he folded his hands in front of him and listened.

"And now you've shown even more trust in me. It's all very overwhelming, so I'd like to do something for you."

Tolistan stepped forward and placed his hands on Narius's shoulders. Narius stilled, unsure what he should do or say. But the scrivener bowed his head.

"May the Singularity go before you, guiding your steps. May the Singularity walk behind you, to watch over your path. May the Singularity walk beside you, strengthening your heart. And may He at last surround us with the rune of light," Tolistan said.

A tremor wormed through Narius, and it felt as though a heavy weight fell upon him. But then, just as quickly, the heaviness was gone, and he felt buoyed and energized. He could take on any challenge. Bring Farga back into the room and show him what he could do!

But just as quickly, the sensation passed, and Tolistan stepped back, a serene smile on his face.

"What was that?" Narius whispered. "A rune?"

Tolistan laughed. "Nothing so spectacular. It's an ancient blessing, one my people have used for millennia." Then the scrivener hesitated. "It was actually something that would be spoken over a *zhannoq'uem* when they entered their time of service."

Narius frowned. "A what?"

"A *zhannoq'uem.* Uh... royal guard in Dynastic. That's probably the closest translation. There are some nuances in the language that don't quite carry over," Tolistan said.

Now an icy wave crashed through Narius. "You just blessed me with something used by the mage-kings?"

"Not exactly." Tolistan sighed. "The blessing comes from some of the ancient texts that describe what the duties of our kings were supposed to be: rulers who sought the Singularity's will, who served as a shield for his people, who ruled for the common good.

"This is a hard truth to share sometimes, Your Strength. The Dynasty's history paints every mage-king with the same brush. Monsters, every single one of them. And that is what some eventually became, but they weren't all that way. At least, not at first. Some remained true to the Singularity and His intentions."

Oh. Narius shifted his weight. He supposed that would be true of any kingdom's rulers. He knew better than most that, in spite of what was taught in the Dynasty's schools, not every king had been good. Some had been barely tolerable, and a few were monsters better left forgotten. That would likely have been true for the Siporans as well.

"So what were these *zhanoi'keem* like?" he asked.

Tolistan's smile broadened. "*Zhannoq'uem*. They were said to be the most powerful toratropic mages in the Ascendancy. Some legends even said that they could cast runes without ink."

Narius blinked in surprise. "I thought that wasn't possible."

"It isn't," Tolistan said. "Like I said, legends. There are some colorful stories about feats performed by the *zhannoq'uem*. One story claims that one of them was able to drain the Sea of Shards in less than a night. Another says that two of the guards once fought an entire legion of Elderreach cultists who were trying to resurrect their fallen gods and defeated them on their own."

Another shudder wormed through Narius. While that fight might have been thrilling, the Dynasty had their own legends about the Elderreach and their noxious followers. The Elderreach cults were said to worship monstrous gods who lived for nothing but carnage and destruction. A single Elderreach god could supposedly destroy an entire region. And those gods inspired their followers to all sorts of vile behavior. Ancient Elderreach temples were said to be abattoirs, places where blood was spilled to resummon the cultists' fallen gods. Better change the subject again.

"One more question, and then I should probably get back to training," he said. "The blessing had something in there about 'the rune of light,' and I've seen that phrase used elsewhere in the texts you had me study. What does that mean?"

Tolistan hesitated. "That's a complicated question. To put it simply, no one has any real idea what it means."

Narius gaped at him. "You're kidding."

"Not entirely. There are a lot of theories. Some people see it as a reference to a rune that could only be cast with the most powerful of inks."

Narius frowned. "I thought human blood was the most powerful of inks."

"In some ways, it is, but remember: using blood for ink is forbidden," Tolistan said. "And the texts actually say that blood connected to the Elderreach cult is more powerful than that. But according to the texts, light is more powerful than any of them."

"How would that even work?"

"That's the thing, Your Strength. It wouldn't. It's poetry. A metaphor. The only one who could paint a rune with light would be the Singularity Himself."

Narius nodded thoughtfully, but then he noticed Tolistan's hesitation. "Is there something more?"

"Y-yes," Tolistan said. "The grammatical construction of 'the rune of light' is fuzzy at best. It could be referring to a rune like the kind the toratropic mages draw. Or the language implies a sort of personification."

"The rune is a person?"

"Not exactly, no. Most scriveners interpret it to mean 'He who draws runes with light,' meaning the Singularity. But in my opinion, that's a bit of a stretch. The way I said it is the best understanding." Tolistan waved his hands as if shooing his own words. "But enough of this. I hope your training goes well, Your Strength. Know that my prayers go with you into the combat."

"Thank you, Scrivener," Narius said.

Tolistan nodded and left the room. Shortly thereafter, Farga returned and set Narius to work, going through a variety of drills. And maybe it was the blessing or maybe it wasn't, but Narius felt like they all went just a little bit better for the rest of the session.

Hopefully that would carry through to the *harsannon* itself.

54

They finally had a name.

Apparently Coran loved the painting. When he got back to Yusra, Coran had shared that the person who had contacted him was a Viscount Lorent. Quartus only vaguely recognized the name, which spoke volumes. That meant he wasn't active in the noble houses' usual machinations. A little more digging revealed that he was something of a hermit, directing his family's finances through proxies. And his family had a lot of finances to manage. As near as Quartus could tell, Lorent's family had been quietly involved with finance, civic infrastructure, shipping, and even high-end restaurants. And yet, as rich and potentially influential as he was, Lorent rarely came to Bastion. Instead, he'd holed himself up in a manor house in a small town in the Right Highlands.

At first, Quartus had worried the reclusive nobleman was out of their reach. He barely had any money left to him, definitely not enough to secure transportation out of Bastion. But Yusra came through again, purchasing two tickets for them on a public skimmer from the Bastion airhub to the one in Irieling. Then it was a two-hour trip south via a public transport until they reached a small hamlet nestled amongst farms and well-cultivated forests. Quartus didn't like that he couldn't pay for anything, but Yusra took it in stride.

He also didn't like the way he was starting to feel about her. He had never really spent so much time with one woman before without trying to sleep with her. And being with someone as brave and smart as Yusra was intimidating. He often found himself at a loss for words. But she had a way of making him comfortable.

They had spent most of their flight in quiet conversation, first discussing strategies about how to deal with Lorent, but once they had their plans in place, they passed the time telling insignificant stories to one another. He told her about his family's personal retreat in Bluerest, of going fishing with his mother or hiking with his cousins. She talked about swimming in the Dalark Channel as a girl, thinking she could cross to the Beachhead on her own. While their experiences were different, a common theme emerged between them. Neither wanted to be held down in the role that others had for them. They both wanted to live their lives on their own terms.

When they arrived in Irieling, the airhub staff assumed they were a married couple. Neither of them objected since it provided good cover, but Quartus found he didn't mind the idea at all. Which only made him more uncomfortable. He had never thought to settle down. Father died before he could broker a marriage for him, and Narius, thank the Moons, had never shown an interest in making up for that lack. But maybe, if he had met someone like Yusra...

But he shoved such thoughts aside as they arrived outside Lorent's manor. They had timed their arrival perfectly. The sun had set about an hour earlier, cloaking the countryside in shadow and thickening darkness. There wasn't a wall or any outward sign of security. That could mean that Lorent thought his presence was too well hidden to need much more.

Quartus pulled their rented transport over, easing it into a small copse of trees on the side of the road. Yusra glanced at him and he nodded. They ducked low and headed through the trees that bordered Lorent's house.

What they found surprised Quartus. The house itself wasn't that large, especially not for a viscount. Only a single story, it was made out of what appeared to be native wood with a dark green roof. Very rustic, very unassuming. A patio was on the side of the house, and a stream burbled in the distance. He smirked. Maybe, once all of this was over and his good name was restored, he could ask his brother to give him Lorent's estate as a reward.

They paused halfway to the house to wait for a reaction. No visible signs of security. Either Lorent was overconfident, or they were about to be caught by his goons. Five minutes ticked by. Then ten. They might be ambushed when they got closer, but they had to risk it.

Quartus tapped Yusra on the shoulder and they closed the distance. They pressed up against the wall of the house and waited. No alarms, still no sign of security.

Quartus stood and studied the windows. They were thick, and if he had to guess, this is where they would find intruder detection sensors. No problem. If he could find a juncture box, he could disable any alarm systems.

"Quartus?" Yusra whispered.

He held up a finger, then took a step back and looked over the side of the house. No sign of a juncture box here. Maybe around back?

"Quartus!" Yusra's voice was more insistent.

What was her problem? He looked to where she stood next to an open side door.

"Wasn't locked," she whispered.

That took him by surprise. On the one hand, this was a rural area and the viscount likely didn't have many visitors. But on the other, if Lorent was really involved, wouldn't he keep his doors locked? He shoved the uneasy feeling aside. He had to focus on what they were doing.

They entered a well-appointed but modest kitchen. There was a stack of dirty dishes in the sink and a slightly rancid smell hung in the air. Quartus wrinkled his nose. Didn't Lorent have servants to clean up after him? Strange behavior for a noble.

Yusra held up a hand, her head tipped to one side. Quartus frowned. What was she...

And then he heard it: the soft murmur of voices. At least three, although he couldn't tell what they were saying. He thought he figured out where the sound was coming from, so he signaled for Yusra to head in that direction. She followed, but she paused near a counter and armed herself with a large meat cleaver.

He should have thought of that. He retrieved an equally large knife and the two of them set out.

They crept down a hallway lined with old portraits of people who wore fashions from the past three centuries. If Quartus had to guess, they were likely Lorent's ancestors, all of them dour-faced men and women wearing clothes from the previous two or three centuries. Not a single smile among them. They passed by a living room area and a modest dining room, but the voices weren't coming from either place.

Then they came to an opening in the wall. Quartus frowned. There was no frame around the doorway, and as he examined it, he realized that a panel had been pushed back and slid aside, revealing a narrow stairway that descended into darkness. A hidden passage? The voices drifted up from below. Quartus jerked his head. Yusra nodded, hefting her cleaver.

Quartus led the way, his knife out and ready to defend himself. His stomach twisted and sweat slicked his brow. This was a bad idea. Why didn't Lorent have any security? Were they walking into a trap? But even as they descended, all they heard were the voices, a few of which sounded familiar although he couldn't make out every word they said.

At the bottom of the steps, they emerged into a surprisingly spacious basement. One wall had rows of wooden shelves, each one with small glass jars filled with liquids. Another had row after row of dusty, leather-bound books. Quartus spotted a desk with multiple scribers stacked on it. And on the wall opposite the stairs was a large communication device. A chair had been pulled up to the array, and an old man sat in it, facing the device.

"...reports of an increase in unrest in major cities throughout the Dynasty's holdings. We're predicting a forty percent chance of major riots by the end of the week in at least three of them." The man's voice was badly distorted.

"The way Istragon's been stoking the flames, they'll riot when Narius fails the *harsannon*," another voice added, this one a woman.

Quartus frowned. That voice was almost familiar. Recognition tickled the back of his mind, but he couldn't place it. The man in the chair chuckled, a sound that descended into a coughing fit.

"Enough of this," a third voice said. "How are the preparations on Maotoa?"

Qaurtus bristled. He recognized that voice. Duke Brencis!

"More troops are arriving daily," a fourth voice said. "Provided that the deliveries are on schedule, we will have more than enough forces ready when the time comes."

Yusra gasped, then slapped a hand over her mouth. Quartus pushed her back into the stairs, then peeked around the corner to see if Lorent had reacted. If he heard her, he didn't let on.

"What is it?" Quartus whispered.

"I know him," Yusra murmured. "Utulgal. He serves Emperor Tirigian as his left hand."

Quartus stared at her, unsure what that meant exactly. But the gist was clear enough. Brencis was conspiring with one of Tirigian's officials? This was just the sort of thing that Tormod would want to know. But they needed more.

"From what I've seen, the deliveries are on schedule. We should be ready when the time comes."

"What of the queen?" Another voice, this one also familiar to Quartus, asked. "She could still unravel all of our plans."

"I wouldn't worry about her," the female voice said. "Should the *harsannon* play out as we expect, she should be effectively neutralized. If not, we have contingencies in place."

"Oh?" the first voice asked.

The woman chuckled. "My left hand has everything in readiness for our contingency. And we have also recruited a high-level asset close to the king and queen. He's come to see the need for Narius to fall. He'll be most useful in the days ahead."

Cold washed over Quartus. Who could that be? His mind raced through the possibilities. A member of Narius's council, like Bokil or Elamek or Masruq? No, they said that it was close to both the king and queen. A guard? One of the servants?

"I will take my leave," the familiar voice said. "There are matters I must attend to that will only benefit our cause. I will update you soon."

The channel clicked, the sound of the mysterious speaker dropping the call. Quartus wracked his brain, trying to determine where he had heard that voice before.

"Is there any other business we should discuss?" the woman asked.

"When do I get my crown?" Brencis asked.

Lorent snorted.

"Patience, my dear duke," the woman said. "All will be set right and very soon. You have my promise on that."

Brencis grumbled something, then the comm channel clicked.

"Will he be a problem, *ar'zhannok*?" Utulgal asked.

"Not at all. He is passionate and dedicated, two qualities that have made him easy to control. As long as we complete our parts of the sundering, he will serve us. Lorent? How are your preparations?"

Lorent cleared his throat and leaned forward. "The last batch finished synthesizing two days ago and should be delivered tomorrow. My part of the plan will be carried out. Never fear, *ar'zhannok*. We will be ready for the sundering."

Quartus frowned. Was that a title? And what was "the sundering?" His fingers tightened on the knife.

"Excellent," the woman said. "Stay on task, focus on what matters, and we shall see the light again."

"We will see the light again," the others said in unison.

Lorent leaned forward and shut off the communications array. Then he sat back in his chair with a heavy sigh. Something snapped, a sharp cracking sound that caused Quartus to jump. Had Lorent just broken a bone?

"You may as well come out, Prince Quartus," Lorent called. "Let's not belabor this longer than we have to."

Quartus winced. They must have missed a security system. He glanced at Yusra, whose eyes were wide. But she nodded.

They stepped out of the stairwell. Lorent swiveled in his chair to face them. He was an old, mostly bald man, his face pockmarked with age spots. He glared at them with rheumy eyes, but oddly, he didn't seem upset.

"I must apologize, Prince," Lorent said, his voice a wheeze. "I know the etiquette for entertaining a royal guest, but I have no refreshments to offer."

"I suppose I'm at fault," Quartus responded. "I didn't give you notice."

Lorent chuckled. "Oh, I had plenty of warning. Coran informed me about your visit. He thanks you for the artwork, by the way."

Quartus's frown deepened. "Then why didn't you leave? Why no goons to protect you?"

Lorent laughed again, but it descended into a hacking fit. "What would the point be? There's nothing you can do to stop us."

"I don't know about that." Yusra brandished her cleaver.

"Oh, my dear, you may capture me. You could even kill me, but then, I have already poured out my life for this cause. I have nothing left to give."

Lorent's fingers twitched, and Quartus glanced at them. Was he reaching for a weapon? No, but the tips of his fingers were stained black.

"I suspect you have more than you know, Lorent," Yusra said. "Give me a few hours, and I'll find out everything you've hidden."

"No doubt you could. But you won't."

In a surprisingly swift move, Lorent opened his shirt, revealing a withered chest. But Quartus's gaze hitched on a pattern drawn on his skin in black, a series of jagged lines and sharp angles that radiated menace. Lorent swiped his hand across the pattern, leaving a trail of black, connecting some of the lines. Then the pattern flared with red light.

Quartus stumbled back a step. Why did Viscount Lorent have a toratropic rune on his chest?

Lorent stiffened in his chair, his fingers digging into the leather. Black lines radiated across his skin, snaking out from the rune. The viscount grunted, his eyes going wide as a red froth dribbled from the corners of his mouth. Then shadows swam across his eyes, and he went limp in the chair.

Yusra dropped the cleaver and rushed past Quartus, kneeling next to the chair. He hurried after her, but he didn't let go of his knife. He had seen too many runes in action to know that he shouldn't face whatever Lorent had done unarmed. Yusra gingerly touched his neck, checking his pulse.

"Still alive but barely," she said. "I don't know what he—"

Lorent twisted in the seat, swatting at her hand, mumbling something under his breath. Yusra knocked his hand away and then leaned in to listen to what he was saying. Lorent mumbled a few more words, then went slack in the chair.

The color had drained from Yusra's face. She touched Lorent's neck again then stumbled back, shaking her head. "He's dead."

"What did he say?"

Yusra sucked in a shuddering breath and started to speak.

Quartus was aware of the heat first, like a tickle of sunlight on his cheek from a summer sun peeking out from behind a cloud. This odd sensation was followed by a glow that snared his sight. He looked down at Lorent. The lines that had carved a path through his skin glowed faintly yellow. But as Quartus stared, the glow brightened, turning first to red, then blue, then a searing white. The heat grew stronger as well until it grew so intense that Quartus snapped an arm up to protect his face.

But the pattern the lines made had been burned into his vision. He had seen them before: the runes that had burned down the half-finished house in the Everhold.

"Yusra, grab whatever you can and run!" Quartus shouted.

Quartus didn't wait to see if she listened. He whirled and snatched up as many of the scribers as he could carry, then bolted for the stairs. Was she behind him? Hopefully, because the world was drowned out by a roar that was chased by an intense heat.

Smoke boiled up from the floor as they emerged from the staircase. Quartus rushed to the front door and shoved it open, tumbling through just as the room behind him erupted into flames. He fell onto the porch, Yusra tumbling over him. Data scribers clattered across the wood. Quartus bit off a curse and scooped up as many as he could as Yusra did the same. But the intense heat chased them off the deck. Hopefully they had something useful.

They didn't stop running until they made it back to the transport. By that point, Lorent's house was a pillar of fire stabbing up into the darkened sky. Quartus collapsed against the vehicle, his chest heaving. But he knew he couldn't rest. Not yet. The nearest town was a long ways away, but that inferno would be seen by someone. Local authorities would come to investigate, and when they arrived, Quartus and Yusra had to be far, far away.

He clambered into the transport and fired up the engine. Yusra joined him, dumping what she carried onto the seat next to her. He glanced from the pile of scribers to her.

"Are you okay?"

She nodded and gulped in several breaths. "You?"

He shrugged one shoulder, but then careened through the dirt onto the road.

"What did Lorent say to you?" Quartus asked.

Yusra took a few deep breaths and shook her head. "I don't think he was talking to me. It sounded like... a prayer."

"But what did he say?"

She turned to him, her eyes wide. "'Nekek shall shine again.'"

55

The world had gone crazy. That was the only way that Everys could explain it. Riots had broken out in a dozen different cities throughout the Dynasty's holdings. An obscure nobleman had been assassinated two days earlier, his house set on fire to cover up the crime. Dalark was fortifying their position on Maotoa, and more troops were arriving in the Beachhead every day.

Yet with all of that happening, her husband was getting dressed to fight in ritual combat to prove his worthiness as a king.

She sat in a corner of a room, a spectator as people scurried around Narius. He stood tall and proud, his head tipped back, a serene smile on his face. He was trying to project an aura of calm confidence and assuredness, but she knew better. She could see the way his hands trembled as he raised his arms so the vambraces could be strapped into place. She spotted the single bead of sweat that rolled down his forehead. Even though the doctors assured her that Narius was fully healed, she had her doubts. And while his attendants were wrapping him in as much armor as they could, she knew this was too dangerous.

But there was nothing she could do.

Everys glanced at the room's perimeter. Zar watched the preparations with a scowl. Paine stood against another wall, his features unreadable.

The attendants stepped back, and Narius turned to face her. Armored plate covered his chest, his legs, and his arms. A helmet obscured everything but his eyes. Rather than shiny metal, they were matte black and looked flimsy. She knew they weren't. Narius's guards had procured the strongest armor they could find. But he looked more like an athlete about to compete in a sporting event than a king about to fight in combat.

Narius slapped the armor on his arms, then on his chest. He nodded. "Well done. Thank you."

The attendants bowed and filed out of the room. As soon as they had exited, an acolyte bustled in.

"Supreme Prelate Istragon has asked me to bless you before the combat." The acolyte's nasally voice grated on her nerves.

Narius waved him forward. The acolyte stepped up to Narius and put his hands on Narius's shoulders. He recited a very formal blessing, invoking the Perfected Warrior's strength and stamina for the king as he faced this new challenge. At one point, Narius looked in Everys's direction and appeared to roll his eyes. She couldn't tell for sure thanks to the helmet, but she stifled a giggle all the same.

After several minutes, the acolyte turned and stiffly marched out of the room. As soon as the door shut behind him, Zar stepped forward.

"All right, Your Strength. Looks like they have you buttoned up." Even after saying that, Zar still tugged on the individual pieces of armor. "I wish we had better intel on what to expect, but we've been over the likely scenarios."

Zar prattled on about how to handle different combat situations: a bigger fighter, a faster warrior, multiple opponents. Everys wanted to scream at him to shut up. He wasn't helping the situation any. But then she realized that this was Zar's way of dealing with his own helplessness. The guard clearly wanted to be in the fight, but he couldn't protect Narius from this threat. So he shared everything he could think of while checking and rechecking each piece of armor.

Narius finally stopped him with a hand on his shoulder. "I'll be fine, Zar, no matter what the prelate's dreamed up."

Everys scowled. Istragon had refused to share any information on what kind of battle Narius faced. All they knew was that he would face combat in Bastion's municipal arena. Thousands of spectators were expected to pack the seats, a mix of nobility and commoners, to witness the outcome. They knew that some sort of spectacle would be involved, but what kind and what it all entailed was a closely guarded secret.

"You and your men did the best you could to prepare me, and I have no doubt that I'll succeed. I'll see you afterward."

With a nod and a final tug on his breastplate, Zar stepped out of the room.

Narius turned to Paine. "Any final words of advice?"

Paine regarded Narius coolly, then shook his head. "I've said my piece often enough, Your Strength. I have no more words of wisdom to offer. Just good luck and—"

Narius crossed the distance and hugged the vizier. Shock flashed across Paine's face, and he stood rigid in the embrace.

"I am sorry for how we've argued, my friend. After all of this is over, I hope we can make things right between us," Narius said.

Everys fought back tears. She didn't like Paine, and she knew the feeling had always been mutual. But the way Narius was behaving, it was as if he was saying his final goodbye.

Paine finally pulled himself free and straightened his robes. "If that is your wish, Your Strength... very well. We'll talk more when this is over. Now if you'll excuse me, I plan to go observe the nobles who are attending to monitor their support."

With that, Paine strode out of the room.

Everys gaped after him. She wanted nothing more than to follow him out and verbally eviscerate him. But then Narius stood in front of her.

A sob escaped her. "I wish I could do something. Draw runes on your armor or strengthen your body for the fight..."

He chuckled. "I wish you could too. But your father wouldn't allow that, and I want to respect his wishes. Besides, I have to win this trial on my own. If there's even a hint that I had any sort of help from you, Istragon would never let it go."

Everys pulled him into a hug, and another sob rippled through her. "I wish you wouldn't do this."

"I do too."

"Then why? Why not go out there and refuse to fight?"

"I can't." He pulled back and snared her hands in his, staring deeply into her eyes. "Everys, if I refuse this combat, the Dynasty will fracture. Istragon will declare my reign invalid. That would just embolden Brencis and rally people to his cause. Some would support me, but we could easily be plunged into civil war."

"But couldn't that happen if you lose?"

He chuckled sadly. "I suppose so. But I have to try, just for a little while longer. But this will be fine. You'll see."

He tipped his helmet back, exposing his face. He cupped her cheek and leaned in for a kiss. It was tentative at first, a mere brush of their lips. But then Everys grabbed the front of his chestplate and pulled him closer, kissing him harder. She screwed her eyes shut to fight the tears. She wanted him to carry this kiss with him, to carry her with him, into the arena. She couldn't do much to offer him physical strength, but if this would help him remember what he fought for, she wanted it to count.

Everys finally released him. "I love you."

"I love you too. Now get to your seat and cheer me on."

She nodded and headed for the door. She cast one last look behind her. Narius had turned away, swinging his arms and stretching out his legs. Everys wanted to say more, but she knew he had to concentrate, so she slipped quietly from the room.

Oluna, Challix, and Rewether waited for her on the other side.

"Are you all right, Blessed?" Challix asked quietly.

No, she wasn't. But she squared her shoulders and nodded. "Let's get this over with."

And as they walked through the arena, headed for her private box, Everys made a promise to herself, to the Singularity, and to Narius. If Narius survived this—no, *when* he survived this—she was going to do everything in her power to make Istragon pay.

56

Narius glanced sidelong at the acolytes on either side of him. The moment he had left the room, they'd escorted him here. Based on the noise that filtered through a large door in front of him, he had to assume the arena was on the opposite side. He also spotted a vid camera when he entered, which was probably broadcasting his image to the entire Dynasty and maybe beyond. So he made sure he stood tall. Proud. Every bit of him a king who deserved his crown.

So how long would he have to wait? He didn't have a chrono with him, but he had to guess that it had been at least fifteen minutes. Was Istragon hoping to make him nervous? Second-guess himself? It wouldn't work. He was ready for this.

Then the sound from the other side of the door died down. Narius's heart stuttered, and he fought to keep from showing any sign of nervousness or anxiety. Any moment now...

A viewscreen lit up on the wall to his right, displaying an image of Istragon resplendent in his robes of office. He apparently was standing in a box overlooking the arena. He raised his hands and held that pose for a few seconds.

"Loyal citizens of the Dynasty, I regret that we have arrived at this juncture. Long have I hoped that King Narius would see the error of his ways, and I know many of you have offered your supplications to the Perfected Warrior that he would once again follow the Warrior's dictates.

"But our king has unfortunately persisted in his apostasy. Tonight, we will determine his fitness to remain on the throne. I wish I did not have to insist on this, but I feel it is necessary for Narius to prove his worth."

Narius bristled at Istragon's casual mention of his name without the title. But then, he shouldn't have been surprised. The prelate was likely trying to provoke him.

"Now I must share that many in the palace have spoken to me over the past few weeks, trying to get me to show mercy to Narius, especially after his ordeal on Maotoa. Both the king and Vizier Paine requested that I temper the challenge. Even the queen herself tried to beguile me so I might shirk my solemn and sacred duties."

She *what?* Narius's lips twitched. He knew for a fact that he and Paine had done nothing of the sort, but somehow, he suspected that Istragon wasn't lying about Everys. When had she done that? What had she said?

Istragon looked down for a moment, as if considering what he was about to say. When he looked up again, though, a predatory light shone in his eyes.

"But I recognized those pleas for what they were: an admission of guilt. The royals know that he has strayed from the Warrior's dictates, and so they try to recruit me into their conspiracy. My friends, shall I allow this to stand?"

The crowd roared, and to Narius, the gathered spectators sounded angry. Sweat trickled down his back, leaving a trail of ice in its wake.

"This is my determination: Narius must prove his worth to us through combat! He is supposed to be the heir of the Perfected Warrior. Let him show his faithfulness through deeds! Tonight, Narius shall follow the path of perfection, the same that the Warrior once trod."

Narius's eyes widened. He couldn't mean—

"Just as the Warrior once faced a pantheon of gods who opposed his desire for the Water Bearer, so too, will Narius face combatants who represent those same gods tonight. He will overcome these defenders and reach the Water Bearer to show he is worthy of his crown!"

A wave of dizziness crashed through Narius. How many opponents did that mean? Who had the Warrior fought? The Gravedigger and Trickster. Chance and Chaos. The Sun? No, according to the myths, the Sun had sat out of the combat, choosing to watch. But the Moons too, right? Weren't there some lesser deities as well? He winced. He should know this!

"And..."

There was *more?*

"For the past one hundred and fifty years, we have not subjected our kings to true combat, using a scoring system to determine the victor. But Narius's offenses have been so grave, I fear we must return to our roots. Tonight's combat will be with real weapons!"

The crowd's roar thundered, shaking the building. Narius's breathing hitched and he wanted something to steady himself.

"I do not wish for Narius to die," Istragon said. "So this combat will not be to the death. Instead, it will continue until Narius has either incapacitated his opponents or gotten them to submit, or until he is no longer able to continue or he has surrendered. And, in keeping with the challenge, Narius will be armed with the same weapons that the Warrior himself used."

The same... But that meant...

In perfect unison, the two acolytes turned away from him. When they turned back, one held out a sword that had been snapped in two. The other held a badly dented shield that was covered in rust and grime. Narius took both, his mind numb.

Then the doors opened in front of him. Bright light poured into the room, and Narius used the shield to protect his eyes. The cheers and jeers of the crowd washed over him, followed by a wave of warm air.

"They're waiting, Your Strength." The acolyte spat his title like it was toxic.

Narius stumbled forward and nearly tripped when he hit low steps. He clambered up into the arena and froze.

The interior of the arena had been transformed for the combat. He stood at the bottom of four tiers, each one ten feet taller than the previous. Low walls and other obstacles dotted each level, but it looked like he would have plenty of room to move. He easily spotted stairs and ladders that led from level to level.

"Come, Narius! Show us that you are still worthy!" Istragon's voice was nearly drowned out by the crowd.

One of the acolytes stepped out after Narius and motioned for him to ascend a ramp to his left. As Narius walked, dramatic music cut through the noise. A sonorous voice declared, "And it came to pass, in days long gone, that the Warrior did look up to see the beauty of the Water Bearer. Thus captured by her charms, he promised to wage war against those who would stand in his way."

Bright beams of light sliced through the arena, illuminating a large statue on the highest tier. Narius wasn't surprised to see that it was an image of the Water Bearer. Only rather than her traditional features, she bore a striking resemblance to Viara. Narius grunted. Istragon likely was trying to twist the knife, but he wouldn't be distracted by such petty antics.

"But when the gods heard of the Warrior's impertinence, they sent emissaries to dissuade him of his plan. And so the Moons left their palaces in the heavens and came down to Pedrevor. But the Warrior's only answer was to defeat them in combat."

Narius stepped onto the first level and tightened his grip on both sword and shield. They wouldn't be much help in a fight, but they were all he had.

As he stepped forward, a door opened in a nearby wall. Two figures stepped through, one a Plissk and the other a Weyfir. The armor they wore appeared to be made out of the same material as Narius's, only theirs had been painted bright colors. The Plissk had a waxing moon on his chest, the Weyfir a waning moon. Both were armed. The Weyfir brandished a scimitar while the Plissk had a razorwhip in his hand. Narius gritted his teeth. He had no idea if the armor he wore would protect him from the sharp edges.

He sighed. One way to find out.

Waving his sword in a tight circle, Narius said, "Let's get this over with."

Everys winced as the Plissk's whip sliced through the air with a sharp crack. Narius raised his shield barely in time, the razor edge clanging against the battered metal. He fell back a step, and the Weyfir pounced, slicing at his legs. Narius spun, ducking behind some of the fake scenery. The Plissk and Weyfir exchanged a look, then crept after him, splitting up to go around Narius's hiding place from both directions.

Oluna reached over and snared Everys's hand, squeezing it tightly.

"Brave face, Blessed," Challix whispered to her. "If the spectators do not see your fear, they might rally to his cause."

And what good would that do? Would they storm the arena, fight for him? Everys wanted to laugh and to cry and to scream, all at once. Her hand twitched to her bracelet. Not many beads left, but she had a few. So what could she do? A smoke screen? Throw lightning as she had to protect Narius in the past? No, she couldn't do any of that. Because if she did, even if she saved Narius, she would only show that Istragon had been telling the truth. Inkstains, smudges, and streaks!

With a shout, Narius charged out of his hiding place, and Everys's heart skipped a beat. He had somehow crept away from where everyone expected him to be, allowing him to flank the Weyfir. The blue-skinned man turned just in time to have Narius barrel into him with his shield, knocking him off his feet. Narius spun the sword around, making it easier to stab the fallen man. Instead, the Weyfir tossed aside his scimitar and raised his hands in surrender.

"Yes!" Everys wanted to crow.

Apparently the crowd agreed with her. They roared their approval as the Weyfir rolled to his feet and stumbled back through the exit. Even Oluna pumped a fist and beamed at Everys.

But Narius's victory was short-lived. The Plissk charged, swirling the razorwhip over his head. He then snapped it at Narius, and the flexible blade cut into Narius's arm. Narius cried out in pain, but then spun the whip around his arm, yanking the Plissk off-balance. The attacker tumbled forward, right into the pommel of Narius's sword. The Plissk crumpled to the floor.

Narius stood over his fallen adversary, his chest heaving. He unwound the whip from his forearm and tossed the weapon aside. Then he inspected the damage to his vambrace. Everys sat up with a jolt when she saw red leaking through the armor.

"He's been hurt," she said.

"Not a surprise," Rewether muttered from his post.

She shot a look at the guard, who held up his hands with a sorry expression.

"It's nothing personal, Blessed," Rewether said. "I want him to win, same as you. But the odds are stacked against him. Don't forget, in the stories, the Perfected Warrior was almost killed dozens of times by the gods. I doubt King Narius will escape completely unscathed."

She supposed that was true. Still, she wanted nothing more than to go down there and help him. Somehow. Some way.

"Do you think I could talk to Istragon?" she asked Challix. "I'm sure we can negotiate some sort of—"

Challix shook her head and nodded toward the opposite end of the arena where Istragon sat in his own box. The prelate stood at the edge of the box, staring down at Narius. Even from that distance, Everys could read the contempt and barely restrained glee in the old man's expression.

"Istragon is too thirsty for his blood, Everys," Oluna whispered.

She was right. This wouldn't stop until Narius either won or lost.

"The Moons, surprised at the Warrior's tenacity," the storyteller's voice boomed over the speakers again, "returned to their place in the heavens. They begged their older sibling, the Sun, to intervene, but the mighty fire refused, saying she did not wish to sully her bright flames. Instead, she spoke a word and summoned the Trickster to stop the Warrior's ascent."

Smoke erupted on the next tier up, multiple colors wafting through the arena. The crowd cheered and clapped, some of them hooting. Narius, though, turned and looked up at the display. Everys could see the way his shoulders slumped. He was already exhausted. But he retrieved the Weyfir's scimitar and tossed the broken sword aside. Everys smiled. That wasn't how the story went. According to the legends, the Warrior had reforged his sword and shield using the Moons' armor. But she doubted Istragon would give Narius a break long enough to do that. So he had to improvise.

Narius crept up the steps to the next tier, the scimitar held out in a defensive position.

Everys hoped nothing would happen while he moved, so she looked around the arena, trying to gauge the crowd's support. If she had to guess, many of them sounded like they were on Narius's side. That was probably because he had dispatched "the Moons" so quickly. Their opinion might sour if he wasn't as successful with the next challenges.

But it wasn't just the commoners Narius had to appease. A row of private boxes ringed the arena, closer to the action. Members of the nobility, ethnarchs and their coteries, and other government officials sat in these. Everys spotted the Plissk ethnarch in one to her left. Thankfully, she didn't appear all that upset about the way the Plissk fighter had fared. The next box over held a number of Narius's advisers. She recognized Elamek and Bokil. And in the next box was Ethnarch Rockflow, Representative Mossglade, and...

Everys's breath caught in her throat.

"Redtale," she whispered.

She hoped she was mistaken, but she wasn't. The former captain of the Queen's Guard sat at the front of the Ixactl delegation's box, studying the action with an impassive expression.

Before she really thought things through, Everys shot up out of her seat.

Oluna snagged her hand. "You can't leave."

"Where are you going?" Challix added.

Everys ground her teeth and pulled her hand free from Oluna's. "To see an old friend."

57

Smoke billowed overhead, and the crowd *oohed* and *aahed*. Narius rolled his eyes. Ridiculous dramatics. Unlike the audience, he couldn't afford to be distracted. His arm still stung from the razorwhip. He had never seen the traditional Plissk weapon up close, but now he could say that his curiosity was satisfied.

The narrator droned about the Warrior's path as Narius trudged up the stairs to the next level. What would he face next? Someone depicting the Trickster, obviously. But how would the Trickster be portrayed? According to the stories, the Warrior and Trickster's battle was more a clash of wits than strength or violence. Somehow he doubted that Istragon would stay true to that part of the story. He shifted his grip on the scimitar. From his clash with the Weyfir, he knew the blade wasn't sharpened. Thank Chaos for that, or the Weyfir might have injured him worse. But that also meant he'd have to work twice as hard to beat whatever incarnation of the Trickster he faced.

By the time Narius reached the next tier, the smoke had mostly cleared, revealing a woman dressed in the robes of a Dunestrider. Narius frowned. First, he faced a Plissk and a Weyfir. Now, a Dunestrider? Istragon was not only having Narius relive the Warrior's path, but he also seemed to be sending a message with who he chose to portray the gods, all peoples the Dynasty had conquered. Either it was a feeble attempt to rally them to Istragon's position, or it was another layer to his narrative, forcing Narius to fight everyone the Dynasty had subjugated. He sighed. Might as well keep going.

With a flick of her wrists, the Dunestrider woman produced two daggers and dropped into a ready fighting stance. Narius took a deep breath and settled into a defensive posture. Why waste his energy on an attack? Let her come to him so he could study her offense and—

His opponent tossed one of the daggers at him. Narius twisted to the side as the blade whirled past his head. He then whipped around, bracing for the attack he knew would follow.

Only the Dunestrider had run in the opposite direction, almost like she was fleeing.

Narius blinked, then frowned. What madness was this? Was he supposed to chase her? She rolled over one of the obstacles, then leaped over another. She started to loop back toward him, but why was she expending so much energy with these acrobatics? It made absolutely no sense.

Apparently the crowd agreed with him. The cheering died out, slowly changing to boos and jeers for the Trickster. Narius was tempted to just head up to the next tier, but he knew that wouldn't be wise. According to the legends, after the Trickster, the Warrior fought Chaos and Chance. Bad enough to face two-on-one odds again, but if he didn't dispatch the Trickster, it would be three-on-one.

Then a thought occurred to him, one that made him straighten up and smile. Maybe this was an opportunity for him to score some points with the spectators, to play the role of the Perfected Warrior. So he strengthened his grip on the scimitar and braced himself.

"Come and face me, coward! You will not escape my wrath! Fight me with honor!" He swung his sword in several arcs, wincing as an ache burned in his right shoulder.

The crowd couldn't possibly hear his voice, but they roared in approval. The Trickster stopped her acrobatics, looked at the spectators, then whipped around to face him. He could read the determination in her posture. Sure enough, she charged.

Narius braced himself. He had better reach with the scimitar, but he knew he couldn't trust that alone. So he took a slow breath and readied himself.

When she reached the halfway point between them, the Trickster threw a small black orb. Narius winced and swatted at it but missed. The orb smashed into the obstacle behind him, and he heard it crack. A cloud of smoke enveloped him, and he choked, waving his sword to clear the air.

Too late. The Trickster slammed into him, smashing him into the waist-high obstacle and carrying both of them over the top.

Narius tumbled over it and slammed into the floor hard. He scrambled for his scimitar, but the Trickster was faster. She snatched it out of his grasp. Narius froze. Should he flee? Wrestle her for it?

But she didn't attack. Even in the middle of the smoke, he could see her pause. Then she held up the scimitar and dagger and deliberately set them on the ground behind her. Narius considered lunging for the weapons, but she held up both hands to stop him. Then she twisted her hands and fingers in a complex gesture, her hands weaving around each other. She clenched her hands into fists and pulled her arms back down to her sides in a sharp gesture.

The air between them rippled and coalesced into a pulsating ball. And suddenly, there was a second Trickster kneeling before him. He jerked back. What was this? Then he spotted another person out of the corner of his eye to his right. He glanced and froze. There was a second him kneeling there.

Before he could say anything, the second him launched forward and tackled one of the Tricksters. They tumbled out from behind the obstacle. Then that Trickster popped to her feet and took off running. The other Narius pursued her, much to the delight of the crowd.

He turned back to the Trickster in front of him. She raised a single finger to her lips, then carefully took off her helmet, revealing not a Dunestrider, but a familiar face framed by short-cropped black hair. The woman from Dreah!

"You!" Narius whispered. "What are you doing here?"

The woman motioned for Narius to stay silent again, then scooted over to the wall. She pressed her hand against it. There was a soft click and a small door popped open. The woman gestured for Narius to crawl through.

He hesitated. This could be a way to escape the combat, but for all he knew, this was a trap. But no, this woman, whoever she was, had helped him on Maotoa. And she had already had many opportunities to hurt him. Although he made it on scant evidence, Narius decided he could trust her. At least, for now. She genuinely wanted him to escape.

And he wanted to. He could already feel exhaustion dragging at his limbs. The longer he waited, the more aches and pains rippled through his body. He may have healed from his wounds, but he hadn't recovered, not fully.

But no, he couldn't, could he? He doubted the illusion the woman had created would last long. His retreat would be discovered and Istragon would decry him for his cowardice. No, he couldn't do this.

Narius shook his head. "I appreciate the offer, but I can't run. I've committed to this, and I have to see it through. Thank you, though."

The woman pursed her lips and blew out a frustrated breath.

He glanced at the ripple in the air that hung between them. "How much more time do we have?"

She considered it, then shrugged and made a small gesture with her right hand.

He frowned. Couldn't she speak? If he had to guess, they didn't have too much time left.

"We'll have to finish our fight," Narius said. "Are you okay with losing?"

She offered him a lopsided grin and nodded.

"Then before we go, is there anything else you can do to help me?"

Her brow furrowed, but she nodded. She motioned for him to scoot closer, then waved her hands over his shoulders, down his arms, toward the floor. Her fingers twisted and wove as she moved. At first, Narius thought she was just humoring him, but then a soothing sensation flowed through him, starting at his shoulders and flowing into his arms and chest. He sucked in a surprised breath. The sensation was eerily familiar. But he couldn't puzzle on that right now. Thanks to whatever she had done, he felt better. Not completely whole, but stronger. At peace. Ready for the next challenge.

"Are you ready?" he asked.

She nodded. She pulled her helmet back on, then shoved the scimitar back to him and picked up her dagger. Then she pulled out another smoke bomb and looked at him. He nodded in return and braced himself.

The roar of the crowd reached a crescendo. Suddenly, the illusions of both him and the Trickster dove over the low wall they hid behind. Narius almost jumped, startled by the movement, but the images vanished before they hit the ground. The ripple in the air dissolved and the woman tossed the smoke bomb. As she did, she rushed forward and slammed into Narius. They tumbled out from behind the obstacle.

He popped to his feet. She did as well. She took several slices at him with the dagger, which he easily dodged. Then he charged in, carefully swinging his scimitar at her in what he hoped was an obvious pattern. She must have caught on to what he was doing, because on his fifth swing, she moved her dagger so that he could knock it out of her hand. She whirled away, but conveniently tripped over her own feet. He was on her in an instant, pressing the blunted edge of his sword against her throat. She held up her hands and froze.

The crowd roared in approval as Narius stood and raised his scimitar overhead in victory. The Trickster scurried off the stage as he turned a slow circle, scanning the crowd. He couldn't see Everys. He winced, disappointed. It would have been nice to see her reaction to his victories so far, a good boost to his morale. He hoped she wasn't too upset. Hopefully this would all be over soon.

From the way the crowd cheered, Everys had missed something exciting. Her heart stuttered. Hopefully Narius had defeated the Trickster and moved on to the next tier. She led the way through the arena halls, Rewether trailing behind and asking her to stop. But she wouldn't. She couldn't. Not until she found out what was happening.

There. Two hulking Ixactls stood sentry outside the entrance to one of the spectator boxes. They turned to face her as she approached. One looked ready to object. But Everys brushed past them and ripped the door open.

Sure enough, Mossglade, Rockflow, and Redtale all sat together near the front of the box. If Everys didn't know their history, she might have even mistaken them as friends.

"What is going on here?" she demanded.

The three Ixactl turned around. Rockflow and Mossglade leaped out of their seats, but Redtale remained seated, her expression unreadable.

"Blessed, what are you doing here?" Mossglade asked.

"I might ask you the same question. Or, more specifically, what you are doing here with her?" Everys gestured at Redtale.

Rockflow glanced at Mossglade before speaking. "We have reached an accord of sorts with the Untested."

Everys's brows shot up. An accord? With revolutionaries that wanted to secede from the Dynasty? What kind of compromise could possibly be reached with the Untested?

"It actually is a workable compromise, Blessed," Mossglade said. "We've found a way for the Untested to have a more official presence in The Stone and our governance. Many of them will be serving in my office and as assistants to Ethnarch Rockflow."

"I'm glad for you," Everys said flatly. "And what did they give up?"

"We need to be the villains," Redtale said.

What? The crowd roared again, nearly drowning out Everys's confused thoughts.

Redtale rose and turned to her. "Rockflow was facing a dilemma. Istragon needed a favor from the ethnarch. But Rockflow knew that, if he helped Istragon, it would look bad for him politically, especially after you returned the *ma-se-kranna*. He was trapped between two impossible choices: refuse the Supreme Prelate or appear ungrateful to the royal family. So we gave him a solution."

A flicker of sadness danced across Redtale's face as the crowd cheered even louder, many of them chanting Narius's name. Everys fought the urge to rush to the edge of the box to see what had happened. If the crowd was cheering that enthusiastically, he had probably won, right?

"Having won his victory, the Warrior continued on his noble path, certain that nothing would deter him," the narrator said. "But one of his greatest challenges awaited him, for the fallen Trickster was mother to two sons, the gods Chaos and Chance. They came to oppose the Warrior's path and seek out their own vengeance."

"Istragon wanted two people who would embody that kind of rage," Redtale said quietly.

Ice swept through Everys. No. That couldn't mean...

She hurried past the Ixactl delegation to the edge of the box. Narius had clambered up to the next tier.

Two Ixactl appeared onstage. One was dressed in red armor, the other in black. They bellowed and swung large clubs with jagged ridges.

"We were able to provide just what Istragon needed," Redtale said. "I'm sorry, Blessed."

She didn't sound sorry. And Everys wanted to scream at her former friend. But she couldn't turn away. She had to watch what was happening. Because she realized that this might be as far as Narius made it.

58

Everys sucked in a sharp breath. The Ixactls charged her husband, both of them bellowing and swinging their clubs in wild arcs. Narius barely managed to duck one of them before rolling in and smacking Chaos across the back of his knees with the scimitar. The Ixactl stumbled and nearly dropped his club, but Chance was right there, smashing the floor with his weapon with such force that Everys was sure she felt the impact in the box.

Redtale grunted next to her. "Frostfall and Gullyborn were so eager to strike a blow for the Untested. Enthusiasm is rarely tempered with strategy."

Everys whirled on her. "How could you? I know that you're upset with me—at both of us!—but you were the commander of the Queen's Guard! How can you possibly justify this?"

"And because I served on the guard, I'm supposed to ignore the Dynasty's faults?" Redtale asked coolly.

"Of course not! Have I ignored the Dynasty's faults?"

"You've certainly grown more comfortable with them," Redtale replied.

Everys bristled. "How can you say that?"

"How can I not?" Redtale laughed. "Yes, you returned the *ma-se-kranna*, but how many artifacts still languish in the archives?"

"After what Rockflow and Mossglade told me, I thought it would be wiser to wait. I didn't realize that bringing the *ma-se-kranna* back to The Stone would cause so much trouble, so I—"

The crowd roared, and Everys's gaze flicked toward the arena. The Ixactls had backed Narius into a corner, but he was holding his own. He ducked and blocked each of their attacks, but it was clear to her that he was tiring.

"Do you hear yourself?" Redtale asked. "*You* thought that it might be too much trouble for the people the Dynasty conquered to receive their stolen heritage, so *you* thought it best to wait. Why is that up to you?"

Everys stammered, her mind racing. She wanted to watch Narius, but she felt that this was just as important. "B-because there is so much happening in the Dynasty, it didn't seem wise to destabilize—"

Redtale took a step closer. "So it's better to keep the old wounds open? To let them slowly bleed?"

"No, b-but—"

"Did the return of the *ma-se-kranna* cause some 'destabilization?' Yes. It did." Redtale jabbed a finger at Rockflow. "But it also brought him to the table. We worked it out."

"I'm glad. But what if..."

"'What if' isn't your question to ask, Blessed," Redtale said. "You still don't get it."

Another cheer from the crowds, with a few boos and jeers mixed in. Everys risked another peek. Narius had broken free of the corner, but it was clear that he was struggling against the two Ixactl. Chance and Chaos were taking turns swinging at him, easily outmaneuvering him at every step.

A fire shot through Everys. She turned her full attention on Redtale. "And neither do you. Did I make a mistake? Yes. I did. I wasn't a good friend to you. I listened to you when you talked about your culture, but I didn't hear you. I didn't understand. And you're right, I should have thought of you immediately when I learned what was in the archives. When we returned the Hearth to the Cold Light, our next stop should have been The Stone with the *ma-se-kranna*. It should have been, but it wasn't. And I am sorry for that. I truly am. I made a mistake and I hurt you.

"I'm not saying that you need to forgive me. That's not something I can control. But I'm going to ask you to forgive me anyway. Please."

Redtale scowled. Everys held back her tears, which wasn't easy. But she knew that if she didn't, Redtale might accuse her of being manipulative. And that wouldn't help the situation at all. She needed to stay strong, no matter what Redtale decided.

Her former guard sighed. "It's not that easy, Blessed. We've been carrying the weight of the Dynasty on our shoulders for three hundred years now. And it just gets heavier and heavier."

"I—" Everys caught herself before saying she understood or she knew. She didn't. She couldn't. So instead, she latched on to an idea, a half-formed hope that might be the salve they both needed. "So let's do something to lighten the load. This is what I propose: each of the conquered people will be invited to send representatives to meet with me personally. While I can't speak for him right now, I'm certain that Narius would be willing to join us. We will listen to what they have experienced at the hands of the Dynasty. And they will tell us what we can do to make things right."

"And you'll be able to act?" Redtale's skepticism was obvious.

"I can't promise that," Everys said. "Not when I don't know what the suggestions will be. But I will give each one a fair audience."

"How is this any different than the Hall of All Voices?" Mossglade asked. "Or even the Ethnarch Parliament?"

Everys jumped, surprised at the question. She had forgotten that Rockflow and Mossglade were still there.

"The Hall and the Parliament were designed to quiet your voices, to filter out your pain and needs through legislative insulation," Everys said. "This time, we will listen directly to the people who are carrying those pains."

Redtale snorted. "You're not offering us much. Promises. Generalities. Easy words to say."

"That's true," Everys said. "But I want you to consider something: do you think you'd get the same offer from Brencis?"

Redtale's jaw clicked shut. She glared at Everys, and Everys couldn't blame her. That was a cheap question, but one that Everys needed to ask.

She turned back to the arena and her heart seized. Narius batted at Chaos and Chance with his sword, but he was clearly exhausted. The Ixactl, though, were going strong. Chaos stood back and laughed as Chance feinted at Narius, threatening to hit him with his club. Narius's armor was scratched and cracked. Too many attacks had hit home.

"We can only take this admittedly small step together," Everys whispered.

Redtale studied her face, and Everys struggled to keep her expression neutral. She thought that she had done a good enough job pleading her case, but if Redtale suspected her of lying—even though she wasn't!—it would all be for naught.

But then Redtale grunted and stepped up to the edge of the box. She unleashed a piercing cry, an undulating sound that somehow cut through the noise of the crowd. Most of the spectators fell silent as Redtale took another breath and somehow shouted even louder. That caught the attention of the two Ixactl on the stage. They stopped their attack and looked up toward the box. Redtale made a small gesture and jerked her head to the right.

Chaos and Chance exchanged uncertain looks, but then Chaos shrugged. He and Chance tossed aside their clubs and lumbered off the stage.

The crowd went silent, but then the booing started. The spectators around them jeered and screamed insults at the Ixactl.

"I'm sorry." Everys touched Redtale's arm and took a step closer. "They won't have to break their horns, will they?"

Redtale snorted. "No. They'll be fine. They obviously fought well, and it's my fault they surrendered. And no one has broken their horns for years." Then she smiled. "Well, almost no one."

Everys choked back another sob. She hadn't seen Redtale's smile in what felt like a lifetime. This brief glimpse nearly dropped her right there.

But then it was gone. "You'd better keep your word, Blessed."

"I will. I promise. We will work to make things better," Everys said.

Redtale nodded, then turned to Rockflow and Mossglade. "I'm going to talk to Gullyborn and Frostfall. Enjoy the rest of the show."

She brushed past Rockflow, and it looked like she deliberately shouldered him out of the way. Rockflow grumbled something, shooting a glare at Everys.

Everys knew she had overstayed her welcome. Best to get back to her seat and see if Narius could capitalize on this.

Narius's chest burned, and he could barely lift his arms. He took several ragged breaths and looked around the arena. The audience had descended into a near riot. He didn't totally understand what had happened himself. The two Ixactl were going to kill him, but then they had walked away.

He looked to the top tier. The statue of Viara glared down at him. Normally, the Water Bearer was depicted with a beatific smile, but not this statue. He could feel her contempt wash over him. A trick of the mind probably. He sighed and looked at his scimitar. The metal was dinged and scratched, and he suspected it was on the verge of snapping in half. He considered trading it for one of the maces Chaos and Chance had left behind, but he decided against it. The weapons were huge, longer than his arm, and he doubted he would be able to lift one, let alone fight with it. So he sighed and headed for the steps.

"With Chaos and Chance, uh... defeated, the Warrior was closer to his goal than ever. But the gods were not yet done with him. For there is one enemy that we all must face, an implacable foe who is relentless in his pursuit of us. The Warrior would need to vanquish the Gravedigger before he could attain his desires."

The arena went still and Narius braced himself. What had the prelate cooked up for this?

A piercing screech cut through the air, an inhuman sound so sharp and shrill Narius winced and the hairs on his arms leaped to attention. Technically, he had never heard that sound before. Very few had. But there was no mistaking it.

In that moment, Narius knew he had lost. Because the Gravedigger he was about to fight was a Diradae.

59

A hush fell over the stadium, and Narius understood why. For many of the spectators, this would be their first chance to see a living Diradae. And while that wasn't true for Narius, he still stumbled back a step as the Diradae clambered onto the top tier.

He was a hulking specimen, encased in black armor that appeared to bleed red streaks through the metal. Narius's heart sank. Visium armor. There was no way his puny scimitar would be able to scratch that.

To make things worse, the Diradae carried a huge club in two of its hands. But what really caused Narius to falter was the Diradae's mask. Rather than the expressionless mask most Diradae wore, this one wore a finely crafted mask that depicted an old man snarling in rage, a depiction of the Gravedigger. Much to his surprise, the mask didn't appear to be made of visium. He noted it as a potential weak spot, but how he would capitalize on that, he didn't know.

The Diradae screeched again, the high-pitched noise slicing down his back. Narius's knees went weak, and his armor felt so heavy.

The Diradae tromped forward and bent down close enough that Narius could see the finer details of his mask. And then, in a voice so soft and thready that Narius almost couldn't hear it, he said, "King Narius, it is my greatest pleasure to meet you. You and the queen are such an inspiration to me."

Narius blinked, surprised at how friendly his opponent's tone was.

"Uh... it's a pleasure to meet you as well..." Narius let his words trail off.

"Oh, how rude of me. My name is He Who Occupies the Lowest Reaches. You can call me Occ."

A faint glimmer of hope warmed Narius's chest. "Occ. I'm sorry we've met under these circumstances."

"As am I, Your Strength. As am I."

"Then I don't suppose you would consider surrendering?"

Occ made a strange clicking sound, but not from beneath his mask. Narius realized that he was knocking his hind appendages together. "I am so sorry, Your Strength, but that just isn't possible. The prelate was most insistent we fight. And my king has asked me to do the same. I don't have a choice. If it's any consolation, I will try to take it easy on you."

Narius chuckled. "I'm afraid I can't make the same promise."

"I wouldn't expect you to, Your Strength. May the Warrior live through your actions. I'll give you a moment to catch your breath."

Occ scuttled backward. Narius took a few steps away as well, swinging his scimitar to loosen his shoulders. The crowd had recovered from their initial shock and many of them were booing and jeering, clearly upset that they weren't fighting yet. Let them. He appreciated Occ's civility in the midst of this stupidity.

What the Diradae said echoed in Narius's mind. *May the Warrior live through your actions.* That was supposedly the point of this—to prove that he did exemplify the supposed god's strength and prowess. Most kings in his position would have offered up pleas and supplications to the Warrior for help. But Narius knew all too well that no one would answer.

But there was someone who could.

Narius wasn't sure how he was supposed to do this. So he simply closed his eyes, took a deep breath, and whispered, "Singularity, I still have much to learn. And I know I may not be worthy of approaching You because of who I am and who my people are. We have done so much to hurt others, but especially Your people. I am trying to do better. But if I lose my throne, I won't be able to make things better. So I need Your help. I don't know what You can do here, but whatever aid You can give me, I'd appreciate it."

He paused, waiting to see if there would be some sort of indication he had been heard or if the Singularity had answered. The crowd still screamed obscenities at them to fight. And Narius felt just as sore and tired as before. But he had said his piece.

He whirled on Occ and brandished his scimitar. The Diradae crouched down, swinging the club in a vicious arc in front of him, then he beckoned with one of his smaller hands.

With a roar of his own, Narius charged. Occ swung at his head, but Narius slid under the weapon. He skidded between Occ's forelegs and slashed at his abdomen with the scimitar. The blade skittered across the armor with a sickening screech. Narius grunted. He had hoped to find an unarmored spot here, but no good. Occ was pretty much encased in visium.

The Diradae jumped to the side, exposing Narius, and Occ swung the club down. Narius rolled out of the way. The blunt weapon slammed into the floor with a loud *crack*. Narius scrambled to his feet. No weak spots underneath. That just left the mask. He sighed. Of course this couldn't be easy.

Occ screamed at him again and charged. But instead of raising the club, he held it to his side like he intended to use it as a ram. Narius dove out of the way, rolling back to his feet. Then Narius ran in after him and swung the scimitar at Occ's head.

The Diradae turned just in time for the blade to ricochet off the side of his mask. The Gravedigger's visage was knocked off-kilter, but Occ grumbled and quickly readjusted it. Narius nodded to himself. That had to be his strategy. How he would exploit this weakness, he didn't know, but this was better than nothing.

But before he could gather his thoughts, Occ swung his club. Narius tried to spin out of the way again, but he wasn't fast enough. The massive weapon slammed into his right arm with a sharp *crack*. The vambrace shattered. Before Narius could react, the club came around again and caught him in the chest. Another loud *snap*, and he fell onto his back with a groan. He looked down. A spiderweb pattern cracked his chestplate. He shook out his arms and the broken armor fell away.

Occ was immediately on him. Narius ducked and dodged, using the scimitar to parry as best as he could. But with each movement, he could feel his arms and legs growing heavier. He just didn't have much left. The club clipped the side of his head, and the helmet barely protected him. He staggered, only to have Occ sweep his legs out from under him. He hit the floor hard, his breath exploding from his lungs. When he saw Occ swing his club toward his chest, Narius rolled. As he did, he lost the scimitar.

Narius popped to his feet in a crouch. He spotted his weapon, but Occ stepped between them. Not a huge loss, considering he couldn't penetrate Occ's armor. But now he had only one option left. The mask.

He nodded to himself and charged. Occ dropped into a defensive stance, but that was perfect. Narius jumped, planting his foot on Occ's club, and then vaulted over Occ's upper arms. He snared the Diradae's shoulder and swung himself onto his back. Then he grabbed the mask and yanked it off.

The crowd roared their approval, but in spite of the cacophony, Narius still heard Occ's anguished scream. The Diradae thrashed, his upper hands clawing at Narius while his lower arms covered his face. Narius held on as Occ bucked and spun. What was happening?

"Too much!" Occ screeched. "Too much!"

One of Occ's fists caught Narius in the side of the head. Stars exploded in Narius's vision. Broken Sword, the Diradae was strong! Narius's hands slipped, and he flew off Occ's back, landing hard on his shoulder and rolling. Pain lanced through his arm and chest, but he staggered to his feet.

Occ continued to thrash, seemingly unaware of Narius or anything else. He covered his face with his upper hands while he groped for the mask with his lower. Narius had no idea what was happening, but he knew an advantage when he saw it.

"I'm sorry, Occ," he whispered, then broke into a run for the Water Bearer's statue.

But Occ stumbled forward, swinging his arms wildly. He slapped Narius hard enough his helmet fell off. Narius staggered and tried to recover, only for Occ to lash out with a vicious kick that caught him in the knee. Narius screamed as his leg bent the wrong way, and he collapsed to the floor. Occ's rampage continued, and the Diradae brought a heavy foot down in the middle of Narius's chest. Agony lanced through his sides, and Narius struggled to catch his breath. Broken ribs. Had to be.

Occ kicked him in the head, hard. More stars, chased by darkness. Narius rolled and tried to rise, but his legs buckled and he collapsed again.

Then Occ slammed into him. Narius fell backward, only to realize that he had been on the edge of the tier. The floor slipped away from under him, and he fell over the edge.

The last thing he saw was Viara's cruel smile as he tumbled, his back hitting one of the obstacles on the lower tier. His entire world descended into an excruciating haze that was mercifully chased by darkness.

60

Slipping out of Irieling was easier than he expected. Lorent's house burning down had the local authorities on edge. But Yusra and Quartus had managed to bluff their way onto a public skimmer and fly back to Bastion. Thankfully no one had looked in their luggage to find what they had salvaged before Lorent's body combusted.

Quartus was still having a hard time processing what he had seen there. He had heard the voices of some of the conspirators. Yusra had identified one of them as a higher-up in the Dalark government. But perhaps the most astonishing thing they had learned was that Lorent had been a practitioner of toratropic magic the whole time. Did that mean he was a Siporan as well? If so, how had his family concealed their heritage and risen so high into the nobility? Were there other Siporans concealing their identities in the same way? What would Everys make of any of this?

Once they were back in Bastion, Yusra had brought him to her safe house, an apartment over an illegal casino in Beyond-the-Wall. He appreciated the sign of trust, but he set to work almost immediately, cataloging what they had collected.

He and Yusra had snagged a dozen data scribers plus about fifty pages of handwritten notes. Yusra had also grabbed a leather pouch. Not surprisingly, the scribers were all encrypted, so Quartus worked on those first, running through as many algorithms as he could to see if he could unlock the contents. Unfortunately, it appeared as if the cipher was different for each scriber. Annoying, but he was positive he could crack each one.

"You sure you don't want to watch?" Yusra asked from the other room.

Quartus snorted. Upon returning to Bastion, they had been overwhelmed with people whispering about Narius's *harsannon*. Bets were flying throughout Beyond-the-Wall on whether or not Narius would win. Quartus tried to tune it all out. Yes, he worried for his brother; given what it sounded like he went through in Maotoa, he knew Narius wouldn't be at his best. But there was nothing that Quartus could do for him from here. The best thing he could do was focus on the task at hand: figure out what Lorent was up to. He waved Yusra off, so she slipped back into the other room.

Did she cast a sad look in his direction before she did? He shook his head to dislodge the ridiculous thought. Stay focused. Yes, Yusra was an attractive woman, and yes, he had entertained the odd fantasy about her. But they were so tantalizingly close to unraveling this conspiracy. He had to stay on task.

He plugged the first scriber into his portable data terminal and unleashed his decryption programs. Once he was sure the process had started, he turned his attention to the leather pouch. He shook the bag, the metal of whatever was inside clinking against each other. He weighed it in his hands and frowned. Coins? Shards of metal? One way to find out.

He gingerly opened the bag and shook out some of the contents. Much to his surprise, a number of metal pieces a little smaller than the palm of his hand tumbled onto the table. Each was shaped like a triangle, with two curving sides and a flat one. The curved sides appeared to be razor sharp. He frowned. Flechettes. While he was no expert, based on the size and shape of the projectiles, these were intended for an assault weapon, probably something the military would use in combat. So why would Lorent have a bag of these?

He turned one of the flechettes over in his hand, still careful about the serrated edge. Again, he could only guess, but he suspected that these would make short work of personal armor if used in the right weapon. Then he noticed the carvings on both sides of the flechette. On one side was the unmistakable logo of TelleGlin. He snorted. Leave it to Clarinda Gaines to advertise on a flechette. But on the other side were little channels, carved into the flat side of the flechette. What were these for? At first, he thought they might be a manufacturing defect, but no, each of the flechettes had the same shallow grooves, forming a pattern of looping lines that crisscrossed and doubled back on themselves.

Toratropic runes, the same one, carved into each of the flechettes. Quartus bit off a curse and dropped the flechette. He had seen what those Gravedigger-inspired abominations could do. So what did these do? He momentarily wished he could talk to Everys about all of this. While they weren't exactly on friendly terms, she might be able to explain this to him.

He sighed. If nothing else, this proved Lorent was mixed up in toratropic magic, which either meant that he really was a Siporan or he was working with them. He turned his attention to the scribers. Hopefully they'd contain the information he needed.

There. Quartus finished decrypting all of the scribers. He wanted to whoop with success, but he knew that any victory they had would be incomplete.

He set the last scriber down next to the others and took a deep breath. In the other room, a roar came from the vidscreen. He glowered at the door. That wasn't helping. He didn't really know how things were going for Narius; based on the crowd reaction from the telecast, it was hard to judge.

Quartus picked up one of the scribers and opened the files. He scowled. More of those notes on chemical compositions. Were these the same formulas they had found a few weeks back? He had no way of telling. As he studied it, he did figure out one detail: whoever was conducting this research had been trying to synthesize two different compounds. They reported success with one and abject failure with the other. Somehow, that gave Quartus a bit of comfort. At least they had struggled.

Maybe there was something he could sift out of this mountain of data. Rather than focus on the chemicals, he looked at who created the reports, if there was any information about where these experiments were conducted or when or how. He uncovered some names he didn't recognize, mostly scientists and researchers. There didn't seem to be a centralized hub for the experiments either. Instead, Quartus found a list of dozens of universities and research centers scattered throughout the Dynasty's holdings. He even found reports from two research centers in Utuaa, the capital of the Dalark Imperium. But what really caught his attention were the dates. Apparently this research had been ongoing for years. Decades, even. As near as he could tell, it started shortly after his grandfather's war against the Cold Light.

He set aside that scriber and moved on to the next one. More scientific data and reports, but this had nothing to do with chemistry. The charts and graphs he found were more straightforward. A team of researchers had been conducting scientific research on the efficacy of different kinds of ink. The experiment was simple enough: They used the same rune, one that produced a gout of flame. They then used various inks to see which one burned hottest and longest. They had used close to a dozen kinds of ink, but the data was clear. The most powerful inks were Cold Light tree sap and...

The scriber clattered to the table and Quartus rocked back in his chair. Blood. Human blood. The flame produced by the rune using human blood had lasted ten times longer than the other inks and had burned five times hotter.

Quartus scrolled through the rest of the data. The researchers had conducted the same experiment dozens of times, using different runes with different effects. While the notes about toratropic runes made little sense to Quartus, the results were clear enough. Blood was the best ink by far, although there were some troubling notes about a theoretical ink that was even more powerful. As near as he could tell, the researchers didn't have access to it. Was that the ink they had failed to create in the other experiments? Maybe. That gave Quartus some comfort, but not much.

He set down the scriber and carefully picked up the flechette again. Suddenly this made sense. Fire a flechette into a victim, and the victim's own blood would become ink in the rune. But what did the rune actually do?

He couldn't find the answer in the scientific data, so he moved on to the next scriber. Maybe the answer was in there.

Unfortunately not. Quartus's frown deepened as he skimmed through construction contracts and reports from multiple construction companies. Apparently all of them had been owned by Lorent, and for the past fifty years, they had been working on a massive infrastructure project in Bastion. Something to do with the city's sewers. How did that relate to anything?

The next didn't shed any additional light on the conspiracy. One was filled with personal letters and missives, again spanning back close to sixty years. He supposed if he spent enough time reading through those, he might be able to glean some information that was relevant. But it didn't seem like a good use of his time. Lorent's conspirators made it sound like whatever they had planned would happen soon. Any sort of delay could be fatal.

The fifth scriber contained more construction reports and contracts. These were more recent and involved Lorent's company installing massive storage tanks throughout Bastion. There were at least fifty of them and were designed to store half a billion gallons of fluid between them all. And while he was no engineer or architect, he was pretty sure these storage tanks had been hidden throughout the city over the past ten years. But why?

"Quartus?" Yusra called from the other room.

He set aside the scriber and grabbed the last one. Hopefully that would have the final piece to this ridiculous puzzle.

"Quartus!"

No, of course it didn't. More personal missives, along with family pictures and some genealogical charts. He tossed the scriber onto the table with a grunt. So what did they have? Old construction projects, scientific research into runes, chemical formulas. So close, so tantalizingly close, but if only...

Yusra ran into the room. Quartus turned to her, but the rebuke died in his throat. She had gone pale and looked on the verge of panicking. She motioned for him to come with her.

Dread oozed through him, numbing his body. He followed her into the other room. The vidscreen still showed the arena where Narius's match was ongoing. Quartus frowned as he watched a playback of Narius fighting with... was that a Diradae? Istragon had not held back at all. On screen, Narius snatched the Diradae's mask, pulling it free. Then the Diradae went wild until it stomped on Narius's chest and sent him flying into a lower platform, where he landed on a half wall back first, then rolled off and collapsed in a heap, unmoving.

The strength and heat drained out of Quartus's body, and his knees buckled. Had he... had he just watched his brother die? Did that mean he had become king? No, he couldn't have. He was outlaw still. But was Narius actually dead? Was Everys okay?

And then Yusra wrapped her arms around him and pulled him into a tight hug. He stood there, not sure what she was doing, but then his confusion broke and he hugged her back. Tears stung his eyes and, much to his surprise, he let them come. Sobs wracked his body. Yes, he and Narius had never gotten along. Narius had always been so stuffy, so formal, so sure of himself. And Quartus, he had chafed at anything that reminded him of who he was. But during the time he had been out of the palace, he had come to realize how fortunate he had been. Not just in terms of material wealth, but how good his brother truly was.

In that moment, held by Yusra, regrets boiled through him. He wished he could tell Narius how proud he was of him, how much he admired him. He wished he could confess how badly he had messed things up with Everys, how glad he was that the two of them had found each other. Now, though, those opportunities could be gone.

The thought of Narius being dead was too much. Too much!

Yusra whispered comforting words to him, stroking his hair, even kissing his cheek. And he let her, because in that moment, he needed her presence. He needed her whispered words. He needed someone. And if that someone was a Dalark spy, so be it.

He finally pulled away from Yusra and swiped at his eyes. He wanted to keep wallowing, but he knew he couldn't. If his brother was truly dead, then his mission had become all the more important, if only to protect Everys from her enemies. "C'mon. We need to go find some underground tanks."

61

Nobody would tell her if Narius was even alive.

Everys sat in the palace medical center, her mind as numb as her body. The past few hours were a haze. If she concentrated, she could remember bits and pieces. The way the crowd had gone silent as Narius fell. The strange screaming of the Diradae who hurt him. Then the rush of people who flooded into the arena to help Narius. Oluna, Rewether, and Challix hurrying her out of her box. The frantic rush back to the palace. And now the hours of waiting while Narius underwent surgery.

She scanned the waiting room. Zar and a number of the King's Guard stood vigil in one corner of the room. Challix and Paine conferred in another. Oluna had excused herself to check in with Masruq. So Everys found herself alone in a crowded room, wishing that her friend had stayed to comfort her. Or Redtale. Or... or anyone, for that matter. But she did her best to keep her expression stoic, to bottle up the raging maelstrom of fear and rage and grief that ate her from the inside out.

She heard someone slip into the waiting room. Everys looked up and her heart stuttered. Papa stood in the doorway, his hands balled into fists at his side. Some of the guards looked ready to shoo him out of the room, but when she rose and crossed over to him, they backed down.

"Papa?" she prompted.

He looked down at the floor. "I saw what happened. In the arena. And I'm sorry, Everys. I'm sorry your husband got hurt."

Heat built up in her eyes, and she had to struggle to keep from weeping right then and there. "Thank you, Papa."

"He shouldn't have even been doing that anyway," Papa muttered. "Stupid waste of time."

Everys nodded. "It was, but he had to do it, Papa. I don't like it either, but this is apparently part of being a king."

"Leaving you as a widow before you're even thirty?" Papa asked.

Everys winced at the venom in his tone. She held up a hand. "I can't do this right now, Papa. I can't. I'm waiting to hear if my husband has—"

The door to the waiting room banged open and a doctor stepped out. The hushed conversations ceased. She forced herself to walk over to him. She held her breath, pressing her lips together, and fought to keep her hands from trembling too much. She had to focus, listen to whatever he had to say. The doctor's expression was so grim.

"Blessed, the king has made it out of surgery. He's in stable condition, but the next few days will be critical."

With that preamble out of the way, the doctor launched into a list of every injury that Narius had received. Everys tried to focus, but she couldn't. Her breathing became ragged, and she twisted her fingers together in her lap, riding out the litany of injuries. Someone else was likely keeping track.

"Can I see him?" she asked, her voice quiet.

The doctor shook his head. "Not right now. He's still under sedation and is being closely monitored."

Everys nodded, but she wanted to scream. She had hoped to have a private moment with her husband, if only to finally ink a healing rune on him. The Dynasty needed him. She needed him. And he needed her help.

At least Papa was here to... She turned back to him, only to realize that he had left the waiting room.

The doctor fielded a few questions from Zar and Paine before he excused himself and returned to Narius. Once again, silence fell. She could feel the others glancing in her direction. Were they seeing how she was reacting? Or were they expecting her to do something? What could she do?

Then Everys cleared her throat and asked the question that burned within her: "So now what happens?"

Paine sighed a mopped a hand over his bald head. "We wait. Wait to see how the king recovers. Wait to see what the judges decide."

That caught Everys's attention. "What does that mean? What possible decision could they have?"

"I suspect that many will consider this a failure. The king did not reach the statue, after all." Paine glanced at Challix. "But Challix has made an intriguing argument. While that is true, the last thing Narius did before he was severely injured was rip off the Diradae's mask. That action apparently incapacitated his opponent. He was even headed for the Water Bearer's statue. So one could make the argument that Narius technically won the combat and what followed was an unfortunate accident."

Everys sat up straighter and looked to Challix. Her assistant smiled and nodded, a quick gesture that sent a wave of warmth coursing through her body.

"Will the judges see it that way?" Everys asked.

Paine grimaced. "Since Tupa Mellisan and Elsrick Bathogen were chosen by Istragon, they will likely follow his lead. Spanica Trentwether and Anadda Leedeke might be more inclined to vote for Narius. But no one can say with any certainty given the way things ended."

Thankfully, he didn't mention her attempt at influencing all of their votes. Either he didn't know about it or, more likely, he didn't feel it necessary to flog her with her failures for once. Everys frowned. There had to be a way...

"So we convince them," Everys said. "We make them see things our way."

"And how would you do that?" Paine's tone was strained, like he was barely holding in his disdain.

Everys's mind raced. They'd need evidence. Everyone in the arena had seen what happened. That was both good and bad; many witnesses, but probably just as many interpretations to what happened. And with Narius unconscious, they couldn't ask him what his thoughts were.

Her head snapped up as she realized the answer. "Where's the Gravedigger? Where's the Diradae? We need to talk to him."

Zar shifted. "That might be tricky, Blessed. As soon as the combat was over, a group of Diradae escorted the Gravedigger out of the arena. No telling where he might be."

"Then we find him," Everys said, her voice cold. "We find him and find out what his thoughts are. Zar, go get him."

Zar's men grumbled, but much to her relief, Zar nodded curtly. "As you say, Blessed."

Good. They could do this. They could find the evidence they needed, make a persuasive case. She was going to do this. For Narius.

The door opened to Everys's quarters, and Zar marched in, followed by the Diradae surrounded by a squad of guards. Everys rose from her seat and Challix stepped up next to her. Everys could practically feel the disapproval radiating off of Challix. Her assistant had insisted they conduct this interview in the throne room, not only to give whatever happened an aura of authority, but to intimidate the Diradae as well. Everys had rejected that notion immediately. If they wanted the Diradae to help them, they couldn't frighten him.

Zar came to a halt and the guards escorting the Diradae stepped aside. Zar gestured toward him and said, "Blessed, He Who Occupies the Lowest Reaches, as you ordered."

"Y-you can call me Occ, Blessed," the Diradae stammered, his voice little more than a whisper, "if it makes things simpler."

Everys stared up at the creature. She hadn't realized how large he was. He towered over her, at least eight or nine feet tall. But he wasn't wearing his black-and-red armor anymore. And he wasn't wearing the Gravedigger mask either. That made sense, she supposed, but she was surprised at how little he actually wore. Just some dull strips of cloth wrapped around his abdomen near his back legs, along with sleeves on his large and small arms as well as his back appendages. He still wore a mask, but it was the expressionless human visage that Diradae usually wore.

She forced herself to smile and gestured toward the kitchenette. "Occ it is. May I offer you some refreshments?"

Occ made a keening sound that set her nerves on edge. "N-no, Blessed, that's quite all right."

"Then please, let's talk."

She started toward a cluster of couches near the fireplace. She had no idea if a Diradae could sit on one, but she hoped he would appreciate the gesture.

"Before we do, Blessed, may I ask? Is the king all right?" Occ asked.

She froze at the quiet question and couldn't bring herself to turn back to him. "Unfortunately, no. He was severely injured. He's stable, but that's all the doctors know."

The keening sound grew louder, more strident. Everys grit her teeth and turned to Occ, only to realize where the noise was coming from. Occ's hind appendages were vibrating, almost a blur.

"Occ, are you all right? Do you need a doctor?" Everys asked.

Occ ducked his head and wrung his hands. Oddly, he did so with one upper hand grabbing a lower on his opposite side, creating what looked like a tangle of limbs across his chest. "It's kind of you to ask, Blessed, but no. Nothing the king did to me really hurt."

"Helped that you were encased in visium," Zar grumbled.

Everys shot him a look, then asked, "Then what's wrong? You appear distressed."

He looked up at her. "How can I not be? Blessed, I adore your husband. You as well. The last thing I wanted to do was hurt him! That's why I volunteered!"

Everys's jaw dropped open. "You what?"

Occ nodded, but the human gesture didn't look right. "I did, Blessed, precisely to keep him safe. When The One Who Bestrides the Darkness sought out someone to participate in the *harsannon*, he had so many volunteers. So many of my people resent the Dynasty and what the king represents. They hoped to injure him. So even though I'm not much of a warrior, I volunteered as well. When I found out I had been chosen, I considered it the Deep's own favor.

"But then to find out that I hurt the king so badly? A being that I've admired since my first molting? And the thought of hurting you as well, Blessed?" The keening grew louder. "I just... I just..."

Everys held up her hands in what she hoped Occ would see as a soothing gesture and took a step forward. "I'll be honest, Occ, I am hurt and upset. But I want to understand. If you didn't want to hurt him, why did you attack him so viciously?"

Sharp clicks punctuated Occ's keening. "I didn't mean to!"

"Then what happened?" Everys had to raise her voice to be heard.

The keening stopped. Occ settled onto the floor, tucking his four legs underneath him and wrapping himself with all four arms. He hung his head.

"He removed my mask," Occ whispered.

Everys frowned. "I don't understand."

Occ didn't say anything for several minutes. He wrung his hands together and made a strange chittering sound. Challix motioned for Everys to keep talking, but she shook her head. Occ was struggling with something, and she didn't feel right to intrude.

"Do you know why Diradae wear these masks?" Occ asked.

Everys didn't, so she shook her head.

"We usually tell outsiders it's a form of protest," Occ said. "The Xoniel forced us to be part of the Dynasty, so we hide our true faces. We wear theirs." Occ's body shuddered, and he wrapped himself in his arms even tighter. "But that's only partially true. Our tunnels are so much darker and quieter than the surface world. It can be overwhelming for us on the surface. The masks are designed to filter the light and noise."

Everys's eyes widened. "So when Narius pulled off your mask..."

"Those lights in the arena. The screaming crowd. It was so much. Too much. Overwhelming. It hurt and I... I panicked. I never intended to hurt King Narius, Blessed. I didn't! But I lost control, and before I knew what was happening..."

Occ started keening again, and Everys wanted nothing more than to hug him. She didn't know if a Diradae would find that comforting or not, so she held back. Poor Occ! As angry as she had been, now she felt pity.

But then part of what he said threaded through her anger and sympathy, rekindling a spark of hope. Everys looked to Challix, whose eyes shone with triumph. So Everys turned back to Occ.

"Suppose Narius hadn't been hurt. How do you think the combat would have ended?"

Occ made a sound that sounded surprisingly close to a human laugh. "Blessed, once he pulled off my mask, there was no way I could have stopped him. He had a clear path to the statue. He should have won."

Everys swallowed a triumphant cheer, mostly to spare Occ's feelings further. But then her excitement fizzled. Would Istragon agree? The prelate would likely ignore Occ's thoughts. If they were going to persuade Istragon and the judges, they'd need someone more influential than just Occ.

An idea seized her. She nodded to herself and snared Occ's hands. His head snapped back, and his keening cut off.

"Would you be willing to tell others that Narius should have won?" she asked.

He nodded, and this time, the gesture looked more genuine. "I would say that to anyone."

"Good." Everys turned to Challix. "I need you to make some arrangements, Challix."

"Press tour?" Challix asked.

Everys shook her head. Speaking to the press might rally the public's support, and that would be important, but that would take too much time. They needed to make a much bigger impact and quickly. And thankfully, she knew just how to accomplish that.

"We're going to make a trip to the Gilded Lock."

62

The next day, Everys headed to the Gilded Lock. She tried not to let on how excited she was. Things were lining up perfectly. Thankfully, Ethnarch Estrid had agreed to her request. Thanks to the *harsannon*, many of his colleagues were still in Bastion. Before she left the palace, she had gotten word that Narius's doctors were seeing encouraging signs that he was recovering. And Istragon still hadn't announced the judges' decision. They had time.

Her plan was going to work. She just knew it.

She glanced over at Challix. "Occ will meet us there?"

"He's eager to help." Challix regarded her with a grin. "You ready for this, Blessed?"

Everys laughed and shook her head. "The last time I did something like this, I caused a minor scandal."

"Only because you didn't know better," Challix said. "But now, you've got everything you need. You're going to do great."

Everys's cheeks heated at the compliment. She and Challix hadn't always seen eye to eye, but it felt good to have her as a partner now.

The transport pulled up next to Ethnarch Estrid's manor. Rewether hurried around and opened the door for Everys. The ethnarch's guard met her at the palace doors and hauled them open. A shudder wormed through her as she entered. The last time she had been here, Alezzar had died. A horrible memory, but hopefully not an omen.

The palace staff led her entourage deeper into the manor, through a winding hallway to a large door, twenty feet tall. It had been formed out of a large block of visium. Toward the top of the door were panels that had somehow been carved into the metal, each one depicting one of the races represented in the Parliament. But two-thirds of the door was still blank, hinting at the Dynasty's long-held dreams of conquest.

One of the palace guards pulled down on a lever, and with a ponderous groan, the door slid aside, revealing the Parliament chamber beyond.

Unlike the Hall of All Voices, the Ethnarch Parliament chamber was a large dome. A number of seating areas formed a ring around a central stage. According to what Everys had read the night before, the architecture was supposed to proclaim that the ethnarchs who met here were all equals in the sight of the Dynasty. But Everys also knew how, like many of the things the Dynasty taught, this was a lie as well. She couldn't help but notice that the seating area for the Diradae was slightly larger and more ornate than the others. And of course, the Siporans would likely never have an ethnarch as part of the Parliament unless something drastic changed.

But she couldn't be distracted by that right now. She had to save her husband's rule.

Occ, who stood next to the Diradae seats, hurried to her side. "It is good to see you again, Blessed."

Everys smiled warmly at him. "Thank you for agreeing to speak."

"Oh, this is nothing compared to the combat." Occ waved his lower hands as if dismissing her words. "It is the least I can do. But do you really believe this will work?"

She forced herself to smile, hoping to project some confidence. In reality, she wasn't sure. Technically, the ethnarchs had no real power. They could only make suggestions to the king and pass along recommendations from the Hall of All Voices. But she hoped that if enough ethnarchs agreed that Narius had won, the judges could be persuaded to declare him the winner. She planned to make a similar plea to the Hall of All Voices in the next few days, but since that body was larger, it would take longer to gather the representatives for a special session.

A low gong sounded and Challix motioned for Everys to take her seat. An ornate chair had been set up for her on the central stage. Everys pursed her lips as she sat down. She didn't like the fact that her back was going to be turned to some of the ethnarchs, but there was nothing she could do about that.

Once she was seated, doors opened along the perimeter and the ethnarchs and their entourages streamed in. She spotted Rockflow followed by a number of his aides. And there was Selestine, the Plissk ethnarch. Numeria, the Dunestrider ethnarch. Sollip Huntermark, the

Weyfir ethnarch. Assumption, the Kolvese ethnarch. Chilyana and Musein, the Grerid ethnarchs. Her eyes hitched on one of the empty seats. She suspected that was supposed to be for the Maotoan delegation. And she wondered idly if someday the Cold Light would have a grafted serve as their representative. Did they even have someone who qualified as an ethnarch? She made a mental note to ask about that. Right now, though, she smiled.

Once the others had assumed their places and sat down, a door behind the Diradae's platform opened and Ethnarch Estrid strode in. He glanced around the room, but with his human mask, it was hard to tell what he was looking at exactly. The other ethnarchs nodded in his direction.

Estrid settled onto his seat. "My friends, I welcome you to my home. I realize you were summoned on very short notice."

A few of the ethnarchs grumbled under their breath, but Everys maintained her cool demeanor. She appreciated what Estrid said. He might not agree with her request, but at least he would take it seriously.

"And we want to thank Queen Everys for joining us today as well," Estrid said.

A frown tickled her brow. That wasn't quite accurate since she had asked for this meeting. But, she supposed, it was a matter of pride. According to Challix, a queen had never convened the Parliament before. This was probably a way for them to save face.

"Thank you for allowing me to speak to you." She rose from her seat and turned a slow circle. "As Ethnarch Estrid said, the matter we need to discuss is of the utmost importance. It is my belief that the king won the *harsannon*. And I am humbly requesting that you, as the Ethnarch Parliament, name him the winner."

The chamber fell silent.

"That is... a bold request, Blessed," Selestine said. "Correct me if I am wrong, but is that not a matter to be determined by Supreme Prelate Istragon and the judges?"

"Under normal circumstances, yes," Everys said. "But the times we live in are hardly normal. Given the uncertainty the Dynasty faces, I feel it is better to not add to whatever Chaos dreams up for us, don't you?"

Selestine's eyes narrowed, and her long tongue flicked out across her snout.

Assumption raised his hand. "Perhaps it would be helpful if you explained your reasoning, Blessed."

Everys glanced between Estrid and Occ. She didn't know if what Occ had shared with her about his people's masks was common knowledge among the ethnarchs. She and Challix had spent a long time hammering out how to best phrase this to avoid revealing uncomfortable secrets.

"He Who Occupies the Lowest Reaches was the Gravedigger who injured the king." Everys gestured toward Occ. "He has shared with me that he feels that, when the king removed his mask, Narius won the combat."

Estrid shifted behind her. She fought the urge to glance over her shoulder at him.

"Why?" Musein asked.

Everys hesitated. "There are cultural reasons. I do not feel that I am at liberty to reveal them."

Occ's head swiveled around, his featureless mask facing her. He bowed his head, crossing his lower arms over his chest.

"So we're to take your word for it?" Numeria asked.

"Not at all. That is why I asked He Who Occupies the Lowest Reaches to join us today, so you could hear it from him directly." Now she turned to Estrid. "If he may speak?"

Estrid made a strange gurgling sound, then scuttled forward. "There is no need. I suspect I understand why Occ believes he lost the combat, and the queen is correct. It is a matter of our culture, and I respectfully request that you inquire no further about it."

The ethnarchs shifted in their seats and shot questioning looks at one another. Everys breathed a quiet sigh of relief. Occ had seemed very hesitant to share the reason for his loss. She was glad she could protect his secret.

"So I'll ask again: why should we weigh in on this particular controversy?" Selestine asked. "Let us be candid, Blessed. You know that while the Dynasty tries to mollify us by calling us 'ethnarchs,' it is a title with very little power. All we can really do is sort through the ramblings from the Hall of All Voices to pass along to the king's council. We do not have any true authority."

"With all due respect, Selestine, I do not believe that to be true," Everys said. "You are all the rulers of your peoples. Your words carry a great deal of weight with them. If you were to make it known that you view Narius as the winner of the combat, your people will listen. Istragon would have to listen, as would the Dynasty as a whole. You could show them all that you are all still rulers to be contended with rather than mere figureheads."

Selestine's eyes flashed and a smile twitched at her lip. She shot a look at Sollip Huntermark, who nodded back to her. He sat up straighter, looking ready to say something.

"Such pretty words!" Numeria stood up from where she sat. "Such wonderful compliments. So inspiring, Blessed. Truly. Your staff has served you well, crafting this speech. But I can't help but notice that you are issuing demands and only offering us compliments. Most of us, anyway."

Everys straightened, heat flashing through her. What did that mean?

"I cannot help but remember what happened during the *harsannon*. Your husband was facing stiff odds against Chance and Chaos. But then you popped up in Rockflow's spectator box and not too long afterward, the Ixactl in the arena laid down their weapons. Is that because you had already returned their precious *ma-se-kranna* to them or did you have to promise them something more?"

Rockflow sputtered and looked ready to object, but Numeria ignored him.

"And I suspect my dear colleague Selestine will vote for you. After all, you did support her people's claim on the Sanctuary Oasis recently," Numeria said.

"I have heard that you recently met with the nobles who served as judges for the *harsannon*," Musein added. "What sort of bribes did you offer them?"

"They must not have taken them. Why else would she be here, asking us to intervene?" Numeria leaned forward in her chair. "So I will be bold enough to ask, what are you willing to offer us?"

Everys stammered, looking over toward Challix for help. Her assistant stared back at her with wide eyes and subtly shrugged. She didn't know what to say either.

Estrid shuffled to Everys's side, holding up all four of his hands. "My friends, this is beneath us. Are we really so crass as to extort the royal family? We are royalty as well."

Huntermark and Assumption nodded emphatically, although Musein rolled his eyes.

"Royalty only in name, not in fact!" Numeria shot back. "I can't help but suspect that if we give the queen what she asks for, she will thank us profusely, and when the king recovers from his injuries, we will be relegated to our usual impotence. So I say we seize the advantage while it is ours."

"Really, Numeria. How can you be so mercenary?" Chilyana asked with a sniff.

Numeria smirked at her. "What can I say? It's my people's cultural heritage!"

The room erupted in heated arguments. Everys stood at the dais, watching as the ethnarchs argued amongst themselves. Estrid heaved a sigh, then turned to her.

"I apologize, Blessed," he whispered. "I wish I could say I am surprised by their behavior, but I am not."

"Is there something I can do?" Everys asked. She wasn't sure if she could make any significant offers to the ethnarchs. She suspected anything they demanded would be monumental.

"I'm afraid not," Estrid said. "The best I can do is try to end the bickering. Would that be acceptable?"

Everys scanned the room, trying to gauge how the ethnarchs might decide. She doubted she could count on Numeria or Musein. But had the Dunestrider's words swayed the others? Only one way to find out. She nodded to Estrid.

The Diradae ethnarch took a step forward and bellowed, one that pitched up into an ear-shattering screech that reminded Everys of Occ's entrance to the arena. She shuddered.

"Friends! Enough of this!" Estrid gestured toward Occ. "He Who Occupies the Lowest Reaches, do you hereby admit that King Narius defeated you during the *harsannon*?"

Occ nodded solemnly.

"Then I put it to this assembly: do we believe that Occ is correct? If we vote 'yes,' I will send for Supreme Prelate Istragon and inform him of our support of King Narius. If we vote 'no,' we will leave the matter to the appointed judges. Selestine? The first vote is yours."

Selestine rose from her chair. "The Plissk vote 'yes.'"

Numeria snorted. "Without considerations from the throne, the Dunestriders vote 'no.'"

"The Kolvese vote 'yes,'" Assumption said.

Sollip Huntermark cleared his throat. "The Weyfir vote 'yes.'"

Chilyana and Musein exchanged a look. "The Grerid both vote 'no.'"

Rockflow rose to his full height. Then, much to Everys's surprise, he glowered at her. "The Ixactl vote 'no.'"

Everys's eyes widened. Why had he done that? After she had returned the *ma-se-kranna* to him? After promising to hear his complaints? But just as she was about to object, she realized she couldn't. She had to let this play out no matter what. She turned to Estrid, waiting to see the ethnarch's decision.

Estrid was consulting a scriber in one of his small hands. Then he rose to his full height. "The Diradae vote 'yes.'"

Everys sucked in a sharp breath. A tie, four-to-four. So what would happen now? Much to her horror, the ethnarchs rose from their places and started to file from the chamber.

"I am sorry, Blessed, but in the event of a tie, the question must be tabled until an ethnarch changes his or her vote."

Everys's heart sank. But that would mean that Istragon and his judges would decide who won the combat. "There's no other way?"

"I am sad to say there isn't." Estrid gestured toward the empty seats. "Without Ethnarch Trevik's participation, we are deadlocked."

And given how Trevik had sided with the Dalark, he likely wouldn't have voted in Narius's favor anyway.

Occ made his mourning keen and Everys wished she could join him. She had failed. Failed the Dynasty. Failed her husband.

63

Everys leaned forward and took Narius's hand in hers. "Wake up, Narius. Please."

He didn't respond, and she really hadn't expected him to. After all, the doctors were still keeping him sedated after his surgeries. It might be days before they weaned him off the anesthetic. But she wanted him to defy the odds, to wake up early, to recover so he could step into the vacuum he left.

So she could see his eyes glowing with love for her.

She swiped at her own eyes, which prickled with tears. She was being selfish. The Dynasty needed him a lot more than she did. And she was being fatalistic. The doctors who'd operated on him were the best the Dynasty had to offer. They had done their jobs well, confidently predicting that, with enough time, Narius could make a full recovery.

But that was the problem. They didn't have any more time. The noose was tightening around her neck even now. Brencis was still on the loose, married to Viara. Dalark controlled Maotoa. And at any moment, Istragon's panel could declare and end to Narius's reign. She couldn't hold this together anymore. She couldn't. She needed him. The Dynasty needed him. So why didn't he wake up?

Just watching him wouldn't help. So she leaned over the bed, kissed his forehead, and then went for a walk through the halls.

As she left the infirmary, she nodded to Occ, who was crouched by the entrance. After the disastrous vote, the Diradae had volunteered to come back to the palace and keep vigil over Narius. Everys had been so touched at his devotion, she had agreed. It took some getting used to, seeing Occ so often. But as she walked past him, he scuttled back into the infirmary to resume his watch.

Tension washed over her as she entered the busy halls. The servants moved at a faster pace, their steps determined and their faces grim. That especially applied to the King's and Qqueen's Guards they passed. And was it her imagination or were there more of them? There seemed to be an armed guard at every corner.

"Everys!" Oluna's voice called.

Everys turned as her friend hustled through the hall. Somehow, Oluna still looked as jovial and cheerful as ever. Everys smiled in spite of herself. Oluna had been a a source of calm the past few days. She was there with a joke or a story or a brewing scandal to distract Everys when she needed it. But she also knew when to back off and give Everys the space and time she needed.

"How is Narius?" Oluna asked.

"The same," Everys said. "No sign of improvement."

Oluna nodded. "So where are you off to now?"

She wasn't sure. Much of what she was normally involved with had been paused during the mounting crisis. No one wanted to invite the queen to a social function with war on the horizon. Few had much time to devote to her charitable outreach programs. So she found herself wandering the halls, trying to stay out of people's ways. She had tried playing Entrench with Papa a few times, but he clearly didn't have his mind in it either.

Oluna leaned in closer. "I didn't tell you this, but Narius's council is meeting in the Amber Office, trying to figure out what to do about the current situation. Without Narius there, I think they're probably seeing a bit of a void where he should be. A void that a royal should really fill."

Everys's head snapped back. "You want me to—?"

"Take your rightful place in that meeting," Oluna said. "Why shouldn't you?"

She could think of several reasons. She didn't have a full understanding of what was happening. She doubted that she would have much to contribute. And she knew how much Paine would disapprove.

A smile tugged at her lips. Maybe that was a good reason to go.

Everys smirked at Oluna, who patted her shoulder, then she headed straight for the Amber Office. As she approached, she could hear raised voices. Not an argument, but the cusp of one. Squaring her shoulders, she pulled the door open and entered.

Governor-General Zammit and Bokil stopped mid-argument. Overturn and several of the other advisers looked content to watch their fight, but their attention snapped to her, surprise painted over their faces. Paine stood near the desk, and he scowled at her.

"Blessed, may we help you?" Paine asked.

"No, but perhaps I can help you," she countered.

He glowered at her, but then sighed and pinched the bridge of his nose. "Overturn, you may brief her."

Everys hesitated in the doorway. That was it? No argument? No snide comments? But then she snapped out of it and hurried to an empty chair. Best not let him change his mind.

Overturn motioned toward a map projected on one wall. "Ever since Dalark took possession of Maotoa, they've been sending over more and more troops to fortify the island. We've also seen an uptick of military forces being deployed into the Beachhead. At first, we thought that they were merely hardening their positions in case we struck first. But this morning's intelligence briefings have shed new light on the situation."

Overturn adjusted the viewscreen's controls. It zoomed in on Maotoa and the Blood Sea which separated the island from the Dyansty's mainland. "Dalark has been repositioning their navy to the eastern side of the island. We thought that this was a defensive posture, but today we spotted this."

He pointed at one section of the ocean. Everys squinted at it, unsure of what she was looking at. Boats of some kind?

"Amphibious landing craft," Overturn said quietly. "Headed for our western coast."

Everys's eyes widened. Overturn adjusted the controls and the image shifted south, to the Beachhead and the Demilitarized Zone.

Overturn nodded grimly. "And we're seeing evidence of Dalark encroaching on the Demilitarized Zone. We could be looking at the prelude to a full invasion."

The room spun around Everys, and for a brief moment, she worried she would faint. But she couldn't show weakness. Not in front of Narius's advisers. And definitely not in front of Paine.

"When will we know for certain?" she asked.

"A few hours," Overturn said. "That is, if this is a genuine threat. This could be a feint. They pretend they're going to invade in the hopes that we'll fire first, thus making us the aggressors in the eyes of the other nations. The troops along the Demilitarized Zone are on high alert, and we're scrambling defenders to the east coast. We'll know by the end of the day if we're really at war or not."

They would be. Everys knew that in her gut. This wasn't a bluff or a feint. The timing was too convenient, coming so shortly after Narius's *harsannon*. Tirigian was going to take advantage of the uncertainty and invade. Well. He could try. And he would fail. She would make sure that he did.

"Is Bastion in any danger?" she asked.

"At present, we don't believe so," Zammit said. "The local garrison is also on high alert, and I've ordered an increase in air patrols. I'm sure that—"

A rumble sounded in the distance, followed by a shaking of the palace floor, little more than a tremor she felt through the soles of her feet. Then another, louder sound, chased by another tremor. Then several more and this time, Everys recognized what they were: explosions.

Zammit bit off a curse and yanked a comm out. She stepped into a corner and spoke quickly to someone, then turned back to the group.

"My confidence may have been premature," she said. "Local forces are reporting at least ten explosions in Bastion just now. No one's sure where they came from."

"Missiles?" Bokil asked. "Skimmers?"

Zammit shook her head. "Nothing indicating aircraft overhead, but then, back when the king was going to marry Innana, her skimmer didn't show up on our skyscans until the very last minute. So it's possible that Dalark has some advanced stealth technology."

"Would've been nice to know that, don't you think?" Bokil grumbled. "Where is Tormod anyway?"

Before anyone could answer, there were more explosions, and one sounded dangerously close to the palace. This was quickly followed by the sound of civic emergency sirens blaring in the distance.

Zammit was still on her comm, barking orders and listening for new information. She paled and looked at Everys. "Blessed, I'm sorry to report, but according to preliminary reports, many of those explosions were in Fair Havens. The bombers seemed to be targeting Siporan residences and places of business."

A chill swept over her. The conversation in the room died, and all eyes turned to her. She swallowed heavily. "Casualties?"

"Uncertain as of right now," Zammit said. Then her comm chirped. She smiled apologetically and turned back to it.

The others resumed their conversations. Paine and Overturn were discussing something near the vidscreen. Nobody seemed interested in talking to her. And no one seemed disturbed about what Zammit had told her.

Fine. Then she would have to act on her own.

She hurried back to the infirmary, passing by servants who looked close to panicking. She wished she could stop to comfort or encourage them, but she knew she didn't have time. She turned the corner into the infirmary.

Occ sat up as she entered. "Blessed? What's happening? Were those explosions?"

She nodded. Before he could ask any more questions, she held up a hand. "Occ, I need you to go to Fair Havens. Look for a woman named Kyna. Most everyone will know where to find her. When you do, tell her that I sent you with this message: 'The days of Downcasting may be upon us again.'"

Occ repeated the message. Everys hoped she wasn't overreacting. The reports Zammit heard might have been incorrect. But if Siporans were being targeted, they should know, especially with the Dalark about to invade. Better to give them a warning and be wrong than to let them all fall into their ancient enemy's clutches.

"Of course, Blessed. You can count on me." Occ turned to the door, but he hesitated, his hind arms twitching in a motion Everys recognized as nervous.

"You can do this," she whispered. "I believe in you."

He straightened to his full height and, with one final glance in her direction, scurried out of the room.

Once he was gone, she plucked a bead from her bracelet and crushed it between her fingers. She smeared the ink on her pointer and set to work on Narius.

She worked as quickly as she could. Everys drew her family's rune on Narius's chest, maybe a bit more sloppily than she should have, but she knew that, with a rune this powerful, neatness wasn't the most important detail. Once it was done, she took a deep breath, braced herself for a possible rebuke, and activated it.

The rune shimmered with light, and the ink sank into Narius's skin. She waited, still braced for the rebuke, but nothing happened. At first, that was a relief. No rebuke, which was good.

But Narius didn't wake up.

His breathing seemed to have improved, his heartbeat continued at a steady pace, and his face appeared more relaxed But rather than the dramatic return to health Everys had hoped for, Narius still lay in the bed, his eyes closed. Maybe it had to do with how battered he had been. Or maybe his previous dramatic recovery had been because of the blood she'd used as ink?

She sighed. Narius was what the Dynasty needed. What she needed. But it appeared that he was going to stay just out of reach.

64

A military transport rolled down the street. Quartus nudged Yusra, and they stepped deeper into the shadows.

The situation had deteriorated. Not only had someone bombed Bastion the previous day, but rumors were flying that Dalark was invading the Dynasty on two fronts, from both Maotoa and the Demilitarized Zone. The criers were oddly silent on the details, leading Quartus to believe the rumors were not only true, but the true circumstances were much more dire. With tensions on the rise, Zammit had declared a curfew, and they were breaking it. But what other choice did they have? They had to find out what was in Lorent's storage tanks. Quartus suspected he knew, but he had to confirm it. And they still had to determine why Lorent's conspirators would want to store millions of gallons of whatever it was throughout the city.

Thankfully, one of the tanks seemed to be just outside of Beyond-the-Wall, down near the banks of the Melgor River. But to get there, they had to avoid the increased military and constabulary patrols. For a neighborhood that was usually neglected, it was heartening to see them, if frustrating at the same time.

Quartus held Yusra close, not daring to even breathe. Her breath, though, was hot against his cheek and her heart thudded into his chest. He gritted his teeth, wishing they could get going, and waited.

Once he was sure that the patrol had moved on, he led the way out of the alley and through the darkened streets. This deep into Fourth Watch, with a curfew in effect, the streets were eerily empty and quiet. Normally they would have come across dozens of people stumbling home from the bars or making their way to a house of ill repute. But they hadn't seen anyone. More evidence of how seriously all of Bastion was taking the situation.

They finally made it to a fence that separated the sidewalk from the hill that sloped down to the Melgor's banks. According to what Quartus had seen on a map, a culvert was supposed to be nearby, which would give them easy access to the sewers. He found a section of the fence that had detached from its post, creating a gap big enough for the two of them to slip through.

The rancid sewage smell was overwhelming as they moved down the hill. Quartus gagged, but he forced himself to keep moving. They eventually reached the river's edge, a concrete embankment built by military engineers decades earlier. And he was pretty sure he spotted a large, circular opening made of dark cement perched over the river. He motioned for Yusra to follow him.

Sure enough, there it was. He broke into a jog, and then slid on some loose gravel. He caught himself against the edge of the culvert. He eased his way to the opening and peeked around the corner, only to groan.

Rows of thick metal bars blocked the entrance. Thankfully, a section of bars was missing. It'd be a tight squeeze, but they'd be able to slip into the sewers through that.

Before he could move, Yusra latched onto his arm. "Someone's coming!"

He tensed. Had they been spotted? They knelt next to the culvert, and he hoped the shadows would be enough to conceal them. His mind raced, forming excuses for why they were out past curfew on the banks of a badly polluted river.

Only it wasn't the military or constables. A lone figure scurried down the hill, then mercifully walked away from them. They continued along the river's edge until they came to a section where the embankment had crumbled, creating a small gully that led straight into the water. The person, whoever it was, pulled something out of their pocket and tossed it into the river. The strange object didn't reflect any of the light, but against the streetlights, he could see it was a small geometric shape, maybe made out of a dark plastic or wood. Quartus frowned. Why would someone risk breaking curfew in the middle of an invasion to throw something into a river?

He turned back to Yusra and whispered, "Let's check the other side and see if—"

A low rumble grew behind him that quickly transitioned into a rhythmic thrumming. Quartus whirled around in time to see the river splash and churn, swirling around faster and faster. The person who threw the object into the river crouched down and watched. Then the water rose up into a mound, almost as though something large was emerging from the depths. The side facing the shore flattened, then a vortex swirled in the center. With a rushing roar, the vortex pulled away from the surface, creating a tunnel in the middle of the water. Quartus sucked in a sharp breath. What was this?

People emerged from the vortex. They crept forward and up the embankment, carefully fanning out. Quartus frowned. They appeared to be armed with military-grade assault rifles and—

One of them turned in their direction and shouted something, a word Quartus didn't recognize.

But apparently Yusra did. She cursed under her breath, then whispered, "Dalark soldiers!"

Her words registered with Quartus just as the soldiers turned in their direction and opened fire. Flechettes pinged off the concrete and one whizzed past Quartus's cheek. He dove for the dirt and covered his head. Where could they find cover?

But then Yusra produced a gun of her own and returned fire. One of the Dalark soldiers grunted and fell back a step. He raised his weapon again only to have red lightning explode from his shoulder.

The energy leaped from the injured soldier, slicing through the other troops. They shouted and convulsed. Yusra shot another one of the soldiers and more electricity ricocheted between them. As soon as the lightning faded, the troops collapsed, some of them falling face-first onto the bank, the others falling back into the water.

Quartus scrambled to his feet and dashed to the mound of water. As he drew closer, he heard an odd droning sound, like someone chanting the same rhythmic tone over and over. He came around the front and stopped short.

The vortex appeared to be a doorway or portal to another place, a brightly lit area filled with Dalark soldiers. A glowing crystal sat on a pedestal just on the other side of the opening. The soldiers shouted and raised their weapons, training them on him. Quartus stumbled back a step just as Yusra skidded to a halt next to him. He quickly yanked the gun from her hands and opened fire on the crystal, shattering it. The moment it did, the mound of water dropped back into the river, the spray drenching Quartus and Yusra.

"How did you know that would work?" Yusra asked.

"I didn't." Quartus hefted the gun, then turned to her. "Why did those flechettes shoot lightning?"

"I don't know," Yusra replied. "I was nearly out of ammunition, so I used some of the flechettes we found in Lorent's house."

Then Yusra cried out, clutching her shoulder. She dropped to her knees and groaned, sweat slicking her hair. Quartus rushed to her side and knelt next to her. Had she been shot? What was going on?

Almost as quickly as it started, her strange fit ended. She gingerly rose and took several gulping breaths.

"What was that?" he asked.

"I-I don't know," she said. "But there was an intense pain in my shoulder that went through my chest and up into my head. I thought I was going to be ripped apart, and then it was gone."

Quartus bit back a curse. Toratropic magic! Had to be! He heaved the weapon into the river. As lethal as those flechettes were, he knew better than to mess with that.

He led Yusra back to the culvert and motioned for her to slip through the opening. Once she was through, he followed.

Thankfully, the sewer tunnel wasn't as cramped as he feared it would be. He produced his scriber and followed the limited map. It took them a half hour of creeping through the tunnels before they came across the top of a massive storage tank, which tapered off to a cylindrical pyramid. A pipe led up into the ceiling, probably to whatever people used to fill the tank, and a cable ran parallel to it. And then there was a hatch on the sloping sides. Perfect.

Quartus hurried to the hatch and hauled it open. An overwhelming stench washed over him. He gagged and backed away. Whatever was in the tank smelled sickly sweet, mixed with an earthy tang. Once his initial discomfort faded, though, he forced himself to look inside. The tank was nearly full with a dark liquid. He frowned. Was this the synthetic tree sap?

"Quartus, over here," Yusra whispered.

She motioned toward a ladder that descended parallel to the tank. She hurried down it and he followed. They landed on a metal floor that circled the bottom of the tank. The cable from up above ran the length of the tank to large device that encircled the very bottom. Based on what Quartus saw, it was most likely a remote-controlled valve that could be used to drain the reservoir. They walked around the tank, looking for any more clues, but they came up empty.

"So now what?" Yusra asked.

Quartus pointed to the valve. "I suppose we could drain it. Hopefully that would slow them down a little, maybe even ruin their plans."

Yusra frowned, but Quartus didn't wait for an answer. He knelt next to the valve and worked at prying the casing open. He could probably jury-rig the device to get it to drain.

"Quartus, wait! Don't do that."

"Why not?" he asked. "We disarm them, and—"

"But we don't know if that's what would happen. And don't you think they have a way of monitoring the contents of the tank? If it suddenly drains, that could alert someone that we're on to them. Right now, we still have at least a small element of surprise."

"So what do you suggest we do?" he asked.

"Find the other tanks. Maybe we can find something that will help explain what all of this means."

He considered Yusra's words. They had been lucky to find the tank unguarded. If they alerted whoever was working with Lorent, they may not be as lucky. He nodded.

"All right, so let's—"

Something clanged in a nearby tunnel, followed by a shuffling sound. People in the tunnels? Or guards?

Yusra whirled and shouted. "Come out now!"

The shuffling sound stopped, and then a hulking shadow emerged from the tunnel. It took Quartus a moment to recognize it for what it was.

"A Diradae?" he whispered.

The Diradae had all four of its arms out in what he assumed was a gesture of surrender. He bowed at the waist and slowly scuttled forward.

"My apologies, ma'am," the Diradae said. "I didn't mean to startle you. I was just seeking refuge. I needed to find someplace quiet and safe, so I came down into the sewers. They're so like our tunnels back home, you see? And I confess I saw the light and heard you talking to your companion and I grew curious, so I—"

The Diradae's head swiveled toward Quartus, and it looked like the strange, expressionless mask the creature wore was staring at him with dead, blank eyes. But the Diradae gasped.

"Prince Quartus?" He moaned, then wrung his hands together. "Oh, this is not good. Not good at all. Why do I keep having these encounters? Have the Depths cursed me for leaving my hive?"

Quartus and Yusra exchanged a look. Clearly the Diradae wasn't a threat, so Quartus motioned for Yusra to stand down. Then he approached the Diradae with outstretched hands in what he hoped looked like a placating gesture.

"It's all right. You just startled us is all. You're right. I am Quartus and this is my friend, Yusra. What's your name?" he asked.

"He Who Occupies the Lowest Reaches, but you can call me Occ."

"Occ. Pleased to meet you."

"You may not feel that way when you find out who I am."

"Why do you say that?" Quartus asked.

Yusra gasped. "I know that name! You're the one who fought the king in the arena!"

Quartus froze. This was the same Diradae who had injured Narius so severely. His fingers twitched, and for a brief moment, he wished he still had the flechette thrower. He would make this Occ pay for what he did to his brother. Narius would be avenged.

Occ keened, ducking his head. "It's true. To my great shame, I did injure the king. And Prince Quartus, I am so sorry for the pain and suffering I've brought to your family. I'm trying to make amends. That's why I was in Fair Havens in the first place. Queen Everys wanted me to—"

That snapped Quartus out of his anger. "You've spoken with the queen?"

Occ nodded. "Quite recently. She sent me with a message to a most colorful character in Fair Havens."

A plan started to form in Quartus's mind. Not a great one, but good enough. "Do you think you could get in to see her again?"

Occ tipped his head to one side. "I suppose I could. She'll want to know if I succeeded in delivering my message."

"Perfect." Quartus fished his comm out of his pocket and handed it to the Diradae. "Take this and bring it to Everys. Have her call 'Yusra' when she gets it."

The Diradae took the comm and tucked it away. "I will consider it my greatest honor to serve you in this capacity, Prince Quartus."

Yusra stifled a laugh, and Quartus couldn't help but smile as well. He had heard plenty of people speak like that in the past. In every case, the flowery language was a poor disguise for the contempt or greed that the speaker felt. But Occ was so guileless, he knew it was genuine.

"Relax, Occ. I just need you to deliver the comm. It's important, but..." His voice trailed off. He was about to say that it wasn't life or death, but he realized that yes, it very well could be. "It's important."

Occ dipped his head and made a chuffing sound with his hind appendages. "Then I will treat this with the utmost care, Prince. I will head straight for the palace and let no one stand in my way."

"Thank you," Quartus said.

Occ turned and scrabbled out of the room. Yusra stepped up next to Quartus and watched the Diradae go.

"So what about us? What are we going to do?" she asked.

Quartus held up his scriber. "We keep looking."

Hopefully they'd find something that explained everything and soon. Because the more he thought about it, the more he realized that what he didn't say to Occ was absolutely true. They were dangling over a precipice, and if they failed, a lot of people would die. Hopefully that wouldn't include them.

65

Everys stared at the vidscreen, her body and mind numb. The news crier continued the litany of disasters, seemingly oblivious to what kind of effect her cataclysmic news would have.

"Reports are coming in that Dalark troops have somehow invaded deep within the Dynasty's holdings. According to the stories we have collected, the troops are moving unopposed through the Right Highlands, the Low River Provinces, the Edge, and the Plotan Expanse. The Dynasty's military is scrambling to find these invaders, but because of Dalark intrusions from the Blood Sea coast and through the Demilitarized Zone, we will not be able to meet them in force."

That was putting the situation mildly. While Everys hadn't been in the Amber Office recently, she had heard rumors as they trickled through the palace staff. Aside from troops at Vetranio's First Stand on the edge of the Cold Light's forest, the Dynasty didn't have many troops stationed in holdings they considered secure. Making matters worse, what few militias and local defense forces were there either disappeared before the Dalark arrived or fled after they did.

The Dalark troops were moving through the Dyansty's holdings relatively unopposed, and all of them were racing to one destination: Bastion. Within two days, the capital would be surrounded. Strategist Overturn was scrambling to pull back defenders, but the troops he had stationed on the west coast of the Blood Sea and along the Demilitarized Zone were tied up in pitched battles.

"In other news, we're hearing rumors that there is chaos inside the palace. King Narius has still not woken up after his grievous injuries in the *harsannon*, and we've also heard reports that Queen Everys has been confined to her quarters. Whether that is for her own safety or as some form of punishment, we aren't sure, but we are investigating the—"

Everys shut off the vidscreen and collapsed into her chair with a groan. That last part wasn't exactly true, but ever since Dalark invaded, the guards had gotten even more twitchy than usual.

"You sound as enthusiastic as I feel, Blessed."

Everys spun around in time to see Tormod step out of the shadows. Heat flashed up her spine, and she popped out of her chair.

"Where have you been?" she demanded.

"Investigating a number of mysteries at the behest of your husband, Blessed." Tormod walked over to her kitchenette and helped himself to a bottle of wine. Without waiting for permission, he popped the cork and took a long drink straight from the bottle. "All of it for naught, given what we're experiencing."

That snapped Everys's mouth shut. She took a moment to examine Tormod carefully. Normally he had a jovial air about him, but he oozed exhaustion. And he appeared to have lost a significant amount of weight. He wasn't wasting away, but his clothes hung on his body like they were too large.

"I'm sorry, that was unfair of me," she said.

He looked at her, then laughed. "No, it's I who should apologize to you, Blessed. I've failed you. You and your husband both. Had I been here, I may have been able to mitigate some of what's happened." He took another long drink. "I've been outmaneuvered, Blessed. Someone has coordinated all of this expertly. Brencis's rise and marriage, the loss of Maotoa, the king's injuries." He raised the bottle in toast to his unseen adversary. "Well done."

Everys clenched her jaw. It wouldn't do for the Dynasty's spymaster to get drunk, not when everything was falling apart.

"So what do we know? Do we know how the Dalark invaded our holdings so quickly?" she asked.

Tormod paused in his drinking and sighed, setting aside the bottle. "It would appear that the Maotoans weren't forthcoming about what their 'special relationship' with the seas actually was. We assumed that had something to do with their shipbuilding or their sailing techniques. Once again, we were wrong."

"How could we have missed that?" Everys asked.

He laughed. "As if you need to ask. How could the Dynasty miss that we have been practicing toratropic magic in their midst for four hundred years? How could we not understand what the Cold Light meant when they asked us to return their Hearth? Sadly, the Dynasty has prioritized exploiting those they've conquered, not understanding them."

Everys's knees went weak, but she caught herself before she fell. "So everything is lost."

"Maybe not everything." Tormod smiled sadly. "It may feel like that, but we can take steps to save what we can. I've heard from my sister that you sent a rather unorthodox messenger with a warning."

Everys perked up at that. "Occ made it?"

"And delivered his message as well. Kyna passed on the message, and as near as she can tell, the scriveners actually took her seriously for once. She doesn't know how many people heeded your warning, but it sounds like many Siporans chose to leave Bastion."

She breathed a sigh of relief. At least her people would survive whatever was to come.

"So what else can we do?" she asked.

He hesitated, then took up the bottle again and took one final drink. "Whatever we can, Blessed. Whatever we can. I would daresay—"

The door to her quarters banged open, and Trule hurried inside, followed by Rewether and Challix.

"What's going on?" Everys asked.

No one answered, not directly. Instead, Challix turned on the vid-screen again. The news crier appeared on screen, but she looked on the verge of panic.

"...reports are coming in from the Demilitarized Zone. The Dalark have defeated the Dynasty's forces and have made it not only through the Zone but have also made significant gains into the Dynasty's holdings. According to eyewitnesses, many of the Dynasty's troops refused to fight, retreating deeper into the Dynasty's holdings. Dalark may have made it as far as Tonraga."

Everys frowned. She didn't know where that was, but from the way the others reacted, that was not good news.

"Our troops in that area are in disarray and putting up less than even token resistance." The crier took a deep, shuddering breath. "This follows the news we learned earlier today that the Dalark navy has effectively routed the Dynasty on the Blood Sea."

The crier kept talking, but a wave of numbness swept through Everys. This was a disaster beyond anything she had ever imagined, probably beyond anything that any military strategist for the Dynasty had ever envisioned as well. The enemy had bested the Dyansty's army. They had pushed deep into the Dynasty's holdings. This had to be the worst military disaster the Dynasty had faced since the Colonial Uprisings. And it had all happened while Narius lay in a bed, unconscious.

Well then. If he couldn't respond, she would. She squared her shoulders and turned to Challix.

"How do I address the Dynasty?" she asked.

Challix's head snapped back. "Bl-blessed?"

"How do I address the Dynasty as a whole? Who do we contact to make that happen?"

Challix hesitated, then said, "Blessed, that sort of thing has—"

"Don't you dare finish that sentence!" Everys snapped. "The Dyansty is fracturing right now before our very eyes. The military is falling apart, and if we don't do something soon, we could have Tirigian's soldiers marching right up to our front door! If Narius could, he'd probably go out there and fight, but he's not able to. And no one else can do it. That leaves me. What do we do to make this happen?"

Challix stared at her, her mouth hanging open. Then she nodded. "I'll get in touch with the crier guilds. Given the circumstances, I doubt they'll object. And if they do—"

"They won't," Tormod said firmly.

Everys was tempted to ask him how he could be so confident, but she turned to Trule instead. "I'm going to need your help with this. You and the girls will have to make me look as regal as possible."

Trule offered her a nervous grin. "That won't be too difficult, Blessed."

With that said, Challix headed out of her quarters, and Trule went to rally the girls. Rewether looked ready to leave, but he hesitated.

"Blessed, I hate to bring this up, but..." He grimaced. "What if Dalark makes it to Bastion? My guards and I will protect you up to our last breaths, but there is little that we can do against an entire army."

She winced at the thought, but she knew it was an all-too-real possibility. So she nodded. "Have a skimmer prepped and ready to leave at a moment's notice. If things appear truly dire, I will leave the city. But not until Dalark is actually at the door, understood?"

Rewether nodded. "And where will we go?"

She frowned. Where could she go? If the reports were accurate, the Dalark were everywhere within the Dynasty's holdings. And it wasn't just them! Brencis was still a factor as well. Maybe she could flee to a foreign country, like Tomma or Rioka. But no, they could just as easily turn her over to the Dalark as offer her sanctuary. So where could she go? Where would she be welcome?

Then she realized she knew just the place.

"The Cold Light," she said. "They have a habit of taking in refugees."

Rewether's eyes widened in surprise, but he nodded. He set off, probably going to make sure everything was ready for that eventual move.

Tormod stepped up close to her. "Any orders for me?"

She scoffed. "I know better than to try. We need you in the shadows, doing what you do best."

Tormod smiled, and a hint of his usual confidence returned. "I shall endeavor to do that as I can, Blessed. Never fear."

She hoped so, because she had a growing feeling that no matter what anyone did, she would be boarding that skimmer for the Cold Light's forests sooner than she expected.

66

Narius still hadn't woken up, and at this point, Everys was starting to wonder if he ever would.

He looked comfortable enough. And the machines hooked up to him pinged quietly, a steady rhythm that none of the doctors or nurses seemed overly concerned about. As a matter of fact, aside from a solitary nurse stationed just outside his room, none of the medical personnel had interrupted her visit. That was both a blessing and a curse. She didn't mind since it meant that she could spend that time with her husband uninterrupted. But it also allowed her thoughts to weigh heavily on her.

She took his hand and gave it a squeeze. His hand was warm in hers but didn't respond. She searched his face for even the slightest reaction, but his eyes remained closed, his mouth open just a bit, his breathing steady.

"I wish you would wake up," she whispered. "I don't understand why you're not. What I did should have taken effect by now. Why won't you wake up?"

Of course, he didn't answer, didn't even give a sign that he had heard her. But what did that mean? Had the rune failed? That didn't seem possible; her family's rune was the most powerful healing rune the Siporans had ever known. So did that mean that he would never wake up? Did that mean that he would have died from his injuries? The doctors didn't seem to think that was the case, but she had no way of knowing.

Tears trickled down her cheeks, and she swiped them away angrily. "I've done too much crying today, and given what I'm about to do, I don't want to look sad. Well, not too sad. Challix and I stayed up all night working on what I'm going to say. I kind of wish my teachers at the Dynastic school could see me. I failed public speaking every time I took it. I think the teacher had it in for me—didn't much like Siporans—but I also know that I was usually a big ball of nerves. And I know what you'd say. I've spoken at Queen's Courts and at that state dinner you threw. But that was nothing. This means something. It's important."

She was babbling and she knew it. But she couldn't filter her words. They gushed out of her, an exhausted torrent. But Narius didn't seem to mind.

"It should be you making this speech, you know. You're the one people would listen to. Get you dressed up in your military uniform, looking all regal. Maybe hit them with one of your family's death glares. I know you say your father was the master of it, but I don't know, I've seen you hit people pretty hard with it. I think yours would cow Brencis into submission and make Tirigian's troops run for the borders. So why not wake up and show everyone?"

Still no response. Her brow pinched into a frown, and she tamped down a surge of frustration. A part of her wanted to shake Narius, shout in his face, slap him until he showed some signs of life. But just that random thought caused her to nearly drown in guilt. She squeezed his hand again, hard enough that she knew he had to feel it, but still no response.

A sob wracked her body, and she hunched over, trying to hold it in but losing.

Then she felt a hand on her shoulder. She looked up. The nurse stood over her, a hand on Everys's shoulder and concern painted across her face.

It felt as though strength flowed into her from the nurse. Everys smiled and hiccupped, swiping at her tears. "I'm all right. I'm sorry. It's just... well, it's a lot, you know?"

The nurse nodded.

"Blessed?"

She looked to the door and her stomach soured. Paine stood in the doorway.

"They've finished setting up in the throne room," he said. "Time for you to get ready."

Every nodded and rose, doing her best to appear in control and regal. She turned to the nurse, about to say something, but she had already slipped onto Everys's seat to check over Narius. She offered Everys an encouraging smile before she turned back to him.

Paine motioned for her to lead the way as they left the infirmary. "For the record, I'm still opposed to this idea."

"Why does that not surprise me?" Everys muttered.

Paine's gaze flicked in her direction. "I know what you're hoping to accomplish, but if you do this, many could turn against you, starting with the Ethnarch Parliament. From what I hear, some of them are still upset that you dared address them at all. If the ethnarchs abandon you and Narius now, it would be disastrous."

"It could convince them to take a stand against Dalark."

"You think they're not already doing that?" Paine asked. "According to what I've heard, Ethnarch Rockflow has mobilized every Ixactl militia he can to patrol the Highlands and fight off the invaders. The Weyfir's coastal patrol units are hurrying toward the Repose and the west coast to harass the Dalark's navy. I've even heard rumors that the Plissk and the Dunestriders are setting aside their differences to defend the sands."

Everys nodded. "That's good, but it's not enough."

"How can you expect more of anyone?"

"I'm not expecting more of them! I'm expecting more of me!" Everys shouted. "Don't you get it? Ever since Narius has been injured, there's been silence from the palace. No official statements. No encouragement. Nothing. Everyone else is scrambling to deal with the invasion, and it looks like the king and queen have abandoned them. All I want to do is let the people know that we haven't."

"And you really think you can do that?" he asked, a sneer laced under his words.

"I don't know. But I have to try."

Paine blew out a long breath through his nose, then nodded. "Very well. I believe your girls are waiting for you. I would say that I hope that the Water Bearer inspires you, but I doubt those words would have any meaning. So instead, I'll say good luck. I think you'll need it."

With that, he stalked away. Everys blew out a held breath of her own and made her way back to her quarters where she knew the girls would hopefully be able to make her look more confident than she felt.

Rather than wear some frilly formal outfit or something more appropriate for a gala or banquet, Trule and the girls dressed Everys in an outfit she once wore to a military base along the Demilitarized Zone. It was simple, functional, and vaguely resembled a military uniform. Not so much that someone might mistake her for a soldier, but enough that she could blend in with them. She definitely approved of the choice. When so many people faced the threat of invasion and death, it made sense for her to dress the part.

She watched as the techs did the final checks on their equipment. The throne room, while spacious, clearly wasn't designed for this type of endeavor. But when they considered the location for this speech, Challix had rejected the briefing rooms in the public relations ministry's offices. She had passed on the main ballroom. No, Challix had insisted that they do this from the throne room and Everys had agreed. They needed the extra gravitas from the setting.

Oluna stood near one of the pillars, watching the commotion. When her gaze met with Everys's, she nodded enthusiastically. Everys smiled in spite of her nervousness. At least she had one willing listener.

One of the techs motioned her to join him, and he directed her to stand at a particular spot just below the thrones themselves. "This is the best place for you to stand, Blessed. We have an audiocaster on you and the lighting will be perfect right here, but if you move too much, we'll have shadows across your face."

Everys winced as she turned toward the camera. Two banks of lights blazed on either side of it, more brilliant than the sun. At least, it felt that way to her. She raised an arm to shield her eyes.

"You'll get used to it, I promise." The tech pointed to a vidscreen off to one side. "That will display what the public sees in real time. We'll keep that muted so it doesn't throw you off too much."

She nodded and took a deep breath. The tech smiled at her.

"Don't worry. You're going to do great." He turned to the others. "Two minutes until we go live!"

Everys shook out her hands and took several deep breaths. Trying not to think of how many people could see what she was about to say.

Challix hurried over to her and gave her outfit a once-over. "Deep breaths, Blessed."

"Want to trade places?" Everys asked.

Her assistant laughed. "There's no way I'd do this half as well as you will."

The tech started to count down, so Challix got out of the way. Everys faced the cameras, squared her shoulders, and waited until the tech signaled for her to begin.

"Hello, my friends. I know that right now, you are all experiencing a great deal of anxiety and fear over what is happening in the Dynasty. You've seen the same reports that I have, that the Dalark have invaded our holdings, not just along the coast or through the Demilitarized Zone, but from the interior as well. You've heard that those troops are now trying to converge on Bastion, no doubt hoping to bring a swift end to this unwarranted and unprovoked invasion.

"I want to assure you that I am just as concerned as you are. And I will be honest: I do not know how this situation will be resolved. I hope that our military will be able to stand against this challenge and turn back the invaders." She struggled to keep a straight face as she said that. She knew that her words sounded hollow, but she couldn't share her honest feelings about the military's poor performance. "But I do know one thing: we are strong enough to withstand this challenge as long as we do so together."

The viewscreen that carried the live feed of her speech flickered for a moment. She hesitated, her thoughts stumbling over each other, but she took a breath and smiled.

"There is great strength to be found when neighbors set aside their differences and stand shoulder-to-shoulder against a common foe. And so I am asking you to do that today. No matter what happens in the coming days, watch out for one another. Protect each other. The time has come for us to make our stand in the here and now, so that..."

The video feed of her speech went awash in static. Everys looked to the tech, unsure if she should keep talking. Maybe people could still see and hear her. But from how the techs were reacting, she didn't think that was likely.

"Hold on!" one of the techs shouted. "We've got some major interference. It looks like... like someone is overriding our signal."

The static on the vidscreen faded away to reveal the face of Duke Brencis. He leered at the camera, and for a brief moment, Everys thought he could somehow see her.

"Oh, my people, are you as tired as I am, listening to these pretenders run their mouths?" he asked. "When I heard that Queen Everys was going to give a speech, I must admit, my morbid curiosity got the better of me. Would she actually say something of substance or would she just offer you empty platitudes of no real value?"

Everys's cheeks burned. She turned to the techs. "Can you stop him?"

"We're trying, Blessed, but someone has overridden our controls and locked us out of the system," one of them said.

She turned back to the vidscreen, her fingers curling into fists.

"And do you hear what she's saying? Take a stand against an invading army. Do your part to resist the people who violate our holdings. But what does she and her husband do? They hide in the palace and expect you to take the risk. But that's not the Perfected Warrior's way. And it isn't mine either.

"Now I'm sure you've heard the reports that the Dynasty's military has fled from the battlefield. But that isn't true. They haven't abandoned you. Instead, they've abandoned Narius and Everys. They now answer to me. And rest assured, I am more than capable of facing this foe. I promise you that I will drive the Dalark back into the ocean. I will punish them for their arrogance. I will force them to abandon their Beachhead and return Maotoa to us. I will make the Dynasty whole once more."

The throne room was silent, but Everys thought she heard some of the techs whispering in approval. She couldn't blame them. Brencis looked like a true incarnation of the Warrior. If she didn't know what a monster he was, she would cheer him on as well.

"I am more than happy to do this for you, my people. All I ask is one thing in return. I need you to remove that witch from my throne room."

Everys's blood ran cold.

"I know that Narius and Everys are cowering in their palace, but Everys had a point. If all of you stand together, you can get rid of her. And if you do, you will have my eternal gratitude, my people.

"Now if you'll excuse me, I have a Dynasty to save."

The camera pulled back from Brencis and somehow rose up, revealing a long column of soldiers marching behind him, with transports behind them, a great army, marching to war. Then the image cut to static, only to switch to an image of Everys's pale face.

She turned to the camera, trying to think of something to say. But she couldn't. No words would come.

"Cut the feed!" Challix whispered.

As soon as the vidscreen went blank, Rewether hurried forward. "We need to get you someplace safe, Blessed. Now."

She tried to laugh, but she wound up choking on the sound. Was anywhere safe anymore? Dalark on one side, Brencis on the other. And nowhere for her to find refuge.

67

Bastion held its collective breath for two days. While Governor-General Zammit reported that the streets were relatively quiet, a palpable tension hung in the air, like everyone was waiting for a spark to be thrown onto a pile of explosives.

As far as Everys was concerned, it was easy to understand why. Brencis had made some big promises when he interrupted her speech. The populace wanted to see if he could or would deliver. When reports started to trickle into Bastion that Brencis's troops had not only caught up with the Dalark invasion force, but made short work of them. The stories were too sporadic for most people to take them seriously. But by the end of the fourth day, the crier guilds had actual video footage of the battles. Brencis's troops were unstoppable. Some slashed through the ranks of the Dalark troops, using weapons that the criers couldn't identify but Everys recognized as *ur-keleshen*. When Brencis's troops shot the Dalark, red lightning tore through their ranks. Within days, Brencis had wiped out the primary invasion force coming up from the Beachhead, then wheeled around to head north for Bastion.

When news of his victory reached the city, Bastion nearly exploded in a riot.

Everys had seen these sorts of civil disturbances before. She had even caused one early in her reign. But this was the largest riot the city had ever seen. According to the reports coming in from the constabulary, two factions had emerged. One wanted to storm the palace and either capture or kill Everys and Narius for Brencis. The other half wanted to defend them. Whenever the two factions met on the streets, the conflict boiled over into rioting. By midday the third day, large columns of smoke rose from the Bastion skyline, and countless sirens blared in the distance.

"We should evacuate now, Blessed," Rewether said. "We've had the skimmer on standby for several days, and it's time to use it."

Everys stood on her balcony, overlooking the royal gardens. The Speartip Mountains rose in the distance. With that view, it was almost possible for her to ignore all the chaos she knew was spilling over in the city.

Almost.

"I can't do that," she said. "If I leave now, I would be handing the Dynasty to Brencis."

"Better to hand it over than have it taken," Rewether countered. "Once he's done with the Dalark, what do you suppose he'll do next?"

She didn't want to admit it, but he had a point. Maybe she should retreat, if only to relieve the pressure. If she left Bastion, maybe the two factions would stop fighting. She could at least save some lives.

Then Rewether frowned and listened intently to his comm unit. He looked up at her. "Blessed, that Diradae is back and says he has an urgent message for you."

Everys frowned. Occ had returned? She hadn't expected that. She had thought that as soon as he had delivered her message to Auntie Kyna, he would leave Bastion entirely, maybe go back to the Diradae Mountains and home. But somehow, the fact that he had come back made her feel happier in spite of the circumstances.

A few minutes later, Occ shuffled into her quarters, escorted by two guards. Much to her surprise, Papa followed them in, although he hung back by the door. The moment Occ saw Everys, he bowed low.

"Blessed, it is such an honor to see you once again," he said.

"The pleasure is mine, Occ. I heard you were able to deliver your message," she said.

"I was. And now I come bearing another."

He reached out with his lower hands, which were cradling a comm unit. She frowned as she took it.

"Where'd you get this?" she asked.

"After I delivered my message, I went into the sewers for shelter, and while I was down there, I ran into Prince Quartus. He asked me to give you this."

Everys's eyes widened, and she looked around the room at the others. As far as she knew, she was the only person aside from Tormod who knew that Quartus was working undercover. Everyone else would assume that he was still outlaw. And based on the looks that flitted across Rewether and Challix's face, they were both surprised and suspicious.

If Occ noticed their reaction, he didn't let on. "He instructed me to ask you to call him on that. Said you could reach him with the name 'Yusra.'"

Surprise rippled through Everys. That was a Dalark name. What had Quartus gotten himself into? She activated the comm unit and found the appropriate ID. The comm unit *chirruped* at her until it connected.

"Everys? Is that you?"

Everys almost laughed. She never thought she'd be happy to hear Quartus's voice again, not after their history together. But she couldn't deny the palpable relief that swept over her. "It is."

"Listen, I think I may have stumbled onto something here, and I could really use some of your expertise."

Any joy she felt was chased away by a wave of ice. "Wh-what do you mean?"

"I was able to track down one of the co-conspirators. It was Viscount Lorent. And Everys, I think he was one of you. He was a Siporan."

She fumbled the comm and almost dropped it. "What?"

"My partner and I raided his estate the other night, and we heard him talking to his friends. My partner was able to identify one of them as a high-ranking official in the Dalark Imperium, and there were a couple of voices that I thought sounded familiar."

Who was his partner and why would he know government officials in the Imperium? But then she remembered that she had called Quartus using an ID with a Dalark name. She shoved aside the curious questions that piled up in her mind. Hopefully they'd have time to exchange stories some other time. "Why do you think he's Siporan?"

"Because his house was filled with drawings that looked like runes. And when we confronted him, he killed himself, but then his body burst into flames, and I swear I saw a toratropic rune on him."

Everys frowned, her mind catching up with what Quartus was saying. She remembered that there had been reports of a nobleman dying in a house fire. Had Quartus been involved in that?

"And the people Lorent was talking to? They kept talking about Nekek the Bright shining again, and they referred to one of them by a word I've never heard before... What was it again?"

A feminine voice whispered something to Quartus.

"Oh, right. *Ar'zadok.*"

Everys's knees buckled underneath her, and a wave of pins and needles swept through her body. She lifted the comm unit closer to her mouth, and as she did, she turned to watch Papa's reaction. He had already gone pale.

"Do you mean *ar'zhannok*?" she whispered.

"Yes, that's it! Why? Do you know what it means?"

Oh yes, she did. All too well. The word was from the ancient Siporan language, a word rarely spoken out loud and then only in whispers, as if their caution would somehow relegate the word and what it meant to the ancient past, trapping it there for the rest of eternity. It was a word that, while most people in the Dynasty wouldn't recognize it, they knew about it all too well.

In Dynastic, *ar'zhannok* meant "mage-king."

Comprehension blossomed on Papa's face as well. He slumped against the door frame and ran a trembling hand through his hair. He met her gaze and started to say something, but then clamped his mouth shut.

"I recognize it," she said. "That's not good."

"I figured as much," Quartus said. "Everys, this conspiracy has been working for years. They've made some kind of special flechette that causes red lightning to explode from a person's body after shooting them. And they've been making this weird synthetic tree sap and storing it underground. I have no idea why, but Yusra and I are trying to figure it out. I'm guessing it's probably not a good thing, right?"

Someone grunted and Everys's head snapped around. Rewether eyed her warily. Inkstains! She had momentarily forgotten that everyone else was here. She could guess part of what the conspirators were up to. They were stockpiling ink, although why they would store it underground, she had no idea. To hide it? But she also knew she couldn't go into details about her suspicions. Not right now.

"Keep doing that, Quartus. If you find out anything else, please let me know."

"Will do. Stay safe, Everys. And tell..." His voice trailed off. "Tell my brother to do the same."

The connection went dead.

Dread twisted in Everys. Had Quartus really heard someone talking to an *ar'zhannok*? Were the mage-kings really back? That didn't seem possible. The Dynasty had supposedly been so thorough in their purge. But then she realized that she shouldn't have been so surprised. If they hadn't realized that there were still Siporans practicing toratropic magic, it was easy to believe they had missed at least one mage-king.

She hurried over to Papa and snared his arm, pulling him out into the hall. "Did you hear that?" she whispered.

He nodded, his face ashen.

"Papa, they're going to be looking to me about how to best deal with this. I could use your advice," she said.

That got his attention. He frowned, fixing his gaze on her. "My advice?"

She nodded emphatically. "You know our culture and history so much better than I do. If anyone will know how to deal with a mage-king, it's—"

"You don't 'deal with' a mage-king!" Papa snapped. "If one of them is out there, there's nothing you can do except run!"

"I can't do that!"

"Yes, you can. We both can!" Papa grabbed her arm. "I know some secret ways out of the city, the ones we used when we started our vigil. We can go back to your mother and Galan. We'll be safe there!"

Everys gaped at him. How could he say that? "I can't do that, Papa. My people need me!"

He scoffed. "Who, the Dynasty? They're your people now?"

"In some ways, yes! I'm still their queen."

He took a step back from her, his gaze hardening. Then, without a word, he turned and walked away.

She watched him walk away. More than anything, she wanted to go after him. But she couldn't. Not when there was so much at stake. Not when she had a room full of people waiting for her to make a decision about what to do next.

She went back into her room and looked at each person one by one. Trule frowned at her, whereas Challix looked absolutely perplexed, as did Rewether. Occ, thanks to his human mask, was completely unreadable. She sighed. They were all trusting her to figure out what to do next, but she hadn't shown the same level of trust in them. She hadn't been fair to any of them, lying to them about who she was and what she was capable of.

"Everyone, please sit down. I have something I need to share with you."

Trule moved to a nearby couch and sat down immediately, as did Occ. Challix and Rewether joined them, as did the other guards. Everys took a deep breath and cast a look toward the door, wishing Papa was still there to help her explain everything.

But as much as she hated to admit it, his absence would make this much easier. She already knew he would never approve of what she was about to do.

68

The beeping finally woke him.

At first, the steady rhythm had lulled him into sleep, kept him submerged in the warm, dreamless depths. But the longer he heard it, the more aware he was that the beeping signaled a wrongness, a brokenness, and the repetitive sound itched at his mind. He couldn't do anything about it at first, just tolerate it. But as time wore on, as the beeping continued in its steady, unending drone, he finally knew he couldn't hide anymore. Taking a deep, shuddering breath, Narius opened his eyes.

He recognized the ceiling above him. It wasn't his bedroom. He knew the mural over his bed all too well. No, he had spent far too long staring at this particular ceiling in the palace. He was back in the infirmary again. But why?

He closed his eyes, a frown pinching his brow. Bits and pieces, little images, flooded back to him. The arena. The combat. The Diradae. Falling through the air and then the sharp pain as he landed on his back. He had been injured? Must have been.

He tried to lift his head, but he couldn't. Not really. Just enough to see a nurse sitting at a nearby station. She hadn't noticed he was awake yet. He tried to speak, to say something, but his mouth was so dry, it felt like the words were glued to his throat. He tried to raise his hand, but his arm felt heavier than his head, as if it was encased in visium.

But then someone stepped into the infirmary doorway, an older man. Narius knew him.

Favid, his father-in-law. Favid leaned over to whisper something to the nurse, motioning for her to step out of the room. She looked ready to argue, but then she glowered at Favid and left, casting a look in his direction. He tried to catch her attention, to let her know that he was awake. But she didn't seem to notice.

As soon as she was gone, Favid crossed over to Narius's bedside. He examined the machines first, almost as if he were a doctor taking stock of his patient's condition. But then his gaze settled on Narius.

"You're finally awake," he murmured. "I suppose it's better this way."

Favid grabbed a nearby stool and pulled it closer to the bed. The metal legs screeched against the floor, sending an unpleasant sensation down Narius's spine. He winced, trying to pull away from Favid, but he couldn't.

"I want you to know, I really did try. For my daughter's sake. I tried to see the good in you. In the Dynasty. I tried to see things the way she did. Because I love her. I really do. I know she may not believe it, but I do."

Favid looked up toward the ceiling, as if he was searching for some sort of answer up there.

"That's always been my problem. I've loved my children and indulged them too much. My boy, Legarr, took advantage of that and got caught up in all sorts of unsavory things. And now I've realized that my Everys has too. I've lost them both."

A frown tickled Narius's brow. That was ridiculous. He didn't know for sure, but he suspected Everys was still in the palace and would love to spend some time with Favid, to let him know that she loved him. He tried to point that out, but his words still wouldn't come. All he could manage was a weak groan.

Favid shot him an angry look, but then his features softened, turned sad. "I suppose I shouldn't be surprised. Once Everys finished her training with the runes, she never showed any interest in attending conclave with us. Galan would go. So would Legarr, if only to try to scam some blades from the other worshipers. But not Everys. Said she would mind the shop. And I let her. I always thought that maybe I should allow her to find her own path and that eventually it would bring her back to the Singularity, to her people. But now I see how wrong I was. She's gone. And it's all your fault."

Narius tried to protest, but again, he could only muster a groan. Favid ignored him, fishing something from his pocket. He snapped it in half and a rancid smell washed over Narius. He recognized it immediately. Ink. Favid had broken a pen in half to get at the ink.

Favid daubed some ink on his hand and sketched something on his left palm. He held it out and his brow furrowed.

"More proof of how far my daughter has fallen," he muttered. "I forbade her from using runes on you, but I see she didn't listen. Your body is swimming with toratropic magic."

Favid leaned over and untied Narius's medical gown at the shoulder, pulling it open to expose his chest.

"I suppose Everys has told you about our family's secret by now, how we have been the guardians of one of the Principalities and its powerful healing rune." He chuckled ruefully and shook his head. "I shouldn't be surprised, given how smitten she is with you. Well, there's something she hasn't learned yet, something that is passed on to each successive head of the household."

He daubed more ink on his finger and traced something on Narius's chest. "Because our family has been entrusted with such a powerful rune, we were also entrusted with an equally powerful countermeasure, a secret rune known only to the heads of the guardian families. It allows us to negate any toratropic spell that has been cast on a person. We were entrusted with it so that, if a member of our family overstepped and did something inappropriate, we could correct it. And I fear that's what I must do now."

He continued his work, humming a quiet tune without a discernible melody. Narius tried to squirm away but couldn't. He stretched for the call button next to him, but his fingers merely brushed it. He took several shuddering breaths and tried to speak, but his voice still wouldn't come. So he pleaded with Favid through his eyes. There was no reason to do this. He wasn't an enemy! He wasn't!

Favid finished his work and sat back. "In just a few moments, this spell will erase all of the toratropic magic from your body. Any spell that my daughter ever cast on you will be undone. Given what she's shared with me, I don't expect you to survive. And that really is for the best."

He leaned in closer. "My daughter would want me to forgive you and your kind for what you did to us. But I can't. Your ancestor destroyed my homeland. He robbed us of our future. And you? I just learned your Dynasty brought back another mage-king. Anyone who allows so much evil to exist should face justice."

Narius swallowed hard, trying to ask about the mage-king, but Favid didn't seem to care. He pressed his palm to Narius's chest. At first, Narius thought that nothing had happened. But then Favid smiled and rose from his chair, tossing the pen away. He took a step away from the bed, then shuddered, his body twisting and his arms spasming into odd angles. Favid shook off the obvious pain and walked out of the infirmary.

Narius took several deep breaths, and then he felt it: a tearing inside his chest. No pain, at first, just an overt understanding that something was wrong, that something had unraveled. His breathing became ragged, and the medical devices' beeping stuttered, becoming fast and erratic before pitching into a wail. Narius clawed at the sheets, trying to escape what he was feeling but it was no use. Pain lanced through his arms, his legs, his back. His vision juked, and it felt like the bed was slowly spinning with him still in it.

And then the nurse appeared over him, panic spreading across her face. Her hands roamed over his body, as if she was trying to feel her way to the problem. He tried to tell her what was happening, but liquid burst from his mouth and dribbled down his cheeks. He choked and tried to cough, but he couldn't summon enough air. She flinched, but then her expression became determined.

He tried to focus on her, to encourage her to keep working, but the world faded around him. The wailing machines gave way to a distant rustling, the rush of wings that flapped with the shadows around him. Those shadows slowly nibbled away at the corner of his vision until the world went gray and he fell, fell, fell into a frozen darkness...

69

Everys braced herself for whatever they might have to say. She knew she had unloaded a lot on them, but once the truth came out, it continued to just tumble from her lips. No one had spoken during her explanation, just listened with varying stages of shock painted across their faces. Once she was done speaking, she made a small prompting gesture with her hands, hoping that someone would break the awkward silence.

"I'll be honest, Blessed, that... that is a lot to process," Challix said quietly.

The fact that she still called her "Blessed" wasn't lost on Everys. That was hopefully a good sign.

Trule gingerly raised her hand. "Bl-blessed, have you ever cast a rune on me?"

The others turned to look at her, the same question lurking on their faces. She almost said no, but then she realized she had. She had cast a toratropic spell on everyone who had attended the state dinner to celebrate the newfound peace between the Dynasty and the Cold Light. But she didn't know if admitting it would be wise, especially given how uneasy Rewether appeared.

"Please forgive my impertinence, but does it matter?" Occ asked. "I realize the chances of her doing that to me are slim, but I have seen the queen's heart and I suspect all of you have as well. Tell me, has she ever given any of you reason to doubt her intentions?"

The others considered it. But before they could answer, the door to her quarters banged open. Zar rushed in. Everys's initial irritation vanished when she saw the near panic in his expression. He locked eyes with her.

"Blessed, you better come with me now. It's the king. He's...he's..."

Everys raced past him, Zar's words chasing her. She tried to outpace them and their meaning. Because if she thought what he said was even remotely true...

She turned the corner and skidded to a halt just inside the infirmary. Three doctors and just as many nurses clustered around Narius's bed, shouting at each other and passing syringes and instruments and other items to each other. Undercutting their voices was the steady drone of medical machinery, a noise that Everys understood far too well.

Everys stumbled forward toward the chaos, offering up a silent prayer that she was misinterpreting, misunderstanding. She had to be. This couldn't possibly be real. A mistake.

One of the doctors noticed her and murmured something to the others. They stopped and backed away, revealing Narius in his bed. His body was limp and ashen, his eyes vacant and staring, blood dried on his lips.

"I'm so sorry, Blessed," one of the doctors whispered. "We don't know what happened. We tried everything we could."

His words barely registered. Everys staggered to the bed and touched her husband's face, hoping that he would react. His skin was cold and felt almost waxy. Her heart tore apart, and she sank to her knees, her body wracked with sobs.

She was barely aware of the people around her, though she heard Trule gasp and Challix curse and Occ make an odd keening sound. But then Rewether stepped in and ordered everyone out of the room. The doctors tried to object, but he simply asked if they could do anything else.

"Give her this much," he snapped.

She didn't want this much. She wanted her husband.

Thankfully,within a few moments, Everys was alone. Alone with her husband. Alone with her empty future.

She looked up at Narius's still form. What happened? What went wrong? She had drawn the healing rune on him. Why had it failed? This made no sense. She knew she did it correctly. Why hadn't the Singularity done anything? Why did He let this happen? Now she was facing the crumbling world on her own, without him. And that wasn't right. This needed to be fixed.

She plucked the third-to-last bead from her bracelet and rubbed it between her fingers, releasing the ink. As she did, she mentally reviewed the runes she needed to draw. A rune of invitation. A rune asking for the Singularity's protection. A rune expressing trust.

This would work. She knew it would. Not too long ago, when Everys had faced a similar disaster at Narius and Innana's wedding, she had cast these runes in a desperate attempt to save a ballroom of guests from Brencis's troops that had been transformed into monsters. She had invited the Singularity to help, and He had. And He would do it here as well.

So she carefully drew the runes on her arms the way she had last time, and with one last look at Narius, she cast them.

At first, nothing happened. Then Everys blinked, and she was no longer in the infirmary, but standing in an infinite black void. Nothing beneath her feet. Nothing overhead. Nothing in front of her or to the side of her or—

"Hello, dear."

She whirled around and was surprised—but not that surprised—to see Auntie Kyna seated in front of her. Oddly, she didn't appear to be actually sitting on anything. She wore her usual rags and had her blindfold pulled down over her eyes. She held her walking stick, idly tracing unseen patterns in front of her.

"Who are you?" Everys asked.

Kyna looked up at her. "You don't recognize me?"

"I recognize who you're supposed to be." Everys crossed her arms. "But you're not really Kyna."

"True, true, but Kyna and I share a similar purpose, so I thought it would help if you saw this instead of, well..." The fake Kyna waved a hand in front of her face.

"Show me."

Kyna paused and, in spite of her blindfold, looked at her. "Are you sure?"

Everys nodded.

With a sigh, Kyna reached up and slid her fingers under the blindfold's fabric and pulled upward—

An explosion of light and fire and heat ripped through Everys. There were wings—so many wings!—and eyes and the roar of a million thunders overlaying the gentle burble of a stream mixed with a hawk's cry and the roar of a mighty beast. And the infinite void, wrapped around shoulders that carried the weight of the world and—

Everys stumbled back a step, clutching at her eyes to block out the overwhelming sight. When she dared look again, Kyna was tugging her blindfold back into place.

"You don't have to be afraid of me, dearie." And as Kyna spoke, the air in front of her shimmered in the pattern of a rune that floated forward and washed over her. As it did, Everys's unease faded.

"So why am I here?" she asked.

"You invited the Singularity, and He showed up. Simple as that."

Everys looked around the void. "So where is He?"

Kyna grimaced. "He's giving you a chance to reconsider the invitation."

Now Everys frowned. "Why?"

"Because He knows you may not like what happens next."

Everys gaped at Kyna. "I asked Him to come here to save Narius!"

"Why?"

"Because we need him. The Dynasty needs him! I need him!"

Kyna nodded thoughtfully. "I thought as much. I'll ask one more time. Do you want to reconsider?"

Everys shook her head. She knew how this would end. The Singularity would save Narius. He would. He had to.

"Very well." Kyna pointed over Everys's shoulder.

She frowned and turned around.

Only to look up and up and up.

A creature of smoke and shadow towered over her, an indistinct nightmare that dredged terror from the deepest parts of her mind. She shrank back from the monstrosity, large as the palace, but then realized that more of the creatures stomped up next to the first. She was surrounded.

But then, with a rumble, trees sprung up around her. Large trees, big as the monsters themselves, slammed into the creatures and drove them back. The monsters bellowed in rage and defiance, but the shadows that formed them melted away, and soon, the monsters had faded into nothing.

Everys stared up at the trees, but then she realized that they were shrinking as well, pulling back from her to reveal an uneven landscape strewn with mountains and rivers and forests and fields. And people no taller than her knees, emerged from the shadows. She saw humans and Diradae and Ixactl and shessu and Plissk and Weyfir.

But then, from across the void, came longboats, propelled across unseen waters by men who hummed their malicious intent. These invaders leaped from their boats and charged onto shore, attacking the people they found. With each kill, the invaders grew larger and larger, until they were almost as tall as Everys herself...

Only to have a swarm of smaller men clamber onto them and topple them. The invaders fell and crumbled back into darkness. The victors then attacked one another. As they fought, the others fought too. Ixactl fought Ixactl, the Diradae struggled within themselves, and the Plissk and Dunestriders were locked in combat. Even the shessu joined the melee, stomping on the people they passed. The individual races grew larger and smaller with every victory and loss.

But then a shock wave blasted through them all, centered on a small knot of people. Everys's eyes widened when she realized that they wore the traditional robes of the mage-kings. They strode forward, wielding runes that appeared like shields on their arms and, with mere gestures, mowed down the people around them. As they marched forward, they grew larger and larger. And as they did, Everys could see the contempt, the malice, the pride on their faces as they consumed the people in front of them, soon towering over Everys like gods among men.

As they continued to stride forward, though, the smaller people fought back. At first, the mage-kings were undefeated, demolishing their opponents and absorbing them, growing taller and stronger. But then they were laid low, their attackers tearing apart their bodies in a vicious slaughter. Once the mage-kings had been reduced to shadows and darkness, the victors turned on the other races and set about subduing them. One by one, they all fell: The Ixactl. The Dunestriders and Plissk. The Weyfir. And soon, a new figure stood before Everys.

At first glance, he turned her stomach. He had the scaly skin of the Plissk, and the horns of an Ixactl jutted from his brow. His legs were like the trunks of two large trees, his arms adorned like that of an ancient Weyfir merchant. His body was swathed in the robes and wraps of a Dunestrider. And he wore a Diradae mask over his face.

Only the mask's face wasn't the usual blank expression. This one was carved to look like Narius.

Try as she might, Everys couldn't bring herself to face him. Just his mere presence turned her stomach. He was wrong, she knew it, and yet she couldn't back away. In spite of the way his proximity made her uneasy, she still felt a strange draw, like she was being absorbed into him. This strange amalgamation stretched out a hand to Everys. And as he did, the expression on the mask changed. Instead of love, hunger. Avarice. The same greed that the mage-kings had worn so proudly.

In spite of her visceral reaction, she still stretched out a hand to him, ready to join him, to be with him, to hold him up and support him...

But then cracks appeared in the mask. His skin turned brittle, and the decay quickly spread down his neck and into his chest. He was going to collapse and crumble.

Everys couldn't let that happen. She hurried forward and began sketching runes on his chest. Healing. Strengthening. Power. Because she couldn't let this happen. She couldn't let him fail. She would save him. She would—

But the runes weren't working. Instead, the rot that consumed Narius had infected her fingertips and spread up her arms. She scrubbed at them, trying to stop it, but it was no use. The cracks raced up her arms into her chest. And as she scrambled to stop the decay from consuming her as well, the strange monstrosity in front of her crumbled into dust and ashes, swept away by a gentle breeze.

A brilliant light flashed overhead, punctuated by a roar that she felt in her chest more than heard. She clapped her hands to her ears and fell face down as a presence bore down on her, ancient as time and heavy as reality. And in the midst of the roar and in spite of the cacophony, three words slammed into her mind.

ALL EMPIRES FALL.

Just as suddenly, the roar faded. She lurched to her knees and looked around. The strange landscape was gone. Instead, she found herself facing... herself?

Multiple copies of herself, forming a ring around her. One wore the simple clothing she had used as a uniform when she ran The Broken Sword after Papa, Mama, and Galan had left Bastion. Another wore the dress she had designed for the state dinner to celebrate the peace with the Cold Light. But the others! One version of her was dressed in scriveners' robes. Another, a Dynasty military uniform. The last two, though, sent chills down her spine, for in one, she wore the royal garb of the mage-kings. And the final was the same monstrosity she had seen crumble just a few moments ago, but instead of Narius, it looked like her.

WHO ARE YOU?

The voice tore through her, and she fell to her knees. The copies of herself stared down at her coldly. In unison, they all reached out their right hands to her, their faces impassive. Then they took a step toward her. Then another. And another. They quickly pressed in around her, and Everys flinched away from them.

WHO ARE YOU?

What did that mean? She was Everys! She was Narius's wife. She was a toratropic mage. She was Siporan. She was...

She risked a peek and realized she was alone. Everys looked over her shoulder, and there was Kyna (but not Kyna), scribbling on the unseen ground her with staff.

"What was that?" Everys's voice was a rasp, as if she had been screaming for hours. She felt as though she had been.

"Not for me to say," Kyna said. "The message was for you, not me."

Everys turned over the jumbled imagery in her mind, trying to sort through it all. But even as she did, the images blended together. All she could hold on to was the violence, the hunger, the unfettered greed. Was that what He was trying to tell her? Is that what He thought of her request? Was she trying to prop up a falling empire, one that only existed to consume?

"But... but if Narius and I can't fix this... what can?"

Light stabbed down from above. Everys shouted in surprise and looked up. Another figure loomed over her. He appeared to be human as well, but His features were blank, His form indistinct. Made of light and shining like the sun, He reached a hand down to her. Unlike with the amalgamation, Everys wasn't repulsed by this Being. She reached up to Him, even though His hand could scoop her up easily. And at the center of His chest was a rune of pure light that blazed brighter than the rest of Him, an unwavering glory that flowed into her own heart and filled her with such—

Everys gasped and jolted upright, suddenly aware of an all-too-real hand on her shoulder. She looked to the bed, half-hoping in spite of what she had seen that it was Narius. But no. Rewether stood over her, a concerned look on his face.

"Are you all right, Blessed?"

Everys stammered, trying to focus, trying to sort through everything she had just seen and heard. But the sights and sounds faded like a dream in the early morning, leaving her with an ache in her chest and echoing words in her mind.

All empires fall. Was that the Dynasty's immediate fate? Or was it a reminder not to put her trust in the Dynasty? As much as she hated to admit it, she had been. Trusting she could manipulate the nobles in their petty games. Trying to influence the people the Dynasty had conquered. Trying to shape people's support for Narius. And yet, in spite of all her attempts, the Dynasty still crumbled around her. Maybe that was the point. The Singularity was trying to get her to see that she needed something stronger on which to stand. It couldn't be herself. It couldn't be Narius. It couldn't be political machinations or military might. It had to be something better. Someone better.

"I hate to interrupt whatever it was you were doing, but we have a situation." Rewether offered his hand and helped her stand up. "There's a group of citizens marching on the palace. It's no longer safe for you to remain here. We have to evacuate. Now."

Everys nodded numbly. Of course she did. Of course they would. She would run. At least her people had fled as well.

As Rewether led her from the infirmary, a new thought occurred to her. Her people. They had put their trust in the wrong things too. Their own empire, their own strength, their own spells. And she had just learned that an *ar'zhannok* was back. If what Quartus had uncovered was true, they were manipulating everything. But she knew in her heart that their trust was misplaced as well.

What could she trust? The being she saw, the one with the rune of light in His chest. The Singularity. That had to be Him. In spite of all the ways she had failed, even though she had rebelled and ignored and ran, He hadn't abandoned her. So maybe, just maybe, she needed to start listening to Him.

So what do you have to tell me? What should I do?

In that moment, an idea built in her mind. Yes, she had to run. But she had something to do before she did.

70

Thankfully, Rewether didn't argue. He didn't question her. Instead, he escorted her through the palace halls. As they walked, they passed servants and government officials, all of them on the verge of panic. Many of them looked to her, but then they continued on, doing whatever it was they thought they should. Everys didn't stop to give anyone orders. She had none to give.

Once they were out of the palace, Everys led the way into the royal gardens. Past the displays of plants taken from all over the Dynasty's holdings. Past the recently planted Cold Light pillar tree. To the very heart of the gardens, the pile of rubble that concealed the entrance to the archives. She stepped to the plinth that disguised the door controls and activated them.

As the door to the archives opened, revealing a set of stairs that descended into the darkness, she turned to Rewether. "Wait here. I shouldn't be long."

Rewether shifted uneasily on his feet. "Don't dawdle, Blessed. We want to be airborne quickly."

She nodded and hurried down the stairs.

Once she was at the bottom, she walked through the displays of objects the Dynasty had plundered from its conquered subjects. Totems. Weapons. A pile of skulls. Statues and idols. She barely afforded any of them a glance. At one time, she might have lingered, trying to absorb the history represented by each object, trying to appreciate the disparate cultures that created them. But she had no time for that. She hoped the people headed to the palace would treat the archives and its collected treasures with respect. She knew that wasn't likely, but she still hoped for it all the same.

And then she reached the heart of the archives, where the Principalities maintained their silent vigil. Here she paused, taking a moment to stare at those sacred plinths, the focus of her people's devotion and the source of so many of their troubles. Yes, the Singularity had given them the Principalities to teach them the runes. Yes, He had encouraged them to grow and learn beyond these foundational patterns. But that sort of knowledge only led to power which led to hunger which led to...

A shudder wormed through her as she remembered the unvarnished desire on the mage-kings' faces in her vision. The *ar'zhannok*. The monsters from her people's past who were supposed to be long forgotten but apparently had only hidden in the shadows, waiting.

She turned and looked at the rack of *ur-keleshens*, both the original and the copies the ancient mage-kings had forged. More evidence of her people's violence and greed. She would have to deal with them first.

Everys plucked the second-to-last bead from her bracelet and smeared its ink on her fingers. She then knelt before the weapon rack and traced a rune along its side. A rune of fire, intense heat, thousands of degrees in a heartbeat. Confine it to the vicious swords' alcove, a layer of protection for the rest of the treasures. Then, holding a deep breath, she activated the rune and stepped back.

A miniature sun blossomed to life, a white-hot sphere that eagerly consumed the cursed blades. In spite of her precautions, the heat still clawed at her face and arms. She took a step back, but then the intense heat blinked out and the room appeared wreathed in shadows. When her eyes adjusted, the rack and the swords were gone. Vaporized.

She turned her attention to the Principalities. She stepped up to the closest and ran the back of her hand over the rune carved in it. Although she wasn't sure, she thought this one was a fertility rune, something a farmer could sketch into his field to guarantee the greatest of harvests. It didn't matter. Not anymore. She tugged the final bead free from its setting on her bracelet, squeezed out the ink, and then traced a rune onto the side of the plinth, one she had used from time to time to thoroughly destroy what was no longer needed.

As soon as it was completed, she activated the rune. And the Principality beneath it shattered.

Cracks radiated out from the rune and tore through the stone. But rather than fall apart, the plinth seemed to fight, holding its shape and form as more and more fractures raced through it. Then, with a mighty tremor, the Principality crumbled into dust.

Everys closed her eyes and willed herself not to cry. She braced herself, waiting for the rebuke. Destroying *ur-keleshen*, that made sense. But the Principalities? Even though she knew in her heart this is what the Singularity wanted, she still worried she was wrong. So she waited. And braced herself. For the disapproval. For the pain. For the revelation that she had misunderstood.

Nothing happened.

She took a shuddering breath and hung her head. These Principalities, gifts though they were, had only served as a foundation for her people's own greed and ambition. The Siporan Ascendancy had created so much pain and resentment and death. Had that remained in the distant past, maybe she would have thought twice. But if the mage-kings were back...

She shook her head. She couldn't risk it. They couldn't have these runes again. Not if she could help it.

So she moved on and set to work painting the rune onto the next one.

71

Quartus swiped at his burning eyes and checked the map on his scriber. They were close to the next storage tank, but the sewer tunnels beneath Bastion were a twisted mess. Passages doubled back on themselves or ended without warning. How Lorent's company had gotten away with creating such a ridiculous mess was beyond him. But then, anyone connected to the project probably thought Lorent had just overused materials to pad his contract, take more money from the government. That was the explanation he would have gravitated to if he didn't know of Lorent's connection to the conspiracy.

He paused at the sound of thunder overhead. Not a storm, he was pretty sure of that. If it had been, these sewers probably would have filled with rainwater, but they remained dry. No, he recognized the sound of marching feet. An army was on the move inside the city.

So far, he and Yusra had found three more tanks of the strange, viscous liquid. But they still hadn't figured out what to do with them. All they could do was confirm where each of the tanks were and, once they were sure they had found them all, contact Everys again and hope that she or Tormod or someone would be able to deal with whatever this was.

Yusra crept down one of the tunnels ahead of him, shining a light along the walls. Quartus couldn't help but smile. He knew she had to be just as frustrated as he was and yet she didn't complain. And even though they'd sloshed through some questionable liquids, she hadn't hesitated. Truth be told, Quartus suspected he was handling the whole adventure worse than she was. He didn't know if he should thank Chaos or Chance or some unknown deity for bringing the two of them together, but he was thankful to whoever was responsible.

"No good up here, Quartus," Yusra whispered. "Another dead end."

She turned and almost collided with him. He reached out and caught her before they did. She stumbled and grabbed his arms, then looked up at him, her eyes wide.

They stood there for a moment or two, just looking into each other's eyes. A smile tugged at Quartus's lips. Not his usual impish smirk. Not the rakish grin he unleashed on the ladies. No, a real, genuine smile that flowed deep from his heart. And she smiled, just for a moment. Heat bloomed in his chest. By all the weapons in the Warrior's arsenal, she was adorable.

But then her smile turned sardonic, and she spun him around. "Back the way we came, Your Strength."

He chuckled but was glad she couldn't see the disappointment he was sure flitted across his face.

Quartus consulted his scriber again and quickly realized what the problem was. They had missed a juncture where they were supposed to go left instead of going straight like they had. He sighed. The sooner they could finish this, the better. He led the way as they backtracked to the intersection and clambered into a higher tunnel. He checked the scriber again and nodded. If they kept going straight, that would bring them right to...

They walked into a large chamber, with a soaring dome ceiling. Channels had been carved into the floor, running through six arches and into the sewers beyond. And in the middle of the room was a massive storage tank, similar to the others that they had found so far. But unlike the other storage tanks, this one had a large console attached to it with a vidscreen. Most of the system looked decades out of date, but newer components had been grafted on.

Quartus hurried over to the system and inspected it. His pulse quickened as he realized that this is what they had been looking for the whole time, the central control system. He examined the control panel and found a large switch that appeared to be the power button. Sucking in a quick breath, he hit it.

At first, nothing happened, but then, with a series of loud clicks that echoed through the chamber, the controls lit up, as did the viewscreen. Quartus laughed as green-and-white letters flickered to life. Positively ancient technology!

But that didn't matter. The user interface seemed simple enough. System status, maintenance mode, signal strength. Quartus tried to pull up the system status, only to have the panel buzz and inform him that he needed a keycard. He frowned. He should have expected some security. Only a fool would leave something like this completely unprotected. He quickly examined the console and found the keycard slot. He snorted. Like most of the system, it was several decades out of date. He didn't need to hack the software. He was pretty sure he could bypass the hardware. He knelt and set to work.

It took a few moments to pry open the casing and rummage through the machine's innards. But after a few creative wire splices, the console *pinged* quietly. Quartus smirked at Yusra, and rather than get annoyed, she smirked right back and motioned for him to proceed.

He tried the system status prompt again and this time, the system responded. While some of the entries didn't make sense to him, he could decipher some of it. There were indeed fifty tanks scattered throughout the city, just like the information in the scriber had said. All of them were reporting that they were ready to discharge their contents. Receivers all working properly.

But then his gaze hitched on the last item. The system had been armed. He had no idea if that was normal. Maybe Lorent's co-conspirators kept the system ready at all times. But that little bit of information was enough to cause his stomach to twist. They still had no idea what any of this was designed to do, and as convenient as it would have been to have an explanation here, he couldn't find one.

He finally selected "system schematic." The console chittered to itself and then an image appeared on the screen, a map of the sewer system with each of the fifty tanks' locations highlighted. Quartus frowned. The tunnels and pipes were a riot of lines, crisscrossing over each other. Quartus squeezed the bridge of his nose. This was less than helpful, but not surprising. The sewer had tunnels that ran over and under each other. Displaying them in two dimensions created this—

Wait, what was that?

At the bottom of the schematic was a checkbox labeled "flow path." It hadn't been selected, so Quartus toggled it on.

The map of the sewers shifted dramatically. Many of the pipes and channels simply vanished, leaving a more coherent pattern. The selected tunnels appeared to be contained within an inverted pentagon, the point facing south. Within the border, the lines looped and swirled around two central straight lines, one bisecting the other two-thirds toward the bottom at a thirty-degree angle. Quartus frowned and leaned in closer. There was something oddly familiar about this pattern. He wasn't sure if he had seen it before or something like it or...

Realization dawned. His head snapped back as if he had been slapped. "Gravedigger's trowel!"

It was a toratropic rune, as big as Bastion itself if he judged it correctly. When Everys and he had investigated a secret lab run by the conspiracy, she had used a rune that he thought might have been similar to this one. What had that one done? He wracked his brain, trying to remember. He couldn't recall. But how was this supposed to work? Where was the ink?

Then his gaze landed on the storage tank and the pieces fell together. Lorent's people had been manufacturing synthetic Cold Light tree sap. Ink! By his calculations there had to be millions of gallons of it, ready to flood the sewers underneath the city at a moment's—

A harsh buzzing filled the room, and a red light on the top of the tank flashed and rotated. Quartus stumbled away from the controls. Had he accidentally tripped an alarm? He dismissed the system schematic and returned to the main screen. Words flashed across the screen: SYSTEM ACTIVATED.

The tank in front of him clanged, followed by a low gurgle. Quartus turned in time to see putrid orange fluid rush through the channels in the room, out through the arches into the sewers beyond.

He spun and grabbed Yusra's hand. "We need to go. Now!"

"Why? What is it?"

While he didn't know what was going to happen, he knew that at any minute, that rune could activate, and there was no way he wanted to be underground when it did. He pulled her back to the exit and hurried her through the tunnels.

As they moved, a disheartening thought chased Quartus through the tunnels. They had lost. And whoever was behind the conspiracy had won.

72

Everys stumbled up out of the archives, her eyes burning. Her hands trembled and her knees wobbled. She sat down on the ground with a *thud* and took several shuddering breaths, trying to get her jangled nerves back under control. Her mind wouldn't let go of the images of what she had just done. Over and over again, she saw the cracks radiate through each of the Principalities before they shattered and crumbled into dust. And yet, even after destroying her people's most sacred objects, the Singularity still hadn't rebuked her. Even though she knew what He wanted her to do, she still expected Him to punish her for what so many of her people would consider sacrilege.

Her guards rushed to her side, and Rewether knelt next to her. "Blessed? Are you all right?"

She gulped down air and managed to shake her head. No. She wasn't. Memories of the times she had spent with Narius, exploring the palace, walking the gardens, watching the city from his balcony. They all washed over her, chased by sorrow that she'd never be able to experience any of it again. She had lost so much and now she had to let go of even more.

A cacophony of sirens erupted in the distance. Rewether froze, then barked questions into his comm. A moment later, he cursed under his breath. When he took Everys's arm again, his grip was firmer, and his pull was more insistent.

"C'mon, Blessed. We need to move. That mob is almost at the palace gates."

Rewether's guards led her back to the palace. They entered the building, only to find it in chaos. Servants and government functionaries rushed through the halls, careening off one another and squeezing through the smallest of spaces. Some of them carried scribers, others boxes or crates. But their near panic seeped into Everys. What was going to happen now? Bastion's citizens would ransack the palace most likely, but then? Given that Brencis had defeated the Dalark's military so handily, she suspected that the duke would be welcomed into the city as a liberator and protector. But after that?

Rewether didn't give her the chance to ask her questions. Instead, he pushed her gently through the hall, bellowing for everyone to get out of her way. They hustled through the halls until they went through another door, out to the palace's private tarmac. A military skimmer waited, its boarding ramp open.

The moment she saw it, she dug in her heels and came to a halt. "Who else is evacuating with us?"

"We've already had your personal staff board: the girls and Challix. They're just waiting for you, Blessed," Rewether said.

That was it? They were only going to take a handful of people? What about Narius's advisers? What about the other staff? They had so much room on the skimmer, why not take more?

She shook her head. "No. We need to get more people."

Rewether grimaced. "We don't have time for this, Blessed. If we're going to leave, we need to leave now!"

"No! What about my father? What about Occ? Oluna and Paine and Tormod and... And my husband's body. I don't want to leave Narius here for Brencis to find. Please. Go get them at least! And have whoever else you find join us out here."

Rewether's mouth pushed into a thin line, but he spun quickly and motioned to the other three guards. "Go. Find Favid, the Diradae, and whoever else you can find. And retrieve the king's body. Hurry."

The guards whirled and sprinted back into the palace.

Rewether turned back to her. "We can't wait too long, Blessed. If I decide we have to go, we go."

Everys wanted to protest, but from Rewether's expression, she knew better than to argue with him. Yes, she was the queen, but he was charged with protecting her. She knew she shouldn't push him too far.

The minutes dragged by. The sirens continued to wail in the distance, and Everys could swear she heard explosions punctuating them.

The first guard returned with Occ in tow. The Diradae looked positively twitchy, and Everys couldn't blame him. With so much panic and uncertainty in the air, mixed with the sirens and noise, Occ was probably on the edge of panic.

"Blessed! This guard says that I am to come with you!" he said.

She nodded. "That's right. After the way that you've helped me, I owe you a debt."

Occ bobbed his head, and he swiped at his mask as if he was polishing it. "Oh, Blessed, that isn't true. The debt is mine after how I injured King Narius. What little I've done hasn't been enough to undo that damage. So..."

Occ knelt on his four legs and bowed his head. "Queen Everys, I pledge my life for yours. I am your humble servant for the rest of my life. Your hive will be my hive. Your will is my duty. I am your servant until honor releases me."

Everys gaped at him. She stammered, trying to think of the right way to respond, but Rewether shot her a look. Clearly this was taking too long.

So she cleared her throat. "Thank you, He Who Occupies the Lowest Reaches. Please, board the skimmer."

Occ scrambled to his feet and hurried to the skimmer.

A few minutes later, the second guard jogged back, holding Papa by his arm. "He didn't want to come with me, Blessed, but I persuaded him."

Papa wouldn't meet her gaze. He glared to one side.

"Papa, we'll talk later," she said.

"There's nothing for us to discuss," Papa grumbled.

The guard led Papa to the skimmer. Shortly thereafter, more people ran out of the palace: random servants, minor functionaries, nobody that Everys immediately recognized. But then Oluna hurried out, two guards at her side. Her friend gave her a shaky but brave smile and ducked onto the transport.

She could practically read Rewether's thoughts as each new person boarded the skimmer. He was likely keeping track, doing the math as to how many people the aircraft could hold. She knew he'd say they had taken on enough, that it was time to go. But she wasn't ready yet. She turned back to the palace and waited, even as dread built inside her. The last thing she wanted to see was a guard carrying her husband's body like a sack of grain.

But when the guard returned, he was empty-handed with a terrified look on his face. Everys took a step forward.

"Where's Narius?" she asked. "Where's my husband?"

The guard wouldn't meet her gaze. "I'm sorry, Blessed. I went to the infirmary but the king... the king is gone. And I couldn't find any of the doctors to find out where they'd put him."

No! She couldn't leave Narius in Bastion. She could just picture what Brencis would do to his body. She wanted to send the guard back, to order Rewether to find more people to scour the palace. Her eyes burned and desperation grew inside her.

But then Rewether touched her shoulder. Gently. Comforting. A shudder wormed through her, chased by a sob that she had to stifle before she lost control.

"Blessed, I'm sorry," Rewether whispered. "I want to bring him too, but we can't wait any longer. According to the reports I've heard, Brencis is just outside the city and could have anti-skimmer batteries set up soon. If we're going to escape, we have to leave now."

Everys wanted to root herself to the spot, to claim this spot as hers the way that the Cold Light claimed the forests as their shade. She wanted nothing more than to stand sentry over the palace, to remind Brencis of who should occupy the office of king.

But Rewether gently turned her around and walked her to the skimmer. She paused at the top of the skimmer's ramp to take one last look at the palace. She never thought she'd come to see this imposing fortress-like palace with any semblance of fondness. Standing there, looking over a place she once considered her own personal prison, she realized she didn't want to leave. A part of her heart would remain here.

Rewether escorted her to a seat and she sank into it. The setting sun stabbed through the window and temporarily blinded her, but a few moments later, the skimmer lurched and clawed its way up into the air.

Everys looked out over the city of Bastion. Ugly black pillars of smoke rose into the air. As the aircraft climbed, she could see people rushing through the streets. The bridges over the Melgor were choked with transports, people trying to evacuate and creating snarls of traffic that might never be resolved. She could feel the panic, the desperation, the sheer terror of the populace, rising like the smoke. Her chest ached from it.

But then she frowned. It looked like one of the streets below them was glowing, like a hint of light shining through a crack in a painted window. But then the light grew brighter, the crack longer, as a jagged line of light shot through the street, careening around corners. She sat up, pressing against the glass to see what was happening.

Others in the skimmer murmured as more and more cracks appeared, a sickly green light shining from beneath the city. At first, Everys thought it was an illusion, a trick her mind was playing on her. But the lines continued to spread, doubling back, crossing each other, creating a pattern of loops and whirls that seemed to encompass the entire city.

Everys's breath caught in her throat. A giant, city-sized rune. And it was one she recognized. She had been taught this rune as a child, used it on occasion. A handy rune to know in the right circumstances. A rune she had just used to destroy her people's most sacred relics.

Within seconds, the pattern was complete. Everys held her breath and waited, hoping against hope that whoever constructed the rune somehow got it wrong. But then the streets broke, shards of concrete tossed into the air. Fissures radiated out from the rune and the buildings lining the streets rumbled. And then many of them collapsed, kicking up clouds of debris and dust. A moment later, an immense roar slapped the skimmer and it shuddered, nearly tossing Everys out of her seat. She held on and closed her eyes, hoping that the pilot would be able to handle the sudden turbulence.

After a few moments, the skimmer leveled off. Everys pressed herself against the window again and gasped.

Bastion was in ruins. Hundreds of buildings had collapsed, and the streets had shattered. Fires blazed all over the city. What had happened to the people? Everys tried to see if she could see anyone, but the skimmer climbed higher and higher, and soon, all she saw was the burning pyre of the city.

She collapsed in her seat. She hadn't wanted to believe what Quartus had told her, that a true *ar'zhannok* was behind the conspiracy against Narius and her. But this proved it. Only a mage-king would destroy a whole city like this using toratropic magic. Only they would be so cruel, so vindictive.

"Serves them right."

Everys turned to find Papa looking out her window. Her mouth went dry. How could he say that? They both had friends down there, people who could have been hurt or killed, people who at the very least had just lost everything they owned. How could he think this was okay? But words wouldn't form.

Papa just snorted and headed back to his seat with a smirk.

She pulled her legs up to her chin and closed her eyes. She wouldn't weep. Not right then. She was too numb. It was all too much. But she knew eventually, the tears would come.

And so would the work of trying to set all of this right.

73

Quartus looked around at the other residents of Bastion. After the cataclysm, Brencis's troops had arrived. Rather than be greeted as conquering heroes, they gathered the survivors and brought them to the most open, untouched space they could find, which turned out to be a decommissioned military base just outside of the city's limits. Quartus and Yusra had been swept up by the patrols and dropped off the night before. Thanks to an impromptu disguise, a bandage wrapped around his forehead and covering a good part of his face, none of the soldiers recognized him. So the two of them had spent a fitful night in a tent. He hadn't slept at all. Most of their neighbors had spent the night groaning or crying or, in some cases, fighting.

When morning came, Quartus hoped they'd be able to slip away, but the number of soldiers patrolling the grounds had tripled overnight. More refugees streamed into the camp every minute. And then, to top it all off, they were all herded into a barely organized crowd in front of the administration building and told to wait.

And then Duke Brencis strode out onto a balcony overlooking the crowd.

There weren't many times when Quartus wished he had received more combat training. This was one of those times. Well, that, and a sniper rifle. Plus a good vantage point. And a clear shot.

Okay, maybe that would be asking too much. Besides, Quartus doubted the Warrior would grant that request given the circumstances.

The crowd muttered to themselves, and Quartus thought they sounded angry. But then someone started cheering. Others quickly joined in, and pretty soon, the adulation almost sounded genuine. It grew louder and louder until a good portion of the crowd was chanting Brencis's name.

Quartus joined in, and he nudged Yusra in the ribs to get her to do so as well. He knew she wouldn't feel like it. He didn't either. But the last thing they needed was to call attention to themselves. He had long since learned that there was always someone watching him. Always, whether they knew he was a prince or not.

Eventually, the applause and cheering died down. Brencis waved to the crowd with a grim smile. "My people, I thank you for that welcome. I know how difficult the past few days have been for you. You have had to endure a false king and queen. You heard the stories of the Dalark Imperium's cowardly attack, slipping into our holdings. And now, this dreadful quake that has destroyed so many of your homes and stolen the lives of so many of your neighbors and family. I feel your pain, my people, I truly do."

A murmur rippled through the crowd, one Quartus understood all too well. Brencis's speech was dignified and measured. And condescending. Though Brencis called the audience "his people," he clearly didn't think of them that way.

"But the worst is behind us," Brencis continued, seemingly oblivious to the crowd's reaction. "In the coming days, I will ensure that Bastion is restored to its former glory. My men will make sure that the Dalark are driven far from our lands. And as for the former king and his witch, well... They are both dead."

Quartus sucked in a sharp breath. How did that happen? He had tried to warn Everys what was coming. Why hadn't she fled?

And Narius... Regrets, old and newer, flashed through his mind. So many missed opportunities. So much pain and strife and fighting between them, both as boys and then as men. The last words they'd spoken to each other, in anger and loathing. Now there wouldn't be any chance to repair that brokenness. As much as Quartus had lied to himself in thinking that he wouldn't care when Narius died, he realized in that moment that he did.

Yusra snared his hand and squeezed it. He wished she would hug him, whisper something comforting to him. But that would only attract unwanted attention. So he squeezed her hand back and tried to be satisfied with that little comfort.

Brencis continued speaking, "Now you may wonder how I am able to make such bold promises. Narius, after all, made similar promises to you. Lofty ones, too audacious for him to ever be able to keep. Promises of reforging the Dynasty into something 'better.' More 'prosperous.' But he would have done so by betraying our greatest legacy. Since ancient times, we have prospered and bettered ourselves through war. Through conquest. You know it and I know it. And there are others who see this truth as well."

He gestured toward the entrance to the building behind him. The doors opened and, much to Quartus's surprise, Speaker Zolkin came out. He waved to the crowd, who applauded for him but not nearly with as much enthusiasm as they had mustered for Brencis. He was followed by four men who wheeled a large vidscreen onto the balcony. While they worked hastily to set it up, Zolkin stepped to the edge of the balcony.

"The Hall of All Voices pledges our support to our new king." There was a definite edge to Zolkin's voice, a hint of stress and pressure. "May he and his queen reign wisely and well."

Brencis nodded, then gestured toward the viewscreen. "And his is not the only one I wanted you to hear from today. For it is not just the Hall that has endorsed my reign, but the Ethnarch Parliament as well."

And suddenly, Quartus understood what the screen was for. Sure enough, just as Brencis gestured toward it, the screen lit up with an image of Estrid. Of course the Diradae ethnarch wouldn't leave his manor. Why break that tradition now?

"My friends, the Ethnarch Parliament also recognizes King Brencis's claim to the throne. And those who hold to the Flail will work with him to ensure the Dynasty's prosperity going forward."

Again, Brencis nodded and launched into some more remarks about his plans for the Dynasty. But Quartus didn't hear a word he said. Instead, he stared at the vidscreen, aghast. He knew that voice. He had heard it before, and recently.

"Quartus," Yusra whispered, squeezing his hand again, this time with urgency instead of comfort. "You heard it too?"

He nodded. They had both heard Estrid's voice in Lorent's lair when the conspirators had spoken with one another. The Diradae ethnarch was a part of the conspiracy.

Quartus shook his head and clicked his mouth shut. He couldn't gape. He couldn't react too visibly. Doing so would only draw attention to Yusra and himself, and that would be disastrous. They had to blend in, just long enough to get out of here. Because in that instant, Quartus realized something.

The conspirators probably thought they had won. They had eliminated Narius and Everys. Brencis had claimed the throne. And while he still didn't know who this *ar'zhannok* was, she probably believed she had succeeded as well. But as far as Quartus was concerned, the hunt wasn't over yet. Only this time, he wouldn't be trying to clear his name. He wouldn't do this for Tormod or for anyone else. Instead, he was going to avenge his brother and sister-in-law. He would find the people who had done this to them and make them pay.

A cheer rippled through the crowd. Quartus jumped, startled, and quickly joined in, trying to summon enough enthusiasm to fake it. Brencis waved again to the crowd.

"My people, I must go now. My queen and I will soon address the rest of the Dynasty to let them know that they, too, are in my safe, capable hands. But rest assured, you will not be overlooked. Bastion will rise from these ruins and once again assume its rightful place as the Dynasty's crown jewel."

He waved again, then turned from the crowd to speak with someone else on the balcony. Apparently the speech was over. The crowd started to disperse, many of them whispering to one another. Some even muttered openly. From what Quartus could glean, no one was all that impressed. More promises from royalty that no one actually expected Brencis to keep. And while he wasn't entirely sure, he thought he heard plenty of people express veiled regret over Narius's death. Quartus turned to leave, but then motion up on the balcony caught his attention. He glanced in that direction and then froze.

Brencis stood, talking quietly with an adviser, a Kolvese man dressed in ornate robes of state. But seeing the two of them together like that knocked Quartus back a step.

Vizier Paine nodded at whatever Brencis was telling him, but he looked out over the crowd.

Quartus stood up a little taller, almost hoping that Paine would see him. Let him. Let him know that Quartus was here, that Quartus knew what he had done. Quartus had been accused of betraying his brother. Well, Paine actually had.

But Paine didn't seem to notice him. The vizier turned back to Brencis and motioned for him to head back into the building. Paine appeared to sigh, then followed in the new king's wake.

Quartus glared at the building, willing it to catch on fire or collapse or... or *something*. But it didn't. Yusra tugged on his arm insistently, drawing him away from the crowd.

He let her, and as they walked, he smiled. No, his work wasn't done yet. He would make all of them pay for what they had done. And he would do it for Narius. He would do it for Everys. He would do it so that, wherever they were, they might finally know some peace.

74

The skimmer banked and Everys rocked with the motion. Her head bounced off the cabin wall and it probably should have hurt, but the pain was a distant reality, something disconnected from her.

Bastion was in ruins. She had personally shattered the Principalities. And Narius was dead. That one was too much to bear. There had been so much that she wanted to tell him, so much that had to be said. And now, she would carry those words with her for the rest of her life.

"Friends, fellow citizens of the Dynasty!"

She closed her eyes and groaned. And how could she forget the best part? She turned to the viewscreen, where an image of Brencis smiled imperiously at her.

"Today is a day of victory for the Dynasty. We have neutralized the vile Dalark, and my troops have secured Bastion. By dint of combat, by the desire of the Perfected Warrior, I have proven myself to be a true king for the Dynasty. I promise that my darling Viara and I will rule by the ancient dictates and traditions of our people."

The camera pulled back to reveal Viara standing next to Brencis. She wore a sleek dress that accentuated her pregnancy, reminding everyone who saw her that she carried Narius's child.

Tears pricked Everys's eyes. That hurt the worst. Narius was gone and now Viara would have his child. Not her. Never her.

"But our enemies dealt us a grievous blow. Bastion, our fair city, is in ruins. We do not know how this happened, but I promise you: we will rebuild. We will rearm. And then we will make the monsters who did this pay."

Everys's stomach soured. Brencis knew full well who those monsters were. He had conspired with them. At least the conspirators wouldn't get their hands on the Principalities, although Everys had no idea how she would ever explain what she had done to her people.

Someone stepped up next to her. Everys glanced out of the corner of her eye and realized it was Oluna.

Her friend knelt next to her. "Everys, are you all right?"

No. No, she wasn't. And it would be a long time before she was even close to all right. A widow. An exile. No doubt hunted by Brencis's forces. And although Brencis made it sound like Dalark had been driven out of the Dynasty's holdings, she knew better. The pilot had reported multiple Dalark units below them. Thankfully, they'd either not seen or ignored them.

But she was queen. As much as she didn't want to be anymore, as much as she'd like to disappear and never come back, she knew she couldn't. So she put on a brave face, smiled, and nodded. "I'm fine."

"You're a horrible liar, Blessed. But things will get better for us. You'll see." Oluna wrapped her arms around Everys and hugged her.

Oluna's warm embrace was almost enough to crack Everys's resolve. A sob bubbled up inside her, but she tamped it down. She needed to remain strong. For the people on the skimmer. For herself. For Narius's memory.

Rewether tromped down the center of the cabin, ducking as he walked. "We've got a problem, Blessed. We're circling over Tall Reach's Shade, but the trees are so densely packed, there's no place for us to safely land. The pilot's talking about heading to Vetranio's First Stand and hoping we can get into the forest from there."

Oluna released her, allowing Everys to slip from her seat. She made her way over to a window she knew would look over the forest. The ground beneath them was an unbroken sea of green. They hadn't had a way of letting the Cold Light know they were coming, but surely they must have been aware that they were circling overhead.

"Very well," she said with a sigh. "Let the pilot know."

And then she saw it: a section of the forest vibrated. Many of the treetops swayed in the wind, but there was something unnatural and unsettling about how some of the trees suddenly twitched beneath them. Then, in one fluid motion, the trees parted. No, they moved, as one, revealing a long strip of bare land beneath the skimmer. Everys smiled. Based on her last visit to the forest, that stretch of land would be perfect for landing.

"Looks like they're ready for us," Everys said, turning to Rewether, and pointing out the window.

Rewether nodded grimly. "I'll let the pilot know."

As Everys made her way back to her seat, she took a quick mental catalog of the people on board. Challix and Trule, along with the rest of her personal staff. Across the aisle, three of her guards, but not Kevtho. She pushed aside the ache that blossomed in her chest. In front of them, Occ had crammed himself into a seat. How he had folded himself into a seat not built for him, she had no idea. Papa glared out one of the windows, just as quiet as he had been for the entire flight. There were the others, the servants and bureaucrats who had sought refuge on the skimmer. And that was it. That was all she could save. And Narius was... He was...

She shoved that thought aside as well and sank into her chair just as the skimmer started its descent. So many thoughts and feelings, warring against each other. She glanced at the viewscreen, where Brencis leered at her with a smarmy grin. In spite of all her conflicting feelings, she knew one thing with absolute certainty: no matter what Brencis might claim, no matter what the Hall of All Voices or the Ethnarch Parliament decided, no matter what Istragon might declare, she was still queen. And she was going to make Brencis and his co-conspirators pay for what they had done to her.

The skimmer bumped along the ground, then came to a halt. Rewether returned to the cabin and signaled for the guards to follow him. Everys smiled. They were likely in the safest place they could be, but she didn't blame the guard for being cautious.

A few minutes later, Rewether returned and motioned for everyone to disembark. Everys let the rest of them exit first, then followed them down the ramp and into the cold air.

She paused at the bottom of the skimmer's ramp to take a deep breath. A sense of peace washed over her. For just that moment, she could pretend that nothing bad had happened. No invasion. No coup. No death and destruction. Just the crisp air, the bright sunshine, and the knowledge that for a little while, she could recapture a little peace.

"Blessed?" Challix prompted.

She opened her eyes, swallowing a groan. Back to reality, then.

Four people emerged from the tree line and made their way to the skimmer. The guards snapped to attention, drawing their weapons, but Everys recognized the newcomers immediately.

"Hold, guards!" she shouted. "They're friends."

And they were. The four people were all grafted, with vines and branches wrapped around their arms, legs, and torsos. While she didn't remember the names of three of them, she knew the one leading the way.

"Yllana?" she called.

The grafted smiled and offered her a short bow. "Queen Everys, welcome back to Tall Reach's Shade. The Yoreroot is honored to give you sanctuary and invites you to stay here as long as you need to. If you'd all follow me, please?"

The other grafted stepped forward and began their own quiet conversations with the rest of the people in Everys's group. The grafted speaking to Occ didn't seem the least bit surprised or put off by talking to a Diradae. Good.

Yllana led her back through the trees toward the settlement near Tall Reach's Shade. Memories flooded over Everys from the first time they had been there. It hadn't been that long ago, but after everything that had happened, it felt like a different lifetime.

Everys shook her head, clearing it. She had to stay focused. Mourning would happen, but for now, she had to focus on next steps.

She stopped short when they emerged from the trees. Instead of a sleepy village, she had stepped into an active military base. Camouflaged transports were lined up on her right, and a squad of troops trotted past on her left. Panic surged through her. Brencis's troops? Had he figured out where she was going?

Yllana placed a hand on Everys's wrist. "You're safe, Blessed. These troops are loyal to you."

"Wh-what are they doing here?" she whispered.

"A few days ago, we found a squad of Dynasty troops within the forest. They had a message from Strategist Overturn. He wanted to know if the troops from Vetranio's First Stand could enter the forest and find refuge with us, promising that he would join us soon if possible. The Yoreroot agreed."

"Why?"

Yllana smiled grimly. "Because the Yoreroot knows what is at stake. We applauded your husband's initiatives and wanted to work with him, to graft our people more strongly together. But with Brencis claiming the throne, we know that will not be possible anymore. So the Yoreroot has made a decision, a choice that they haven't made in over eight thousand years."

Everys felt dizzy, but she waited for Yllana to continue.

"The Cold Light will go to war. For you. For your husband. For the Dynasty's future and ours as well." Then a shudder passed through Yllana's body and she straightened up, seemingly taller and stronger. "Everys Queen, I swear to you by root and branch, by sun and water, by the Below and the Hearth itself, we will not rest until you have reclaimed your throne."

Tears welled in Everys's eyes at Tall Reach's words. It was all too much. This was never what she wanted, nothing she had ever even dreamed of. But even still, even with the uncertainty and the pain, even with the grief and the anger that simmered inside her, underlying it all was a sense of peace.

She nodded and turned to Tall Reach. "I thank you, Tall Reach."

"And there is yet more. The last time you visited my Shade, I shared with you that there were other Siporans who have taken refuge in our forests. At the time, they were too frightened to meet with you openly. But now..." Another shudder passed through Yllana, and her features softened into a shy smile. "Our community is ready."

Now a sob choked her. Everys hugged Yllana and the grafted hugged her back. They stood there for several minutes until someone cleared her throat behind them. Everys released Yllana and turned to find Papa staring at them.

"There are Siporans here?" he whispered.

Yllana glanced at Everys. She nodded.

"There are, sir," Yllana said. "And we are glad to have all of you here. You will be safe in Tall Reach's Shade."

Papa stared at Yllana and then walked away. Everys frowned. She motioned to Rewether, gesturing after her father. The guard captain nodded and signaled for one of the guards to follow Papa. The last thing they needed was for him to get lost in the forest.

Then Challix walked up to Everys and drew her aside.

"The grafted say that we'll have the run of the embassy," Challix said. "I've set the girls to getting the place cleaned up and ready for you. What are your orders, Blessed?"

Everys blinked away her tears and nodded to herself. She stood up taller, straighter, trying to draw strength from the people and the trees around her.

"We settle in. We heal. And then we show Brencis that we still have some fight left in us."

Challix smiled and Everys thought she even heard some muted cheers from the passersby. But she remembered what the Singularity had shown her. All empires fall. And maybe it was the Dynasty's time. But until she knew for certain, she would keep fighting. Not for the Dynasty, but for the people who lived under it, who would now be subjected to Brencis's cruelty and the mage-king's machinations. On her own, there'd be no way to do that. But she wasn't alone. She had her friends. She would find new allies. But most importantly, she would walk with the Singularity and see what He had in store for all of them.

75

The first thing he was aware of was the ache. Dull and persistent, it soaked through every fiber of his being. He groaned, stirring and trying to roll away from it, but he couldn't. With every move, a sharper pain shot through his arms and legs. He whimpered and rolled onto his side.

That motion set off a storm of dizziness that crested through him. His stomach lurched, and he worried that he would vomit, but the sensation quickly passed. Instead, he released a shuddering sigh and clawed at the blanket, trying to pull it over his head. But the fabric was rough and scratchy. It felt like thorns raked his skin.

What had happened to him? His last memories were a blur, and trying to dredge them up only caused him more discomfort. All he wanted to do was go back to sleep, to drift off into the darkness and—

Someone nudged his leg. Gently at first, but then harder.

He rolled onto his back and sat up, setting off a riot of sparks in his vision. He groaned and pitched forward so he could claw at his temples. Why did he feel like this?

Someone nudged his leg again. He looked up. A young woman sat at the edge of his bed, regarding him with an impish smile. He frowned. He recognized her from... from where? From before the darkness. She had been his nurse. And in the arena. And Maotoa.

Narius gasped. "You!"

The young woman's smile broadened, and she gestured, her hands twitching and twisting together. Then she thrust her hands toward him, her palms open, and a wave of peace washed over him. The ache didn't vanish, but it did fade enough for him to gather his thoughts.

He could remember... Favid drawing a rune, and then... and then...

He looked at the young woman and frowned. "You saved me?"

She nodded, repeating her gestures again, this time cupping her hands on either side of his head. Once again, a wave of peace crested within him, and some of the tension slipped away from him.

"Why?" he whispered.

"Because I asked her to. You're fortunate Kavi was able to infiltrate the palace and place you in deep hibernation before you succumbed to your injuries. Otherwise you'd likely be dead. You're welcome, beloved."

Narius froze. He knew that voice. He hadn't heard it for a while, and the last time he had, it had been breathy and thin. Definitely not as rich and strong as it was now. But the voice was unmistakable.

He turned, and sure enough, another young woman sat in a chair at the opposite end of the cramped room. She regarded him coolly with green eyes, her auburn hair pulled up into a style reminiscent of a crown. She smiled at him with a confidence and assuredness he had never seen in her before.

"Innana?" he whispered.

The sister of Emperor Tirigian, his former fiancée, nodded. "Welcome to Utuaa, my love. We have a lot of work to do."

Acknowledgements

Fun fact: I've never actually written a trilogy before. Oh, sure, I have my *Failstate* "trilogy," but that's more of a series than anything else. But an actual, honest-to-goodness trilogy? Where a massive story is stretched over three books? Never done it before. It's kind of daunting, actually. But the fact that you're reading these words right now is thanks to a number of people:

First of all, thank you to Jim Schroeder for helping me to create Spanica Trentwether. This was part of a Kickstarter reward for *Drawn in Ash* and, when I first worked with Jim on the character, I thought that he would play a minor role in this book and then shuffle off the stage. Actually, it turns out that Spanica had a lot to do in the Dynasty. He'll be back in the next book, and he even popped up in the Paine novella, *The Storm's Eye*. So thank you, Jim, for creating such a useful character!

I also couldn't do this without the help of my beta readers, Lisa Gefrides, Chawna Schroeder, and Katie Vincent. Your insight was invaluable. And Katie, thanks for saving Narius.

What can I say about my editor, Megan Gerig? Megan's insights into this story were incredible. Her enthusiasm for this storyworld and its characters is truly humbling. It's always so much fun to read through her notes and comments. Everys and Narius's story wouldn't be nearly as strong if it wasn't for her.

Kirk DouPonce, you once again delivered an incredible cover. Thank you so much for bringing Everys and Kevtho to life!

Thank you to these Kickstarter backers who went above and beyond in their support: Timothy Bicknase, Meghan Clark, Edward Cloetier, Megan Gerig, Rosie and Lydia Houze, Jill McConnell,

William Merrell, Chawna Schroeder, Jimmy Schroeder, and Jason "Yanc" Worley.

Thank you to my patient and long-suffering family. They had to listen as I worked through different scenes and ideas, usually when I was supposed to be eating dinner. And a special thanks to my oldest for helping me figure out Occ.

Most of all, though, thank You to the God who called me His own through the waters of Holy Baptism. All empires may one day fall, but Your Kingdom will endure forever. *Soli Deo Gloria*!

About the Author

John is a PK, a pastor's kid. He grew up in Columbia Heights, a suburb of Minneapolis, with his parents and younger sister and brother. They were the terror of their local library because, every few weeks, they would come and check out crates full of books, increasing the workload of the poor librarians. In high school, though, John worked at the same library, so it balanced out.

After high school, John attended Concordia University in St. Paul, Minnesota, where he majored in theatre. Upon his graduation in 1996, he moved on to Concordia Seminary in St. Louis, Missouri. He graduated with his Masters of Divinity in 2000. He served as a Lutheran minister in Blue Earth, Minnesota, and South Saint Paul, Minnesota. He currently serves as an associate pastor in Blue Springs, Missouri, where he lives with his wife and kids.

John is a lifelong writer. He started with badly drawn comic books in the fifth grade. When he realized that he was a lousy artist, he moved on to badly written novels in middle school. He's tried his hand at screenplays (don't ask), stage plays (a little better), fanfic, teen mysteries, and religious fiction. But his first love has always been speculative fiction.

His debut novel, *Failstate*, was published by Marcher Lord Press in April of 2012, and was a finalist for the Christy Awards in 2013. He has gone on to publish four more novels with Marcher Lord Press/Enclave Publishing, two of which, *Numb* and *Failstate: Nemesis*, were finalists for the Christy Awards in 2014 and 2015. *Drawn in Ash* won the Realm Award for Science Fiction in 2023 and was a semi-finalist for the Carol Awards that same year.

John looks forward to telling even more strange tales that point people back to God and His incredible grace.

Also By...

The Failstate Series

Failstate
Gauntlet Goes to Prom (ebook exclusive)
Failstate: Legends
Kynetic: On Target (ebook exclusive)
Failstate: Nemesis

The Ministrix Duology

Numb
The Hive

The Legacy of Ink Trilogy

Drawn in Ash
The Storm's Eye (ebook exclusive)
Drawn through Blood

Cage and the Outpost of Monolith (short story)

Anthologies

Into the Bewilderness
Just Dumb Enough (Contributor)
The Memory Eater (Contributor)
Spirited: 13 Haunting Tales (Contributor)

Kickstarter Backers

This book wouldn't have made it to print without the invaluable support and financial help of my Kickstarter backers. So thank you to those who joined me on this adventure:

David Beagley, Jake and Faith Bellinghausen, Scott Casey, Joshua C. Chadd, Ivan Ruel Cload, B. Cluppert, Ashley Cook, Tatianne Dobbin, Jennifer Dyer, Tom Evans, Leila Rose Foreman, Noah G., Chris "My Brother from Another Mother" Gordon, Andrew Gunsch, Clint Hall, Pamela Hart, E. A. Hendryx, Jenny Herschbach, Lee Hillshire, Lizzie Hite, Luke Italiano, Pauline Baird Jones, Jason C. Joyner, A. F. Kopp, Joel Kovach, Ryan and Kate Kuecker, Tom Langemo, Bob and Sandy Logan, Mark Lundgren, Corrine Lussier, Brian McCauley, Alex Mellen, C.J. Milacci, Alberto Mohammed-Dawson, Mom and Dad, Meagan Myhren-Bennett, Marie Norris, Josh Olds, Mark Otte, Aaron Plattner, Dominik Plejić, Tracy Popey, Rachel Reinke, Lisa Sauter, Tamara M. Slaten, Rachelle Y. Sperling, Amanda Trumpower, Kaitlin Vincent, Dona Watson, Joseph Wernecke, Jill Williamson, Tracy Workman, Peter Younghusband, Beth, Brandon, Catherine, Nick

Learn more about Vizier Paine

Haven't gotten enough of Vizier Paine? Find out more about his rise to power in the ebook exclusive novella, *The Storm's Eye*.

Get a free short story!

Did you enjoy this book? How'd you like to get a free short story set in the Dynasty?

Head over to John's website and sign up for the Geeky Grace Newsletter. When you do, you'll receive the short story *Cage and the Outpost of Monolith* absolutely free!

johnwotte.com/subscribe

Made in the USA
Monee, IL
02 October 2023